About the Author

Mary-Anne O'Connor has a combined arts education degree with specialities in environment, music and literature. She works in marketing and co-wrote/edited *A Brush with Light* and *Secrets of the Brush* with Kevin Best.

Mary-Anne lives in a house overlooking her beloved bushland in northern Sydney with her husband Anthony, their two sons Jimmy and Jack, and their very spoilt dog Saxon. This is her fourth major novel. Her previous novels, *Gallipoli Street* (2015), *Worth Fighting For* (2016) and *War Flower* (2017), have all been bestsellers.

Also by Mary-Anne O'Connor

Gallipoli Street
Worth Fighting For
War Flower

In a Great Southern Land

Mary-Anne
O'CONNOR

AUTHOR'S NOTE

In a Great Southern Land is a work of fiction and, although it has been based on true events in history, artistic licence has been employed at times to ensure cohesion is maintained.

First Published 2019
Second Australian Paperback Edition 2020
ISBN 9781489295118

IN A GREAT SOUTHERN LAND
© 2019 by Mary-Anne O'Connor
Australian Copyright 2019
New Zealand Copyright 2019

Except for use in any review, the reproduction or utilisation of this work in whole or in part in any form by any electronic, mechanical or other means, now known or hereafter invented, including xerography, photocopying and recording, or in any information storage or retrieval system, is forbidden without the permission of the publisher.

This book is sold subject to the condition that it shall not, by way of trade or otherwise, be lent, resold, hired out or otherwise circulated without the prior consent of the publisher in any form of binding or cover other than that in which it is published and without a similar condition including this condition being imposed on the subsequent purchaser.

All rights reserved including the right of reproduction in whole or in part in any form.

This is a work of fiction. Names, characters, places, and incidents are either the product of the author's imagination or are used fictitiously, and any resemblance to actual persons, living or dead, business establishments, events, or locales is entirely coincidental.

Published by
HQ Fiction
An imprint of Harlequin Enterprises (Australia) Pty Limited (ABN 47 001 180 918),
a subsidiary of HarperCollins Publishers Australia Pty Limited (ABN 36 009 913 517)
Level 13, 201 Elizabeth St
SYDNEY NSW 2000
AUSTRALIA

® and TM (apart from those relating to FSC®) are trademarks of Harlequin Enterprises (Australia) Pty Limited or its corporate affiliates. Trademarks indicated with ® are registered in Australia, New Zealand and in other countries.

A catalogue record for this book is available from the National Library of Australia
www.librariesaustralia.nla.gov.au

Printed and bound in Australia by McPherson's Printing Group

For my husband Anthony, always kind.

Few, and taken by surprise,
Oh! the mist that hid the skies —
And the steel in diggers' eyes —
Sunday morning in December long ago;
*   And they grapple and they strike —*
*   With the pick-handle and pike —*
Twenty minutes freed Australia at Eureka long ago.

— 'Australia's Forgotten Flag', Henry Lawson

The Letter

One

Killaloe, County Clare, Ireland, April 1851

Playing games, whether for opportunity, mischief or seduction, was a pastime Kieran Clancy should have quit long ago. But 'should' was a word he seldom obeyed.

'Check.'

Maeve O'Shannassey frowned at her cornered king.

'However did you manage that?' she muttered, perplexed. Her pretty face suited consternation. Hell, she looked delectable no matter what she was feeling, and Kieran further warmed to the contest at hand.

'You'll find I have many hidden talents, Miss Maeve, games of chase being one of my specialities,' Kieran told her.

'And yet I continue to outrun you, Mr Kieran,' she replied, rather brazenly for her, before moving her queen to block his knight. 'Check, I believe.'

Kieran barely glanced at the table, raising his eyebrows instead and leaning in close to take the queen. 'You may well run, fair maid, but you cannot hide.' The words were spoken in her ear and he could smell her hair, still damp from the outdoors and sweet with the honey-scented soap she favoured. He held the breath in to savour it, momentarily intoxicated, before adding 'checkmate'.

Maeve stood in a rush, almost knocking over the board, and Kieran cursed himself for breaking one of his own rules in life: appear bold but never cocky.

'T...tea?' she suggested, her earlier confidence gone.

Kieran sighed as she made a swift exit to the kitchen where her mother was ostensibly baking but really keeping guard over her daughter. Leaning back against the French settee, he reflected that Maeve was proving far more difficult to court than any of the local girls he'd been interested in over the years. That was probably part of the attraction – but not all of it.

The rain pelted hard against the pane and Kieran looked out, glad to be away from the fields for a change. Green and lush the farmlands near Killaloe may be, but when the wet set in it lost much of its appeal, turning soggy and grey. He studied the parlour window itself instead. Aside from the luxury of glass, it was framed by polished oak and had lace curtains, a step far above most other homes in the area, and the fine furniture and thick carpets herein further emphasised how remote the chances were that he, Kieran Clancy, a poor Irish farmer, stood any real chances with this girl.

Listening to Mrs O'Shannassey's lofty tones drift through the door he knew he should just leave. But of course, he wouldn't.

Kieran stood to pace the room and plot instead. It was simply a matter of evening the scales somehow, offering more than other suitors, more than material wealth and all the trappings her family prized.

Such as? he asked himself.

Well, he could work on his charm; she seemed to enjoy some of his more humorous witticisms and compliments. Hopefully that might lead to delicious stolen moments of shared desire. Noting the nervous knot twisting in his gut at the thought, he acknowledged he could well end up giving her his heart. Then he paused to look across towards town to where Mr O'Shannassey would be working today and he knew that, even if that were enough for Maeve, it would never be enough for her father.

The man was quite a success story, and it wasn't just the impressive house that bespoke the fact. He had a thriving business at his new store, which sold everything from silk stockings to imported perfumes, but by far the greatest attraction to the locals were the apothecary vials that lined the counter, a curious assortment of concoctions, handmade, mostly, by Mr O'Shannassey himself. It seemed people couldn't get enough of the often ill-tasting liquids that promised cures for maladies from ear infections to rheumatism.

It didn't hurt, perhaps, that he had so desperate a clientele. Most had suffered these past few years and ill-health was commonplace. Overworked by English landlords and robbed of much of their crops by Queen Victoria, the final straw for many in the village came when the potato crops had failed a few years previously. Starvation had led to disease; consumption, cholera and smallpox. In the end many lives had been taken, including those of Kieran's own mother and father. Where were Mr O'Shannassey's 'miracle cures' then?

Kieran shoved his hands deep into his pockets, pushing resentment and grief away. It wasn't the man's fault that Ireland suffered so. Perhaps some of his remedies even worked, although Kieran placed far more faith in his sister Eileen's tonics. Still, he supposed O'Shannassey was giving people hope and that was a gift in itself, even if, on their meagre wages, they could ill afford it.

Money. Kieran sighed at the enormity of the word, acknowledging that the odds against him were stacked high in this particular game. Maeve might well fall for Kieran's romantic overtures but her parents would require a man of means, especially if he had any chance of actually marrying her.

Unless his brother Liam could pull off what he had planned.

Maeve returned then and that last glimmering thought evaporated as Kieran turned to watch her move, her creamy skin pushing against her dress as she bent to pour the tea.

'Milk?' she asked.

'Please.'

Kieran returned to the settee and he was pleased when Maeve sat beside him, slightly closer than before. Near enough for him to see the flecks of green in her otherwise brown eyes and smell that hair once more. He closed his own eyes momentarily, memorising the scent, his determination to win her returning with force.

'Are you feeling poorly?' Maeve asked.

'Not with you around,' he told her. Her lovely face flushed and it gave him a heady rush that he could affect her so. A small tip of the scales.

'Perhaps I should fetch you one of father's tonics.'

Kieran smiled at her. 'I'm perfectly fine, I promise.' He was tempted to add that he doubted her father had invented a cure for desire but that was, of course, a flirtation too far.

Maeve looked to her tea and circled her spoon about her cup demurely. 'Father's had some rather wonderful news actually: Lord Whitely has agreed to fund mass production of some of his inventions.'

Kieran swallowed his distaste with his tea at the mention of Lord Whitely's name. Long how he'd ached to tell the owner of their small farm to stick his power over the tenanting Clancy family up his pompous Cambridge arse.

'Is that so?' Kieran said, feigning what he hoped was a mixture of mild curiosity and politeness.

'Yes, there's a factory in Kilrush that will start producing them next month.'

'Truly?' Kieran said, trying to maintain his composure, but all he could envisage were those scales dipping dramatically back against him.

Maeve nodded, her face alight with excitement. 'Lord Whitely has invited us to dine at the family estate this Sunday to celebrate the partnership. His son is returning to Killaloe.'

Those scales weren't only dipping now; they were set to fall over. He'd heard from Eileen that Maeve's mother was distantly related to an earl, rendering her just passably genteel, and, even though it was slightly beneath a gentleman to work in commerce, this fact also seemed forgiven of O'Shannassey now. Such social elevation meant any hope Kieran had with Maeve was fast disappearing. Whitely's rich but unattractive son was known to be looking for a wife and he would surely take an interest in her. And Maeve's parents would never choose the tenant over the lord for their daughter; an aristocratic Englishman would win such a battle without contest.

Kieran had little choice but to seize this rare opportunity to win her affections, right now, while he still had any possible hope.

'Sounds grand,' he said, opting for nonchalance and changing the subject. 'Another game of chess?'

'I do believe you are a better chess player than I, Master Kieran,' she said. 'Perhaps I should challenge you to a game of cards instead. My cousins taught me well as a child and I don't mind telling you I could fair whip you at whist.'

Bold but never cocky, he reminded himself.

'I'm sure you could fair whip me at many games Miss Maeve.'

He was rewarded with another blush. 'Really, Master Kieran, you shouldn't say such things…' She looked to the open kitchen door and he took advantage of her momentary distraction, taking her hand before she could stop him.

'Maeve, I...' He'd been about to declare his feelings but instead he took one look at her shocked face and parted lips and found himself kissing her, a sudden, heated event that took them both by surprise. Passion flooded through him as he poured all that yearning for her into the moment, before pausing to read her expression, knowing her first reaction to him was crucial. *Kiss me back*, he pleaded silently, and his heart leapt as she swayed towards him, but they were interrupted by a distant voice.

'*Kieran!* Kieran, where are you?'

He would have done his best to ignore it but Maeve had pulled away, startled, and Kieran took a deep breath, cursing his brother Liam for his unbelievably confounded timing.

'Excuse me,' he said, sending her what he hoped was his most irresistible smile before standing and walking over to open the front door.

'Here,' he called, stepping out and bracing himself against the unwelcoming day. The rain was still falling and he pulled his coat over his neck, wishing he'd grabbed his cap. Liam turned and spied him, letting out a whoop of excitement as he ran down the cobblestone road, nearly losing his footing as he skidded to a halt.

'It's arrived. We got it!' he panted. 'It's ours, Kieran. All ours!'

Kieran's annoyance with his brother evaporated as he stared back, barely believing the news as he took the outstretched letter from Liam's hands and read it under his coat to shield it from the rain. But there it was, in black and white.

'Land,' Kieran breathed and they looked to one another in a moment of pure joy before embracing right there in the street.

'We have land,' Kieran cried as they danced about now, drenched by the rain but uncaring as passers-by stopped to watch, sensibly beneath umbrellas.

'*Land*, Mrs Flannery, *land*, Mr Leary,' Liam yelled to their neighbours who were smiling with them.

'It came then, lads?' Mr Leary said.

'Aye, it came.' Kieran patted the letter, now safely in his inside pocket, barely able to hold back his tears.

'You're lucky you've got such a way with words there, Liam,' Mr Leary observed. 'They don't give it away like they used to, from what I hear.'

'We'll have to pay some money off over time, but it's nothing we won't be able to handle,' Liam told him, still beaming.

'So they're providing free passage for you to cross the ocean then they'll just hand it over,' Mrs Flannery said, shaking her head in wonderment. 'Imagine that.'

Rainwater poured down upon Kieran as he looked at those old, familiar faces, lined by grief and hardship as so many of the locals were, yet finding it within themselves to rejoice in their neighbour's good fortune. He tried to take in the enormity of what this could mean. He wasn't the only one to leave; the Irish were emigrating in droves, forced to seek whatever work they could find in foreign cities or, worse still, taking to the crowded poorhouses – a wretched existence indeed. But this...this was something else altogether. This was opportunity. A fresh start in a new game. A chance.

'The great southern land,' Liam said, looking at him, then laughing at his own incredible words. 'I'm still trying to believe it.'

'Aye, you can believe it alright,' Kieran said, grinning at his brother before spying Maeve as she stood at her parents' door. 'We're going, the whole lot of us,' he said, more meaningfully now, 'as a family.' He let the emphasis rest on that last word and Maeve sent him a tremulous smile, the scales tipping back with force.

'Your father'd be well proud, lads – and your good mother too, God rest her soul,' Mr Leary said and Kieran felt the tears well and fall now. 'Never forget your roots though, boys. You're Irish first and foremost – make no mistake.'

He watched as Maeve dipped her gaze and closed the door and wondered if her father had a vial that could alter the loyalty to Ireland that ran through all their veins. It had brought them nothing but heartache so what use was it in the end?

'Not for much longer, Mr Leary,' Kieran told him, 'we'll be Australians. Free men…on Clancy land. Clancy owned.'

Far away from the weight of English oppression, no longer mere Irish pawns, pinned in their corner of the chessboard.

The dark clouds rumbled above and Kieran bared his face to the lashing sky, letting the wonderful news wash through and consume him.

'Checkmate,' he told the rain.

Two

Eileen Murphy was dancing. Not just a waltz or even a quadrille, this was a fully impassioned, whirling Irish jig. But why not? It wasn't every day you found out your prayers had been answered and you were moving hemispheres with your entire family to New Holland, or 'Australia' as people now called it. Not as a convict like so many other poor souls from her country, but as free men and women to own land and build homes, with a legacy to pass down to their children. She had three already, Thomas, James and Matthew; her husband Rory often boasted he wanted a dozen sons named after all twelve apostles by the time they were done. Eileen wasn't too sure about that. A little girl named Mary would be nice too.

Rory picked her up in his burly arms and twirled her high and she laughed with rare abandon. Life had been harsh living as a tenant all these years, bowing and kowtowing to Lord Whitely and his horrible family like they were some kind of undeserving gods. Then there were these recent, cruellest years when there'd been barely enough to eat. She still blamed her parents' deaths from the pox on the widespread starvation, no matter what anyone said. They'd been so weakened none of her cures could save them, despite nursing them both around the clock.

But that terrible grief was behind them now, thanks to Liam's cleverness with words, and they had their ma and da to thank for that. The English didn't allow the poor Irish masses an education but their parents had schooled them anyway, passing down a family tradition of teaching each generation to read and write.

'Knowledge is power,' her father often used to say. 'You don't know what you don't know until you learn.'

That adage had always confused Eileen somewhat but Liam, in particular, had taken the concept on and was always burying his head in whatever books he could find. Unfortunately they were rare commodities but the newspapers came to town once a fortnight and Liam would pore over every word before penning versions of what he read himself. His writing had consequently flourished. And now her youngest brother had used this skill to its utmost advantage, convincing the powers-that-be that a country on the other side of the world needed their farming skills and non-criminal selves. They'd even been granted free passage!

And land of their own. Oh, how her dear parents would have wept at the news. Autonomy at last.

Eileen could barely hold all the joy she felt inside her petite body. It was as if someone had opened up her chest and filled it with sunshine, and her Rory was basking in it too, kissing her more times in public tonight than was decent and drinking far too much ale. But how could she possibly chastise him when she was downing a fair share of the stuff herself? And the kisses, well, she never tired of those.

Her husband held up his glass in the air and began to sing 'Whisky in the Jar', his handsome face alight, eyes twinkling at her with more moisture than usual. How kind life could be when tears were for joy, not sorrow.

The little pub filled with voices as one by one all their friends and neighbours joined in and she acknowledged that she would miss her home, feeling a little misty herself. But such independence wasn't something any one of them would turn down. It had simmered there all along, in their Clancy blood, and her grandfather John had spilt his in the name of rebellion, trying to bring it home. Perhaps one day independence would be gained in Ireland too but until then his descendants would find it on far-flung land. On soil of their very own.

'*Singing Tooral liooral liaddity,*' Rory boomed and the throng joined in, swaying and drinking as one.

Singing Tooral liooral liay
Singing Tooral liooral liaddity
And we're bound for Botany Bay!

Liam came over and put his arm around her and she hugged her youngest brother close. He'd always been a special boy, kind to a fault, but it was his wonderful mind beneath their mother's fair hair that had given them all this opportunity and she knew she'd be forever grateful.

She looked around for their middle sibling and spied him in the corner, singing to that Maeve O'Shannassey who looked far too buxom and ripe for the picking to Eileen's liking. It was one thing if Kieran wanted to marry the girl but quite another if he was just having his usual fun. Her brother was a wild one when it came to drinking and womanising but Maeve wasn't just some local wench; in fact, she was quite likely out of his reach.

Still, he did look quite smitten, Eileen had to admit. Maeve looked to be so too, her pretty face shining as Kieran bent his dark head towards hers to whisper goodness-knows-what. Perhaps she would have a sister-in-law for company on the long voyage south, Eileen mused, pleased at the prospect, but the idea faded as she noted Maeve's glowering father nearby.

Just then the pub door banged open and to her annoyance Lord Whitely walked in with a young man in evening dress. It was his eldest son, William, Eileen realised, recognising the red hair and rat-like features of the teen who'd plagued her in her youth. He was a man now, of one-and-twenty years, same as herself, and on the lookout for a wife, she'd heard, now that he'd finished university. Education was just one of the many advantages he'd always had over her. Shame he'd do nothing useful with it, Eileen mused, figuring he'd likely be set to join his father in managing their estate and making Irish lives miserable. Quite an aspiration, she thought darkly, then shook herself out of such bleak reveries. Tonight was a celebration.

Lord Whitely and William were greeted by Mr O'Shannassey, and Eileen watched as Maeve was summoned to join them, their party taking a table at the back, as far away from commoners as was possible in this cramped pub. Maeve didn't look very keen to go and Kieran was doing a poor job of hiding his disappointment as he worked his way towards the bar. Eileen moved to stand alongside him.

'Drink?' he offered, tossing two pennies on the counter.

'Aye,' Eileen said, 'if you're offering.' She studied her brother's dark expression as he tapped impatiently, waiting. 'Don't tell me you're giving up on the lass already.'

Kieran shot her a glance, his blue eyes flashing. 'Don't meddle, Eiles.'

'Who's meddling?' she said, shrugging her shoulders and taking the arriving ale. 'Although it seems to me news of our good fortune hasn't got around to all corners of this room as yet. Might even things up a bit.'

Kieran sipped his drink and gave the table in the corner a thoughtful glance. 'Aye,' he said, flicking his gaze back to his sister and flashing a quick, sudden grin. Eileen couldn't help but feel a sense of gleeful anticipation as he pushed away from the bar and she followed his weave towards the Whitely–O'Shannassey party.

The crowd began to quieten down as everyone in the room paused to watch, all keen to see how the high and mighty Whitelys would react to the news that they were about to lose their long-suffering, hardworking tenants.

'Good evening, my lord,' Kieran said jovially.

'Evening, Clancy.' Whitely's greeting was reluctant at best.

'And what brings you out on such a cold night as this?' Kieran continued.

Whitely gave Kieran a weary look, unused to being addressed so casually, no doubt. 'William's in town and wanted to have a nightcap at the village,' Whitely replied shortly.

'Ah yes, William. Marvellous to have you back, sir.'

William's eyes narrowed as he stroked a white silver-tipped cane that he held by his side. 'Who is this person?' he said, raking his eyes over Kieran with disdain.

'Just one of your tenants, sir. Be off with you, Clancy. None of us are interested in listening to your nonsense,' Mr O'Shannassey said, leaning forward in front of Maeve to shield her from view. Apparently, Kieran's earlier familiarity with his daughter had taken its toll.

'Certainly, sir, although there was one thing I wanted to address with Lord Whitely…'

'Tell it on the morrow,' Whitely said dismissively. 'I'll be coming to inspect the state of those southern fences. They won't do for my Moileds once the snow comes.' The man was obsessed with his prize herd of cattle, valuing their wellbeing far more highly than that of the humans who tended them.

'No, sir, only I'm afraid it may prove impossible to get them rebuilt in time.' Eileen and Liam had moved to stand close during this exchange and Eileen watched the scene with held breath, noting the entire pub seemed to be doing the same.

Whitely flicked his eyes around the crowd, taking in the engaged audience, then stared down his long nose at Kieran, contempt in his voice now. 'If I say they be built, they be built. That's the end of it.'

'Yes, sir, only I'm afraid it won't be by me. Or by any of my family,' Kieran added, clapping his hand on Liam's shoulder and nodding at Eileen and Rory who stood behind.

'Are you refusing to do your job?' Whitely spat.

'Not refusing, sir, we just won't be able to physically do it from south of the equator.'

There were quite a few chuckles rippling through the crowd as Whitely's jaw fell open.

'What…what are you saying? Are you joining the navy or something?' It was William who spoke and it caused quite a few more sniggers.

'Well, that wouldn't be possible for a woman and three infants now, would it? Can't see much use for a sailor who hasn't learnt to use his legs properly yet, let alone find sea ones.'

This made Rory chortle and Eileen had to dig him in the ribs, fighting laughter herself.

'Out with it, man, and watch your tongue,' Whitely said, his face red by now. 'Are you seeking servant work in the colonies – is that it? I won't be giving any of you Clancys letters, if that's what you're thinking.'

'Oh, we won't be requiring letters from you, my lord. We've one of our own, in fact. Shall I read it to you or perhaps just give you the general gist?' He paused to observe a furious Whitely then smiled broadly. 'Just the bottom line, I take it then? Very well. The fact is we have been given paid passage to Australia; the entire family.' The Whitelys and Mr O'Shannassey all gaped as Kieran continued on. 'Oh, and we've been given a land grant too.

Choice farming area in New South Wales as it happens. We're thinking sheep, isn't that right, Liam?'

Liam nodded, grinning at his brother. 'Perhaps, although cattle seems tempting. I wonder if we can purchase a few Moileds to take with us.'

'Marvellous idea. Interested in making a sale, my lord?'

Whitely looked tempted to punch him in the face but instead he slammed his drink down and stood abruptly. 'Come along, William,' he grated before marching straight out of the pub, the O'Shannasseys in tow, although Maeve managed to sneak a conspiratorial smile at Kieran as they went.

No sooner had the door slammed shut than the place erupted with applause and laughter.

'Ah, but that did feel good,' Kieran said, shaking his head, Liam still chuckling alongside him. 'Drinks all round!' he declared and the violinist in the corner struck a merry tune as the crowd resumed their dancing.

'Whitely's got no answer to that now, does he?' Rory said in Eileen's ear happily. 'We'll have the open seas between us and them in no time, Mrs Murphy.'

'Aye,' Eileen said, but as she looked over at the door she couldn't help but feel there would be more obstacles ahead of them yet, not the least the contest over a pretty girl. Still, that was Kieran's battle, not hers, Eileen decided, turning to wrap her arms around Rory who kissed her soundly for the umpteenth time that evening. It probably wasn't doing the family reputation any good but she just couldn't bring herself to care. Not tonight. Not when they'd made their declaration and at long last had thrown off the shackles that had weighed on their clan for generations.

'To Australia,' Rory said, handing her another ale and clinking her glass. 'And to you, my lovely. I'll have you draped in finery like a queen in no time.'

Eileen laughed but such nonsense meant nil to a girl such as herself. 'The only riches I've ever wanted are right in here,' she said, placing her hand over his heart, 'with no lord or master to dictate our lives.'

'The fates will be kind from now on,' he promised, breaking back into another song with the crowd.

Over the mountains high and steep,
Over the waters wide and deep;
Oh Séarlas Óg will win the day,
Over the hills and far away.

Eileen joined in, the yearning she'd always found in the song replaced with something new, something foreign to her until this day. She knew she'd seek it again and again from now on. It was powerful, this first taste of freedom.

Three

Liam heaved the bale onto the wagon, sweat running down his back despite the cold. It was exhausting work but Whitely had put William in charge and he was riding them hard up until the last of the month. Liam couldn't wait until they finally set off on their journey and could leave the bastard to his own devices. He pitied the Collins family who would take over their tenancy. The son was only fourteen but would be expected to do the work of a man, Liam well knew.

Kieran was working alongside him but was distracted, and with good cause. Maeve O'Shannassey was standing next to William outside her parents' store and had been listening to whatever inanities came out of the man's mouth the good part of half an hour. Not something an interested suitor welcomed at the eleventh hour of their almost-courtship, especially when the other man had her father's approval, something Liam was fairly certain Kieran had little hope of now.

She was the first girl his brother had ever taken seriously and having the wealthiest heir in the county showing an interest in her was dire news indeed. He doubted land on the other side of the globe held much weight in comparison.

'She won't be genteel enough for his father's liking,' Liam muttered to Kieran, trying to ease the sting.

'She's far too bloody good for the likes of him,' Kieran returned, throwing a bale angrily. It slipped and fell to the road and William turned at the sound.

'Watch what you're doing there, Clancy,' he called loftily, pointing his white silver-tipped cane. The brothers now knew it to be his constant companion. 'Father's expecting the herd fed and watered by sundown and won't put up with your slackness today.'

Kieran stood, hands on his hips, and if looks could kill Liam figured William would evaporate in a puff of smoke.

'Don't just stand there, man, get a move on,' William ordered before turning back to Maeve and offering what sounded like some kind of apology. Kieran picked up the bale and threw it on the tray furiously, not noticing Maeve's look of pity, which was probably for the best.

Liam wondered at the true extent of William's intentions and supposed they could well be serious. The connection to an earl, however distant, was certainly in Maeve's favour and O'Shannassey had a fair bit of coin, owning both their house and the large shop as well as a merchant ship in Kilrush, by all reports. It wasn't great wealth by Whitely standards but with a face and a figure like Maeve's thrown into the deal a marriage arrangement wasn't unrealistic.

Not that he would say such a thing to Kieran. His brother had been in a foul temper all week since Maeve's family had gone up to the Whitely estate for high tea the previous Sunday. They hadn't returned until dark; a fact his brother knew because he'd waited hours in the freezing street to watch for their return. Liam wouldn't put it past the Whitelys to be considering a betrothal partly as revenge against the Clancys; punishment for the 'betrayal' of leaving.

The last bale was loaded and the brothers boarded the wagon, setting off down the street, past the rows of brightly coloured houses towards the couple on the corner.

'Wait,' William called, halting their progress. He walked around to the back of the wagon and inspected the load, his pointed face looking for any fault he could find, Liam knew. He hadn't long been overseeing their running of the farm but already he was proving himself every bit as condescending and unreasonable as his father. Maeve watched anxiously nearby, her expression transparently guilty as she studied Kieran's face, but he stared straight ahead, ignoring her, his mouth set in a grim line.

'There's twenty bales on here. I thought father instructed only eighteen.'

Liam spoke, halting anything derisive Kieran might have come out with. 'Mr Leary gave a good price for twenty at fifteen per cent off the usual cost.'

'How would you know how to calculate such a thing?' William scoffed. 'I'm sure he played you for a fool. How much was it?'

'Seventeen shillings.'

'Good God, man,' William exploded. 'How dare you waste my father's money in such a manner!'

'Please, sir, the cost of a bale is usually a shilling each so...'

'So you've wasted a shilling on your purchase, you stupid oaf.'

Kieran was gripping the reins tightly now and turned to stare William in the face. 'You may want to calculate that again, *sir*.'

William's face was contorting in self-righteous anger but he paused as he opened his mouth to respond, his mathematical error obviously registering.

'I was...just making sure you weren't lying. I've met enough crooked Irishmen in my life to necessitate laying such traps; apologies, Miss Maeve. Irish people of your class withstanding, of course.' He bowed slightly towards her and attempted a smile that did little to improve his sharp features.

'Of course,' Maeve said, but she looked upset. Liam found himself sorry for her, having to put up with such a man's intentions, especially as her worried gaze drew back again to Kieran and he saw genuine affection there. Kieran was still avoiding her eyes, looking straight ahead once more.

'If there isn't anything else, sir?' Liam queried.

'No, get back to work and make sure you remember to lock the northern gate this time.'

Liam didn't bother reminding him that the gate had been left open by William himself. The afternoon was already escaping them.

It was another two hours and near dark by the time they'd finished tending to the Moileds. Within that time neither brother had spoken a word but they broke their silence now that they could draw breath, sitting alongside each other on the bench outside the barn to light their pipes.

Liam stared out to a clearing sky, the horizon ablaze in pink and gold above the rich emerald folds of the hills below. The thick blanket of greenery dominated the greater landscape but it was split by the Shannon River, which shone like a satin ribbon as it flowed steadily through the town. Brightly painted village walls were richly reflected and the arches beneath the long stone bridge glowed in the burnished light, adding to the overall prettiness of the scene. There was something almost penitent in a Killaloe sunset, Liam reflected. Like the cold and the wet were apologising for the discomfort they caused by offering this brief, glorious beauty in atonement.

This view outside the barn was one they had taken in every day of their lives once the work was done, rain, hail or shine, just as their father and forefathers had done before them, through their characteristically clear blue Clancy eyes. It was something he would miss, Liam knew, committing it to his memory as early stars began to appear. It wouldn't be long until a different set of stars soared above them, southern constellations that they would follow to the other side of the world.

'Fifteen days and counting,' he reflected out loud, 'and we'll have different skies above us.'

'Aye,' Kieran said, glancing up as a crow sailed against the spectacular sky. 'I was wishing them away but now I feel as if I...' He stopped with a shrug.

'That you're running out of time?'

Kieran nodded, dragging on his pipe.

'If you want her then court her. It's no use sitting back and letting William take over – it's not only up to her father.'

'I know that.'

'I know you know that. You wrote the book on chasing lasses but this is different. If it's marriage you want, you'll have to get serious about this, Kieran.'

'I am serious about it.'

'Well, ignoring her and brooding about it isn't a very good plan. You really *are* running out of time; every minute counts now.'

'*I know that!*'

'Well, what the hell are you doing sitting around whining at me then?'

Kieran slammed down his pipe and stood up, striding off to the gate without a backwards glance, his expression so determined Liam could almost feel sorry for William now.

Almost, but not quite.

It was a precarious position to be in but Kieran really couldn't think of any other way to see her. Her father had firmly shut the door in his face and she was well and truly ensconced inside under lock and key for the night, hence his perch upon the roof above her windowsill. He was hardly comfortable, hanging with his head at an angle that had the blood rushing to his ears, but it was the only way he could spy when she arrived. *Fortune favours the brave, if sometimes foolish,* Liam often liked to say. Kieran wondered which one he was tonight.

Dinner must be well over by now, judging by the rumbling of his stomach, and Kieran knew Maeve enjoyed writing in her journal in her room at night. She'd even confessed to a few entries about him but not the details, of course.

Just then she appeared, beautiful as ever in a blue and white flowered dress, and Kieran had a terrible urge to wait for her to lift it over her head and reveal what lay beneath, but shook his head clear. He leaned over with a stick he'd picked up earlier instead and tapped lightly on the window. It was louder than he'd intended and he winced.

Maeve heard it immediately and walked over cautiously, staring out then jumping as she saw him, dangling half upside down. Possibly looking a bit mad. But to her credit she regained her composure and lifted the latch to open the window.

'What on earth are you doing?'

'Visiting.' Kieran said it with what he hoped was a light-hearted, daring manner and she seemed to think it was, letting out a small giggle.

'Goodness, you could fall to your death.'

'At least I'd see an angel before I pass,' he said and she giggled again. Kieran would have loved to continue to coax more amusement from her but his legs were beginninΩg to ache. 'I need to talk to you, Maeve. Meet me by the river,' he pleaded, changing his tone.

'Now?' she said, scandalised.

'Yes. Please. It's important; I must speak with you.' He slid slightly and her hand flew to her mouth.

'Oh dear lord...alright. Give me a minute though.'

'I'll wait near the bridge,' he said before clambering away, glad to get down at last and run off to wait for her.

The water was dark as it eddied against the shore and the moonlight shone across it, lighting the ripples in liquid silver rows. Kieran watched, impatient for her arrival, although still unsure what he would say. It would be better to say nothing, of course. He father would never allow them to be together and the only sensible thing to do was to walk away. That was what he should do, anyway.

Ten minutes or so later she finally came, and he was so happy she had turned up he forgot about protocol, wrapping her in his arms, and it felt so natural, so right. Kieran knew then, suddenly without question, that he had to have her by his side in life. She was his. It was unthinkable that she ever belong to another.

'What...what was it you had to tell me?' she said, her words muffled against his chest, the sweet scent of honey assailing his senses.

'Just this,' he replied, throwing words aside for the second time in their relationship and kissing her in the same sudden way he'd done in her front parlour that day, in a rush of unrestrained longing that stole their breath. 'I love you, Maeve,' he said, the confession like a weight lifting off his heart. 'Come with me to Australia. Leave all of this behind.'

Her face crumpled and she fell against him, crying as she told him what he'd feared. 'Father...Father is hoping for me to marry William.'

'And what do you want, my love?'

She pulled back, wiping at her cheeks, and the moonlight lit the tears still swimming in her eyes. 'I want you,' she whispered.

He kissed her again, her soft body pressed against his, and his passion for her was so strong he had to fight against himself to restrain from taking her, then and there on the grass near the old stone bridge with that dark, silvery river lapping nearby. He pulled his mouth from hers and held her in a long hug instead, trying to calm the raging heat in his veins.

'Ah, my girl, my beautiful girl. What are we to do?' He rocked her against him, his chin resting on her fair hair and she sighed, the gentle lap of the small waves the only other sound.

'I won't be able to fight it if Father and Lord Whitely come to an arrangement.'

'No,' he had to agree, 'but…but you could avoid it altogether.' He pulled her back, holding both her hands to watch her face as he asked the next. 'Run away, Maeve. Elope with me to the other side of the earth and take your chances on a life filled with love and adventure. It's what you want in your heart. You know it's true.' He was taking a big risk in the game now but Liam was right. He was running out of time for any more caution.

'But it's…it's so far from my family…' She was hesitating so he tried again, using every bit of persuasion and charm he'd ever possessed.

'I will be your family. I will be your sun and your moon.' He threw his hands towards the sky, where that brilliant orb glowed above them, before kneeling before her. 'I will worship you all the days of your life. Marry me, Maeve. Choose a life with me.'

She bit her lip. 'Father says you're nothing but a smooth-talking rogue.'

'I'm using words because they are all I have for now. The only proof of my love…and I do love you, Maeve, more than the fields love the rain…'

'I'll have no money this way, no dowry…'

'More than the river loves the sea…'

'Kieran…'

'More than life itself, Maeve. *Marry me.*'

Maeve's lovely brown eyes bore into his as her mouth slowly stretched into a smile. 'Aye, then, how can I say no to such smooth talk as that?'

Kieran felt his whole life turn on a pin in that moment and he stood up so fast and kissed her so urgently it made him dizzy, but that was quickly overridden by his desire once more. And something else. Suddenly it wasn't just about winning a game; it had become something far more sacred. A blending of their entire beings, an entwining of hearts.

'We'll have to keep it a secret from everyone, even your siblings. No-one can know,' Maeve whispered, her forehead resting against his.

'Aye,' he agreed. 'I'll come for you before dawn's light on the day and we'll marry before anyone can stop this from happening.'

'What about my passage?'

Kieran frowned. He hadn't thought about that.

'I'll figure something out,' he promised. 'Just make sure you're packed and ready to go and I'll take care of everything else.'

Maeve smiled at him, her trust evident. 'I expect it goes without saying but I…I love you too, Kieran.'

Something melted inside him at her words and he kissed her long and slow, a new reverence there now. It may well go without saying but he was damn glad she had.

Four

He was turning it over in his hands when Liam found him.

'Thinking about wearing it around town now, are you? Can't say you won't get mugged.'

Kieran started, then wrapped up the fob watch in the velvet cloth it had always lived in, placing it back in the drawer. 'People aren't so desperate that they'd rob a friend.'

'They might not do it for the watch, just on account of you lording about the place now that you've got land.'

'Ha,' Kieran said, but there was deep thought in those eyes.

'What's going on?' There'd never been room for anything less than straight honesty between them.

'I may need to sell it,' Kieran said. 'How would you feel about that?'

'Will you tell me what you're needing to sell it for?'

'No.'

Liam nodded slowly. 'Well, sell it if you must. You'd have good reason, I know, but don't forget we'll need as much money as possible to build a farm. It'll take more than trees and hard work, Kieran.'

'Aye, I know.' Kieran looked worried as he rubbed his face.

'I trust you,' Liam said simply and his brother sent him a grateful smile before he walked out. Liam had no idea what Kieran would need so much money for right now but he'd bet his own last shilling it had something to do with Maeve O'Shannassey. And whichever way you looked at things, that didn't bode well. The girl was being seriously courted by William Whitely now and everyone knew a marriage betrothal was inevitable, despite the fact she and Kieran could barely tear their eyes from one another whenever they crossed paths. His brother was destined for a broken heart when they left but there seemed little to be done about it now.

Liam shoved such thoughts away, busying himself with the last of the packing instead and focusing on the new life that beckoned come tomorrow. The past few weeks had dragged by so slowly it seemed impossible that the mundane, exacting existence they were all well used to would change so drastically. Even just the idea of being on a tall ship seemed ridiculously exciting. Liam had waited his whole life to push out from the shoreline into the great oceans of the world, to follow the gulls until land was so distant even they disappeared. To let go.

It promised to be a day he would never forget and it tingled through his skin every time he thought about it.

'Here's the last,' Eileen puffed as she dragged a case out of her and Rory's tiny bedroom.

'Good lord. How have you managed to accumulate enough stuff to fill another trunk?'

'It's mostly seeds 'n' herbs and vials and the like, and warm blankets of course. The children will need them on the voyage.'

'Not so much when we get there, I'd wager. It's not near as cold as here, from what I've read.'

Young Thomas could be heard terrorising his brothers outside. They were playing Captain again, a game they'd invented that involved Thomas, the eldest, always playing captain of the ship they would soon board in real life, his little brothers James and Matthew his hapless crew. Eileen rolled her eyes as she went to the door. 'If you don't behave I'll have you tied to the mast when we go,' she yelled and a quieter game soon followed. 'What were you and Kieran discussing?' she said, turning back into the room and walking over to the fire to put the water on.

Liam shrugged. 'He had Da's watch out. I think he plans to sell it.'

'*What?* What on earth for?' Eileen asked. It was the only thing of value the family possessed and she looked suitably concerned.

'He didn't say.'

She sat in the rocking chair then, tapping the teapot thoughtfully as she waited for the water to boil. 'Mr Leary said he saw him down in Kilrush last week. Said he was at the shipping office for some time.'

Liam frowned. 'I've got the letters of passage so I don't know what he was doing in there.'

'Maybe he was just confirming things again,' Eileen said.

Liam felt the blood drain as another possibility occurred to him. 'Maybe he feels we're one ticket short.'

Eileen stared at him, aghast. 'But he…he would need Maeve to elope,' she said. 'Good God, what will Whitely do then?'

'Let alone her father. They have connections everywhere in port. They could have him chased down and thrown in gaol.'

Eileen paled and stood to pace the room. 'We'll have to talk him out of it. 'Tis sheer madness.' She shook her head angrily. 'What the hell is he thinking, doing this?'

'He's thinking he'll bed the girl so fast it will be too late and Whitely won't want her.'

She paused, considering that. 'He'll have to wed her before we board. Perhaps even tonight.'

'Looks like we have a decision to make then, you and I,' Liam said, 'whether to halt this thing or help him do it. If he's made up his mind there'll be no stopping it; maybe it would be best we say nothing and I follow him – make sure someone has his back.'

'Aye,' Eileen said, sitting down heavily. 'I suppose that's an idea. Stupid fool, endangering all our futures with his reckless ways.'

'Fortune favours the brave, if sometimes foolish.' Liam looked over at her and gave a helpless shrug. 'And they say there's no fool like a fool in love.'

Eileen sighed. 'Except the fools who help those who are.'

Kieran checked the watch again, thinking it was nice to hold the time for a change. Like he was holding fate in his hands. It was almost three. Perfect. He clicked it shut and wrapped it carefully, stuffing it in his bag and tiptoeing his way out. The letter on the table would tell his family that he would meet them in port at midday when the ship was due to sail and to take his things on board. They were all packed on the back of the cart, along with everything else the Clancys were taking with them, and Mr Leary would return the dray along with the horse once he'd waved them off.

There was only one thing left to do and it was the most dangerous part of the plan of course: getting Maeve to Kilrush. He hoped she'd made it to the bridge with her father's horse and hurried his steps.

It was pitch black as he arrived and he trod carefully now, aware she could have been seen or caught.

'Maeve?' he whispered and a figure came out of the shadows.

'Kieran,' she said, rushing to him, and he held her for a relieved moment.

'All ready, my love?' he said and she nodded, her eyes filled with apprehension. He kissed her, putting what assurance he could into the act, and she relaxed a little in his arms. 'Let's go.' Kieran mounted the steed and pulled her up behind him, instantly glad of her warmth and form at his back. The stallion's name was Midnight and he was a fine animal; Kieran just hoped he wouldn't be caught as a horse-thief as well this night. Woman-thief would be bad enough.

They rode swiftly, putting distance between the past and the future with every mile, and Kieran urged Midnight on, conscious that he needed to meet the man from the pawnshop at dawn to get the cash, pay for Maeve's passage and get to the church on time for their nuptials. Quite a heady schedule.

The moon shone brightly above as it danced through the clouds and Kieran was grateful for its pale light. A lame horse was the last thing they needed now. On and on they went, streaking along the road, the wind sharp against their cheeks, the bite of the last Irish spring night they would ever know cutting through their clothes as they made their escape.

Then finally they could smell the sea salt: Kilrush was there at last. Kieran slowed Midnight to a walk as they entered the port town, mindful of drawing any attention to themselves as they clopped along the shadowed streets towards the pawn shop where the sale would take place. It was eerily quiet, save the lash of the sea that pushed and pulled like a restless animal against the docks, and Kieran had every sense on alert as he drew up near some stables and lifted Maeve down.

'You need to stay well out of sight,' he said, checking the watch. 'Don't worry, we've half an hour yet. I'll wait with you.' He took her to the stall he'd paid for last week where her travel trunk was well-hidden and tethered Midnight before settling her on a hay bale with a blanket to wait. 'Are you too cold?' he asked solicitously, drawing her close and kissing her forehead.

She shook her head. 'Not really.'

Kieran kissed her mouth then and she kissed him back with an eagerness that matched his own. 'Not much longer, my girl.'

Checking the watch again he saw it was time to make his sale and he tasted her lips once more before moving off. It was freezing near the shop, the wind that whipped off the water bitterly cold, and Kieran willed the man to come as the faint light of dawn crept over the horizon. Fortunately, he arrived, right on time, and Kieran went into the shop, fetching the sum he'd been promised before exiting. So far so good.

He reached the stables once more and hurried over to Maeve, puzzled to find her crying, her body pressed against the wall.

'I'm sorry, Kieran,' she managed, but he didn't hear any more. He couldn't see anything either, only the blur of bodies and the flash of a white cane. Then a sudden terrifying void of pain-filled pitch black.

Liam was getting worried, more and more so with every passing minute as they searched every street and corner for Kieran. The sun had been up a good few hours by now and the situation was moving on towards critical. Kieran had left a note saying he'd meet them at the ship but Liam and Eileen knew the chances of him turning up on time, let alone unharmed, were greatly diminishing. Not now that they'd seen Maeve O'Shannassey being led out of town by her father in Lord Whitely's carriage, the family horse in tow. If she'd been caught it was highly likely Kieran had been too.

Liam cursed his decision to follow Kieran at a distance on their neighbour's mare, knowing that if he hadn't lost sight of his brother due to the O'Shannasseys' far superior mount he might have prevented this from happening.

'Kieran,' Eileen called desperately. They'd checked the gaol; they'd even checked the morgue, but he was nowhere to be found. And the boat that promised them all a better life was sailing in half an hour's time. Liam knew he wouldn't get on it without Kieran; he could never leave without finding his brother first, no matter what the cost.

'I tried the shipping office,' Rory said, running towards them, panting. 'They've not seen him.'

'Did you try the docks?' Eileen asked, her voice tight with worry.

'Aye. Not there either.'

'Did you try beneath them?' Liam said and three pairs of terrified eyes collided.

'I'm coming too...' Eileen said.

'No, we have to get back to the children. They need to get on board,' Rory said.

'Mr Leary...'

'Has done enough.'

Eileen looked mutinously at her husband before her shoulders slumped. 'Will...will we still go?'

'You will,' Liam said. 'I can follow later, if need be.'

'You may never save the money...'

'I'll no' leave without him, Eiles.'

His sister's eyes filled with tears as she gave him a brief embrace. 'God go with you.' Liam held her tight then drew away to shake Rory's hand.

'If I don't...'

Rory simply nodded, his eyes wet, and Liam turned away to run towards the docks. It was dank underneath and filled with the rot of refuse and the stench of fish remains among the polluted water and seaweed.

'Kieran,' he called, straining to see under the boards in the darkness after the brilliant sun of moments before. He moved along, his heart freezing every time he thought he saw something human. There was a discarded stained shirt then a seafarer's boot;

a broken china doll then a ripped sailor's coat. But no beaten, bloodied man, dead or alive.

The ship sounded its bell and Liam broke into a sweat, despite the cold.

'Kieran,' he said brokenly, hope beginning to fade. There would be no new life now and no old life worth living without his elder brother beside him. His closest friend in the world.

'It's me, Liam,' he said pointlessly to the dark, terrible place. Sunlight was slicing where the boards didn't quite meet, more like blinding walls than comforting rays, and he walked through them with blurring vision as dread took its inevitable hold. *'Kieran.'*

Just then there was a faint moan from further down and Liam turned his head, scarcely believing he'd heard it. But no, there it was again. He trod carelessly now as he pulled his feet through the sludge of the putrid ground, moving even faster as he saw an arm, then legs, then a face.

'Dear God,' Liam breathed, his tears running unchecked as he looked at his brother's swollen countenance, so badly beaten he was barely recognisable. But he was alive. The bell sounded a second time, spurring Liam into fast action as he lifted Kieran and strode as best he could towards the sound.

'Eileen! *Eileen!*'

She had all but lost hope as she scanned the docks, immoveable as she stood her vigil at the ship's prow, a stiff wind drying the tears on her cheeks as soon as they landed. Rosary beads in hand. They were pulling up the gangplanks and Eileen heard the sound like the building of a casket, wooden slabs sealing Kieran's fate.

'*Eileen!*'

Her name was being carried on that wind now and she turned to find its source, gasping at the sight of her two brothers, one straining to carry the other who looked lifeless in his arms.

'Stop!' Eileen screamed, running to halt the sailors from dragging up the last planks. Rory rushed by her, thrusting Matthew into her arms and running to help Liam carry Kieran to the ship and get him on board.

'Oh Kieran, oh dear God, what have they done to you...' Eileen moaned, kneeling down next to him. His dark hair was matted with blood and his face was mottled in angry welts that warped his handsome features like a grotesque mask. Her earlier fear turned to shock and it stole the air from her lungs as she fought to fill them in great gasps between her tears. 'What have they done...' She choked again, gently touching his poor face, her fingers trembling.

Someone had called the ship's master, Captain Reynolds, and he came over to investigate the scene as the children looked on with large eyes.

'Get Dr Stewart,' he ordered. 'What's happened here?'

'He...he must have been robbed,' Liam said.

'They've certainly made a fine mess of him. Look out there,' Captain Reynolds said as the doctor arrived and the crowd moved back. He gave him a quick grim-faced examination and looked over at Eileen.

'You his wife?'

'No, sir,' Eileen managed, clearing her throat and fighting for composure. 'I'm his sister.'

Dr Stewart nodded, nothing in his expression offering any comfort. 'I don't need to tell you he's in a bad way. I'd be surprised if he makes it a day on the seas. Best take him ashore.'

'No,' Liam said firmly, 'he stays with us.'

'Brother?' Dr Stewart guessed.

'Aye, sir. There's nothing for him back there. Please, Captain,' he said, desperation seeping through as he looked at the man, 'we're his only kin...'

'Don't you want to find the culprit who did this?' Captain Reynolds said.

Liam avoided his gaze. 'He's probably long gone by now.'

The captain looked to hesitate and Eileen stood her full five feet two inches next to Liam, finding courage by his side. 'I'll take care of him, Captain. I've tended the sick many times before and I can do it again…under your instructions of course, sir,' she rushed to appease the doctor. 'Please,' she said, putting her arms around her young sons, 'don't make us leave him behind.'

'Not only up to you, miss, is it?' Captain Reynolds returned. 'God will have a say in this one.'

'Then I'll pray for him too.'

She searched the man's face, hoping for a flicker of compassion, knowing all of their fates lay in his next words.

'Take him inside,' he relented and Eileen let go of the breath that was squeezing her chest tight.

'Thank you,' she said. 'Oh thank you, sir.'

He gave her a gruff smile. 'Just make sure you keep him alive, young lady,' he said, turning to walk away. 'Captains never like to be proven wrong.'

'No, sir,' she muttered as they lifted Kieran and carried him off, 'neither do Clancys.'

The sailors lifted the last of the planks and the great ship began to pull away, cutting the water slowly as it sought momentum. It wasn't the wondrous start they'd all dreamed of but they were all on board and moving towards the open sea, and somewhere within, Eileen felt her determination lift and swell. Their longed-for future had arrived at last and if her first call of duty was to nurse Kieran back to life so he could be a part of that, so be it.

The English had taken many things from the Clancy clan on Irish soil, she reflected, taking one last look at her homeland. But no more. Now they were as free as the elements that would drive them forward and Eileen knew she would find strength in that; enough to let flow from her healing hands into her brother's broken form. The Whitelys would not have this final piece of vengeance, she vowed with quiet ferocity. And no more Clancy blood would ever be shed at an Englishman's hand.

Eileen collected her bag and made her way towards the infirmary as the immense white sails unfurled above, stretching their arcs towards the sun. They caught the wind and she felt the ship pull with its power, making her lurch momentarily before she moved on, the water stretching before them like a shimmering blue highway; the waves fanning against the prow in encouraging spray.

The canvas billowed strongly and already she knew she'd forever welcome that sound; a beating drum of promise that would deliver them from any more injustice. And lead them all to freedom in a great southern land.

The Price of an Apple

Five

Liverpool, England, August 1851

The grandfather clock ticked loudly in the hall, marking the time with solemn finality as each minute slipped away, just as life was slipping away from the man beyond the door. Eve Richards stared at the solid wood barrier, wishing the doctor would hurry in his ablutions, trying to hold onto hope even though that precious emotion had slipped away days ago. It had been the same with her mother when Eve was five years old; few people ever survived the last stages of consumption. She'd known her father wouldn't make it once the blood stained the pillows. It wouldn't be long now.

Footsteps approached, brisk clicks on the polished floorboards, and Eve knew it was Mrs Matthews, the housekeeper. No-one else would be allowed up here at such a time. Sure enough, as Eve raised her eyes they collided with the bespectacled gaze of the woman who'd become like a mother to her these last twelve and a half years of her life.

'Where's your wrap, Evie? You'll catch your death...' she chastised, then pursed her lips tight at the unintentional slip. 'Here,' she said, more gently now as she took her own shawl and wrapped it about Eve's shoulders. She sat next to her on the bench that lined the wall opposite her father's room and Eve knew she was searching more carefully for her words now. Not that it would guarantee any subtlety from the woman; Mrs Matthews was renowned for speaking plainly. 'Dr Hallows knows what he's doing, child.'

Eve simply nodded, too numb to remark.

'Mind you, you'd think he'd change his name considering his profession,' she whispered, giving Eve a small, conspiratorial smile. 'Hardly a reassurance now, is it? Hallows indeed.'

Eve's mouth tugged at the corners into a small smile too. Mrs Matthews was likely the only person on earth capable of coaxing such a reaction from her now.

'I've spoken to Sir Humphrey,' Mrs Matthews told her, patting Eve's hands with her own work-worn one. 'I think he'll allow you to go if that's what you wish.' Eve looked down at those familiar fingers, rarely idle, and swollen at the knuckles these days; red where the single wedding band lay. Her husband had passed many years ago but that ring would remain all the days of Mrs Matthews's life, Eve knew.

'I'm not sure what to do,' Eve said, her voice barely a rasp after hours of silence.

'Doris is a good woman and Lady Margaret's children are of a manageable age. You'll do well to take the position, Evie, although I'll sorely miss you.' The admission made the older woman's eyes fill but she brushed the tears away immediately. A servant's tears were reserved for only the cruellest of life's moments. Some would be shed soon enough this day.

'But Master Robert…'

'…will do as his father orders,' Mrs Matthews said brusquely. They were brave words but ultimately they both knew she would have little power over Eve's future.

'He...he said...' Eve began but she was interrupted by the turn of the doorknob and whatever admissions she would have made died on her lips as Dr Hallows appeared. His face was grave, and Eve thought vaguely that he appeared almost spectre-like in the early morning light.

'I'm sorry, Miss Eve, but he hasn't long.'

She'd expected it, of course, there was no other outcome from here, but each syllable dragged at her heart and her body felt otherworldly as she moved into the darkened room. The lamp burnt an orange glow across the bed where her father lay, ravaged by months of disease, a bare imprint of the man who was once, in his prime, considered robust. He'd even been approached to take up boxing in his youth but he'd declined, of course. An aspiring butler was a gentleman, not a rogue. Still, he'd told the tale of being forced to defend a young damsel in distress on more than one occasion; a maiden at the markets so pretty a lout had approached her right in the middle of the square, demanding a kiss. Those eager lips were met with her father's fist instead and the maiden... well, she became a butler's wife: Mrs Emma-Kate Richards.

Eve sank to the chair alongside him now, delaying the pain of watching his last, laboured breaths by looking across at a sketch someone had once made of her mother instead. Her image sat on her father's bedside table as it always had, pride of place in its frame; a face much like Eve's, people said, heart-shaped with large hazel eyes.

There were other items there too: a jug of water no more to be drunk from, bloodstained cloths that Mrs Matthews was already whisking from the room to wash or perhaps throw away. A bowl of porridge, untouched, a wooden comb with a few silvered hairs that still clung. An unfinished novel by Charles Dickens that Eve had been reading to him since his hands had become too weak to hold the tome. Life was passing in this room, every item within it screamed that truth inside the silence, from the starched butler's uniforms to the polished shoes that would ever remain waiting for their owner to don them. Just traces and shadows now as a body farewelled its soul.

Eve fought against that rare comfort of tears to give the man who was dying her only strength in his last moments. He deserved that much. He deserved far more.

The impeccably dressed, ever-patient, consummate gentleman: Graham Harrison Richards. Butler, widower, father to Eve, his only child.

The last words dropped into her mind as she looked to his face at last. Then the strength she'd hoped to impart began to wilt as she traced every crease; lines that showed the gentleness of his nature marked his forehead, once darting dimples sank into hollow cheeks.

His eyes flickered and she sensed he wanted to speak.

'Evie,' he said, barely audible, and she leaned close, clasping his hand against her cheek.

'I'm here, Papa, I'm here.'

His hand gave hers the slightest of squeezes and her heart ached at the realisation of just how weak he'd become.

'Emma...Kate...' he managed.

'I know, Papa, I know...it's alright. Go to her now. She's waiting with a choir of angels for you.' She hoped that idea would comfort him, about the angels. Evie had been chosen to sing at Liverpool Cathedral once, when she was a girl. Her father had beamed with undisguised pride the entire time. He'd always been proud of everything she did, from learning to read and write by candlelight under his nightly instruction to speaking in his genteel way, unlike the rest of the household servants.

'Ave...'

'...Maria,' she finished for him, trying to smile as she brushed back a wisp of his hair.

'Sing,' he said on the faintest of breaths and she tried to do as he asked, softly, brokenly, until the fingers entwined in hers lost their warmth and the shallow rise and fall of his chest stilled, like an ocean losing the tide.

'I love you,' she whispered but his soul had departed and all that was left to do was relinquish those tears at last; it was time now. And so she gave them to that room, to all the traces and shadows, knowing from this day forward she would no longer be a butler's daughter.

No longer protected. No longer a child.

The sky was the colour of lemon flesh at the horizon with heavy clouds drifting above in a thick, slate blanket. Nearby the priest was droning on in Latin but Eve wasn't really listening. She was thinking about that colour and the times her parents took her down to the seaside at Blackpool to learn how to swim when she was young. She'd been allowed to eat fish and chips and enjoy a drink people called 'lemonade'. She wished she could taste it again sometime; it was like nothing she'd ever tried, both sour and sweet at the same time, and with wondrous bubbles that had tickled her nose.

'...*in nomine Patris et Filii et Spiritus Sancti*...'

A clump of cold earth was thrust into her hand and Eve looked at it dully.

'Toss it in, love,' Mrs Matthews whispered in her ear and she did so, feeling disconnected to the whole affair as it landed with a thud on the coffin. She held no faith in funerals improving anyone's chances of going to heaven, placing far more stock on how a life had been lived as to whether or not you 'graduated' as a soul. Her father had been a religious man but more importantly a good one, and he would be with her mother now, of that Eve had no doubt. It was her own mortal soul that was potentially in peril.

The gravedigger began to pile on more earth and Eve watched the wood disappear, her throat tight with grief.

'He was the best of men,' Mrs Matthews said, holding her arm about Eve's waist, 'and your mother was one of the kindest women I ever knew, bless her soul. They'll never leave you really, I promise.' Eve nodded, wondering at the truth of such a notion. Heaven and earth had always seemed very separate places to her.

The crowd of people slowly began to disperse and Eve realised it was all over as she turned to walk back towards the cart with Mrs Matthews, bracing herself against the wind.

'Miss Eve,' boomed a voice and she paused to face her employer, Sir Humphrey Arlington, and his fur-clad wife, Lady Sophia. 'May we convey our deepest sympathies, my dear. Richards was a marvellous butler. I daresay I will never see the likes of him again in my household.'

'No, sir. Thank you, sir,' Eve responded, knowing that was true. Quite a few of Sir Humphrey's friends had tried to poach her father for themselves but he had remained, characteristically loyal to his original master all of his days.

Lady Sophia nodded at Eve, engaged for a change, before moving on with her husband. She was 'a strange fish', as Mrs Matthews liked to say, cold and uninterested in anything or anyone save her prize cavaliers who were already yapping from the carriage, impatient. Still, it meant something that she had come today, Eve supposed, in fact many of the Arlingtons' friends had come in all their finery, and her father certainly deserved such recognition.

Watching them depart her breath caught sharply as another voice came from behind.

'My condolences, Miss Eve.' She turned and knew she was blushing, although whether from nerves or fear it was hard to determine. Master Robert, Sir Humphrey's youngest son, stood before her, his hat in his hand and his dark eyes sincere beneath thick strands of brown hair. They were whipping about wildly in the breeze and Eve chose to be distracted by that rather than hold his gaze. 'He will be much missed by us all.'

'Thank you, Master Robert.'

'I thought perhaps today you might enjoy the warmth of the carriage,' he offered, gesturing ahead.

Mrs Matthews was rigid with disapproval but Eve could hardly refuse such an honour so she walked with him down the path and allowed his assistance up the steps, trying not to flinch at his touch.

'Thank you,' she said, settling her skirts then gripping her gloved fingers tight.

He was studying her, even more intently than usual, and Eve could feel the heat in her cheeks as she waited to hear what he would say.

'It suits you,' he finally declared. 'Black, I mean.'

'I wouldn't imagine mourning dress could suit anyone, sir.'

He shrugged. 'It does you.'

The carriage struggled along the cobblestone streets as they left the cemetery near the cathedral and traversed across the city for home. Eve tried to appear composed, although he was unnerving her with that stare. And surely telling a woman she looked well in mourning was bordering on unchivalrous. What would Mrs Matthews have to say about that?

'Father tells me you're serious about moving on.'

Eve blushed again and looked out the window to avoid those probing eyes. 'Yes, sir. I have applied for the position of nanny with Lady Margaret Houghton. Mrs Matthews's sister is the cook there.'

'Yes, I know,' Robert said, still staring intently and Eve regretted her impulse to meet his gaze. His eyes were so dark they sometimes lost the brown within the centres, part of his mother's Italian heritage, apparently. 'I hope they don't accept it.'

'Why is that, sir?' she asked, clenching her hands harder.

Robert smiled then, causing her stomach to knot. 'I think there may be better prospects for you here.'

That made her uneasy. He'd said something similar a few weeks ago, flippantly to his parents but designed to be overheard; something about her 'potential' and how he couldn't imagine her ever being released to another household. He hadn't elaborated further but there was a private glance delivered to her at the time and, despite her naivety, she knew there was a message within it. Something beyond propriety.

Mrs Matthews seemed to have picked up on it, whatever 'it' was. It was the same message that underscored his tone whenever he addressed her of late and it was in his touch whenever their fingers should collide; a cup and saucer here, hat and gloves there. It left her on edge, affected by the tiny shocks each encounter produced and ever wary of his presence.

Perhaps he was trifling with her, perhaps it was more.

'Mrs Matthews is making the arrangements...'

'It isn't Mrs Matthews's life though, is it?'

She levelled a gaze of her own then. 'No, sir. It is mine.'

He smiled again, in his quick, sudden way that so easily disarmed. 'It certainly is, Miss Eve, and you are free to make your own decision in this matter, of course. Although you may want to consider what you'd truly be giving up by leaving.' He leaned closer and she could smell the scent of tobacco and cologne clinging to his coat, a masculine scent that seemed to suddenly fill the carriage. 'The only people you still consider family, a guaranteed place within the household, the potential to rise to lady's maid or perhaps even housekeeper one day...' She knew all of these things. The only reason she really had for leaving was a fresh start. '...and employers you can trust.' His eyes were intense now and as dark as his cloak. 'You do trust me, don't you, Evie?'

'Miss Eve,' she said faintly as his face drew ever closer to hers.

'I prefer Evie. It can be our little secret. Along with this.' And to her shock his lips were suddenly on hers.

Eve had been kissed before, well, the odd chaste peck on the cheek, but there was nothing even remotely chaste about the urgent kiss Robert was suddenly stealing. She hadn't even known such kisses existed until Molly, the maid, had told her of secret trysts she'd shared with the stable hand, John Jackson. 'Tongues and all, Evie, and so busy with his hands I had to wriggle like an eel to stop things goin' on so fast.'

Evie wasn't wriggling, she was paralysed by shock. Then her father's face came to mind and she found her resistance, pushing Robert back in indignation that he would do this today, of all days.

'No,' she gasped. 'Please, sir...I cannot.'

'You're so beautiful,' he whispered, his breath short against her face as he looked down at the dark material across her breast. 'I cannot rid you from my thoughts.'

'Y...you should not say such things, sir,' she said, trying not to lose all composure. Her hands grasped at the bench arms as she strained away from him, her heart beating like a wild rabbit, but he followed and kissed her again. It was difficult to move away now, with his chest close and his hand curving around her chin to the nape of her neck, and it was no longer rushed and desperate, this second kiss. He was turning it into something else, some kind of hypnotic dance, filled with longing and unspoken questions.

'It's unbearable, watching you,' he said in a brief, drugging pause, 'wanting you.' Robert took to kissing her neck then and she felt a strange, curling warmth unfold as skin met skin; foreign and dangerous, like her body was starting to betray her mind.

'Evie,' he said again. Too familiar. Too intimate. Too close.

But that warmth was running down her arms, her chest and deep into her core. Crowding her logic. Stealing her breath.

'*Robert.*'

The word felt separate from her, unbidden and removed from sense, and it took a moment for her to register she'd even said it. Then reality slammed its way back through.

'No! *I don't want this,*' she exclaimed, pulling away and dropping any address, even the customary 'sir' in her sudden anger at both him and herself. Fortunately, the carriage began to slow as they arrived at the house and he drew back to his seat, breathing hard and dark eyes burning. Then the footman opened the door and Eve scrambled to alight, trying to avoid any further contact, but she couldn't avoid hearing his final whisper.

It followed her to bed that night and deep into her dreams.

'Then why did you say my name?'

Six

Liverpool, September 1851

Mrs Matthews was prattling but Eve didn't mind too much tonight, especially as the conversation was focused on Lady Margaret and the position with her they both hoped Eve would secure. Surely the letter would arrive soon, Eve thought nervously. Autumn's chill now laced the air, which marked near three weeks of waiting.

'Doris says his lordship owns some prize horseflesh; even lets the servants ride some of the lesser beasts for exercise, which is generosity itself, if you ask me. A good man, Evie, you'll do well to mind your manners and see if you don't earn his approval. Speaking of which I've a mind to send Doris another letter, just to check, like…'

Eve drifted off as Mrs Matthews elaborated on her idea of sending a reminder to her sister for the third time that evening. Still, it was better than the constant singing of her potential new master's praises. Eve wasn't keen on overly impressing the man of the house. The woman would do just fine.

Thinking about her own younger master she looked out the sitting room window with growing consternation. He was in town tonight with his set which meant he would likely be coming back late, a good thing, but also likely to be inebriated, which was very, very bad. It was hard enough trying to ignore him when he was sober. When he was in his cups it became pointless. One could hardly disregard the heat in his covert stares, the uncensored desire he now confessed in close whispers as she passed him by. Wine was a truth serum, so her father had always said, and when Robert drank the truth spilt out, like a cup running over, across her body and into her soul.

'*You're so beautiful I can scarcely think, nor talk with sense.*'

'*It's intoxicating, watching you. Like a delicious torture.*'

'*I couldn't sleep last night for tossing in my sheets, knowing you're just one floor beneath.*'

Then last night, the most dangerous of all.

'*You know it's just a matter of time until we're together, don't you?*'

It had made her heart beat hard against its cage, yet there were other sensations at play too. Her own breathing seemed to stop each time he neared, and her skin became strangely more alive, like a sudden hot breeze brushed across it, raising each tiny hair on her arms. An entity ran through the very air between them now and the house seemed heavy under its spell, charging her senses and paralysing all rational thought.

Eve was being chased down by it, the prey in a hunt, running out of places to deny its existence as Robert pursued her, like her namesake through Eden. And her greatest fear was what she would do if caught. If she would be betrayed by the flaw that cursed both first woman and man.

Temptation.

Eve knew she had to resist him; it was sheer madness to succumb. There would be very little sympathy for a young female servant if she was found in a compromising position, favoured butler's orphan or no. Women had ever carried the weight of consequence when it came to sins of the flesh; the curse of holding the apple during that first tempted bite.

Her father had often told her she'd been named Eve to remind her to always listen for truth and never be fooled by the lures of the serpent. Yet, there he was, barely cold in the ground and already the snake was hissing in her ear, offering her forbidden fruit and placing her in danger of losing everything her father had worked so hard to give her: safety, security, respectability. Her only hope at fulfilling his planned destiny for her was this new position – far away from Robert's presence – but it was becoming an ever more dangerous wait now. Each look and whisper coiling tighter, daring her to awaken sensual pleasures and give in to the oldest sin.

Mrs Matthews went to make the tea and Evie stood, trying to stretch away such preoccupations as her neglected mending fell to the side of the chair. Outside it was very windy once more, with rain streaking the windows in travelling rivulets and Evie placed her hand against the cold pane, feeling the confines of the house keenly. Dangers lurked without, dangers lurked within. And dangers lurked deep down, inside.

The door opened and Molly came into the room, struggling with the firewood in her arms. 'Go on and help me then,' she huffed and Eve stood to assist her, even though she'd already filled all the grates in the main rooms that afternoon on her own. 'Don't see why it's always up to me to fetch it. Got a splinter for me trouble,' Molly grumbled, investigating her small injury. 'Pass me one of them needles and look quick about it,' she ordered, pointing over at Eve's sewing basket.

'Get it yourself, y'baggage,' Mrs Matthews exclaimed, overhearing as she returned. 'I've said it before, Molly Brown, if you're not the laziest girl to grace God's green earth I don't know who is.'

Molly said nothing but poked her tongue out at the housekeeper behind her back as Mrs Matthews poured the tea.

'Make sure you burn the tip of the needle properly then,' Mrs Matthews said, turning to pass Eve a cup of tea. Molly mumbled something back and Mrs Matthews rolled her eyes at Eve. 'Ever acting the poor martyr.'

Eve sipped at her tea and tried not to smile. Molly wouldn't appreciate any amusement from her, she knew.

'I hope you can still carry your basket on Saturday. I've a long list for the market this week,' Mrs Matthews told Molly.

'Are we expecting guests?' Eve asked.

'It ain't you expecting 'em, is it? It's the master,' Molly muttered as she tended her finger.

'Actually, it's the young master this week. He has friends stopping over Sunday who'll travel on with you to the hunt.'

'I could make two trips to the market if you like,' Eve suggested, thinking the more time away from the house right now the better.

'No, I want two trips...ow,' Molly exclaimed, pausing to pull the splinter out. 'Bloomin' stupid thing.'

'We'll see how we go. We may make do with some of those leftover pears and have Cook make a cobbler...' The sound of the heavy front door opening interrupted her, along with a chorus of barking from Lady Sophia's dogs and the low drone of men's voices.

'Master Robert's 'ome early,' Molly said, blowing on her finger.

'So it seems,' Mrs Matthews said offhandedly, yet she sloshed her tea. 'Why don't you trot off to bed now, Evie? I'll finish off that sewing for you if you like.' Eve obliged, ignoring Molly's jealous sniff over what she would undoubtedly view as favoured treatment. Such competitive trifles would usually have bothered Eve but not tonight.

Her heart rate rose immediately, thumping against her ribs as she made her way swiftly but in silence, the noise of her own blood in her ears; every instinct alert to any sudden movements or noises.

Passing by the stairs that led to the library she heard conversation, deep and muffled. Eve stilled, pausing to listen, then allowed herself to relax a fraction. Robert was now chatting with his friends and Sir Humphrey over cigars, which should last for some while, as was their habit.

Robert's voice seemed to trail her, like a hound on her scent, but it faded once she arrived at her room and locked the door behind her. By the time she'd changed out of her dress and put on her night-rail she'd managed to banish his sound but not his imprint; that seemed to cling to her in a thick, disorientating cloak. Would he come to her this night, filling her veins with that drugging heat? Conflicting both body and mind? She dreaded hearing the tap of his boots, the click of the doorknob, the murmur of entreaties and demands. Yet shamefully the thought somehow excited her too. Both emotions left her restless and she tossed in the blankets and sheets.

I do not want this, she reminded herself in frustration, tears at the corners of her eyes, yet the memory of whispering his name mocked her. How could she have let her guard down so? She'd never crossed the line between servant and master in her life, not even to forget a curtsey or a teaspoon or a lowering of eyes. She'd been raised to be better than this.

Eve stared across at her mother's portrait, now at her own bedside, and her thoughts turned once again to her father, her grief raw as she remembered his favourite advice.

Look for truth and act truthfully, Evie, and remember: you teach people how to treat you, with each and every thing you do and say.

The dull tick of the grandfather clock swinging its pendulum echoed in the hall as Eve contemplated that philosophy, guilt tinging each thought. *Have I taught Master Robert to treat me this way? To attempt seduction on the very day of my father's funeral? To proposition me with acts of sin?*

Then the clock struck the hour, interrupting her thoughts, and she forced herself to focus on filling and emptying her lungs instead, slowly and deeply with each tick of the hand. Whatever her part in this flirtation, it was unthinkable anything would actually come of it. Time would save her, she reassured herself. Soon she would be well out of temptation's way.

It left her feeling strangely empty but she ignored all emotions now, concentrating on that rhythmical passage of time until, eventually, her alert senses were lulled into slumber.

It was some time later when she was awoken by a noise at the door and her eyes flew immediately wide. *It's locked; I locked it*, she reminded herself. Then Robert's voice came in an urgent whisper.

'Eve. Eve, open the door.'

She rose slowly from her bed to stand, barefoot and shivering, and disbelieving as she stared at the thick wood that separated them.

'Evie…'

'You cannot be here,' she hissed back.

'I have to talk to you, Eve, please,' he pleaded. 'Don't let a door come between us. Open it, I'm begging you.'

She knew better than to oblige but his tone was unravelling her good sense once more, seeping its way back into her blood.

'You know I cannot…'

'Yes, you can,' he interrupted, his voice low and close through the edge of the frame. 'You can do anything you want behind a closed door…not that I would make you, of course. I only want to talk. To see you before I sleep.'

'I'm not sure I believe you,' she said, wishing the door invisible now in order to read his expression.

'I just want to say goodnight.'

The great clock chimed three times and it gave Eve further pause. Anyone could hear them in this still, quiet hour.

'I won't touch you, Eve,' he said solemnly. 'I swear it as a gentleman.'

Such a vow swayed her and before she could further question herself she sprang into action, unlocking the door in a rush lest she change her mind. His handsome face replaced the barrier of wood in sudden revelation, his expression reassuringly earnest with his promise before he entered, and it relaxed her. Slightly.

He was swaying a little, however, and to her shock he perched himself on the end of her bed, steadying himself then patting the space alongside him. Eve's wariness returned with force.

'You can trust me. I gave my word, remember?'

Eve re-locked the door and sat down stiffly, placing as much space between them as she could. Pulse hammering hard. 'I am trusting you, sir.'

'And so you can, my Evie. So you can.' He looked at her properly then, their faces too close, and she could see the faint stubble on his chin, the loosening of his cravat at his throat.

'You should not be here, sir. What if someone hears or sees you?'

'Then I will insist on their silence,' he muttered, tracing his eyes over her before returning to her face once more. 'It would be worth it to take this visage into my slumber.' He was slurring his words slightly and she could smell the wine on him now. It was acridly sweet and mixed with tobacco.

'You risk too much, sir.'

'You risk too little.'

His dark eyes were boring into hers and she swallowed against the flutter of nerves it caused. 'There is more at stake for me than there is for you. Sir,' she added.

'You almost dropped the address then. Perhaps you could also drop more of your guard.' He lifted a hand to her hair, touching it gently where it fell from across her shoulder. 'You called me Robert once, as I recall.'

'You promised you wouldn't touch me...' she objected faintly, forgetting all formalities now, and distracted from any real outrage as she watched him slide the strands between his fingers.

'I plead an amendment,' he whispered, leaning closer, 'if the lady will allow it: I will keep my vow unless you want me to break it.'

'I...won't...' His mouth was drawing in now, stopping an inch away from hers as their breath mingled, a heady, strange sensation for Eve. It was as if the wine and tobacco was flowing into her, too, or some kind of intoxicant.

'Kiss me, Eve,' he whispered, a rawness in the plea, and watching that mouth somehow she fell, despite every possible reasoning, every danger, every last thread of her deserting sense.

The fall instantly became a dive, deep into an abyss, as the curling he'd awakened in the past burnt into a sudden eruption of intense desire. Oh, how she wanted this. And how wretched that she'd have to break it and speak.

'Master Robert...' she rasped, clutching at his shirt as she pushed away. 'I cannot...'

'Let me love you, Evie. I will take care of you, I promise,' Robert replied, pulling her back. Kissing her face and running his hands through her hair.

'But we can't...'

'Yes, we can.' His tone was so persuasive and his touch so intoxicating Eve was fast losing her fight against temptation now.

'I can't do this,' she tried once more, in a desperate attempt not to yield. *It will ruin you*, her battered mind tried to shout through the cloud of sensation consuming her. 'Please, sir, I am a...a virgin...'

'I know you are, sweet Evie, and I won't take that from you, I promise. No-one will ever know,' he reassured. 'You need fear nothing – *just feel*.' He swept his fingers softly down her neck then kissed where they had been, causing Eve to close her eyes as surrender took over. *Feel*.

Robert undid her night-rail slowly as he continued his journey, exposing her naked body to the cool air. 'So beautiful,' he said, gazing at her. No man had ever seen her thus but she had no time to wonder at the fact as other wonders took over. He seemed to know exactly where the places were that ignited such feelings and soon guided her to where her touch could also pleasure him. They became fevered then, in a sensual exchange filled with discovery as mouths and hands explored. She did things she didn't even know women did and felt things she had no idea she could, not only giving in to temptation but revelling in it. He kept to his word, protecting her virginity, yet finding ways to satiate them both until the sheets were pooled on the floor and the clock struck another hour.

Then the door of her room opened and closed once more, reclaiming him to his rightful, elevated quarters, and Eve listened dazedly to the continual tick of that great clock, registering the passing of time once more. But it was forever altered now.

I did not want this, she told the night. *I didn't want a life of sin.*

But as the rain lashed at the window pane she knew that's exactly what she was living, now that she'd taught Master Robert how to treat her. Now that he could influence and would impact everything she would do or say.

Seven

The fire crackled merrily but it was the only thing that was cheerful in the stuffy work chamber that afternoon. Mrs Matthews was 'out of sorts', as Molly had warned her earlier, and Eve knew full well the reason why.

'Tea?' Eve offered, putting aside the silverware she'd been polishing to pour it.

'Humph,' Mrs Matthews replied. She flicked the linen napkin she'd been folding briskly before taking the proffered cup.

'Cake?' Eve asked, lifting the tin from the shelf.

'Not today,' Mrs Matthews said stiffly. That was enough indication in itself that she was in an ill-temper. Cake worked like some kind of mood compass on the housekeeper; enjoyed with gusto on happy days, firmly declined when anything foul was afoot. Eve sighed. The tin was definitely being left shut today.

Eve sat to rest and sipped at her tea, desperate for a way to improve the situation, but this wasn't just a small rift running between them. This was a gigantic chasm.

'You could write to her again...'

'I wonder if the weather might...'

Both paused, their colliding words registering. 'Please,' Eve invited softly, already knowing what Mrs Matthews would say.

'You could write to her again. There must be some mistake, making y'wait so long.'

'Perhaps the children have taken ill,' Eve suggested.

'Humph,' Mrs Matthews said again. 'There's sommin' fishy's goin' on and it's nowt for good.' Not only did Mrs Matthews's appetite for cake alter according to stress, so did the thickness of her Leicester accent. 'Someone's sticking their nose in, I'm reckoning, someone with no truck an' that's a fact.' Eve heard the accusation and whom it was directed at plainly.

'Why would anyone do that?' she replied, as lightly as she could manage.

'Humph,' Mrs Matthews said for the third time, 'why indeed.'

Eve fiddled with her cup, trying hard not to look guilty as the night of illicit passion she'd engaged in floated at the back of her mind. Surely Robert wouldn't stand in the way of such a position for her. Surely he was only interested in something sweet and brief – Molly had told her many times that men soon tired of a woman once the chase was done. Eve hated that the concept depressed her.

'Anyway, there's much to occupy us as we wait,' she said, opting for a change in subject. 'We've plenty to do before the hunt.'

'Aye, the hunt.' Mrs Matthews was 'dead against' Eve being on staff at the country estate for Sir Humphrey's annual event but they had a large crowd coming. Only a handful of servants would stay to tend to the Liverpool residence, including Mrs Matthews. 'I've been meaning to have another word to the master 'bout that. It may be better for y'to stop here with me.'

'But they'll be needing me to tend the young ladies...'

'It's not the young ladies worryin' me.'

Eve felt herself blush, cursing such a telltale signal. 'Well, I suppose if you don't trust me to go...'

'It's no' that I don't trust *you*, child,' Mrs Matthews said, her voice softening now, 'I always have, it's the young master...'

'I...'

'No, hear me out, Evie, you need to realise a few things, my girl. Aye, you're so young in so many ways.' Mrs Matthews took off her spectacles and rubbed at her eyes as she sat, looking tired all of a sudden. 'I don't think you understand what could happen to you if...if things got out of hand, like. A young man has needs, Eve. Perhaps, with your mother gone, I should have explained things sooner to you, I don't know.' She pinned Eve with a concerned look then. 'I just hope I'm not already too late.'

'Too late for what?' Eve said, hating herself.

'To warn you of the dangers of letting a man...have his way with ye.'

'I won't let that happen,' Eve assured her, glad that there was some truth there. She hadn't taken a proper bite of the serpent's apple; the full sin had not come to pass.

'Bad sense can rule good when there's passion in y'blood.'

Eve stood, almost knocking over her cup as she placed it on the table. 'I really don't know why you're saying all of this. I'm not in any danger...'

'You're a terrible liar, my girl. You always were.'

Eve's voice was shaking now, as were her hands, and she hid them in her skirts. 'I haven't let him do that, Mrs Matthews. I swear it.'

She nodded slowly. 'Aye, but something changed, I can see it plain as day. Just beware, Evie. You're playing with fire and fire burns. You should be praying hard as y'can for that letter to arrive and get you well away before it's too late.'

Eve said nothing about the concept of praying. Truth was she feared God wouldn't want much to do with her now.

'It'll end in heartache, it always does, and I'll no' be able to help you if that's what comes to pass.' Mrs Matthews finished her tea with those words and stood to fold the linen once more, putting her spectacles back on and blinking back tears. Eve felt so wretched then that she went over and hugged her, something usually reserved for birthdays or special occasions.

'Go on with ye,' Mrs Matthews said, patting her back briefly, but they both knew that embrace held more truth than any guarded half-confessions would allow. And more gratitude than words could ever say.

The early autumn sunshine landed mid-morning next day, just in time for Eve's weekly trip to the markets. She'd always loved Saturdays for this very reason, a chance to walk down past the fine houses along their road with all the sights and sounds and scents they conveyed. Even better, today Molly had gone to the markets earlier on her own to further the chances of filling the large order the household required for the evening. Eve doubted she would have made much progress. Molly was as lazy at shopping as she was at everything else. Eve figured Mrs Matthews was simply trying to even things up a bit in the favouritism department by sending her early instead of Eve. Time at the markets was highly prized. However, the rare opportunity to travel alone was welcome respite from the tension at home, so the decision suited Eve just fine.

The streets were clean in this neighbourhood and the houses were large and stately, mostly fronted with enormous bay windows and adorned with rose gardens that were the pride of their gardeners. Judges, traders and men of industry vied for prominence here, along with the occasional noble gentry such as her employer, and Eve knew she was very blessed to have such a privileged address.

But thoughts of privilege provoked thoughts of Robert whom she'd promised herself not to dwell upon today, so she sought another preoccupation, taking out Mrs Matthews's shopping list which Molly had conveniently left at home.

It was long and she contemplated it carefully as she waited for the omnibus, and she was still calculating what she would need to budget for certain items as she clambered on board. That task complete, she placed the list back in her basket and turned to enjoy watching the familiar route.

The great cathedral was always in view, whatever part of Liverpool you were travelling through, and her eyes often rose to it in between her observations of the streets, although she forced herself not to ruminate on the cemetery that lay behind.

The architecture turned more industrial as they crossed town. Men, women and children worked long hours in those new rows of factories, Eve knew, and she supposed they would be grateful for a way to feed themselves, despite the hardship of such work. The city was becoming increasingly over-populated.

Eventually they rounded the corner to where the markets were held. They could be smelled before they came into sight, a mixed concoction of animal and produce that both tantalised and offended, depending upon the waft of the breeze. There were freshly baked goods and sweet stone fruits in the air, hay and manure, a faint aroma of honey and the easily detectable, mouth-watering scent of smoking hams. Eve hoped she'd be able to taste a piece, knowing Mr Jenkins who loaded and unloaded crates from the docks would sneak a sample for her if asked. He'd always held a soft spot for her, having been her mother's neighbour during her youth.

The Mersey could be seen from the square, sitting in quiet greys and blues beyond the crowds that gathered at the edge of the fray, serene enough from a distance but poisoned with refuse up close.

Eve knew that stench all too well, from visiting her grandparents there with her mother as a small child. The family were long gone now, as were so many who lived down and around Scottie Road in Vauxhall, as the area was called. Disease seemed to thrive in the damp air and sanitation was appalling in the rows of back-to-back houses where Emma-Kate had spent her youth. Few, if any, ever bathed and most were forced to share communal toilets. Those were mere cesspits, often unemptied for months on end, and Emma-Kate had refused to let her daughter use one when they'd visited.

Eve held few fond memories of the poorer parts of this town and felt the injustices that thrived there deeply, if from afar. Her mother had never quite let the Vauxhall brogue go, nor the memories of those hard, early years of her life, often reminding her little daughter to 'pray for the Africans' when she said her prayers. Slave trading had been rife when she was a child.

These days it was the sight of convicts being taken up the Mersey to be transported and interred in hulks on the Thames to await deportation that haunted Liverpool. 'Go for row' her mother had often termed it, a simple, child-like phrase but it had made Eve shudder with its dark connotations.

The omnibus came to a rattling halt and Eve shrugged away her melancholy thoughts, allowing the excitement of the markets to consume her now. Hawkers called out constantly, promoting their wares, and there was a kaleidoscope of vegetables on display, although not as much summer fruit as previous weeks. Cheese wheels were being cut, the pieces weighed, and chickens darted about, chased by small children. There were wines, breads and cakes, cured meats and the constant delicious waft of that smoking ham that almost overpowered the smell of rotting piles of garbage on the fringe.

Eve soaked it all in, waving to Mr Jenkins who returned her greeting cheerfully.

'Morning, my beauty!'

Numerous Irish accents could be heard, one of many changes Eve had witnessed so far in her young life. Immigration had long fed this growing town and the Irish were the latest to flock in large numbers to her shores, many having been starved out of their own country due to the famine. Eve smiled at their brogue, which she found rather musical, although not all shared in her fondness for this age-old enemy who clashed, in particular, with the Protestant poor of the town.

Eve's father had always considered the distinction between the two Christian faiths a man-made division, something that God would surely consider as relevant as choosing how one approached eating a boiled egg. *We all end up nourished, no matter how we dine*, he'd often say on the subject. Eve saw the undeniable logic in this radical view, although it wasn't something she dared voice in public. Not everyone shied away from religious opinion so easily.

'Bloody Paddies,' Molly said, finding her in the throng and rolling her eyes at one woman who was haggling for some meat for her brood. A gang of grubby-faced offspring were racing around her skirts, adding even further mayhem to the place, and Eve smiled at them.

'They're only trying to get by, just like the rest of us. Have you bought any fruit yet?' she asked Molly, guessing that she hadn't. It would likely be up to Eve to do the lion's share of the purchasing, not that she really minded. It was fun, choosing what the family would eat, almost as if she had some say in Robert's life. Eve rapidly shook that thought away.

'No much there, really,' Molly shrugged. 'Peter!' she called and waved. 'Now this looks a bit more promising. Ripe for the picking, I'd say,' she whispered to Eve, giggling.

Peter Williams was a tall lad, just gone nineteen, and Molly had been pointing him out to Eve for some time at church, having now tired of her stable boy beau. Personally, Eve couldn't see anything terribly interesting in him, with his pointed face and roughly cut hair, but Molly was all smiles, looking up at her new would-be conquest coquettishly.

'Well, there y'are! I was beginning to think you was hiding from me.'

'Hello there, Molly,' he said with a nod before turning to Eve. 'Sorry, don't know that I've met y'friend...?' He looked at Eve questioningly, his eyes running over her in inspection, and she held her basket a little more tightly in front.

'This here's Eve,' Molly said, not looking too pleased to have to introduce her.

'Very nice to meet ye,' he said, grinning now.

'Hello,' Eve said, moving further behind Molly to avoid his stare.

'I've seen you round, ain't I?' he said, leaning to keep her in full sight.

'Perhaps. Molly and I attend most of the same places together.'

'"Attend", do ye?' he said, amused. 'My, ain't we nice and posh?'

'She's always puttin' on them fancy airs and graces, just ignore her,' Molly said, moving in front and tapping his arm. 'Now where's them nice juicy plums you promised me? You was licking your lips last week and I been waiting to taste them ever since.' She drawled the last and Eve would have been tempted to chortle at the thinly veiled flirtation if she wasn't so busy trying to be inconspicuous.

Peter laughed. 'Just over at me da's table. Come on, you too, *Lady* Eve.'

Eve felt obliged to follow although she would have preferred to wander and explore on her own. Fortunately, Peter was as good as his word and the sample piece of plum they were given was delicious.

'How much?' Eve asked.

'Tuppence a pail.' It was a little steep but Eve had tasted Cook's plum pie in the past so she paid for two lots, placing one in her basket and asking Molly to do the same.

'Nuh, I'll carry the potatoes later,' Molly said, although Eve doubted that. She'd probably talk this Peter character into doing it for her in the end. 'Come on, let's check out the sweetmeats. I've a few coins of me own to spare this week.'

Peter went willingly enough to earn his free treat, although he looked back at Eve with a strangely knowing stare and she had the ridiculous thought he knew what she'd been up to in her room with Robert. The thought of his name invited thoughts of his person, and she tried in vain to stop them intruding but lost the battle this time. It had been the same last night when he'd stayed in town. She'd felt bereft in his absence, with images of him flickering in random sequence through her mind, and she'd found sleep elusive in a bed she now associated with pleasure.

'Evie!' Mr Jenkins was calling and she turned and hurried towards him gladly, relieved to have something else to occupy her. 'There's our girl, getting prettier each day – spittin' image of your mother, you know that? And your father's dimples to boot,' he added as she smiled, but it faded at his last words. 'Ah, sorry to mention him, love,' Mr Jenkins said, his craggy face filling with sympathy. 'He was a good man and he loved y'ma and that were enough f'me.' Eve nodded but the sudden tears scratching her throat prevented comment. 'Anyways, here,' he said, taking out a package from the dray and holding it towards her. 'Think you should have this now.'

'What is it?' she said, both surprised and touched.

'Just something from the old days; something your da gave me once. Figured it should be yours.'

Eve gazed up at him, speechless as tears filled her eyes.

'Now, now, none of that. Have a look and see if it don't make you smile instead.' She tore at the paper, wiping at her cheeks and gasping as a bound book was revealed. 'It's a Bible – see? With pictures and all. Your da knew I couldn't read so he said I should have it to learn more 'bout scripture and stuff. Think he were worried for me soul,' he added with a wink.

Eve had wondered at the whereabouts of this precious family heirloom but of course her father would do something this generous and thoughtful. Not that Mr Jenkins needed to know how she'd missed it. 'He was always very grateful to you, for looking after Mother when she was young,' she said instead.

'She looked out for me too, Evie. We Scottie Road lot have to stick together,' he told her, nodding solemnly. 'It's the same for you, y'know that, don't ye? Whenever you need anythin'...'

'...come find you at the old pub near home.'

'Aye, that's where I'll likely be. You may be a fine lady working in a fine house but ye'll always be Emma-Kate's baby girl to us.'

Eve nodded, too moved to comment, so she gave him a quick hug instead.

'Aw, come on then. Enough o'that. Let's see if we can't rustle up some of that smoked ham you're always partial to, eh? Joe!' he called to his friend who was working on that stall. Soon Eve was munching on a delicious piece of meat as she continued her errands and by the time she struggled onto the omnibus with Molly her basket was overflowing. Not so her companion's. Molly had managed to get Peter to lift the potatoes on board but had achieved little else, save eat sweets and bat her eyelashes for a few hours.

The omnibus rumbled along, eventually arriving at their stop and the girls alighted, Eve pausing to pat one of the familiar horses that drew it before she went.

'There now, Clover,' she said, stroking his soft nose one more time before moving off, only to see Mrs Matthews running down the road towards her, skirts and petticoats swishing about, her face red from exertion.

'Evie! Evie!'

Molly had paused to laugh at the sight and Eve would have joined her if not for the reason behind such excitement suddenly dawning as she spied the letter in Mrs Matthews's hand.

'You've got it, my girl! They've taken you on!'

Eve opened the letter slowly, reading its contents and searching for an appropriate response. 'Well, that's a relief,' she said, although in truth it felt more like resignation.

'God has listened to our prayers,' Mrs Matthews said, still breathless as she grasped Eve's hands tight and beamed at her. 'You've quite a future before you now.'

'Half yer luck,' Molly said, no longer laughing.

'Yes, very lucky indeed,' Eve said, forcing a smile.

'Goes to show y'never know what fate has in store for ye! And to think they need y'so soon after all this waiting. Ye'll be off straight after the hunt!'

'You mean I'll have to do the unpacking all by meself...?' Molly began to complain but Mrs Matthews cut her short as they turned for the house.

'In all my born days, I've never known a girl so bone lazy! Who d'y'think does most of it for you anyways? By the living saints.'

But Eve had stopped listening now because there was movement at the front parlour window and a man with eyes so brown they were almost black was watching her as she approached the gate.

He already knew her news; she could read it in his stance. And even from here she could sense the tension that ran through him, predatory and intense. Unyielding and unwilling to let her go.

She hadn't wanted this, it was true what she'd said that first day, and yet it was hers, just the same. It seemed desire was not a choice; it actually chose you. And now the hunter would close in and it was her heart that was in peril; the trophy in any true game of chase. Staring back at those eyes, she wanted to run the gauntlet, to see where the hunt would lead. But of course, there were only two possible outcomes, willing prey or no.

To escape to safety before the time ran out or to end up, eventually, being caught.

Eight

It was raining again, running in tears down the pane, and Eve watched the fall as if from a distance, trying not to feel the overwhelming weight of mixed emotions that ran within.

She would leave this house tomorrow, and every memory it held, and her mismatched bags stood by the door in a bulging, haphazard pile, as if confused to be filled to bursting for the first time. They contained every possession Eve owned, including her dresses and shoes and an assortment of knickknacks the family had collected over the years, with her mother's portrait in careful wrapping near the top.

She was taking her father's books too and would add the precious family Bible to the pile when she could bear to pack it away. For now it sat in her lap and she turned up her lamp to look through those old, familiar pages. She hadn't seen the images since she was a child: Samson in the temple, Moses parting the sea, the fall of Babylon.

Eve flicked to the beginning and her eyes traced what used to be her favourite page: Adam and Eve in the Garden of Eden. They were dressed in animal skins and running from huge dark clouds that represented the wrath of God as the serpent watched them from the trees. There was an apple drawn in the margin and Eve remembered her father putting it there after reading her the passage in his deep, cultured voice. Eve hadn't had a very good afternoon that day, getting herself in trouble with Cook for climbing on a chair to reach the biscuit tin then falling hard, cutting her chin. Her father had been less than impressed to find Cook yelling at his injured daughter but he'd also been aware a lesson needed to be learnt, something he'd delivered in his own gentle way as Eve held her bandaged face and sniffed back tears beside him.

'This is your time in history, Evie,' he'd said as he drew the apple. 'Not the original Eve but an Eve just the same, and with the same lessons to learn. But you get chances, you see, never forget that. When times are darkest remember that God forgives; He brought the Saviour to us in the end. This Eve went on to be the first mother, to be penitent, and showed great humility. She made amends.' He'd patted her head then, adding, 'All of us fall down at some point, my dearest girl, but the best among us learn from our mistakes.'

Eve smiled in memory, touching the faint scar that still ran along her chin and missing him so much at that moment that tears clouded her vision. *Oh Papa, I have fallen hard.*

Still, it was almost done. Only one more week with the family at their country estate to assist at the hunt then her days in their service were over. From there she'd go straight to her new employer and her new life to forget all about her brief flirtation with sin. She supposed she'd see out the rest of her days a spinster. Not many nannies found husbands, locked away on remote country estates, nor would temptation likely cross her path evermore.

Eve braced herself to face that sin one last time, sure that Robert would come and longing for his touch, knowing there would be little chance for them to be together at the crowded hunt. But she dreaded it too. Tonight, temptation would shine brighter than ever before as it offered one last taste. Eve prayed she would remain strong enough not to take a full bite, after all, and earn God's wrath. To somehow escape to a respectable, if loveless, fate.

Robert had been preoccupied with his guests all night, but now, at last, the tread of footsteps and the click of the door sounded and Eve gasped as he wasted no time, ripping off his dinner jacket and falling in a rush to kiss her with more urgency than ever before. The rest of their clothes were quickly discarded and sudden, desperate confessions exploded; words of longing, of rebellion, of desire.

'You cannot leave me,' he said, between aching kisses. 'One night apart…was hard enough…forever…it's unthinkable…'

'I…I don't know how I shall bear it,' she admitted, already missing him even though he was in her arms.

'My sweet girl…'

Eve grasped his dark head close against her chest, unable to stop her next words. 'My love.'

Robert lifted his black eyes, searching into her soul. 'And I love you, my Evie. Let me show you how much this last time…please.'

She'd been prepared for his lust but not his love and it made that apple shine and beckon unbearably. Then he stroked her chin ever so gently, touching her scar that lay there in imprint; a reminder of past recklessness. Robert kissed it, softly, and it felt like a worshipful plea to embrace the sinner within; to let go.

Eve felt surrender overtake her in an irresistible wave. There was no more restraint as he took her to new places of pleasure, places she knew she should deny him but could no longer withhold. For he'd taken her heart now, along with her body, and the force of it drowned out any sense from her mind.

There was a moment of pain but then something sweet and wondrous, a true union of man and woman; a glorious revelling in the Garden of Eden that ended far too soon. It left her with no regret and she doubted she'd ever feel such an unworthy emotion when she remembered it, in years to come. It may well be considered immoral and depraved by others in their world but right now it felt pure with love. And it belonged only to them, and the sound of the rain as she lay against his chest, her ear on his heart. Holding on to each precious second before they slipped away.

'I will find a way to be with you...at the hunt.'

'You know it's impossible,' she told him, 'the guests, the servants' quarters...'

'I will find a way.'

She knew she should discourage the idea. It could potentially endanger her entire future, but that was the strangest thing about temptation.

When it overtook the heart it no longer felt like sin.

Nine

Normally, cleaning up after breakfast was no great challenge for Eve but that following morning it was turning into something of a catastrophe. For starters, Robert's guests were a demanding duo. She'd been spared their presence the night before by having to help Cook in the kitchen but today she was needed upstairs and feeling more rattled by the minute. Lady Augustine had twice complained about the temperature of her eggs then ordered the bacon be re-fried to a 'respectable level of crisp'. And her brother, the overweight and leering Sir Bixby, had insisted Eve pour the tea at least half a dozen times, she suspected merely to have her in his close proximity.

Meanwhile, Lady Sophia was fussing over her lap dogs to the point of obsession, demanding Eve fetch brushes and powders and even tonics in preparation for 'the little biddy babies'' big trip to the country.

Robert had adopted an expression of boredom towards the whole proceeding, a necessary enough stance, but it depressed her to have him ignore the way they all treated her, just the same. Molly was also behaving in a particularly superior way which was grating on Eve's nerves.

All of this, coupled with the knowledge that she was leaving Mrs Matthews, the closest person to her in the world today, *and* soon to be giving up the man she now loved, had her almost to the point of tears. Her hands shook as she cleared away cutlery and her throat ached to find a quiet corner and have a good cry.

But of course there was no time for such self-indulgence. The entire party would leave at noon and Eve was starting to wonder how on earth she would ever get on that carriage but somehow, one by one, each chore was done. The packing of refreshments, the stowing of blankets, the scrubbing and cleaning and lugging things about, until finally, unbelievably, it was time to depart.

Robert was already in his carriage, his black eyes finding hers in one fleeting message of desire as he boarded, leaving her riddled with longing then guilt as Mrs Matthews came over to say her final goodbye.

'Have you got your good shawl?' the housekeeper asked with a forced lightness but her chin was already quivering and Eve swallowed against her own building tears.

'Yes. In my basket,' Eve told her, putting it down. 'I...I suppose this is it then...'

'Aye, and no tears mind. 'Tis a happy occasion for you, let's no' forget.' Eve nodded, trying to remain composed, but then Mrs Matthews placed a parcel in her hands, adding, 'Just a little departing gift, child. It's a cake tin. Perhaps you'll think of me oft times, when you have your tea, like. I know I'll...' she paused then as her voice began to break, 'I'll be thinking of you.' Eve fell into her arms, unable to hold back her tears now and Mrs Matthews let out a sob of her own. 'There, child. There now, my girl. Off you go,' she finished, patting her back before pulling away. 'Write to me as soon as you can, won't you?'

Eve nodded. 'Of course...of course I will.' Her step was unsteady then as she boarded the carriage, the last to depart, and it took off immediately, allowing Eve only seconds to settle herself before leaning out to wave goodbye.

'Be good,' Mrs Matthews called, clutching her handkerchief, tears streaming now.

Eve couldn't bring herself to respond to that but she managed to nod and call out 'goodbye!'.

The stately house was passing from sight now as the carriage moved onto the street and Mrs Matthews walked out to the footpath, a lone figure in grey, still crying and waving. Now left behind.

'*Goodbye*,' Eve whispered, to the only home she'd ever known, to the street that had carried her to market every Saturday morning of her life, to the woman who'd been like a mother, all these years. To the cathedral that watched over them all, rich and poor alike, in this city of Liverpool, until most found their end in the graveyard behind. The place where her parents lay.

Goodbye, Eve told her mother and father silently. *I'm sorry that I've been so true to the worst traits of my namesake, but I will try to repent. There'll be time, you see…the rest of my days.*

Eve drew back from the window and closed her eyes, too exhausted by the emotions of the past twenty-four hours to reflect anymore. But her body ached with the irrefutable truth that this really was the beginning of the end now. She was taking leave of more than people and places in these last, precious moments, she was farewelling herself – or at least the only version of the person she had always been. In a matter of mere days she would be a stranger in a strange home living a strange, new, loveless life.

The wheels rattled and Eve looked along the line towards the fine family carriage up ahead and a now-familiar flutter of excitement unfurled, despite her grief and resignation, for there were still hours to be filled before that lonely new life. Moments to find dark eyes and perhaps whispers or precious more. Until she said goodbye to the last person she loved and left her reckless days of sin behind.

Ten

Arlington House, North-East Lancashire, September 1851

The glass balls shone as Eve lowered them in their crate onto the table, relieved she hadn't tripped and smashed such a delicate delivery. It was painstaking work, filling each one with feathers and powder, and she'd been up preparing them since before dawn, figuring Molly would sleep in and leave the lion's share of it up to her, which, predictably, she had. That task accomplished, she paused briefly to look at the scenery, which was distracting in the early afternoon sunshine.

The grazing paddocks were lush beyond the stables and dog pens, and the gardens were thick with early autumn flowers. It was very pretty, of course, but it was the forest and the bare gritstone fells above it that enticed Eve. They looked wild and inviting and Eve longed to explore them on horseback as the young gentlemen had been doing this morning. It wasn't just because she had happy memories of clambering across the open hillsides and through the shadowed corridors in years gone past, it was because one man in particular rode up there today. And in such raw surrounds that's all he became: a man. And she a woman.

Horse hooves sounded and Eve's stomach lurched at the sound of their return.

'Excellent house party this year, my friend, truly excellent,' she heard Sir Bixby saying to Robert as they dismounted nearby. 'You must let me return the favour by staying with me in London for the season. Young Alice Morley is coming out, so I hear.'

'Last I saw she looked to be quite a beauty,' one of the guests, Nigel Rawlings, joined in. 'Ripe for the picking, I'd say.'

'I remember her sister Pauline was fair,' Robert said, patting his white country stallion Zeus and handing over the reins to the stable boy.

'Bit pasty for my taste, although perhaps it washes off. Honestly, why do women insist on wearing so much powder these days?' Bixby exclaimed. 'Give me the soft pink cheek of a country lass any day,' he added loudly and Eve made a hasty exit over to the refreshments table to help lay out the sandwiches and pastries.

'What took you so long?' complained Molly under her breath. 'Put the glasses out and be quick about it.'

Eve couldn't be bothered objecting so she did as she was told, trying not to notice how handsome Robert looked in his country attire as the men lined up for the trap shoot. She wasn't the only one admiring him, if the coquettish comments coming from the approaching ladies were anything to go by.

'I've a wager on you, Sir Robert,' one called out, a woman by the name of Samantha Wiggins whose blonde hair was wound in tight ringlets. 'Shoot them all for me, won't you?'

'He doesn't have every ball to himself,' said Martha Harrison, a lady Eve remembered from previous years as being rather dry, 'the men all take turns.'

'Well, perhaps he'll be the only one to hit any,' Samantha said. 'Get them all and I'll partner you at whist tonight,' she promised him across the lawn.

'Surely that's more of a punishment than a reward,' Martha muttered. Samantha heard but merely giggled along with the others.

'If Samantha gets to partner you at whist then I want the first quadrille,' Augustine said with an exaggerated pout. Eve thought the expression made her look rather like one of Lady Sophia's cavaliers then immediately regretted such an unkind comparison.

'Now, now, ladies,' Lady Sophia said airily, seeming vaguely amused at the feminine interest directed towards her son. Not that it had her full attention of course; there were dogs to be petted, after all. Randolph, the eldest and most spoilt, lay on his back in her lap, snoring, meanwhile Rosebud was chasing sparrows and falling over herself in her excitement at being outdoors. Eve couldn't help but smile at her antics as she worked but it was soon replaced by a frown as another woman joined the party under the marquee, a tall redhead named Bernice Burrows. Eve remembered her well from the previous year's hunt. It was difficult to forget a woman with a bustline like hers, particularly when she had it on continual display. Today it was showcased in a daringly low-cut blue silk dress, not an entirely appropriate choice for day-wear.

'Have I missed anything?' she asked, smiling at the other ladies before planting her gaze firmly on Robert.

'Just about to start,' Robert told her, and Eve noticed he managed to keep his eyes on the woman's face. Not so Bixby, unsurprisingly.

'Splendid. I've been watching my figure all week in anticipation of your famous high tea afterwards, Lady Sophia. Whatever do you feed your cows to get such rich cream?' She nodded over at the herd who were, indeed, rather fat as they grazed on the thick, emerald grass.

'Best udders in England,' Bixby declared, giving Bernice's bodice a good leer.

'Really, Sir Bixby!' Bernice protested, but her smile was smug.

'Least the cows keep their udders to themselves,' Molly said under her breath and Eve stifled a smile of her own.

Robert cuffed his friend's shoulder before signalling for the first ball to be thrown and everyone watched as he took aim. He missed the first but hit the second and the glass exploded in a delightful rain of feathers and powder.

'It seems an angel has misplaced his smelling salts,' said Robert and the ladies all tittered and clapped both his skill and wit. It made Eve want to roll her eyes at the trivial pursuits of the wealthy and their equally trivial games of charm but she was jealous too, despite that.

Bixby went next, hitting his third target, followed by Nigel and a few others who had wandered down to join in, and by the time high tea was served all the glass balls had been smashed, much to the party's entertainment and amusement.

And all the while Eve poured and served and tried hard to focus on her work but it was becoming increasingly difficult. It was horribly dejecting standing on the edge of Robert's world, never to belong; knowing even the simple pleasure of watching him was about to be taken away too. She and Robert may well be equals when the costumes of society were removed and they lay bare-skinned against one another, like Adam and that first Eve. But as soon as they donned those costumes once more and resumed the roles the world expected them to play any pretence of equality was gone. She would ever be a servant, unimportant and behind the scenes, there to provide service to people like him. Aristocrats born into privilege, destined to spend their lives strutting on society's stage.

Eve passed by Bernice and offered her refreshments from the tray, her grey cotton dull alongside the redhead's blue silk.

'I really shouldn't,' Bernice said, not looking at Eve, of course, as she lifted a buttered scone covered in jam and cream and stuffed it past her lips. Eve tried not to watch but it transfixed her. This woman could devour anything she wanted, whenever she wanted it. Any pretence of worrying over her figure was just part of the play, lines she intoned to lure men close; have them focus on what lay beneath the layers of silk. Her only challenge in life would be choosing which wealthy man she would ensnare and, for someone like Bernice, that shouldn't prove too hard. Her life was one of indulgence and Eve supposed it would always be so.

'Robert,' Bernice called, moving over to stand close and he turned and smiled his handsome smile. Augustine and Samantha glowered alongside them, obviously envious, and Eve could almost feel sorry for them, only she was too busy feeling sorry for herself. Then Robert leaned in and whispered something that made Bernice blush and suddenly the injustice of it all was too much to be borne. Eve walked to the table and put down her tray, trying not to let it slam.

'Where d'y'think you're off to?' Molly said as she cleared away plates and forks.

'We need more cream,' Eve said, grabbing an empty bowl. She rushed across the lawn, ignoring Molly's objection, her only focus putting space between herself and this farcical world. Eve ran down the stairs to the cellar, needing the darkest, quietest space to calm down, but instead of taking deep breaths or perhaps just crying she found herself hurling things instead. Bags of sugar and flour and oats. Stacking them in piles then hauling them back. Anything to release this pent-up tension. This anger. Because yes, she was angry now, angrier than she'd ever been. It wasn't her fault she'd been born into a life of servitude. It wasn't her fault she'd fallen in love with a member of the gentry. It wasn't her fault and it wasn't fair.

'Argh!' she grunted, lugging another sack.

'What are you doing?' asked a voice from the door and she turned in shock to see Robert standing there.

'I...I...'

He walked over and Eve could only watch, mesmerised and heart pounding, as he lifted his hand to graze a tear off her cheek and trace the scar.

'It's killing me too,' he said softly.

Then she was in his arms and he was kissing her mouth, her neck, tearing at buttons and pulling the grey uniform away. Baring skin to skin. Robert pushed her hard up against the shelves, his hands running along her legs. 'I can't be away long,' he panted. She nodded and pulled him between her thighs and it was fast and urgent and so intense she stood shuddering afterwards, needing a minute to calm her breathing once he'd gone, blinking in the dim light as her senses returned.

Eve made her way to the kitchen and collected the cream, returning to the guests and resuming her part. But it wasn't Robert's renewed flirtation with Bernice that worried her upon her return, nor was it Lady Sophia's insistence that her dogs eat the cream. It was the fact that Molly had merely delivered her a long knowing stare.

Without a single, admonishing word.

Eleven

'The red or the green?' Bernice held the brooches against the neckline frill of her riding habit, trying to decide.

'Both would suit well, ma'am.'

'True,' Bernice said. 'I think the green brings out my eyes more and Robert did call me a green-eyed vixen last night so...' Bernice smiled at her reflection as she fastened it and Eve tried not to feel any jealousy. She could hardly warrant it after the incident in the cellar yesterday. 'I wonder should I take an extra cloak... goodness, who's here now?' she added, rising to walk over to the window at the sound of carriages arriving. Eve stood nearby, watching as the two vehicles came to a standstill and the step was lowered from the first, allowing a lady and gentleman in very fine riding attire to alight. 'Why, it's Lady Margaret and Sir John Houghton. I didn't know they were joining us this year.'

Eve stared at her future employers in shock. *No*, her mind rebelled. *What are they doing here? I'm not ready to face them yet. I'm not ready!*

'I think I will take that cloak. Fetch it for me, will you?' Bernice ordered, turning to take one last look at her reflection as Eve did so automatically. Bernice left the room then and, with her service to the lady now complete, Eve had no choice but to make her way to the kitchens.

She descended the great stairs filled with apprehension, wondering how she could avoid the newcomers and find somewhere to compose herself instead. It was only a difference of a few days but their presence at the hunt was intruding on these last stolen moments of desperate love. The Houghtons were an unbearable reality, an inevitable conclusion, but she wasn't supposed to have to face them for four more days. Eve clenched her fist as voices sounded from the entryway and that sense of injustice rose within her once more.

'...terribly ill, I'm afraid, but they've all recovered well now and we really couldn't resist your kind invitation.'

'But of course! You must meet young Eve too, while you're here,' Sir Humphrey was saying and Eve tried to slip past to the kitchen stairwell but failed. 'Ah, but there she is! Eve, come greet your new employers. I must say we were very reluctant to let her go.'

Eve turned and walked towards them, trying not to appear nervous. Or guilty, which would be worse. 'How do you do, Lady Margaret,' she said with a curtsey. 'Sir John.'

Lady Margaret assessed her with keen eyes. 'Eve,' she said with a slight nod.

'Marvellous to meet you, young lady. Cook says her sister can't sing your praises highly enough,' Sir John said in a booming friendly way.

'Mrs Matthews is very kind, sir,' Eve said, searching for something else to say. 'I'm very grateful for her recommendation and for your generosity in offering me this position. I will endeavour to serve you to the best of my ability.'

'She mentioned you had some learning. Certainly your accent is rather genteel,' Lady Margaret said, casually taking off her gloves as she spoke, her expression still sharp.

'Eve's father was a cultured man and taught his daughter well,' Sir Humphrey told her.

'I can't imagine why anyone would bother educating a maid,' Lady Margaret said. 'Still, John seemed quite taken with the idea.'

'Well, surely it will come in handy as the children's new nanny; I dare say some positive influences will rub off on them,' Sir John said. 'Do you read well, my dear?'

'Well enough to pass the time on rainy afternoons, sir.'

'Marvellous, marvellous.'

'I suppose you've brought books with you then?' said Lady Margaret. 'I'm not sure we'll have room in the carriages.'

'Only a few, ma'am. I can leave them behind if it inconveniences you.'

'Nonsense, nonsense. Let the lass have her tomes if it pleases her,' Sir John declared. 'I find the notion of a learned servant rather refreshing.' He beamed at her in approval and, Eve suspected, a fair dose of self-congratulation. The mystery behind the delay in her offer of employment was fast becoming clear.

'She's from fine stock, aren't you, Eve?' Sir Humphrey said. 'An intelligent father and a beautiful mother. You'll have to keep her under lock and key, my good fellow; we barely let her leave the house.'

The men chuckled but Lady Margaret's mouth was set in a rigid line now. Eve felt a trickle of sweat run down her spine as the woman's gaze flicked up and down, taking in every inch of her person. Suddenly the grey uniform felt too tight; the costume of obedient servant an absurdity upon Eve's naked, sinful skin. Then, just as she tried to thrust such discomforting thoughts aside, footsteps sounded and Robert came down the stairs.

He looked resplendent in his red coat and riding attire and Eve wondered if she would actually pass out from the stress of being in his sudden, damning presence.

'Robert,' said Sir John, smiling broadly. 'Good to see you, young man.'

'Hello, John, Lady Margaret. You're looking very well.'

Eve watched as the lady's expression transformed from disapproval to undisguised appreciation. 'Robert,' she said, all smiles and fluttering eyelashes. Eve noted she was rather attractive when her expression softened. 'You're a dreadful beast, keeping us waiting for you to visit when we were last in town.'

'I recall I had some pressing business to attend to, although looking at you now I wonder what on earth it could have been.'

She laughed and the party wandered off, leaving Eve to melt away into the invisible domain of servitude. But resentment stirred where compliance should appropriately reside.

And a flicker of black eyes followed her as she closed the door.

Twelve

The breeze was rippling the ferns that lay in thick undergrowth on the forest floor but the subtle sounds of such whispering nature were drowned out as the large party prepared for the hunt. Horns blew and hooves clattered and there were so many dogs underfoot and barking madly Eve could barely think straight. On top of all this, men were shouting and testing their guns while the few women on horseback attempted to appear poised and graceful among the mayhem.

Eve's job was to help them set off so she could assist in preparing luncheon although that seemed an almost impossible eventuality. There was little hope of any structure descending upon this disorganised chaos. As it turned out, in the end they simply disappeared into the forest in sporadic, excited groups until at last the servants were left in peace. Mostly. Lady Sophia's lap dogs, Randolph and Rosebud, were scratching in their wicker basket and Eve was ordered to let them out.

'Keep a close eye on them, mind,' warned Miss Baird, the estate housekeeper, and Eve sighed, knowing that would make the morning far more trying. As if it hadn't been difficult enough. The cavaliers ran out in excitement, licking and jumping, and she smiled a little before hefting rugs from the cart and lugging them over to where the other servants were already beginning to set up the picnic. It wouldn't be difficult setting out the prepared food and refreshments but it would be a challenge keeping Rosebud, in particular, from messing everything up. Everyone tried for a while but in the end Miss Baird ordered Molly to take her for a walk.

'Why can't Eve do it? She's the one s'posed to be looking out for 'em.'

'Yes, yes, alright then. Just go!'

Eve took off, glad to get away from Molly, at least, whose smug expression since yesterday was adding to Eve's growing list of concerns. How much did Molly know? Had she seen Eve and Robert together or was she just making an educated guess that something was going on between them? Add to that the loss of her old life, a disapproving new mistress and a pending broken heart and Eve could really say she was quite miserable. The only thing keeping her from breaking down was the sweet, torturous anticipation that there could still be stolen moments of passion for her and Robert over these last few precious days. Somehow.

The sounds of people and activity began to fade as Eve walked on and the forest embraced her. The early autumn trees swayed gently, dappling this green and gold, canopied world in patterns of shade and light, the turning leaves bowing on heavy boughs as she passed. She picked one that was already tinged with crimson, twirling it in her fingers, thinking it had been a long time since she'd done so. It had been a long time since she'd felt that carefree, then she wondered what had motivated her to do it now. It just seemed like an easy thing to do; a simple, little act on a complicated day.

Rosebud trotted along in front and Eve watched her happy form, envying the dog's freedom from worry. Hers was the most pampered life of all, although she couldn't begrudge the pup as she looked back at Eve with beseeching brown eyes. She would miss her really, despite Lady Sophia's ridiculous mollycoddling.

The forest beckoned her on and she clambered over a moss-covered hedge, deeper into the hardwoods now. The leafy roof thickened and it grew colder as the sunlight dimmed, appearing only in occasional rays now, catching tiny particles that looked like fairy dust, or so she would have mused in her younger days. How comforting it felt here, how familiar, despite the fact she only ever came to these parts once a year. Perhaps it would feel the same in any forest of the world; a welcoming back as you walked in. Some kind of homecoming. Maybe it arced back to primal existence, an ancient echo of living in Eden, before mankind chose a more complicated fate and temptation corrupted their right to paradise.

Distant horns could be heard and she closed her mind against the sound, not wanting to think about the violent games at play nearby and the poor animals whose hearts would be hammering hard as they ran a desperate race for their lives.

Eve sat to rest at the base of an oak tree as Rosebud explored the edges of the stream nearby, relaxing her aching shoulders as she leaned on the bark. It allowed her some small respite from the emotional turmoil rupturing within as she watched the water trickle and pool, then meander on in a steady, constant flow. Like it washed through her mind too.

Rosebud came to lay her head in Eve's lap, and Eve stroked her velvety snout absently, closing her eyes and drawing the earthy, damp air deep into her lungs. Resting here, in the woods, she took comfort in its refuge, letting Mother Nature cloak her briefly in her unique, quiet wisdom. It felt almost like prayer, yet it was less confronting; the mother held no judgement and asked no atonement for sin. She simply said 'live' with every swaying branch, every flower, every insect. In the gentle flow of the stream.

She seemed more forgiving than God right now, filling Eve with the courage to face the harsh realities at hand. To take stock here, against the oak, away from the games of chase.

Robert was her hunter, yet she was more than willing prey. That much she could never, in any good conscience, deny. And of course there was only one feasible option left now: to make her escape lest she be caught. It was her only hope for a decent life; no other way.

Such was the verdict of a rational mind but it fell deafly against the forest surrounds. For she and the mother both well knew that logic was a poor foe against passion, that humanity was ruled not only by the mind but by the body and the heart. It harked back to that very first garden when that first choice was made. When temptation tipped the sway.

Eve ran a great risk on this final run, the hounds of fate on her heels, as she made a last desperate dash to survival. Yes, there are always choices to be made, paths to be chosen, decisions along the way, but right now such power felt well beyond Eve's conscious control. For her mind was no longer in charge and even her body wouldn't dictate her fate. Both were now ruled by her captive heart.

It was the rain that woke her, in droplets large enough to break through the canopy and land on her startled face. Eve was disorientated at first but quickly remembered that she was in the forest and that some time must have passed because the clear skies were now slate grey through the leaves, her fingers numb with cold.

'Rosebud,' she called anxiously, but there was no patter of little paws or grateful bark and Eve supposed she had found her way back. She could only hope to do the same, trying to remember the way as she peered through the rain in the dimming light, feeling suddenly very alone.

She stood and began to walk carefully, stumbling as her boots navigated the slippery earth that was now running with building rivulets. The earlier breeze had whipped into a strong wind that lashed the rain against her freezing body, bending the heavy boughs and howling in a low moan, transforming the charming forest of before into a menacing, frightening beast.

Mother Nature was in a fury now, no longer softly nurturing. Blinding sheets of lightning flashed, intermittently illuminating the wildly thrashing landscape in stark white, and clouds rumbled and roared in angry thunder. The comforting oak trees of before now seemed like dark giants waiting to grab at her as she passed and she let out a scream as a branch snagged her dress, ripping it as she fell against the hedge, grazing her knees. Eve wished desperately that Rosebud was still with her; any company would be welcome about now. Then the sound of approaching hooves made her reconsider that last thought and she shrank into the shadows, pushing mud and soaking strands of hair from out of her eyes.

'Eve! Eve, are you there?'

'*Robert!*'

She clambered over the hedge to run to him as he leapt from Zeus, relief flooding her as she stumbled into his arms.

'Good God, where have you been? We've search parties scouring...'

'I took Rosebud for a walk and rested...for a while and I just... fell...fell asleep.' Her entire body was shaking as she forced the words out but he was here, her Robert, and she was safe now. Eve buried herself against his warm coat, no longer caring about the cold or the rain or the dark.

'When she came back on her own I didn't know what to think,' he told her, a desperate edge to his voice as he took her face in his palms and stroked back her soaking hair. Then he kissed her and her love for him was so great her ruling heart dictated her body and mind. She clutched at his coat now, filled with a sudden urgency to be consumed by the force of it, all risk thrown to that whipping wind as she drew him down against her breast that he soon exposed. Robert tore at her skirts, pushing her against the rough trunk of a tree, unheeding of the other raging forces of nature that savaged them. Urgent in turn as their nakedness met the shock of the elements.

'If she isn't down this way I'll go back to check...'

Eve's senses were so consumed she thought perhaps she imagined the voice, but then there were dogs barking and another voice, louder this time, as the lightning lit everything and everyone into sudden, stark revelation. Men on horseback. Thrashing branches. Skin on skin.

'Good lord! Robert...is that you?'

Then she was suddenly, brutally exposed as Robert's body drew away. Then there were more voices and she was dragging wet clothes over bare, icy flesh. And someone was demanding explanations and Robert was mounting his white horse and someone else picked her up and threw her on one of her own, leading her through the night, back to the estate.

And all the while the rain poured and the wind ripped and a horn sounded, far away, signalling that the hunting was done.

Thirteen

The grandfather clock ticked loudly in the hall and Eve listened to it with the vague thought that a great clock had kept her company the last time she had sat outside a room, awaiting a verdict. How quickly time had moved since that sad day. How much had changed and would now change further, uncertainty growing with every slow, inevitable beat.

Eve had heard them all through the walls: Lady Margaret's triumph that she'd poorly disguised as outrage, Sir John's disappointment and attempts at pacifying his wife, Sir Humphrey's disgust – with Eve or his son she was yet to fully discern – Lady Sophia's condemnation, and now this, Molly's damning testimony. Her voice rang out clearly over the sound of the clock, designed to be heard from the hall.

'Off with Master Robert day 'n' night, shirking her duties, but the likes o' her don't care. Too good for the rest of us, she'll have you believe...'

'Do you mean to tell me this has been going on for some time?' Lady Sophia demanded.

'I'd say for months, m'lady – right behind your back and all. High and mighty as she is, no wonder she's lifting her skirts for gentry...'

'Yes, yes, that will do then, Molly,' Eve heard Sir Humphrey say. He was beginning to sound tired and Eve wondered if they would call for her soon, announcing her sentence and so putting an end to this household trial. How she longed for Mrs Matthews, hoping she would be allowed to go home. Perhaps Robert would be sent abroad and she would be permitted to stay in the kitchens or work here at the country estate. *Perhaps I would even be able to see him at times*, her heart interrupted her thoughts.

Shut it, she told it firmly, but it was impossible to fully do so.

Robert was yet to make an appearance and Eve was beginning to wonder if he would. Maybe he'd headed back to Liverpool or London to spare her a more emotionally charged scene. Funnily enough, she felt devoid of emotion right now. Blank. Probably exhaustion, she supposed, having not slept all night. But it did feel eerily familiar to that other day in the hallway. She knew by now that sometimes, when you desperately dread something happening and it finally comes to pass, it seems, strangely, not quite real; to the point that you doubt you will feel any emotion at all. But emotion would arrive, and with it that rare comfort of tears. She knew that much as well.

The door burst open and Molly walked out, casting her a look so superior Eve could almost have slapped her, if she'd had any energy available for such things. But then Eve's name was called at last and she dragged herself forward to face yet another of life's verdicts.

'Sit down, Eve,' Sir Humphrey said, gesturing at a hard-backed chair.

'Thank you, sir.' Her voice sounded faint and other-worldly beneath her protective cloak of non-reality and Eve forced herself to concentrate hard and answer as carefully as she could.

Sir Humphrey looked over at Lady Sophia who sat stony-faced as he cleared his throat. 'Firstly, I must say I am both surprised and disappointed. I can't even imagine what your father would have to say about this.'

Eve swallowed hard as tears found her throat and her previously numbed emotions sprang to life in a sudden wave. 'Yes, sir,' she managed.

'I'm sure I don't need to tell you of the seriousness of the matter. Whatever you were thinking, disgracing yourself in such a way...Seducing the young man of the house is an unforgivable offence for a servant. We cannot protect you, you understand.'

'I...I...did not mean to...'

'Nevertheless, you have committed this crime, Eve. It cannot be undone.'

'But...but Robert told me he...'

'Silence,' Sir Humphrey thundered as Lady Sophia let out a gasp. 'How dare you use his name in such a familiar manner? Have you lost all sense of propriety?'

'N...no, sir. It's...it's just that he was the one that wanted t-to... initially...he said he...'

'A woman's role is to curb physical attention from a man,' Lady Sophia scoffed. 'You were hardly forced, by all accounts, unless you are attempting to lay such accusations upon my son.'

Eve stared at her, scarcely believing they meant to lay all fault at her door and scrambling for a way to explain. 'No, ma'am, but he did tell me he...he said...the first time...'

'Are you seriously trying to defend this sordid behaviour by even telling us there was a *first* time?' Sir Humphrey raged. 'I'll not hear any more of this.'

'If you could only ask him to speak for me...'

'My son will not be "speaking" for you, nor shall I be speaking further on this matter,' Sir Humphrey told her with quiet fury.

'You are to pack your things and leave our service immediately. There's an omnibus due in an hour. You will meet it at the gate.' He stood then and Lady Sophia raised her brows as they waited for her to obey but Eve could only stare at them both in disbelief.

'Leave?' she whispered, tears gathering in her eyes.

'Immediately,' Sir Humphrey reiterated coldly, although he looked uncomfortable as the tears began to stream down her face. 'No hysterics now, girl. I'm sure you have people back in Liverpool you can turn to.'

Eve managed a nod, sobered even further by the thought of the options left to her now. Liverpool. No longer a word associated with service in a fine house. Now it meant the backstreets. Hardship. *Vauxhall.*

Sir Humphrey and Lady Sophia waited as she somehow managed to stand and make her way to the door.

'Oh, and Eve,' called Lady Sophia as Eve reached the door, 'tell Molly to fetch the tea before you go…and to bring me my babies. Such a trying day.'

Eve nodded once more, leaving the room and mounting the stairs to pack her things in a daze then wait, hands clenched in her lap until they lost all feeling. Then she descended and left the house to wait at the gate and watch the very last ties to her old world roll by. Molly stood at the window and Eve sensed her victory through the pane. *Fetch the tea, bring the dogs*, Eve told her silently, too late.

She looked out at the barn where the fine horses were tethered, beside the hunting dogs in their pen. Then her eyes fell to the fields where the fat cattle grazed and the turning forest lay beyond in the mother's arms, at peace today.

And above it all rose the barren slopes of the gritstone fells, raw against the pale morning sky, marked only by a lone horseman astride a white horse.

Perhaps only a mile, yet an entire world away.

Fourteen

Vauxhall, Liverpool, September 1851

Eve woke with a start as the omnibus door was wrenched open and the driver yelled the destination to the passengers.

Vauxhall. Even as she reinforced it over and again in her mind she still couldn't believe this was actually where she was supposed to be. Surely this was just a dream, a terrible nightmare. But no, sleep had just been broken and she was wide awake now, standing in the drizzling rain, all her earthly possessions at her feet.

'Excuse me,' she called to a woman passing by but she was ignored so she tried a man instead. 'Excuse me, can you tell me where I might find the old pub on Scottie Road?'

The man paused then laughed, displaying a row of rotting, uneven teeth. 'Every few yards, love.' The information was both confusing and unhelpful but he did point her in the direction of the road so Eve set off, figuring it was either do so or stand in the rain and get similar responses. But trying to remember her way back to the old neighbourhood would be a challenge, as tired as she was. She hadn't been there since she was a small child.

It was difficult work, carrying all her bags, but she didn't dare ask anyone for help for fear they'd run off with one. Besides, the only money she had was a few shillings and she knew she'd need every penny if she were to survive in this part of town. Scottie Road turned out to be 'Scotland Road' and Eve felt foolish for not having remembered such common knowledge, but there was little she recalled in general about this part of town. Although she did remember the smell. It permeated everything; a dank, horrid stench, rancid and almost unbreathable. The road itself was in poor repair and it was impossible to avoid the manure and human waste that lined the edges. Eve was forced to move towards it whenever traffic rolled by.

A pub came into view and she read the sign *Ye Olde Alehouse* hopefully, peering inside at what didn't seem too debaucherous a scene for a Saturday night. Then again the town clock had only just struck six.

'Excuse me,' she asked one young man as he approached the door, 'I wonder if you could ask if a Mr Jenkins is within?'

'Blimey,' the young man said, grinning at her, 'what's a girl like you doin' 'round 'ere?'

'Looking for my uncle,' she said, supposing that might improve her chances of him helping her.

'Right you are then, miss.' The young man went in and Eve waited with her bags, trying to appear inconspicuous to the work-roughened locals but earning plenty of suspicious stares. The young man returned and gave her a shrug. 'Not in 'ere, I'm afraid. Sorry, miss.'

'Oh. Well, thank you,' she said, picking up her bags and moving on. She tried not to feel disheartened but the same news was returned at Ye Scottie Tavern, Ye Olde Public House, Ye Streets of Scotland Alehouse and a few others besides and the clock was now striking ten as she sat on a low stone fence, exhausted, her bags now seeming almost impossibly heavy. Buses didn't seem to travel down here and she debated whether or not to spend some of her precious savings on a cab back to the house and ask Mrs Matthews if she might hide overnight in the cellar.

The sounds of wheels approaching made up her mind but disappointingly it wasn't a cab, it was a large dray making its way along and Eve gathered her skirts close, hoping not to be sprayed with street filth by the wheels, when she recognised the driver. At first she couldn't place him then something suddenly clicked.

'Peter? *Peter!*' she called, standing to wave.

'Who's that then?' he said, pulling up the horse and peering over at her.

'It…it's me, Eve. I met you with Molly…at the market a few weeks ago.' She pulled off her bonnet to allow him a better view of her face and he frowned for a moment before recognition hit.

'Oh yeah, Lady Eve,' he said, grinning and looking her up and down. 'Watcha doin' down here then?'

'I'm…er…looking for Mr Jenkins. My mother's friend, well, more of an uncle really. He said to find him at the old pub but I'm afraid I don't know which one he meant.'

Peter stared at her bags then back at her face as she watched him nervously. 'Running away from 'ome, are ye?'

'Pretty much, I'm afraid,' she said, figuring that was probably the best way of putting things for now. She didn't trust him but at this point she had no-one else to turn to, unless she could find Mr Jenkins or a cab.

'Well, hop on board then. There's a few more pubs further on but they'll mostly be shuttin' down soon,' he told her. 'Jenkins… ain't he the one who unloads for Joe's Meats?' he asked, jumping down to throw her bags on board.

'I think so,' Eve said, climbing up on the bench, her legs heavy with the exertion. 'He works at the markets…and he does have a friend called Joe who sells smoked hams,' Eve said, remembering.

'Yeah, I know 'im. Drinks down at the docks on Saturdays. I'm heading down anyways so it looks like tonight's your lucky night, Lady Eve,' he said, clicking to the horse as they moved off.

'Oh…that's such a relief; you're too kind.'

'Can't 'xactly say no to a damsel in distress. 'Sides, any friend of Molly's…' He looked a little too knowing when he said the last but Eve chose not to read into it. All she cared about was finding Mr Jenkins and having somewhere to stow her things and lay her head, safe and secure after this terrible, endless day.

The horse pulled the dray and they cluttered along, passing various drunks and seedy-looking men as they made their way towards the docks. Eve was starting to realise the depths of her good fortune in finding Peter and looked over at him thankfully.

'So, what is it you're carrying in the back?' she asked.

'Never ask a man what he carries to the docks,' he muttered darkly, then grinned as her face fell. 'Just jokin' there, Lady Eve. Mostly potatoes. It's what I'm pickin' up that's got me out so late.'

'Never ask a man what he picks up from the docks,' she guessed and he laughed.

'Nuh, it's just some early apples, but they're so fresh the worms can't even squeeze their way in,' he told her and she laughed a little too. It felt strange to do so, after such a day.

The street grew darker and Eve could hear the Mersey now, lapping on its polluted fringes. This was another stench altogether, like they'd taken the Vauxhall brew and added sea salt and rotting fish. Eve wondered momentarily if she would vomit but managed not to. She was hungry, she realised, despite the smell. She couldn't even remember the last time she ate.

'Peter,' she said, thinking to ask if there was any food to be bought nearby, but he lifted up a hand to silence her and she followed his line of vision. Men were down by the nearest dock and one of them flashed a lantern twice. Peter reached over for his own and flashed a signal back before turning to Eve.

'Wait 'ere for a mo',' he told her quietly. 'I won't be long then I'll take you over to the docks pub and your Mr Jenkins.'

'Alright,' Eve said, getting down and preparing to wait. She was so tired by now she could barely stand and she leaned against a large crate, drawing her shawl close. It was the one Mrs Matthews had given her, made from thick Yorkshire wool, but it did little to stem the raw chill in the rising mist. By the time Peter finally returned she felt half frozen.

And hungrier than she'd ever been in her life.

'Thank goodness! Peter...'

'Shhh, not now. I have to go see a man about somethin' first. Just a minute, mind.' He jumped down from the dray and took off on foot.

'But I'm starving!' she called after him.

'Have an apple,' he suggested before disappearing in the grey.

Eve went to the back of the dray and lifted a basket lid to find it full of waxy red apples and she took one, biting into its sweet flesh. Peter was right. This apple was so firm and juicy she doubted a worm actually could burrow its way in. She finished it quickly and took a large bite of another, hoping Peter wouldn't mind.

Her hunger was abating but she was still exhausted and horribly cold so Eve put the apple in her pocket and climbed into the back of the dray. She found a heavy blanket and huddled under it between the baskets, almost comfortable now and grateful. That feeling surprised her. How much she had lost in this past twenty-four hours: life in a great house, the man she loved, her place in the world. Yet, as her father would say, we all have lessons to learn. Eve half-smiled at the memory of his voice, considering that advice from long ago. *But you get chances, you see, never forget that.*

Perhaps this was her chance; a new life. A fresh start. Maybe it would even be a better existence, something she could negotiate on her own terms, for despite its poverty and contamination, Vauxhall held something her old life could never offer. Down here, at the least, she was free.

'Freedom,' she murmured aloud, tasting the word. How precious that seemed, suddenly. How overlooked, until now.

Eve's eyes began to close as she thought upon it but the sound of a light whistle roused her as Peter emerged from the fog, heaving a sack into the back and looking at her huddled form with amusement.

'Make yourself at home, why don't you?'

'Oh, I'm sorry. I'll get out,' Eve said, starting to push herself up.

'No, no. Mebbe I'll join you for a while.' He clambered in and sat close, his leg against hers, and Eve felt instantly uneasy, her tired mind now suddenly alert.

'I think…it's getting late. I don't want to miss Mr Jenkins.'

'I'm sure Mr Jenkins can wait while I claim me coachman's fees.' Peter leaned in and kissed her and Eve pulled away.

'Please, Peter, I'm not willing to…' He kissed her again and she tried to twist away but he held her fast this time.

'You're a beautiful woman, Lady Eve,' he muttered against her ear as his hand felt its way along her rib cage. 'We'll do well together, you and me.' He grabbed her breast and she cried out, struggling against him.

Peter stared, angry now. 'Not good enough for you, am I?' Then he slapped her across the face, telling her to shut her mouth before tearing her dress open, the rending splitting the damp air.

Eve was terrified but she was also angry, and heartily sick of men taking what they wanted, whether by persuasion or force. Well, she wasn't completely defenceless. And she did have weapons of her own.

'*Help!*' she yelled as loudly as she could, pushing at him, scratching and clawing, and causing the dray horse to shift and snort nervously.

'I told you to shut it,' Peter said angrily, locking his hand over her mouth and looking around, but it was too late. A policeman's whistle sounded and approaching footsteps could be heard across the boards.

'Who is it? Who's there?' called a voice and lanterns glowed in the fog.

'Shite,' Peter swore, pulling away and jumping to the ground to crouch and look out. 'Don't say nuthin',' he warned but Eve took her chances.

'Over here!' she called as loudly as she could.

Peter swore again, adding, 'Stupid bitch,' before taking off at a run. The lanterns moved closer and something clicked in Eve's brain. *Lanterns*. Signals. Dock deals late on a Saturday night. She looked around at the bounty of first-rate fruit and climbed down from the dray herself. This wasn't a place to be found by the authorities.

Eve crept away, cursing her own naivety, sticking to the sides of the sheds and straining to see anything in the misted, shrouded night. The docks had seemed a cold, dank sort of place before but, with dangers now lurking in that disorientating fog, they had transformed to an eerie hunting ground. Eve's heart hammered as she took to the shadows, the prey once more, begging God with both heart and mind to spare her stained soul. She'd been cast from the garden, she'd lost it all, let her at least have that precious freedom now. Her chance. *I've learnt my lessons now, Lord. I swear it.*

Crack. The sound of the pistol tore the night and Eve's heart fairly slammed in its cage as she took off, not knowing where the shot came from or where she ran to. It was simply instinct and adrenaline that made her move, the desperate will to survive. To outwit, outmanoeuvre, outrun.

Crack. It came again; her leg hit metal and she fell, and her head landed hard against the damp, rough boards. Then grey turned to black as something rolled from her pocket to rest at her cheek.

It was a perfect apple, red and waxy, marred by one single hunger-fuelled bite.

Fifteen

Liverpool, November 1851

She was trying to walk but it was merely a shuffle, her muscles wasted after weeks in a solitary cell. No-one had bothered giving her a clean dress nor did she have any way of mending the one she had worn that night at the docks and it remained ripped and bloodstained. Eve had tied her shawl around it to hide what she could and scrubbed at her face. She even used some of her precious water ration to ease some of the grease from her hair and comb it out with her fingers before tying it back, but all of these ablutions couldn't hide the dirt, the stains, the stench of prison that clung to her now.

Mrs Matthews was there, as she'd promised she'd be, but there was no-one else here for her. Eve had long given up any hope that Robert would come to her defence, his loyalty to his family and position an obvious choice in the end. The only other person who would care was Mr Jenkins but of course he wouldn't know she was here and Eve didn't want him to. Better he remember her as Emma-Kate's fortunate daughter living a life of respectable servitude. It seemed like a dream to Eve now; a lifetime ago.

'Miss Eve Richards,' intoned the judge.

She stepped forward and they removed her chains and she rubbed at the chafing on her wrists absently. Her fate would be announced now but she had little hope it would be a kind outcome. It seemed her destiny would be one of full repentance. A complete casting out. Eve felt that old cloak of non-reality descend; the one that protected her from feeling anything at the most dreaded of life's moments.

'...transporting stolen goods including two bushels of apples, one sack of American tobacco...'

Eve wondered if Peter had ever intended to take her to Mr Jenkins, if indeed there even was a pub down at the docks.

'...previous employer had fired you from service for acts of depravity and seduction...'

Perhaps he'd made that up too, taking advantage of her naivety and emotional state that night; her weak, exhausted mind.

'...acts of thievery including several books, a decorative cake tin...'

'No,' called out Mrs Matthews on a sob, shaking her head.

'Silence in the court,' called the bailiff and the judge paused to look up at the housekeeper then at Eve.

'Do you contest this accusation?'

There was little point trying to convince him the contraband wasn't hers seeing as she'd been caught red-handed with the stolen apple. No-one in authority had believed her so far and she knew none ever would. Facts were all that mattered in the courts, places where so many lied. Still, this one fact could be disproven – Mrs Matthews could vouch for that much.

'They were my things...in the travel bags in the cart,' Eve told him.

"Tis true, Your Honour. I gave her the tin meself,' Mrs Matthews dared to add.

The judge shook his head. 'It is of little matter at this point, I'm afraid.' He cleared his throat and Eve awaited his next words. What price would the Crown exact for the sum of her sins?

'Miss Eve Richards. you are hereby found guilty of being an accessory to grand theft and sentenced to transportation to the colony of Australia –' he shifted his parchment to raise his eyes towards her '– for the term of your natural life.'

Eve blinked, tears blurring her vision as Mrs Matthews collapsed and begged him for mercy; meanwhile the guard took Eve's wrists and reattached her chains. Then they took her away to live the most feared fate in Liverpool, to be taken up the Mersey to be a suffering soul awaiting deportation in a hulk on the Thames. To 'go for row', as her mother would say, always with a shudder.

Eve had earned God's wrath and she couldn't fully blame the serpents, those hungry hunters of the prey. For her sins were real too; a weak body, a weak mind. Perhaps she'd even taught others how to treat her with certain things she'd said, and done.

However unjust, however cruel, atonement must be paid now, and the cost was that once-overlooked freedom. She would mourn it for the term of her natural life.

It was simply the price of the apple.

Fever

Sixteen

Sydney, Australia, January 1852

The afternoon sun was brilliant as it danced across the cerulean blue of Sydney Harbour and Kieran paused in his hammering to squint up at it, wondering how much hotter this summer could possibly become. Dave Tumulty, his new friend and co-worker, said it got so scorching in Sydney in February you could cook an egg on a spade. Kieran was starting to think that might actually be true. The bushland along the foreshores and headlands well looked as if it had withstood millions of years of such treatment, seeming bleached of colour to an Irishman's eye. There were no emerald fields and dark green woodlands here, even the soil was more sand than earth, proving difficult for the settlers to farm.

Kieran pulled his cap lower to avoid the sun's glare but didn't bother unrolling his sleeves to protect his burning arms. Truth be told, he loved the feeling. In fact, he doubted he would ever tire of the heat that permeated every corner of this new land after so many years in the cold. His friend Dave didn't seem to mind it either, singing merrily as he worked and punctuating the sea shanty with each hammer of a nail.

And it's all for me grog, me jolly, jolly grog
All for my beer and tobacco
Well, I spent all my tin
On the lassies drinking gin
Far across the Western Ocean I must wander

Kieran chuckled and hammered in time himself, acknowledging that Dave made building at shipping yards far more enjoyable than it should be. Indeed, he made any job they took on a bit of a lark. Hailing from Limerick, Dave had arrived eighteen months earlier and had quickly made Sydney his own, turning his hand to just about anything and learning what made the place tick as he went. Consequently, he now knew everything there was to know about trade ships, imports and, more importantly, the black market. He also knew more people than Kieran could possibly count, especially those in the notorious Rocks area nearby.

After three months in his company Kieran knew he really should get a move on and follow Liam, Eileen and the family out across the Blue Mountains to Orange where they were already setting up the new farm. As it was, he'd already stayed far longer past his period of recuperation here than he'd intended but that old 'should' issue seemed to have crossed the seas with him from Ireland. And there were strong incentives to stay put.

For a start, the money and the associated perks of working alongside Dave were proving too lucrative to pass up. Kieran had a fair amount of coin stashed away, not to mention some furnishings that he knew would appease his worried sister when he finally showed.

Well, perhaps a little bit, anyway.

Eileen's last letter had been tersely worded and she'd obviously had some help from Liam, the wordsmith, when she'd informed Kieran that she was 'heartily sick of false promises of impending arrival' and tempted to come to Sydney to drag his 'unrepentant, ungrateful self west' if he didn't turn up soon.

It wasn't that he didn't look forward to seeing their land at last and carving out a new life with his family, he was just enjoying himself a bit too much right now. This time spent in Sydney was taking some of the sting out of having Maeve torn away and the horrific beating he'd suffered back in Kilrush. It was also helping him to come to terms with the subsequent struggle for life he'd endured as the family crossed the Atlantic. If not for Eileen's ministrations he'd certainly have died on the voyage, yet the pull of that guilt wasn't quite strong enough to drag him away from Sydney.

And there was another compelling incentive to stay, for it wasn't just the financial benefits that attracted Kieran to the underhanded dealings he took part in with Dave, it was the knowledge that he took it straight from the hands of those who least deserved more wealth. People who had never had a moment of deprivation in their aristocratic lives, along with their corrupt associates in the military. Lord Whitely's face came to mind then and Kieran paused to clench and unclench his right fist that still ached from the bones that had been broken that cold morning in Kilrush. Yes, the desire for vengeance against oppression burnt deeply in Kieran now and he would exact it whenever he could, from every man who treated other, less fortunate people with contempt.

You didn't have to look too far here for the chance to do so. There were many injustices here in Australia; they'd been transported as surely as the convict men and women who'd been forced aboard the tall ships and made their passage. But there was also something new drumming through the heart of this colony, something fresh and untamed. If he had to put a word to it he supposed he'd call it 'opportunity', yet it was more than that. Whatever it was, it felt like a living thing and it coursed through his veins and fed that vengeance along with his ambition, filling him with a new type of excitement, one he'd never before experienced.

He was playing games again, essentially, and, couple that with the drinking and gambling Dave kept exposing him to, it was little wonder Kieran chose to recover here in Sydney a bit longer. The place was addictive.

'Quitting time!' Dave announced suddenly, tossing his hammer and rubbing his face and hands on a cloth rag.

'Y'sure about that?' Kieran queried, looking at the half-finished job with uncertainty.

'Aye, 'tis thirsty work, Kier, and I've a hankerin' for some sweeter company than your ugly self.' Dave began to whistle the sea shanty now, putting on his favourite green waistcoat and combing down his hair, and Kieran joined him as they made their way to The Fortune of War, a favourite pub. Kieran wished he had time to wash up and rid himself of the sweat of the day but he was too keen for an ale to do so. Besides, no-one else seemed particularly bothered about hygiene in this part of town. Still, he did have his new cap, the ink barely dry where he'd written his name along the brim only this morning, and he put it on to smarten himself up a bit.

Rows of buildings painstakingly constructed from the local sandstone cast shadows that relieved their heated skin as they passed through The Rocks but it did little to relieve the stench of humanity living in squalor. Refuse lined the steep, narrow streets and the faces that passed by were streaked with dirt, mostly workmen such as themselves and the occasional woman, some hauling children back to the crowded terraces where people here made their home.

Troopers, the colony's policemen, mostly court-martialled exsoldiers, were notably absent and with good reason: this was the convict side of town. Kieran had been surprised to learn on arrival that many of the convicts hadn't ended up in gaols when they docked in

Sydney. They lived here, mostly, conducting normal lives, marrying and having families if lucky enough; some even ran businesses, although most had to work for the government a portion of the time as part of their debt to society. Poverty was rife as a result; resentment ran high, despite some of the freedoms granted, and a knife could easily be pulled from a pocket and plunged into the hated troopers. In fact, there were streets that were considered so dangerous no-one dared enter them, save the gangs who held their control.

But despite the base undercurrents flowing through the town, Kieran loved it here. Sydney seemed made for a man who was starting life over, from its cream-coloured buildings to its busy wooden docks, and it drummed with constant action, especially at its centre, where drunken sing-a-longs, betting rings and pub brawls were commonplace. The natural harbour saw plenty of action too, with constant shipments moving through the Heads from all over the world every week. They delivered plenty of colourful characters to match, and it seemed to Kieran that every nation on earth had representation on these shores.

The immigrants should have been left to make their own fates, but of course the troopers had other ideas, as did the gentry. Class distinction had been transported too and the aristocracy resided separately in stately buildings among exclusive gardened pockets to the east, along with military and government officials. It seemed the Crown's long reach was strong, even in this remote corner of the chessboard, but somehow that didn't make Kieran like Sydney any less. If anything, it made him more protective of his new countrymen living on this side of town, firing a nationalism that surprised him in so short a time.

'Did you see your girl in that green dress last night?' Dave said, jumping aside as a woman led a donkey through. 'Had her eyes falling out of her head for gawking at you, although lord knows why.'

'She's not my girl,' Kieran said firmly, trying not to think of Maeve. He doubted he'd ever have a sweetheart again, not now that he knew just how brutally something that precious could be ripped away.

'She wants to be, I'm betting. I might even get some punts goin' on you doing the deed tonight.'

'I can't stop you if you're that keen to lose your money,' Kieran told him, moving out of the way of a man awkwardly trying to push a covered barrow over the uneven stones, his expression determined. Kieran wondered what lay beneath the hessian, knowing it could be anything around here.

The sunlight was burnishing the sandstone now as they walked into the cooler interior of the pub, still blinking from the glare. It was busy already, then again it was Friday, and the refreshing ale was downed quickly as they quenched their thirst. Dave soon took court and Kieran had to laugh at the way he entertained the crowd, sharing tall tales of his past adventures and telling some rather ribald jokes. By the time it was near dark he was reciting limericks from his hometown and Kieran was well on his way to feeling good and drunk.

There was a young man from Brighton
Who thought he'd at last found a tight 'un.
He said, 'Oh my love,
It fits like a glove.'
Said she, 'But you're not in the right 'un.'

The pub erupted with laughter and Kieran shook his head at his friend, who took a bow before landing on a chair alongside.

'You're a sick man, y'know that, don't you?'

'I'm simply sharing some homespun culture about the place. Can't let the troopers and toffs create another bloody England o'er here – Australia needs a good dose of the Irish, I'm reckoning.' A young woman walked by and Dave tipped his hat with a grin. 'Hello there, lovely. My, my.'

'You seem determined to add a fair dose of Irish kiddies to the place too,' Kieran said over his ale. 'You've a new lass in your bed every week.'

'A challenging task yet someone has to take it on,' Dave declared. 'You could help a little, you know – just as a contribution to your new country an' all.'

'Aye, I could,' Kieran said.

'What's the hold-up then?' Dave pushed. 'Are you still heart-sick over some lass back home? I've told you, nothin' fixes getting over a woman better than bedding a dozen more. Don't bother denying it. It's written all over your long face there.'

'Who says I've a long face?'

'The horses outside were all talking 'bout you. I think the grey mare's taken quite a fancy...unless you finally goin' to give in and claim your girl.' Dave nodded at the door where the woman who'd been showing interest in Kieran these past few weeks was arriving. 'Speak of the she-devil.'

Kieran watched her through bleary eyes and she caught his gaze, smiling in immediate, open invitation. She was just his type really: blonde, curvaceous, pretty, or she would have been before Maeve O'Shannassey had come along. The thought curbed his lust and he drained his glass. 'No blondes for me.'

'It's what's beneath that green dress you should be thinking of, not the colour of her fecken hair,' Dave told him and Kieran noticed she had indeed worn the same outfit tonight. It was obviously new and she seemed keen to show it off. And indeed, what was underneath it, besides. Her bodice strained against a generous expanse of skin as she sauntered towards him, turning heads as she made her way through the appreciative, leering crowd. They doffed caps and whistled and offered all kinds of greetings her way but she ignored them all, focusing on Kieran alone.

'Hello again,' she said, hand on hip. It was a stance of confidence and expectation.

'Hello,' said Kieran, too drunk to bother standing but sober enough to realise his lust hadn't quite been curbed, after all.

'Good evening, miss, can we fetch you a drink?' Dave asked and Kieran supposed he should have offered to do that himself. 'Please, have a seat there,' Dave added and Kieran figured he really should have been the one offering that, too.

She didn't seem too perturbed by his lack of manners, however; in fact it seemed to encourage her if the way she sat down and challenged his stare was any indication. 'Please,' she said to Dave and he headed off to the bar.

Kieran studied her, taking in the smaller details of her person: the powder her skin didn't need, the reddened lips and the tightness of her dress. He wondered then if she expected money in return for favours, knowing he wouldn't be willing to pay if, indeed, he did end up bedding her. Perhaps she'd already had customers tonight, hence her late arrival. The thought curbed his lust once more.

'Busy evening?' he asked, more arrogantly than he'd intended.

'Not really,' she said, sliding her hair off her shoulder with her hand, exposing even more of that creamy skin. 'You?'

'Busy watching,' he shrugged, flicking his eyes at the young woman Dave had noticed earlier, trying to bring her down a peg or two.

She ignored the ploy. 'Busy drinking, more like,' she countered, eyebrows raised as if daring him to deny it.

'It's my duty as an Irishman, isn't that right, Dave?' Kieran said to his friend, who was returning with the drinks.

'I sincerely hope you're not on the same bloody topic as before,' Dave muttered to Kieran, then he smiled at the woman. 'I don't think we've been properly introduced. David Tumulty's the name, although please call me Dave.'

'Nice t'meet you, Mr Dave. I'm Shelagh Byrne.'

'Shelagh Byrne. What a fine Irish name for a fine-looking lass, eh, Kieran?'

'Kieran, is it?' she asked, looking at him half-amused.

'Kieran Clancy,' Kieran said, knowing his manners towards her had really been appalling so far but not caring all that much. She brought out the worst in him for some reason, probably because he knew she was trying to make him pander to her ego just for sport and it made him determined to resist her, which she seemed to pick up on.

'Clancy, eh? A fine name too,' Shelagh said and Kieran could almost feel the gauntlet being thrown down between them.

'Those who passed it down to me certainly were fine Irishmen.'

'I can well believe it, Mr Kieran,' she said, running knowing eyes over him as she took a long drink of her ale then trailed a single finger across her lips to wipe them. The action made him catch his breath and this time the lust returned with a vengeance, flooding through his alcohol-heated veins and coiling in his gut.

'Er...I think I'll just go see a horse about his long face,' said Dave, moving away, but Kieran was engaged in her game now, despite himself, his gaze never leaving hers.

'What else do you believe, Miss Shelagh?' he asked, taking a deep drink too.

'That you should take what you want in life,' she said, leaning in closer. 'That time goes by too fast to waste even a second.' Her face was close now and her mouth within range for him to kiss her if he wanted. The thought further stirred his blood.

'Don't you want to just sit and savour it sometimes?' he said, still trying to remain cool even while that mouth was sorely tempting him.

'What's to savour here in a pub full o' drunks?' she asked, shrugging her creamy shoulder dismissively. It made the green material slip a little further and Kieran itched to rip it off her altogether.

'Oh, I don't know; the knowledge that you have a fine Irish name...'

She moved even closer now, her lips mere inches away, and his inebriated mind slipped and fed her ego after all.

'That half the men in this room want you...'

Shelagh smiled, claiming victory in the flattery. 'Only half?'

She kissed him then, just a touch of her lips but the hunger caught like sudden fire.

'You don't waste any time,' he murmured against them.

'Not even a second,' she reminded him, then she kissed him again, a longer dance this time, and he was so drunk with both grog and lust he could have taken her on the table, right there and then.

Instead he pulled back and grabbed her hand, leading her outside, past the leers and whistles and a grinning Dave who was taking a leak near the horses, but any other awareness was drowned out by desire. And no amount of ale was going to affect his ability to unleash it now. She took him to her room, which wasn't far away, leading him up twisting stairs to the back of a building that was crowded with add-ons, their progress hampered by urgent kisses against the sandstone walls. Then they were on her bed and the green dress was shed and all the angst Kieran had felt since he'd left Ireland behind was funnelled into an explosion of desperate, hungry sex.

The alcohol blurred it but Kieran awoke to memories of exploring every inch of Shelagh's creamy skin and feeling the satiating if exhausting effects of bedding a woman who didn't like to waste even a second of time.

There were coins on the bedside table as he dressed and he paused to stare at them then over to Shelagh who was watching him from the sheets.

'Should I be adding to the pile?' he said, not really sure whether or not to ask.

Shelagh stretched her naked form and smiled what seemed a very satisfied smile. 'I took what I wanted last night as well, Mr Kieran. In good conscience, I'd have to pay you too.'

She closed her eyes then and he saw little other choice but to take his leave, stepping outside to make his way down the stairs in the pre-dawn light. It felt strange to have spent the night with a woman again, even stranger that it was for pure lust. He'd had little interest since he'd left Maeve behind, thinking without love it would mean nothing to him now.

Kieran stood and stared out at the harbour, observing ships that had sailed from all corners to rest here, beneath a new set of stars. To bring people who needed to start again. People like himself.

This was part of that process, he supposed, and he searched for feelings of regret, finding none. The indifference disturbed him.

The thought came to him then that Whitely's ambush had beaten more than his flesh; it had taken some of the goodness inside him too. Filling him with ambition and vengeance was one thing, he was glad to give the experience that, but it was quite something else if it had left him cold inside. If it had actually broken his heart.

Seventeen

Sydney, August 1852

'Rise 'n' shine,' Dave called out cheerfully as he banged open the door of the small room Kieran was renting near the shipping yards. Winter had long arrived since the one night he'd spent with Shelagh and Kieran had been fast asleep under the blankets, choosing his own bed despite her offer of a repeat performance last night.

'Go away,' Kieran mumbled into his bed, pulling the bedclothes over his head and groaning.

'Time's money, Kier, and there's work to be done.'

'Don' care.' Kieran's head was throbbing from the foolish decision he'd made to accept a challenge to a Scotch-drinking contest from a Scotsman. He'd done it to divert himself from the temptation of re-bedding Shelagh and feeling soulless once more, but surely feeling like you were in hell afterwards nullified the purpose.

'What kind of attitude is that?' Dave proclaimed, hauling the blankets off and pouring a mug of water from the jug on the stand.

'Look sharp. I've got a hot tip on a fight this morning and I need your arse with me up the river.'

'That's not work,' Kieran told him, retrieving his blankets.

'All manner of making money is work. Sweet Mary, Jesus and Joseph, it's like I've taught him nothing 't all,' Dave said, looking up at the ceiling as if to address the spirit world.

Kieran groaned again and Dave picked up the jug, holding it above his friend. 'Three seconds or you get this over your head. One...'

'Can't a man be left to recover from an evil Scot in peace?'

'Two...'

'Alright, just give me...'

'Three.' Dave dunked the water over Kieran's face then put the jug down to brush his palms together with satisfaction. 'Right, see you outside then.'

Kieran closed his eyes in defeat as the chilled water trickled down his face and hair, soaking the bed, and he groaned anew as Dave's cheerful voice carried through the walls.

What shall we do with the drunken sailor
What shall we do with the drunken sailor
What shall we do with the drunken sailor
Earl-eye in the mornin'

'I'll get that bastard one day,' Kieran muttered to himself before sitting up and looking around for a clean shirt. There was no use trying to argue with Dave when he was hell-bent on making some coin, especially when you were in a fragile way.

Ten minutes later they were boarding a steam ferry headed for Parramatta and Dave was greeting the ferry-master like an old friend. Kieran wondered if he actually knew the man but the ferry-master was chatting cheerfully to him, regardless. For his own part

Kieran didn't bother making pleasantries as he gripped the cold rail tight, wondering if he'd make the journey without throwing up.

'Sit down, go on,' Dave said, finishing up his conversation and turning to point Kieran towards the bench near the doors. 'What kind of Irishman are you, anyways? Turning down a woman then letting a Scot out-drink you like that.'

'You're just sore because you lost money betting on me.'

'Who says I bet on you?' Dave said, taking a seat next to him. 'I may be your mate and all but I'm not stupid enough to back you in a Scotch duel against a man called William "Haggis" McDougall.'

'I'll never touch the stuff again,' Kieran said, meaning it.

'Don' try to eat none o' that haggis either. Disgusting it is. Some part of an animal's innards just shouldn't be consumed by man. Entrails and the like...where you off to?'

It was a good ten minutes until Kieran returned, holding onto his stomach and wishing he'd never opened his eyes that morning.

'All better now, are you? Better out than in, as me da always used t'say.'

'Shut it,' Kieran told Dave, taking his seat gingerly.

'My, my, we are a bit cross this mornin'; maybe a spot of breakfast might perk you up? They have some lovely fresh oysters on board headed for the market. Mind you, y'can never be too careful with them slimy buggers. If the wrong one slides on down it can churn your stomach round and round and leave you retching for days on end until...what ho? Off again, are you?'

Dave played this wicked game all the way up the river until Kieran was quite sure there was little chance there was anything inside of him left to bring up. It was with shaky legs that he walked down the gangplank at the journey's end and paid a woman a penny for a drink from her pitcher of water. It helped settle him somewhat and he stood for a moment to regain his equilibrium and soak in his first view of Parramatta.

It was a busy place, especially near the docks where men were loading and unloading produce from the farms nearby and a mixture of society was on parade: soldiers, troopers, convicts, farmers, traders spruiking their fare. It was cleaner than The Rocks area and the more affluent rode across the stone bridge in fine carriages, the women holding on to brightly decorated hats alongside men sporting ties and coats. They looked uncomfortable and Kieran didn't envy their attire as they walked into churches for weekly Mass or Service. Eileen came to mind then and he felt a wave of guilt that he had stopped going himself without her around to prod him.

Quite a few church spires rose above the scene but Kieran looked past them now, taking in the neat rows of cottages interspersed with shops, pubs and larger buildings that he supposed were factories and government houses. In all, it felt far more cosmopolitan than the Sydney he'd been exposed to so far and he began to forget about his nausea as they walked alongside the river towards the main part of town, the fresh sights diverting him.

Dave had been to Parramatta several times and he started giving Kieran a bit of a tour as they went. 'That there's the Lennox Bridge where I fell off a cart last summer and hurt me rear end and that's Julia's brothel where the lady herself kissed it better later on,' he said, pointing. 'And that's Tim Hanley's eatery; best Irish stew in Sydney and that's a fact.'

The delicious scent was almost enough to whet Kieran's appetite and he made a mental note to try it another time as he peered about in the warming sunshine. ''Tis bigger than I expected,' he said, 'and the river looks like it might be nice for a dip in summer. Do many people go swimming?'

'Usually just the Aborigines. There's some o'er yonder.'

Some people were indeed visible and Kieran paused to watch them with interest. They were partially dressed in animal furs, cooking on a fire nearby and going about their daily lives as he supposed they'd always done. The men were in conversation and the children splashed in the shallows, seemingly oblivious to the white people on the other side, living a very different existence. The water looked inviting despite the cold and Kieran was tempted to have a quick dip himself.

'Quit your gawking and look lively,' Dave called over his shoulder a few yards ahead and Kieran hurried to catch up.

'That must be strange for them, having us land here and take over,' Kieran said, panting a little from the exertion of running with a hangover.

'Fewer of them to offend at this point; smallpox wiped out most and a lot of them were shot,' Dave told him.

'What for?'

Dave shrugged, but his tone was bitter. 'Objecting to dying, I suppose.'

Kieran took one last look, disgusted and sorry for them now. 'Poor buggers.'

'Aye, well at least they got to keep the original name alive. Parramatta is their word; it means place of eels.'

'Eels?' Kieran repeated, looking back at the water doubtfully now.

'Good eating apparently. Although they tend to have a rubbery texture and you have to get past that greasy skin o'theirs...you feeling alright there, Kier?'

Kieran swallowed against the rising bile and grimaced. 'Keep it up and I swear you'll be wearing what's left.'

Dave laughed then and they rounded a corner, dodging a loaded cart as they went. A large crowd was gathering in the park ahead and Kieran wondered if this was the location of the fight. 'Is this it then?'

'No, that's the Hanging Green. Some poor blighter's about to swing.'

Kieran looked at the eager faces of the crowd in disgust. 'Sick bastards.'

'People need entertainment I suppose,' Dave said with a shrug. 'Hopefully they're not executing a lass. That there's the Women's Factory, well, it was anyway, until they stopped bringing 'em here. Now it's an asylum for the sick ones and the lunatics.'

'Just what they need to see out their window then,' Kieran joked, gesturing at the Hanging Green, although the concept of those wretched souls looking out at such a place was making him feel sicker still.

'Maybe we should rescue a few later, see if we can't cheer them up. The mad ones probably aren't too particular so there's hope for you yet...ah, here we go: The Royal Oak Hotel.'

Kieran peered up at the sign that crowned the pub, a rather elegant building, painted in cream and green, that sat on the corner of Church Street.

'After you, sir,' Dave said, reaching for the door and Kieran walked in to a sea of mostly working-class men like themselves, all itching for a cold ale and a flutter today.

'Jacko, mate! Angus, you ugly dog – get yourself a haircut before I put a collar on you! PJ McLaren! Y'know last I saw this idjit he was face down in a horse trough and a trooper was eyeing off his arse for a right kickin'. Jock McCock – as I live and breathe. Where've y'been hiding that sorry mug o'yours?'

Kieran followed Dave through the throng, laughing at his friend's comical greetings and grabbing a beer for them both at the bar. It went down better than he expected, although his stomach made some noises of objection, and by the time he was on his fourth the inebriation had overrun the hangover at last and he was rather enjoying himself.

'Where's this sorry bastard about to get a whippin' by our lad Brick?' Dave asked Jock.

'On his way, on his way. You'll be eatin' your words soon enough though,' Jock told him.

Jock was betting on Brick's opponent, Big Pete, a Welsh convict with a fierce reputation, and Dave had squeezed a sizeable bet out of his optimistic friend. Kieran wondered if the man had any idea just how rarely Dave ever lost a wager. He was also wondering if McCock was really his surname.

About ten minutes later the boxers arrived and as they moved through to the centre of the floor Kieran was beginning to doubt Brick's chances. Brick worked with them at the docks and was heavyset, certainly, but Big Pete turned out to be a monster of a man, towering over the crowd with his enormous shoulders and seemingly non-existent neck. Last-minute bets were flying fast and Dave was taking full advantage, committing himself to a big payout should he lose.

'Y'sure you want to make that one?' Kieran questioned him as he agreed to yet another large wager.

'Course I am – the man's pure fat. I'm reckoning he couldn't swing an ale let alone a fist with those pudgy arms o' his.' Big Pete heard and Kieran swallowed hard as he stared over at them, his eyes narrow above a crooked nose. Unfortunately the look only encouraged Dave. 'The bigger they are, the smaller the willy I've heard too. This one'd be lucky to find his among all that lard. Maybe we should send 'im over to the Women's Asylum to see if they have any luck.' There was a lot of laughter but Kieran was hiding behind his beer now, hoping the man wouldn't recognise them afterwards.

Not that Big Pete would be able to do much. He was flanked by several troopers, all armed with bludgeons, and they looked mean enough to use them unsparingly.

'Go on then, and mind I've a fiver on ye,' said one, unlocking Big Pete's manacles and pushing him forward.

'Wait,' said another, and Kieran recognised the pock-marked face of Sergeant Toovey, a well-known and much disliked man. Kieran watched as he whispered a few things to Big Pete on the side and whatever it was it caused the convict to narrow his eyes even further. Kieran wondered what kind of threat or reward was on offer. Then he wondered what crime Big Pete had committed to be under such heavy security, a sobering thought.

The two boxers squared up and someone rang a bell that caused the crowd to erupt in excited cheering and jeering. Big Pete looked dangerously determined, landing his first punch with a resounding thump, and Brick reeled back, shaking his head before lifting his fists higher. Big Pete punched again and this time it hit Brick's shoulder, which he took quite well, but there were plenty more to absorb and by the time five minutes had passed Brick's lip was bleeding profusely and Kieran was seriously doubting his ability to come back. Dave seemed unperturbed, however, merely smiling and shrugging at the jibes thrown his way.

'I hope you've brought a full pocketbook with you,' Jock yelled over the din.

'It'll be full o' your money when I leave,' he yelled back.

Sergeant Toovey heard and sent Dave a derisive sneer before turning back to watch the fight. It looked set to arrive at a violent conclusion now as Big Pete drew back to deliver what would surely be the killer punch.

'Shite,' Kieran whispered to himself. He could barely stand to watch as the big fist flew but somehow it met with air as Brick ducked faster than a man his size should be able to, then, seemingly out of nowhere, his own fist landed in Big Pete's sizeable stomach. It shocked the Welshman, that much Kieran could see, but the next one shocked him more, landing straight on Big Pete's nose, which cracked loud enough for the room to hear before he fell backwards in a heavy heap. The pub erupted and Kieran jumped up and down, clapping a smug Dave on the back and joining the chant with several other lucky punters. *Brick! Brick! Brick! Brick!*

Brick was hoisted in the air and there was general mayhem as bets were paid up and celebratory drinks were purchased but little attention was paid to the bleeding man on the floor. Kieran watched as he slowly found his feet and Sergeant Toovey gave Dave a filthy glare before angrily grabbing Big Pete's wrists and locking the manacles once more. The giant convict seemed pitiful now with his face covered in blood, his expression beaten too as he looked over and noticed Kieran staring. It made Kieran want to say or do something to help but there was nothing to be done, so he did the only thing he could think of: he tipped his cap.

Some kind of reaction flashed in Big Pete's eyes but Kieran had no more time to consider what it was as an oblivious and jubilant Dave stood on a chair and announced that the drinks were on him.

It was a merry afternoon that followed as Dave did his best to mollify his less fortunate mates.

'Just couldn't see it coming,' muttered Jock for the umpteenth time.

'Aye, I've heard the ladies sayin' that about you,' Dave replied.

By the time they left Kieran's insides were sore with laughter and the beer had added to the Scotch the night before to render him very wobbly indeed. Dave was equally the worse for wear and the walk to the ferry in the cold night air seemed far further than it had that morning.

'Piss stop,' Dave declared, pausing to relieve himself against the asylum wall. 'Wonder how lonely those poor lasses are up there?' he added as he stared blearily at the barred windows above.

'Some wouldna seen a man for years,' Kieran said, leaning on the wall to steady himself and peer too.

'Seems a shame not to drop in and say hello. Just to be friendly, like.'

Kieran swayed, considering. 'Can't just walk...walk on in.'

'Can't just walk on by neither.'

'True,' Kieran said. 'It's just *rude*.'

'It would be *rude*, wouldn' it? You know those walls look pretty climb...climbabable. That's a word,' Dave said.

'Surely,' Kieran agreed.

'I'm gonna have a go,' Dave said.

'Fortune favours the brave if...hic...sometimes foolish,' Kieran declared, and they stumbled over to the wall, hoisting themselves up with varying success before somehow reaching the top.

'Wonder why no-one's ever done this before?' Kieran whispered as they peered over at the main building. 'Seems stupid not to.'

'It does seem stupid,' Dave agreed. 'Now all we have ta do is get down...easy now...arrghhh.' Dave had attempted to crouch down to climb and promptly fallen arse first to the prison ground, which made Kieran laugh so hard he fell too.

'Shite,' Dave said, 'I think I've broken me old fella.'

'Well that...that kinda defeats the purpose of being here, now doesn't it?' Kieran said, laughing so much he could barely get the words out. 'Oh shite, are those dogs?'

'Oh for fecks' sake,' Dave said as they got up and grabbed at the bricks to climb out. A snarling mongrel came around the corner and lunged towards them in the dark as they clambered up and Dave swore again as it ripped at his pants. 'Argh, he's got me! Feck off, you hellish beast.'

'Get off him!' Kieran told the growling dog, still laughing to the point that he could barely climb but somehow he made it to the top with Dave and they jumped over to the other side, landing just as a policeman's rattle sounded.

'Shite, shite, shite,' they both swore, crawling at first then somehow managing to stand and make a run for it.

They twisted their way through backstreets until the rattles faded and Kieran figured they were in the clear as they rounded a corner near the docks, but unfortunately someone had piled a bunch of crates on the path. Both men fell over them with an almighty crash and the ruckus earned the attention of a group of troopers nearby, the absolute last ones Kieran and Dave needed to see right now.

'Hello then, what 'ave we here?' Sergeant Toovey said, a dangerous grin spreading across his face as he sauntered over. The others followed, obviously intoxicated themselves, with Big Pete still in tow. No-one had bothered washing off the blood from the fight and it was darkening and crusting on his face. How he felt about that fact was impossible to discern, especially now that he was being shoved to the back as the sergeant began to circle Kieran and Dave, taking out his bludgeon and stroking it threateningly. It gave Kieran flashbacks of a white cane and fear began to pool in his stomach as the adrenaline pumped through.

'You've had a busy day, 'aven't you, boys? Winning money on y'dirty ol' Brick and drinkin' y'selves senseless…then again, you are only Irishmen. We can't expect too much from them, can we, mates?' he addressed his men and they sniggered, each taking out their own bludgeons.

'Just on our way home t'sleep it off, Sergeant,' Dave said, almost succeeding in his attempt at sounding cheerful.

'Oh, I think we can be of assistance there, can't we, boys?'

'We can make 'em sleep orright,' agreed one.

'Can't guarantee they'll wake up but,' said another, smiling with a row of crooked, yellowed teeth.

Kieran tried to focus through the alcohol distortion, looking for a sudden punch, a flash of a bludgeon, a lunge. It came all at once, in a blur, and he and Dave were next to useless in defence as the troopers rained blows upon them, laughing as they grunted, ridiculing as they groaned.

Dave fell to his knees and they began to kick him, taking turns. Kieran tried desperately to help his friend but the troopers held him back.

'Nuh, you just watch,' the sergeant said. ''Bout time he learnt his lesson.'

Another kick landed and Kieran winced as Dave cried out in pain.

'Gutless bastards,' Kieran yelled, unable to hold the words back as he fought to free himself.

'What did you say, Irish?' the sergeant said, coming close to his face.

'I said you're gutless. Easy enough to hurt a man when he's down.'

'How about one who's standing up then?' Sergeant Toovey struck Kieran with his bludgeon then, straight on Kieran's chin. Kieran reeled but he wasn't done.

'Can't fight...a fair...fight, can ye?' Kieran countered, too drunk and angry to care about caution anymore. 'I suppose you don't even know how to fight man to man, y'yellow Pommy bastard.'

Toovey's face contorted at those words. 'Oh, I know how to fight man to man, only you're an animal, aren't ya? A filthy bogtrotter. Good for nothing but this.' He drew his bludgeon back to strike again and Kieran closed his eyes against the impending pain, only this time it didn't arrive.

Crack.

Kieran opened his eyes once more to the sight of Sergeant Toovey reeling backwards, instantly unconscious from the force of an enormous fist.

'What the bloody hell do y'think you're...'

Crack, and another man fell. Big Pete was fast with his fists, even with manacles on, and the inebriated troopers were slow to react, dropping before they could even think to raise their bludgeons. In what seemed like a matter of seconds they all lay in a defeated pile and Kieran and Dave straightened on shaken legs to stare at them in stunned silence.

'Well,' said Dave, still holding his guts. 'That was...right nice of you. Dave's the name. Dave Tumulty.' He held out his hand to shake Big Pete's but the effort seemed to cost him.

'And I'm Kieran Clancy,' Kieran said, turning to face Big Pete, rubbing his jaw that was painful from the effort of speaking. 'You must have been...agh...wanting to do that for a long time, I'm guessing. Why'd you choose...' But then rattles sounded again and the three men took off at once, not wanting to be found anywhere near that pile. Down to the docks they went as best they could manage, keeping to the shadows along the river and trying not to stumble and make too much noise. As luck would have it the ferry was pulling in and Kieran and Dave turned to Big Pete, wondering what to do with him. Big Pete assisted by nodding at a loose steel spike on a fence and placing his wrists either side of a rock. The task of breaking the chain was done wordlessly as Kieran obliged until they stood back, at a loss at what to do once more.

'So...do you want to come with us to The Rocks?' Kieran offered, not knowing what else to suggest.

'I don't think that'd be in ye best interests,' he replied. It was the first time Kieran had heard the man speak and the gentle tone of his voice surprised him.

'I know the captain. I'm sure I could smuggle you on board,' Dave said, still nursing his stomach, his expression pained. 'It's the least we can do.'

'No, I'll make me way west now. I've heard plenty of talk about the goldfields and I think it's me best shot for hiding out now. Nuggets the size of apples, they say; streets paved with the stuff.'

'Aye, I've heard that,' Dave said, 'but I think some of the stories are a bit tall.'

'Ye hear a lot of things when people forget you have a brain. There's gold out there alright, and I know just where to find it.'

'That so...?'

'But if they find *you* you'll be shot,' Kieran interrupted Dave.

'Better off dead than a circus act,' Big Pete said, bending over to dip his sleeve in the water and wiping at the blood on his face.

'Here,' Kieran said, handing him his handkerchief. 'Take me cap too; might make you less recognisable...and some coins while I think about it.'

Dave reached in his pocket and pulled out some of his winnings, adding it to the pile. 'Glad you didn't fight like that earlier today or I'd have nothing to give you.'

Kieran put it all in the cap and held it out but Big Pete stared for a long moment before accepting, his expression difficult to read. 'Ye asked before why I chose now to give those bastards what they had comin'...truth is it's because o' ye.'

'What did I do?' Kieran asked, surprised.

'Ye gave me somethin' today no-one's bothered to offer me in years.'

Kieran looked at the cap and thought back to the fight and the moment he tipped it at the convict. 'You mean pity?'

'No,' said Big Pete, putting the cap with its contents hidden within on his overly large head. 'I mean respect.'

He shook hands with them both then before walking away, disappearing into the darkness as the ferry docked nearby.

'Reckon he'll be alright?' Kieran asked, looking back as he and Dave limped towards the steamer.

'Him wearing your cap for camouflage is about as useful as putting a tin cup on a watermelon but aye, he'll be right enough.'

Kieran laughed, wincing as it hurt his aching jaw, but by the time they reached Kieran's place back in Sydney both men fell mercifully asleep, practically unconscious from alcohol and injuries.

Next morning it took Kieran a while to remember what had transpired the night before as flashes of brick walls, rattles, bludgeons and something to do with a watermelon passed through his mind. No, he couldn't quite recall everything but looking at Dave's naked arse exposed by a dog-ripped pair of breeches nearby he knew one thing for sure: it really was time to get the hell out of Sydney.

Eighteen

Sydney, September 1852

Eve had never considered that darkness had multiple personalities before. It had always just seemed like a gentle friend that lulled her to sleep at night; a welcome purveyor of rest. She knew better now. Darkness could be insidious, hiding truths; ugly inconvenient facts that offended the eye, like bodies covered in faeces and filth, weeping sores. Phlegm and infection. Vomit.

For the most part this was welcome; one could almost pretend they weren't chained here, in the dank depths of a convict ship, surrounded by the sorriest souls ever born to earth. Yes, it could almost be done if the other senses could be so easily fooled, but there was no way to trick her sense of smell, her hearing, her taste and her touch. If she survived she was sure the stench of this place would never leave her, the pitiful moans would never quite be silenced, the constant rising bile would never be far away. And the pain of shackles would weigh upon her wrists and ankles forevermore.

This new, wicked darkness hid other truths too: violence and fornication. Danger. The human soul found new shades of depth when the light was gone. They'd come for her too at first, the soldiers, but blood had soaked her skirts and Eve knew it was more than a monthly discharge. A baby had been formed during those last days of her freedom but of course a child was too pure a being to come into this dark world. It was a blessing and she hadn't mourned it. They'd even allowed her a short stay in the infirmary and she'd been given new clothes before being transferred from the hulk on the Thames to this transport ship.

The soldiers had no interest in any of them now, as putrid and skinny as they all were. For her own part, Eve had become so weak she supposed she might die, and these past few weeks she'd begun to wish she would. No care for her own existence – yet another sin to stain her soul. But who would want to live on such terms? Who would want such an unnatural life?

Others had died along the way. Martha, an older woman who had tried to beg for more food and was thus denied any for days. Mercifully she'd gone in her sleep and no-one even questioned why. Ginny had died too, a young girl Eve supposed no more than sixteen or so. She'd been sick from the start and so small Eve knew she'd never make it, although the sadness of her passing still clung. It wasn't easy watching someone fit then die, her eyes open as she lay on the deck, blue as the cloudless sky above and just as empty.

They'd stopped taking the women above deck now as they approached Sydney at last. The soldiers seemed otherwise preoccupied and Eve supposed they were watching for the coastline and getting the ship ready to dock. Shirley, the only woman here who spoke very much, swore she'd heard one of them say it was today. Eve supposed she should be grateful for that: an ending to one phase of the horror her life had become.

After months of being rocked by the sea, at times terrified they'd sink as storms lashed in the night, it would be reassuring to stand with solid land beneath their feet once more. The soldiers were whistling as they worked and the other women around her were peering up at the cracks around the hatch that allowed a tiny amount of light into the dark, almost like an offering of hope but not quite. For it never actually touched them, that sunlight. Yet another comfort denied.

'It's calm,' noted one, a dark woman called Stella. She spoke only rarely and her voice was barely a rasp.

'That's because we're coming into the harbour,' Shirley said. She knew quite a lot about ships, having spent time on them in her youth as part of a large fishing family, although she feared the water itself, having never learnt to swim. Perhaps that's why she spoke about it so much, to reassure herself with logic as they made their perilous way across the ocean.

For whatever reason it was, Eve had clung to her knowledge these past months like she was the only voice of reason left in the world, which to Eve she was.

The waves are building because the storm is at its peak.
The swell is receding so the worst of the danger is over.
The water is calm because we are in shelter now, never fear.

Without Shirley Eve doubted she would have maintained any sanity at all on this voyage but she'd never got around to telling her so, having lost the will to speak long ago. Perhaps one day she would find it again and be able to thank her, maybe even tell her own name and story. If such things ever mattered again.

Suddenly the hatch was opened and the tiny light exploded into a blinding force of white.

'Alright, you lot. Time to get your miserable souls up and out.'

Keys were being turned now and iron fell away as they formed a line, legs aching in fleeting, terrible pain from wasted muscles experiencing unexpected use. Faces blinked up at the white sails in the sun and Eve climbed with the rest to take in her first glimpse of Sydney, not that it would be her home. Convicts were no longer transported to this port, according to Shirley, and the ones that currently lived here, either independently or rotting in the gaols and hospitals, would be the last.

She and her pitiful inmates were merely stopping over for a few days before continuing on to a place called Tasmania. Eve was terrified even at the mention of the name. Apparently it was at the ends of the earth and so wretched a place actual devils lived there, snarling black beasts that bit you in the night, or so one woman had told her back on the Thames. But at least this ship had taken the east coast route and they would likely get there alive. Many perished when approaching from the south, navigating along what was terrifyingly termed 'the Shipwreck Coast'.

'Get a move on,' one of the soldiers said, shoving Eve along, and she stumbled as she reached the deck and took her place. The first thing she noticed was the air, sweet with the scent of land but still salted by the sea. The sun was warm and overly bright but her eyes were adjusting now and she could see the town at last, a bustling, sprawling port filled with sand-coloured stone dwellings on one hillside, great houses and parks on the other.

That old feeling of non-reality suffused her as her senses tried to adjust to so much detail after so little, for so long. Colours she'd forgotten existed fed her eyes as humanity moved about, a purple dress here, a crimson jacket there. And green. So much of it as the land spread before them. How she loved green, Eve realised. How clean and alive it now seemed when you hadn't seen it for such a length of time. And what an odd colour to take for granted, the shade of so much life. She supposed it took death and despair to really notice such a thing.

Movement was mesmerising her too, after continuous stillness and shadows, and this busy port was filled with it as industrious Sydneysiders moved about. The centre seemed all about shipping and sails whipped in the breeze as men busied themselves furling and unfurling them, tying ropes and moving cargo about. It was reassuring to see the ships come to rest and unload, marking the end of seemingly impossibly vast journeys. She wished with what was left of her might she'd never have to step on a boat again, but it was a pointless wishing. Supported by very little might.

Steamers were in the mix as well and one was pulling in nearby, a fairly small vessel that the soldiers were pointing at and discussing. Eve wasn't interested in its capabilities. She was simply staring at one of the crewmen. He was eating a sandwich. A humble, brown bread, miraculous sandwich.

But taste was one sense she really couldn't bear to ruminate upon so she went back to focusing on sight instead. She drew her eyes from humanity and back to nature, tracing the harbour's coastline. It was surprisingly beautiful with its thick bushland, golden beaches and inviting blue water, unexpectedly paradisiacal, although the bushes themselves were strange looking. As were the birds, she noted, watching some brightly coloured ones flock onto a tall, silver-coloured tree. The sun was directly above and still brilliant; in fact it seemed brighter than anywhere she'd been, and hotter too. Eve grew parched as she stared at the clear water now, longing not only for a drink but to bathe and be clean once more. Perhaps they would allow it at some point. She'd gladly go in fully clothed and wash the stench out of her garments as well.

Rowboats were arriving and Eve felt suddenly overwhelmed by the sight, almost disbelieving that they'd be letting her off this wretched ship at last. But sure enough she and the others soon climbed down and were rowed to the dock where they were directed onto the steamer that had been under discussion. The walking and climbing soon took its toll and by the time Eve sat to make the journey to somewhere called Parramatta her whole body felt exhausted. And that thirst wasn't going away. Her tongue was so dry it felt like paper and the scenery seemed to mock her distress, those strange bushes appearing thirsty now too, their pale greenery alike to shrubs underwatered.

The soldiers were drinking, ale from a barrel in fact, and Eve longed for a cup although she'd never even tasted the stuff. She was so tempted to ask she had to bite her poor dry tongue, but better that pain than one they would surely inflict.

By the time they drew into Parramatta she was almost faint and the others looked so too, then Shirley dared to ask if they would drink when they disembarked.

'Drink this!' the soldier said. He was well in his cups by now and swaying as he picked her up and to Eve's horror threw her overboard.

The water looked fairly shallow but Shirley was very short and she struggled immediately.

'Help!' she screamed. 'I can't swim!'

No-one moved to help her and Eve watched in horror as the woman who'd kept her sane for so long fought for breath, her face falling below the water, eyes terrified.

'She...she's...' Her voice came out a whisper after months of disuse and she went to try again but Shirley's screaming silenced her. A terrible gurgling sound followed as she fell beneath once more, her hand the only part of her left above water. *Drowning, she's drowning*, Eve's mind screamed.

'Give her a wave then, lads,' said a drunk soldier, and the sound of their laughter twisted something in Eve's chest. Before she really had any time to consider it she lifted herself up and over the ferry wall, jumping overboard to land in the river, the cool water coming as a shock to her overheated skin. Eve dragged herself towards Shirley, her skirts an instantly heavy weight, and used her old swimming experience and comparative height to help her to the shore. The soldiers didn't seem to mind her rashness, still laughing and jeering as they watched Eve settle the woman on the sand, patting her back as she coughed up brackish sludge and calming her as best she could.

'A drink, I need...a drink,' Shirley gasped, '...*please.*'

Eve pulled herself upwards and stumbled towards another woman selling ladlefuls of water from a pitcher, finding her voice at last.

'A drink, I beg of you.'

'One penny,' she said, her tone gruff as she looked Eve over. Eve pushed back wet strands of hair and rubbed at her face, trying to appear more composed.

'I apologise, madam, that I have no way to pay you,' Eve told her, forcing the words through a painfully dry, disused throat, 'but surely you could find it in your heart to help this poor soul,' Eve said, pointing over at the distressed Shirley who had collapsed on the sand.

'One penny,' the woman said firmly, as the soldiers continued to jeer.

'Ask her to take off that dress and I'll pay ye!' called one and Eve looked around in despair, tears threatening now at the cruelty on display. Non-reality back in play.

'She's...she's so thirsty...' Eve said, her strained voice beginning to fail. 'Please...'

Then someone spoke from behind, an Irishman with a lilting brogue.

'You seem to be in a spot of bother there, miss. I'd be honoured if you allowed me to assist you.'

Kieran knew he was being worse than foolish. He and Dave were lying as low as they possibly could as they loaded their wagon with illegitimate cargo in Parramatta today and certainly putting himself in the eyes of some rowdy, drunken soldiers here was bordering on insane but he just couldn't seem to help himself. He'd been about to go in to help the near-drowning woman when this mad girl jumped off the boat and he'd felt instant admiration for her bravery. Not to mention the fact that someone refusing to give the lass water for the shaken, parched woman she'd rescued was just plain wrong.

But now, as she turned and he saw her up close for the first time, there was additional motivation to aid this damsel in distress: she was, quite simply, beautiful. Her wet hair was drying in fair strands and it framed a face filled with features so exquisite the grime and mud simply couldn't hide it. And her eyes...well, they were hazel, he supposed, but seemed a hundred shades of brown and green and were so wide with surprise at his small offer of assistance that Kieran could have wept for her. How could such a lovely girl ever have ended up here?

'A spot of bother...' she echoed.

'Aye, and I won't take no for an answer now. Two please,' he told the now disgruntled seller and she dipped her ladle as Kieran handed over the tuppence. With the commotion over, the soldiers had lost interest and Kieran handed the girl the water without interference. 'Drink yourself first, lass.'

'No,' she said, seeming to collect herself. 'I'll drink after her.' Kieran watched, his admiration growing, as she took the water over to the other convict who drank so desperately it hurt to watch.

'Now you,' he insisted, holding up the second ladle. She returned and drank thirstily herself although her eyes were drawn to the other poor wretches who watched on from the steamer. She frowned and Kieran immediately turned back to the woman, asking her how much to give them all a drink. She looked over at the soldiers hesitantly at first but they were so absorbed in their ale consumption it was obvious they wouldn't care. The woman took Kieran's money then, moving over to the steamer's edge and ladling water up to the convicts above.

Eve watched on, relieved, and he felt rather ridiculously pleased when sudden shallow dimples flashed in her cheeks.

'That was very kind of you, sir.'

'Well, it's worth it now, to see such a pretty smile.'

The girl touched her fingers to her face at his words, as if surprised. 'It's been so long since anyone showed kindness...I was starting to doubt anyone ever would again.' She spoke in a soft, well-educated tone, still watching the convicts drink, and Kieran took in more tiny details of her while she was thus distracted. There was a small scar on her chin and her wrists were red and chafed, and she was painfully thin, her graceful neck reed-like, her wet clothes hanging off her frame. 'Anyway, you'd be best not to risk speaking to me any longer, sir,' she said, turning her face back towards him, those wondrous eyes finding his once more. 'I've put you to too much trouble as it is, I'm afraid.'

Kieran looked over at Dave near the wagon, frantically motioning him to move away, then at the disinterested soldiers and shrugged. 'I'll take me chances,' he decided. 'It seems you need a better welcome to Parramatta than the one you've received so far. Where are they taking you?'

'I'm...I'm not sure...' she replied, looking around with trepidation now as her gaze took in the government buildings lining the streets. 'They don't really tell us much.'

She looked ashamed at the admission and Kieran chastised himself for asking an uncomfortable question, but it wasn't an easy thing, trying to charm a convict girl while in the middle of committing your own criminal activities. In front of a bunch of inebriated soldiers.

'At least it will be on land anyway,' he pointed out. 'I'm guessing you're fresh off the ship.'

She nodded. 'Only just arrived.'

'Well, you should get at least a few days in to get your land legs back. Do you know where you're headed after?' Kieran asked before cursing himself for his own stupidity again. There was only one possible, terrible answer to that question.

'Tasmania.'

She said it with a lowering of that graceful neck and she appeared to Kieran like a swan then, a beaten one. But he could understand why. Tasmania was the last place in Eastern Australia to still be taking convicts and it was home to some of most notorious gaols on earth, which spoke volumes about the extent of her crimes. Perhaps he really should move away. But he didn't.

'I'm sorry,' he said instead. 'I shouldn't pry.'

'It's more that you shouldn't bother,' she whispered, her eyes darting over to the soldiers, fear there now as they laughed loudly and made obscene gestures over some dirty joke. Kieran was afraid for her too – already they were beginning to look over. She was wet, her dress clinging, and he knew they would order him away soon, leaving her vulnerable and alone once more. The thought made him want to grab her, run over to Dave and hide her in the wagon, before kidnapping her out to Orange where he was finally headed to on the morrow, after this one last, lucrative job.

Just then a carriage drew up and people paused to watch as a naval officer alighted. He spied the convict women and soldiers nearby and strode over. Kieran listened as he addressed the soldiers.

'Who's in charge here?'

'I am, sir,' said one, trying his best to stand upright and salute but doing a rather poor job of it. 'Sergeant…Sotheby.'

'Captain Cartwright,' the officer said, pausing to look Sergeant Sotheby up and down. 'For pity's sake, man, have you been drinking on duty?'

'No, sir, I mean, yes, sir, but we were told to wait here until dismissed and we figured a little...er...refreshment after so long at sea wouldn't do no harm.' Sergeant Sotheby managed to sound coherent but then belched and ruined the effect.

'Look at the state of you,' Captain Cartwright said, shaking his head in disgust. 'Have you even bothered feeding and watering these convicts?'

Kieran bristled at the way the women were referred to like horses but at least the man was taking some interest in their welfare.

'They've had water, sir.'

The captain looked over and scowled at Eve and the other wet woman. 'It seems you've thrown it all over some of them.'

'They...er...fell in the river, sir.'

'Humph. I won't even ask how you managed that! Get them all down on shore; I want to inspect them at once.'

'Yes, sir.' Sergeant Sotheby gave the order, and the women were shuffled off the steamer as the officer spoke in quieter tones.

'I've just been down to the asylum and I've never seen a sorrier bunch of women in my life, not that my hopes were high. All I need is one half-decent wench to act as a maid for my wife down near Melbourne but so far I wouldn't let *any* of them within ten feet of her.'

'Aye, sir. I've heard most are bloody mad...er, I mean, beyond help.'

Kieran listened on as the captain further described his needs, probably little realising that Sergeant Sotheby was unlikely to know one convict from the other, even if he were sober, and it spurred Kieran on to make his second rash decision of the day.

'What's your name?' he whispered to the girl who was still beside him.

'It doesn't matter. I'm very grateful to you, sir, but you should go, *please*. You'll get yourself in trouble,' she urged.

Dave was motioning desperately now as a crowd of curious onlookers gathered and Kieran knew he really *should* move away, but not until he had his answer.

'Your name, love. Hurry.'

The girl looked surprised at the endearment but the words slipped out. 'Eve Richards.'

'Grand,' he said, moving off into the crowd now.

'What game are you playing at now, you daft bastard?' Dave hissed as soon as he could get close. 'Why don't you just put a sign around our necks while you're at it?'

'I couldn't just stand by and watch.'

'Aye, you could and you should have! Anyway, let's get out of here before any troopers recognise us.'

'Not yet,' Kieran said and Dave threw his hands in the air in frustration.

'You realise *we* could go to gaol if they check the cart?'

'Aye, we could.'

'And you're consorting with a *convict*.'

'Aye, a lovely one, don't you think?'

Dave gaped now in disbelief. 'I suppose you're planning to just kidnap her then? Should I make room in the wagon next to the contraband?'

'Thought crossed me mind.'

'*Are you...?*'

'Shhh.'

The women were lined up now, a sorry, starving bunch, and Captain Cartwright marched along, inspecting them.

'I am in need of a maid,' he announced in a loud clear voice. 'Someone without lice or disease who can string two words together is becoming my only criteria. Can any one of you meet it?'

They all looked too frightened to respond until one timidly raised her hand. 'I ken cook, sir, and I ain't got no vermin.'

'Yes, but you're as disgusting a woman as ever saw daylight so that's out of the question.' She was, indeed, an unfortunate-looking woman with her blackened teeth and matted frizzy hair and Dave stifled a chuckle, despite the tension.

'Shhh,' Kieran hissed again.

'I...can...' Shirley began but he simply shook his head.

'You look like you just swallowed half that disease-ridden river, my dear, and I need someone who'll survive the journey.'

Shirley's eyes went wide but that devastating comment silenced her.

'Who else have we got?' None dared respond at all now and Kieran noted Eve's chin was very low as the captain sighed. 'Looks like I've wasted my time. Take them off to the asylum now, man, and make sure you...'

'Excuse me, sir,' Kieran called out, taking his chance. Dave grabbed at his arm but he shook it off as he moved forward towards the captain. 'I believe I recognise one woman here who fits the bill nicely.'

'Who said that? Speak up then,' Captain Cartwright boomed, turning.

Bold but never cocky, Kieran reminded himself, taking a deep breath before continuing. 'The name's Kieran, sir, Kieran Clancy,' he said, doffing his new cap. 'I said I recognise one of these women. She worked in a fine country house in Ireland where I was a stableman for a while. The family brought her all the way out from London, she was so skilled a maid.'

'Which family was it?'

'Lord and Lady Whitely,' Kieran said, detesting the reference but knowing it held clout.

'Hmm, yes, I've heard of the man. Rather particular about his servants, as I recall. Which woman is it?' he asked, interested now as he perused them again.

'Eve Richards, Captain, one of the ladies who unfortunately fell into the river, but I can assure you she didn't, er...ingest the water and isn't normally prone to accident,' Kieran said, walking the captain over and standing before Eve, 'except the one that landed her here, of course.'

Captain Cartwright looked Eve over slowly, taking in every detail of her person from the wet, grubby dress, to the red-raw shackle marks, but his grim expression softened somewhat when it reached her face. 'What kind of "accident"?'

'She was involved in a runaway cart disaster. A wealthy man was killed and the poor girl was blamed but everyone knew it wasn't her fault. A terrible shame for a young lass.'

'Cart, eh?' said the captain. 'And what were you doing driving one as a maid?'

'Oh, she wasn't driving, sir...'

'I was addressing the girl.'

Kieran watched nervously as Eve searched for words, praying for her own sake she'd play along. 'It was my friend who was driving, sir, only he ran off and left the blame with me. I am guilty though, in a way. I trusted far too easily and my own foolishness landed me here. I cannot say otherwise, if I am entirely honest.'

The captain looked both taken aback and impressed. 'That's quite a cultured accent you have there. How did you acquire it?'

'My father, sir. He was a learned man.'

Kieran saw a glimmer of tears but Eve blinked them away and he held his breath as the captain made up his mind. 'Well, at least we won't have to put up with some godawful cockney wailing all day. You'll do, Eve. Get your things and let's get moving.'

Eve blushed but this time that elegant neck didn't bow in shame. 'I have none, sir.'

'Eh? Well, never mind. Say your goodbyes and get in the carriage. Must be some blasted papers to sign, there usually are. Where's that drunken fool got to?'

'Here, sir,' said Sergeant Sotheby.

The captain went over to sign his ownership of Eve and Kieran turned to take his leave, wishing he could do more but knowing this was, at least, a better fate for her than a Tasmanian gaol.

Her eyes were fixed on him now, her mouth parted in shock at what had just transpired, he imagined, her life completely altered on a stranger's whim.

'Well, I guess this is goodbye then,' he began, wishing it weren't so as those incredible eyes filled once more. 'Hey now, lass, don't cry. 'Tis a better future for you now. You may even earn your freedom with him, you never know.'

'It's not that,' she whispered, 'it's just that…you're so kind to do this and I can't possibly ever repay you.'

'It was your kindness that motivated me in the first place. You should be thanking yourself.'

'No,' she said, shaking her head, 'I'm thanking you, sir, from the bottom of my heart. You've given me so much more today than you'll ever know.'

'Maybe I'll see you again someday, down near Melbourne, and you can give me a kiss for me troubles.' He said it to lighten the mood but she looked around then and did just that, kissing him quickly on the cheek and whispering in his ear.

'I'll never forget you, Kieran Clancy, not for as long as I live.'

They called for her then and Dave sidled up to Kieran, grabbing him and pulling him into the crowd. Kieran reluctantly obliged but kept watching as Eve whispered something to the other river-soaked woman before boarding the carriage and being driven away, not taking his eyes from her back until she disappeared from view.

'One of these days you'll get me killed,' Dave said, shaking his head. 'Whatever were you thinking to do such a thing? Your brain's gone soft! She could have murdered kittens for all you know.'

Kieran found he actually didn't care what crime she'd committed; he'd seen a kind woman in action today, a good soul in those eyes.

'She deserved a better life.'

'As if you can be the judge of such a thing! You weren't using your brain at all, I'm betting. You moony idjit.'

Dave was right about that much. Kieran hadn't been using his brain when he'd made decisions about Eve, he'd been ruled by his heart, which meant it wasn't quite broken after all. Not even when the lass had blonde hair, although hers was more white than gold.

She was just as out of reach as Maeve O'Shannassey but, as he watched the carriage disappear, he vowed he would find Eve Richards again one day. He knew he would do it too, with absolute certainty, as he rubbed at the place where she'd kissed him just now. He knew it because their fates were inextricably entwined forever now. And because it was exactly what he really shouldn't do.

Nineteen

Orange, New South Wales, September 1852

The early morning clouds laced the sky like sea foam, silver and white against the pale blue, and Liam watched them glide contentedly as he drank his tea on the front porch. Well, Eileen liked to call the roughly built lean-to a 'porch' anyway, but then again she liked to call the three-bedroom cottage Liam and Rory had constructed this summer a 'homestead' too. It could hardly be termed such but Liam indulged his sister such folly. He'd even helped Rory and the kids make a sign for the front gate that read *Welcome to Clancy Homestead, may God bless our home sweet home.* Thomas, James and Matthew had done their best to paint flowers around the edges but they were rather blotchy and smudged. It was just another reason Liam hoped the new baby would be a girl. In his limited bachelor experience they tended to take more care in the finer arts. The fact that they were a good half hour ride out of town and Eileen could use some female company was a larger reason for the preference, of course.

The sunlight filtered through the trees in rays, almost celestial as it shone in between the twisting branches. They were strange, these Australian gums, twisting upon themselves in all manner of arrangement, their bark peeling back to fall at their base almost banana-like; long dark strips that frayed at the edges. A few held strange markings, intricate curling patterns made by some kind of insect on the smooth grey trunks. Liam had told the children faeries carved them at night, writing secret messages to each other. The astute Thomas hadn't been fooled for a moment.

'As if the faeries would bother to come to Australia, Uncle,' he'd scoffed. 'They'd melt in this sun and that's a fact.'

'I didn't mean Irish faeries, Thomas. I'm talking about Australian faeries; tougher little creatures than the ones back home, I'm reckoning. Go on and ask your teacher if you don't believe me.'

Thomas had still looked sceptical but Liam knew he'd ask her anyway. He was a curious young fellow.

Liam and Rory spent most days working the land, building fences and holding yards, and a decent enough barn that had sheltered their small herd of cattle that winter. It got 'bloody cold mate' in these parts, as the locals liked to say, but even after these past frosty months Liam doubted he would ever really consider it so. Australian cold just couldn't compare to Irish cold. Still, it was a bit chilly this early spring morning and Liam cupped his fingers around his mug of tea to warm them as voices began to sound from inside.

'...but I have a tummy ache,' James was complaining. 'I can't go to lessons today, Ma.'

'Go on with you,' Eileen said, 'and why have you room for porridge then?'

'It's moved to me brain,' James told her, his mouth obviously full as he spoke.

'You can't have a tummy ache in your brain,' Thomas said, 'that's called a headache, like the ones you're always givin' me.'

Liam chuckled as Rory came out to join him, shaking his head.

'I'm sick too, Ma. My tummy aches in me nose,' Matthew said.

'How's a stomach sitting there, right on your face?' Thomas said. 'Are you gonna sniff your breakfast down then?'

A sniffly, gurgly noise sounded, followed by the clatter of a bowl and spoon and much giggling.

'Jesus, Mary and Joseph!' Eileen exclaimed. 'By the living saints, you three try my patience. Thomas Murphy, go and fetch a rag, and you younger two, go fetch your satchels.'

'But me tummy ache...' James protested.

'I'll give you an ache you won't forget in a minute! Go on – get!'

Banging and muttering followed and Rory sipped his tea in silence, trying not to laugh and get in trouble with Eileen, Liam knew. Minutes later the trio ran out of the house, Matthew sporting a milk stain down the front of his shirt, and they yelled their goodbyes as they went down the dirt drive, satchels bouncing as they ran the mile or so to the small school.

'That Thomas will be the death of me yet,' Eileen declared as she joined the men, with a well-earned cup of tea herself now that the children were out of the house.

'I don't know how Mrs Backside copes with him,' Rory said, watching the three heads bobbing down the lane.

'It's Blackslide, not Backside. I can't believe you're calling the poor woman that too,' Eileen said with exasperation as Liam and Rory both lost their battle in trying not to laugh.

'Seven going on seventeen, that boy I'm afraid, me love,' Rory said, still chuckling as he put his arm around her, 'and as full of mischief as a boxful of leprechauns.'

'Aye, and I wonder where he gets it from,' Eileen said, shoving him a little but smiling now.

'Don't blame me, blame that prodigal brother of yours,' he said, holding up his hands in innocence.

'Should have been here weeks ago,' Eileen said, holding on to her swollen belly as she sat down heavily in her rocking chair to sip her tea. It was her favourite spot, and Liam was glad Rory had insisted on bringing the chair all the way from Ireland then out across the mountains to Orange. Eileen said it warmed her heart to have the comforts of home make the journey too, and there were a few precious, familiar items about the place, most of which had been handed down over generations: the big iron teapot, the statue of Mary in pride of place on the mantle. Eileen often put flowers in front of it as their mother had always done, like a shrine.

There were plenty of wildflowers on the hundred-acre property but Eileen had taken to watching the view rather than walk among it these past few weeks. The porch was where she spent most of her days now, to sit and take in the green and gold fields beyond those strange twisting trees and look south towards the craggy purple mountain that dominated the landscape, Mt Canobolas. But it was the northern view Liam saw her contemplating most, the rise on the hill where Kieran would eventually appear. Just as she was now.

'He'll come, Eiles, and he'll fall in love with the place just as we have,' Liam reassured her. 'Kieran's always needed time to… you know, get over things.'

'Ha! Get over things, is it? Wallow in ale, more like.'

'Probably,' Liam said with a shrug.

'Well, I'm glad you're alright with doing all the hard work setting up our family farm while your brother runs amok in Sydney doing goodness knows what.'

'If that's what he needs right now…'

'What he needs! Since when does copious amounts of drink mend anything? Not to mention the fact that he still isn't fully recovered – what if he gets into a pub brawl or beaten up by one of those convicts in those hellish Rocks?'

'He can hold his own, Eiles.'

'Bah! You're too soft on him, Liam; you both are,' she added, levelling a stare at Rory. 'He doesn't deserve such…such indulgence.'

'Indulgence, is it?' Liam said.

'You're not the only one with a vocabulary, Liam Clancy.'

Liam said nothing, letting Rory take over.

'You can bluster and bristle all you want, love, but it'll no' bring him home any faster.'

Eileen went to say more but then Rory bent over to kiss the top of her head and it silenced her.

They finished their tea without further conversation, each lost in their own thoughts as the sun broke free above the treetops to shine brilliantly across their land. Liam had meant it when he'd said Kieran would grow to love it here. There were no words to explain the incredible sense of belonging he felt, knowing every tree, every blade of grass and patch of brown earth lay on Clancy land, Clancy owned.

Everything they worked for was for family, not an English landlord; every tree they stumped, every fence they built, every cow they milked was part of their collective progress. A legacy to build together, and, with their payments to the Crown nearly done with, something to hand down to the next generation and the next. Liam knew Kieran would feel the same about the place, when he finally showed up, but until he did they would all remain restless. Without Kieran here none of them could feel truly settled, nor truly home.

No, Eileen wasn't alone in her worrying, although Liam didn't begrudge their brother the opportunity to 'run amok', as she put it. He couldn't blame Kieran for that, perhaps he'd do the same under similar circumstances, but he also couldn't stem the fear that pooled in his guts whenever he thought of Kieran in danger. Nor could he ever block out the moment when he'd found him, half-dead, unable to outrun the consequences of his actions back in Ireland.

It was that still-fresh, terrible memory that drove them all to gaze at that spot on the track each day, praying for Kieran to appear. Perhaps it would be today, perhaps tomorrow. Perhaps the day after that. All Liam knew was that longed-for day would arrive; God wouldn't have spared his brother's life for no reason. Surely his miracle survival was a sign that Kieran was destined for great things, that his life had purpose. For some reason Liam's mother came to mind then and he found himself humming her favourite blessing as he watched and he waited for his brother to come home.

May the road rise to meet you,
may the wind be ever at your back.
May the sun shine warm upon your face,
and the rains fall soft upon your fields.
And until we meet again,
may God hold you in the palm of his hand.

Twenty

The wagon clattered down the western side of the Blue Mountains, past thick woodlands of mountain ash and occasional pockets of rainforest, and Kieran breathed deeply of the aromatic air. It was said the eucalyptus oil from the trees gave the area its unique perfume, the haze of which coloured the atmosphere and turned the mountains 'blue'.

They certainly were that, a striking hue that rendered them quite beautiful in Kieran's opinion, and he was thoroughly enjoying the journey across the newly, and remarkably, built road that traversed the Great Dividing Range. The locals had told them tall tales of its construction last night, how men had lost their lives attempting to cut through this rugged country, and he could well believe it. The craggy mountain range stood like a wall between the coast and the fertile western plains beyond but finally, after several decades trying, access had been achieved ten years ago. Thriving communities had risen quickly, lured by the mining, timber and trade in the area and the opportunity to provide accommodation and refreshments to pioneer settlers, such as himself, as they made their trek across.

They came in droves to the vast west, not just for rich farmland but for an even greater opportunity to make their fortune now: gold. The hunt for burnished riches was spreading like fever, sweeping across Sydney these past few weeks and reputedly far beyond her shores. Thousands were making the pilgrimage to Bathurst and Orange to find out if the rumours of fist-sized nuggets were true, and Kieran had been surprised at how busy the roads and towns were.

Crisply cool, the alpine belt had an aura of excitement about it as people stopped for supplies and shared theories on how best to extract the precious stuff from the earth. Blackheath, in particular, was a bustling haven of industry and growth, bursting at the seams with wagons and people carrying all manner of mining and building materials.

It all felt incongruous somehow to Kieran, to see such strangely modern undertakings among a prehistoric landscape. One local had told him that scientists now theorised the whole area was once a volcano, and the deep ravines were really an ancient crater. Millions of years of weathering had further sunken valley floors and Kieran observed that these mountains felt somehow in reverse, with sheer sandstone cliffs crumbling deep into the rainforest pockets below.

It would have been an ideal place to pause for contemplation; to perhaps revel in the memory of a beautiful, river-soaked girl and even turn this wagon south, if only he hadn't allowed the suddenly gold-obsessed Dave to come along at the last minute. Instead he'd been incessantly badgered by his mate to join him on the goldfields a good part of the way, although Dave's campaign had been generously interspersed with almost every limerick, sea shanty and dirty joke known to mankind. Kieran's plans to have a quiet overnight camp had predictably been hijacked and he'd spent a rowdy night in a pub called The Scotch Thistle Inn with Dave instead.

His head was still thumping from yet another hangover but he had to admit it'd been worth it to watch Dave get up and sing with the band, prancing about in his green waistcoat. There was no way to censor him, of course, and the publican had been laughing so hard he didn't even attempt to stop it, not even when Dave sang his own version of 'Randy Dandy O'.

Kieran was able to enjoy a little peace and quiet now though, with Dave fast asleep in the back, and he didn't attempt to wake him as the first sight of the western plains came into view. Dave wasn't much of a one for appreciating nature anyway, unless it came in a dress. The tablelands stretched out before them in glorious invitation beneath a vast blue sky, extending as far as the eye could see. It reminded him of the vista from the shed back home in some ways, although the sunlight here seemed different, like someone had turned up a giant lantern. The green was paler and some of the areas were covered in a soft yellow hue, which Dave actually might have been interested to see, undoubtedly considering golden fields a good sign.

He could see the small town of Lithgow below, then open country beyond, leading to land unexplored and unnamed by Europeans. Beyond it they'd find Bathurst and eventually the fast-growing town of Orange. *My new home*, Kieran reflected, *well, for now, anyway*, his heart added as Eve's face flashed by once more. But then the enormity of this moment soaked through, and he gave in to the dream he'd been holding onto all those months back in Ireland. *Clancy land. Clancy owned.*

The west looked wild and untamed from up here, an expansive frontier filled with possibilities, and that wondrous feeling consumed him once more, the one that had been building these past few months. It washed through him with force as he took it all in; a heady mix of excitement, wonder, gratitude and anticipation. Kieran felt an overwhelming need to express it and found himself whistling the last song he'd heard.

The sound awoke Dave and he climbed over to sit beside him with a grin.

'You know you just can't *whistle* a sea shanty, Kier.'

Kieran grinned back and soon both men were singing at the top of their lungs.

Soon we'll be warping her out through the locks,
Way, ay, roll an' go!
Where the pretty young gals all pull up their frocks,
To be rollickin' randy dandy O!

'Just two more for the road,' Dave said, holding up his fingers to the barman. 'You said yourself it's only a few miles away.'

'We've been travelling all bloody day and I just want to get there,' Kieran said, running his hands through his hair and putting his cap back on, although he had to admit the beer tasted pretty damn good after all the dust along the road for hundreds of miles.

'Go on,' Dave coaxed and Kieran relented.

'May as well make some friends while we're here, I suppose,' Kieran muttered, looking around at the building crowd. This was a country pub and it looked to have stricter rules than the ones he was used to back in The Rocks. For one thing, it was men only, although there was a women's parlour next door. Kieran wondered how Eileen felt about the segregation after being able to go to the public bar with men and women alike back home, then he wondered if she even went out these days with the baby nearly due. The thought made him want to leave sooner but Dave was handing him another ale and he supposed it wouldn't really hurt to stay for one more, especially as Dave was now working on that 'making friends' idea.

'Well, we heard there was gold in Orange and looks like we found it!' he was saying to a group of locals who laughed as he held up his ale in the late sunlight. 'Although I don't understand what you were thinking naming the place after the wrong colour!'

'We don't even grow oranges, this here's apple country,' one man told him and Dave seemed to think that a grand joke.

'Where are you lads headed then?' asked another.

'Kieran here's off for home but I'm going over to Ophir to find me fortune.'

'Let me know if you find mine. I've been diggin' for weeks with barely anything to show for it.'

His friend rolled his eyes. 'I keep telling you, mate, we need to go to Victoria! They're picking nuggets up off the ground in Ballarat.'

'Where's that then?' Dave asked, interested.

'Near Melbourne,' the man replied. Kieran was interested then too.

The conversation flowed fast from there on, along with the ale, and by the time the sun was approaching the horizon Kieran already felt at home in his new town.

'You must be keen to get to your farm, lad,' said the apple farmer, whom the others had introduced as 'Seedy' George. He was actually a pretty nice fellow, just a little apple obsessed, which made a change from most of the others who shared in Dave's gold fever.

'Aye, and I should have been standing on it by now, only this thirsty bastard's trying to corrupt me with liquid temptation,' Kieran said, taking an ale from Dave's hands as he passed yet another round along.

'You could always say no,' suggested Al, who they'd been told was Seedy's nephew.

'True, true, he could do that, young Al, but for an Irishman saying no to a drink is like saying no to a woman,' Dave announced to the group at large. 'Your brain gives off a warning but your body tends to disagree.'

'But surely your brain fills you with regret the next day,' Al said. 'Don't you ever learn your lesson?'

'Aye, well I *would* but you see the fecken thing can't remember what it should be regretting,' Dave said, tapping his forehead, and the surrounding group roared in appreciation.

The late afternoon fell to dusk among other such merriment and someone began to play the fiddle, which had Dave hopping about singing in no time.

I am a true-born Irish man
I'll never deny what I am
I was born in old Tipperary town
Three thousand miles away

'We really had better go,' Kieran called out to him but he was shouted down by the crowd.

'Nuh, let him finish!' Seedy protested and Kieran couldn't help but enjoy the rest.

Hooray my boys, hooray
No more do I wish for to roam
The sun it will shine in the harvest time
To welcome Paddy home

The kookaburras were making a loud racket in the gums and Eileen listened and watched, still fascinated by their late afternoon ritual after all these months. Such strange-looking birds they were, almost ugly compared to the brilliantly coloured parrots that often landed upon the rail. The 'kookies' were her favourite, however, with their raucous laughter and strangely loyal ways towards each other; they were families, not flocks, and Eileen could relate to that.

She'd become rather superstitious of their behaviour, often looking for signals from them as she sat and watched from her chair, her eyes drawn over and again to that place on the road whenever they would break into song or land on the welcome sign at the gate. She'd been quite hopeful this morning when one had tapped at her window and looked quizzically inside, and she'd wondered if this was the day Kieran would finally come. More likely the bird was looking for crumbs from the bread tin that she sometimes threw when no-one was looking. Rory, in particular, would tease her for spoiling wild birds in such a manner.

She'd felt particularly hot today, although Liam had said the frost had been thick on the grass, but perhaps it was just the baby making her warmer than usual. It was certainly making her more uncomfortable. Eileen stood to lift the hair off her neck and stretch her back, kneading at the soreness on her hip that oft played up this late into her pregnancies. It made it harder to sleep. Harder to do most things, in fact.

'Thomas! James! Matthew!' she called, shielding her eyes from the lengthening rays as she searched for them. They didn't answer but she could see them playing on the wood pile that she'd told them several times to stay clear of since Liam had told her about the giant brown snake he'd seen nearby.

She sent up a prayer to St Patrick as she watched the children, wishing he were still alive to drive the serpents out of here as he'd purportedly done in Ireland.

'Come on home now!' she called but they still ignored her, despite being well within earshot. 'Of all the living saints,' she grumbled, making her way carefully down the stairs and across towards them. The pain in her hip was worsening and she muttered something less religious and more unladylike under her breath.

Thomas was climbing to the top of the pile, a stick in hand as he declared war on his brothers. '...an' if you don't do as I say I'll have ye walk the plank!'

'I wanna walk the plank!' James yelled.

'Me too!' Matthew joined in and the younger two giggled as Thomas clambered down and raced towards them.

'I'll have ye for that, ye scurvy blighters!'

Eileen paused, out of breath and blinking back pain now, as the boys ran about and she could scarcely get the words out to call. 'Boys! Come up home for your tea.'

'Aw, but Ma, we have t'kill the sea beast first!' James complained.

'There's no...no beasts about except the ones I'm looking at. Now come up for tea and no more of your nonsense.'

'Are you alright there, Ma?' Thomas said, pausing.

Eileen grimaced, trying to hide the hurt from him. 'Aye...I just...'

'Look!' Matthew interrupted, pointing. 'It is a beastie.'

'It's a serpent!' James exclaimed, staring transfixed as a brown snake moved from the pile right where Thomas had been standing only moments before.

'Oh dear lord...*run!*' Eileen screamed and the boys took off, startled by her panic, and she tried her best to follow. Unlike most local snakes this breed was notoriously aggressive and her hip seared in agonised protest as she lumbered after her children, too terrified to do otherwise. It seemed miles instead of yards to the porch and then the door, and Thomas closed it behind her quickly as she collapsed against the table, recognising other pains now.

'Ma...?'

'Get your da,' she grated out, leaning heavily on other furniture as she dragged her body towards the bed. James ran out with Thomas to the south paddock where Rory and Liam were working but Matthew stood transfixed, his little face afraid as Eileen blinked to focus on it.

'Get my vials from the medicine chest, me love, then go…go and do your letters for y'teacher.'

'But Miss Backside's away, Ma.'

'Black…slide,' she corrected, vaguely registering the irony of the words as her world turned dark.

There was no moon tonight, the stars providing the only light as the horse thundered down the track towards town and Liam prayed to God he wouldn't fall off and break his neck, focusing hard on the approaching town lights. Something was wrong; he didn't need to note the empty apothecary bottles and the desperation on Rory's face to know that much. The pouring sweat on his sister's pale countenance and her cries of pain told him all he needed to know: his sister had a fever and the baby was coming. Fast.

The main pub was in the full throes of a party that rang down the street but Liam galloped past towards the doctor's house nearby, unheeding as someone called out his name until he realised he recognised the tone. One he knew all too well.

'Kieran?' he called back, slowing his mount to turn around and stare at the sight of his brother stumbling out of the pub and swaying in the middle of the street in disbelief.

'When did…?' He jumped down as Kieran ran towards him and they embraced, Kieran all smiles until he looked Liam in the face.

'What is it?' Kieran asked immediately. 'Eileen?'

'Aye, she's having the baby but she's...I'm not sure but something's wrong. She has a fever.'

'A...a fever?'

'I'm here to fetch the doctor. Come on.'

Kieran followed Liam as they ran over to the doctor's house, a man by the name of Sherman who Liam had met a few times now. Liam knocked hard on the door and he was knocking again by the time an older woman answered, the doctor's wife.

'Sorry to trouble you, ma'am, but we need Dr Sherman to come,' Liam began. 'Our sister...'

'He's not here,' she interrupted him. 'I'm afraid he's gone to Ophir. A bunch of miners have come down with scarlet fever, bless them,' she added, making the sign of the cross.

'Shite,' Kieran muttered before apologising. 'Sorry, ma'am.'

'What of Mrs Jenkins or Mrs Kershaw?' Liam asked.

'Over at Ophir too, I'm afraid. One poor woman's been in labour for two days with twins, so I've heard.'

Liam bit his lip from swearing again. They were the town's only two midwives. 'Is there any other doctor around tonight?'

'Only Dr Sloane,' she replied, looking doubtful, as well she might. The man was a notoriously snobbish Yorkshireman and was known for regarding the Irish in town as beneath him, rarely treating them. Liam had never met him, but he knew when he did he'd need every ounce of intelligence and charm he'd ever possessed to come to the fore.

'Thank you, ma'am,' Liam said and she closed the door. 'Shite, shite, shite,' he muttered, unleashing his own frustration now.

'What's the problem?' Kieran said, stumbling slightly. 'If he's a doctor let's just go and get him.'

Liam looked at his inebriated brother, knowing he wouldn't like what he was about to hear. 'You can't come with me for this, Kier. Make your way home and I'll meet you there.'

'What d'you mean I can't come with you?'

'Just that. You'll have to trust me on this one.'

Kieran stared at him, frowning. 'I'll shut my mouth if that's what you're worried about.'

The pub party echoed in the night and Liam paused, considering. 'You're going to have to promise me on that. The man's gentry, or some such guff, and he hates the likes of us.'

'I'll no' say a word. I promise.'

Liam sighed, wondering if that was possible, but there was no time to argue and he strode down to the end of the street with Kieran towards Dr Sloane's newly constructed fine house, considering what he'd say carefully. Kieran knocked this time and Liam took a deep breath, Eileen's pale face paramount in his mind.

Conversation could be heard and the tinkling of glasses as the door opened.

'...and leave room for the brandy, Niles. Yes, what is it?'

Dr Sloane had answered the door himself, dressed in an evening suit and seemingly unimpressed at the interruption. Liam looked at the face of the man who could potentially mean the difference between his sister and her baby's lives, wondering if that would be enough for him to leave what was, obviously, his own dinner party.

'We're sorry to trouble you, sir,' Liam said, trying to force out the brogue from his accent, 'but it's our sister. She's having her baby but...'

'First time?' he all but barked.

'No, sir, her fourth.'

'Oh, for goodness sake.'

A woman entered the hall, elegantly attired and holding a champagne glass. 'What's going on, Charles? Are you being called out?'

'No, no. Serve dessert, Elizabeth, and I'll be along shortly.' She left and he turned back to Liam, impatience etched on his features now. 'I'm sure your sister will be fine.'

'But…but you see she's got a fever…' Liam tried again.

The doctor sighed, looking over them both before speaking again. 'It's no use fearing the worst. She's probably just heated from the exertion, which is quite common, I assure you.'

'No, sir, but…'

'Women have babies every day and if she's brought three others into the world there's hardly anything here to worry about.'

'Yes, however this time she…'

'…will be perfectly fine as well.'

He looked to be closing the door on them and Liam tried again. '*Please*, doctor…'

The pleading in his tone seemed to annoy the man then, or perhaps it was just the brogue, after all. 'I'm sure your sister will do well enough with whatever midwives you have in your clan.' He said the last with a trace of contempt and Liam felt his own eyes narrow as Kieran stepped forward, breaking his silence.

'What do y'mean by…'

'We've no-one with us to help her, doctor,' Liam interrupted him. 'Mrs Jenkins and Mrs Kershaw are both over at Ophir and we would very much appreciate your professional help and expertise. I'm told you're a very experienced and learned physician; the best in town.'

'I'm the *only* doctor in town tonight, as you're obviously aware, but otherwise engaged, I'm afraid. Go home and make sure your sister has plenty of fluids to keep her strength up. And for goodness sake don't just stand about saying your Hail Marys – get her to push when the time's right.'

'How will we know when that is?'

'If it's her fourth baby, she'll know well enough.' He began to really shut the door then and Liam looked at Kieran, at a loss what else to do, which prompted his brother to put his foot in the way of it closing.

'What the devil do you think you're doing?' the doctor demanded.

'Just making sure you have all the facts,' Kieran said forcefully, but his stance was a little unsteady.

'Wetting the baby's head already, are you? Typical,' the doctor said with disgust. 'Get your blasted foot out of my door and go home to sleep it off, Paddy.'

'Not quite yet, I don't think. My sister is sick and she…req… requires your help. You'd best get your things and come with us, if you don't mind me insisting.'

'I'll do no such thing,' the doctor said, kicking Kieran's foot and slamming the door.

Kieran pounded hard, enraged. 'Open up and come with us now!'

'Get off my property before I fetch the police,' the doctor stormed from the other side.

'Leave it,' Liam implored, looking nervously about. Altercations with the law would only delay them further and he needed to get home urgently now, since Eileen would just have to rely on what he'd read to help her. And what she'd taught him herself over the years.

'You can't just refuse to help us!' Kieran yelled, kicking the door.

'Kieran, come away…' Liam said, grabbing his arm to pull him back, but Kieran shrugged him off.

'Open it before I break it down, y'fecken' bastard,' Kieran yelled.

Horrified gasps and murmuring could be heard within. 'Elizabeth, send Gerald for the constable.'

'Come on, Kieran…' Liam begged but his brother was lost in a rage.

'If she dies the blood will be on your hands,' he shouted.

'There's too much Irish blood pouring into this damn town as it is!' came the answer, prompting Kieran to pick up a rock and hurl it through the man's window, shattering the pane. A policeman's rattle sounded and Kieran reluctantly moved away, both brothers mounting the horse and taking off down the street. And, as they passed the crowded pub, an Irishman's voice rang out to cheers of appreciation and applause.

The sun it will shine in the harvest time
To welcome Paddy home

Twenty-One

'Not long now, not long, my Eiles.'

Rory was holding her hand but he seemed far away, his voice becoming muffled in her ears, and she was trying to focus on him but the lamplight hurt her eyes. Eileen squeezed them shut, wishing the black would return but searing pains were keeping her wretchedly conscious and she was so hot she couldn't seem to stop her exhausted body from thrashing about.

'Liam,' she managed to say. Her brother would come and bring help. He was always a smart boy, and kind too.

'On his way,' Rory told her, patting her face dry with a towel.

Eileen stared out the window, towards the place on the rise where her brother would come. And her other brother, eventually. One day soon. A kookaburra had tapped on the window only this morning and she'd foolishly believed it might be today. Then all thought was obliterated by agony and she clenched uselessly against it.

'Argh,' she grunted, and Rory returned to hold her hand tight.

'Not long now. Not long, my Eiles.'

But the struggle was hard. Fighting for family always was.

'Thank god,' Rory said, clasping Liam's hand then staring in shock past his shoulder. 'Kieran? Oh lord, of all the days...' Rory hugged him tight then pulled away to wipe tears from his eyes. Kieran wiped at a few as well.

'I'm afraid I'm a poor substitute for who you really need.'

Rory looked to Liam then at the door. 'Where's the doctor?'

'At Ophir treating scarlet fever, apparently.'

'Did you try Dr Sloane?'

'Aye.' Liam didn't elaborate and Kieran figured that was probably best for now. Repercussions would arrive soon enough and Rory looked shaken enough as it was.

'How is she?'

Rory shrugged, looking more worried than Kieran had ever seen him, and a terrible knot began to twist in his stomach, churning with the alcohol from before. They walked to the bedroom and Kieran's guts fell further as Eileen came into view. She was a pitiful version of the sister he loved, with her face drained of colour and her hair lying in damp, dark strands against the pillow. Liam bent over to place a hand on Eileen's forehead.

'How are you feeling, Eiles? Are the pains coming closer?'

'Aye...they...argh...they are.' Her expression was so tortured it hurt to watch but Kieran knew she needed his strength tonight. That realisation and the sight of Eileen's now-empty tonic vials on the bedside table sobered him fast. The healer of the family would need everything they could give her now that her own concoctions couldn't help and her health was in peril.

'I've a present for you,' Liam told her, moving aside, and Kieran stepped forward to take her hand.

'Hello, my Eiles.'

Her eyes fluttered at first but then recognition lit their depths and she began to cry, squeezing his hand tight.

'Kieran...you came home. You came.'

'Aye, love. I'm here. Everything's going to be just fine.'

She smiled briefly and he took a cloth to wipe her tears. 'The kookie was right.'

Kieran frowned. 'What the hell is a kookie?' But then another wave of pain distorted her face and he held on with her.

'How far along, Rory?' Liam asked, moving closer.

'I don't know,' he said, shaking his head. The midwives had always taken care of the women giving birth back in Killaloe. None of them had ever seen someone going through this before.

'Eiles? Eiles, stay with us now,' Kieran urged as his sister turned paler, looking set to faint.

'Has she passed out at all?' Liam asked, obviously thinking the same.

'Aye, several times,' Rory confirmed. 'What does it mean?'

'It means she's weak from the fever. We have to get it down so she's strong enough to push,' Liam said, walking over to wash his hands in a bowl and dry them. 'Kieran, fetch more towels and put the kettle on.'

Kieran jumped to do so, glad to be able to do something to help and more grateful for his brother's clever brain than he'd ever been in his life.

'Is there anyone else we can fetch to help?' Rory asked, sounding desperate.

Liam's tone was gentle as Kieran listened from the kitchen. 'There's no time for that now, but, look, she's done this before and she can do it again; we've just got to make sure everything is clean, or so I remember the women always saying back home. Fetch me some fresh sheets and a new pillow, alright?'

'Aye,' Rory said and Kieran heard some relief in his voice too now, feeling some of what he'd been carrying alone these past few hours.

By the time they'd completed the tasks assigned, Liam had positioned himself to see how far along Eileen was, which was extremely brave, in Kieran's opinion. Nursing your sister through childbirth was no small undertaking but Liam faced it calmly, talking in reassuring tones as he went.

'I can see the head, Eiles. It won't be long, just a few big pushes now.'

Kieran wondered what he was basing that prediction on then he recalled that Liam had helped quite a few of the Moileds give birth back in Ireland. He sincerely hoped his brother's knowledge on the subject extended further than cows.

'How's her temperature, Rory?' Liam asked, looking up at Eileen's face.

'I'd say it's come down some,' Rory reported after feeling both her arms.

'Good. Time for a big push now, Eiles, that's the girl.'

'I...can't...' she moaned, thrashing her head from side to side.

'You have to do it, Eiles. Push for me now.'

'Come on, me love. For our baby's sake,' Rory said, kissing her hands.

Eileen focused on his face and Kieran watched as she somehow found enough strength to push although it didn't last long. Liam coaxed her for the next few minutes before a darker fear passed over his countenance, almost imperceptible to most but Kieran saw it straight away.

'What is it?' Rory asked and Kieran held his breath.

'I can't be sure but the baby isn't progressing, which could mean several things but I think...well, I'm guessing it has the cord wrapped around its neck,' Liam told them and Rory slumped to a chair.

'Can you...can she...'

'I'm going to have to help her deliver it.'

Rory nodded, ashen now. 'Alright.'

Kieran watched his brother wash his hands once more, preparing himself, and a swell of rage returned towards Dr Sloane who should be here. Saving Irish blood.

Rory and Kieran each took one of Eileen's hands and Liam prepared her.

'I know you're exhausted, I know you think you can't do this, but you can and you will. Just one more push, Eiles. On the count of three, alright? One, two…'

Eileen's face contorted and her arms shook from the exertion but somehow she pushed and Liam pulled and in an agony of pitiful screaming she delivered at last. Liam held the baby gently but his eyes were filled with tears as he brought her to her mother.

'I'm so sorry, Eiles. I…couldn't…' His voice broke then as the baby was lowered into Eileen's arms and she looked over its tiny, perfect form, heartbreak in her eyes.

'It was a girl,' she said before dissolving into devastated sobs, holding the little child tight against her chest.

'Aye, my love,' Rory said, breaking down and kneeling alongside to wrap his arms around them both.

Liam stayed to help while needed but Kieran left the parents to mourn their baby's loss in private, with heavy steps and a heavy heart. He walked outside, gripping the rail and weeping too. The sun was crowning on the horizon as the dawn arrived and a strange-looking bird sat on the branch of a tree, watching him. It let out a chorus of sounds unlike any he'd ever heard, almost like a laugh, as the beauty of the sunrise mocked the tragedy of the day.

Kieran watched the scene with the realisation that he was looking at his very own land for the first time in his life. The place he had longed for, worked for, dreamed of and now found. Clancy land. Clancy owned. But blood had been spilt now and the oppression they thought they'd left behind in Ireland had managed to find them here, after all.

They still weren't really free.

Hatred welled within, and even though he knew logically Dr Sloane may not have been able to have saved Eileen's baby, he blamed the Englishman just the same.

The man had taken something from them all today, even if he couldn't quite be held accountable for the death, for he'd stolen the joy from the land they'd call home. A place that would forever be marked by the grave of a tiny life whose blood was considered 'only Irish', even here, in their own far-flung corner of the world.

The sound of an approaching wagon disturbed his thoughts and, as he looked over to see Dave arriving, he knew immediately he would be leaving this longed-for place the same day he'd arrived. There was no cheerful whistle or wave, which meant word had got around and the law would soon be on their way, looking for an Irishman who'd dared to cast a stone.

Liam came out to stand beside him, his eyes bloodshot and red-rimmed, and Kieran put his arm around his brother's shoulders, knowing no words would ever suffice to bring comfort to this day but trying anyway.

'You did everything you could.'

Liam nodded, fresh tears forming but he wiped them away. 'Friend of yours?' he said, changing the subject and nodding over at Dave who was taking out his pipe from his green waistcoat.

'Aye.'

There was a pause as the inevitable sat between them. 'Where will you go?'

Kieran shrugged. 'Somewhere far away, just for a while until things calm down, although I hate to leave you to carry this.'

Liam sighed. 'Aye, but you're no use to us in gaol, Kier. Go. We'll manage until you come home.'

The word hung in the morning air and Kieran looked out across the farm, committing it to mind before he left. 'I'll write when I get there, wherever that may be.'

'I get the feeling you know where that is already.'

'What makes you say that?' Kieran said, although he knew Liam was right.

'Just something in your expression I've seen before,' Liam said with a shrug. 'You always follow your heart.'

Eureka

Twenty-Two

Sovereign Hill, Ballarat, Victoria, February 1854

There was a stiff breeze and flags fluttered outside the rows of tents; Union Jacks, Irish tricolours, Scottish thistles, French Tricolores and even Texas Stars vied for prominence. Kieran ducked his head beneath their own flag above their tent flap, the green corner whipping his cheek as he stooped through and threw his bag down on the table. It was strewn with the usual paraphernalia he and Dave had amassed: tobacco, eating utensils, paper bags filled with flour and salt, a hammer, the local gazette and a few empty beer bottles they had yet to return to the pub.

'Any luck?' Dave asked.

Usually they worked their claim together but today Kieran had spent a bit of time panning further up the creek with some newcomers, teaching them the ropes, just to make a change.

'Not really, enough for supper I suppose,' he told him, patting his pocket where the gold of the day lay in its leather pouch. 'Yourself?'

'Enough for me grog,' Dave told him with a grin and a shrug. His teeth were almost obscured by the long beard he'd grown since they'd arrived and he would look every bit the rough goldminer if not for that amiable expression he usually wore poking through. Most miners, or 'diggers' as they termed themselves, weren't quite so cheerful. Tensions were high since the government brought in the unpopular thirty-shilling gold licence law, and pushing through the daily grind of hard labour for even smaller rewards left many disgruntled. Not to mention the lack of fresh food and water and the corrupt police force. Hungry, thirsty, poor and bullied made a strong recipe for unrest and Dave and Kieran had been lucky not to have been drawn into the many scuffles that took place.

Kieran scratched at his own beard, deciding to shave it off before they headed to Melbourne in the morning for a much-needed break.

'Have you packed the wagon?'

'Aye, not that we're taking much,' Dave told him, brushing off his boots. Most of the furniture and supplies they'd brought from Sydney to Orange had been left at the Clancy farm and they lived simply down here, their needs few.

'Just the important stuff, I see,' Kieran said, nodding over at a barrel of rum Dave had placed in the corner, 'or is that staying here with Jock?' Dave's old mate Jock McCock was down in the goldfields seeking his fortune too and would mind their claim while they travelled.

'He hasn't the self-control to care for this girl properly,' Dave said, picking it up and hugging it tight. 'You have to court her properly, show her a little respect.'

'She might roll about and break her pretty waist,' Kieran said, tapping the iron ring around the barrel's middle.

'No fear o' that. She'll sit up front with me in style, won't you, me love?'

Dave went as far as to kiss it and Kieran chuckled. He hadn't felt much like laughing these past months but this latest trip was buoying him up, especially as they would traverse through quite a few new towns. That meant he could continue his search for the gold he sought most in Victoria. A white kind of gold, framing a face so beautiful it was imprinted on his brain, keeping him company through the long, lonely nights in this muddy, male-dominated hellhole.

'Have you weighed up?' he asked Dave.

'Aye, and I've eaten besides. A full pouch and a full stomach, my friend,' Dave said, patting his belly. Dave was one of the few men here who never seemed to tire of the daily fare of damper and mutton. Personally, after over a year of the stuff Kieran would be happy never to taste either again.

'I think I might do mine first thing before we go,' Kieran said, looking down the road towards the bank shed where a bunch of miners stood in line to have their gold weighed and exchanged for coin. It wasn't that important anyway. There was enough money still left from their dealings at the docks to finance them for a while yet and the amount of gold they mined at their claim was more than most. Enough time had passed for it to even be possible to go home by now, Kieran supposed, but somewhere along the line he'd caught the fever too. There was a sizeable vein to be found at their stake on the creek beds, he was sure of it, and besides, there was the matter of the other gold to consider, however illogical that pursuit may be.

'Pub then?' Dave suggested, hiding the rum barrel under the table. Liquor was expensive and illegal sales were rife, despite the strict punishments inflicted if hawkers were found out. The government seemed intent on inflicting sobriety on the miners on top of everything else. Dave had been careful this time though, ordering the barrel through the general store to avoid any trouble.

'Why not,' Kieran said. Tomorrow was a holiday, after all.

They made their way past the other tents where most of the miners were now cleaning up for Friday night and the scent of soap made a nice change from the usual stench of sweat in the air. Mining equipment was piled up near most dwellings, along with water barrels, timber, and stores. They lived simply on Sovereign Hill, their needs met well enough if the pan glinted in the sun, doing without if not. It was a life of hard work, base fare, dirt, grime and grog, and when he looked back on it one day Kieran knew he would consider this time spent on the goldfields the most masculine existence he ever knew.

Everything here seemed manly, from the beards to the brawls to the constant betting. They competed with each other over the smallest things, perhaps from boredom, perhaps from the frustration of waiting for the 'big find' or perhaps, quite simply, because they missed female company so they challenged one another instead. In some ways Kieran found it easier than being in society. Here at the diggings he could just be his essential self, raw and uncensored, comfortable in his own, dust-covered skin. But in other ways Kieran found it oppressive and he missed the comforts of a real home, the nurturing and love of a family. Or of a woman.

There wouldn't be any of the fairer sex around tonight, or if there were they'd be painted, cheaply perfumed yet expensive company, and far more likely to frequent the better hotels in town than the miners' pub he and Dave favoured. A few Aboriginal miners sat around outside, unable to go in, and Kieran and Dave nodded and said hello. The injustice of the fact that these men worked just as hard as the rest of them, and were likely just as thirsty, but were refused entry to the pubs just seemed to be accepted by most. But that, coupled with the fact that their land was being mined or sold off without consultation, let alone permission, weighed on Kieran's conscience.

He sighed then, entering the pub, knowing he was helpless to change the laws against them. Hell, he couldn't even change the law for miners' fees being set at thirty, unaffordable shillings.

The building was really little more than a large shed filled with benches and a long narrow bar and, as he and Dave walked in, the raucous chorus of men's voices filled it to the rafters. Pubs were the only real source of entertainment for the miners and this place, in particular, was notoriously rowdy, setting the scene for many bloody fistfights. In fact, Keiran couldn't remember a night here without one, but no serious injuries ever seemed to result. Just a black eye or two and a split lip, here and there.

Dave knew everyone in it by name or nickname, of course. 'Johnno! Pickle-eyes! How's the willy, Willy?'

Kieran followed him through, amused by his antics as usual, and they arrived at the bar amid a lot of ribbing and back-slapping to down beers and get on their merry way. It flowed easily and Dave was dancing about and singing sea shanties by the time Jock came running through the door, eyes wide as he relayed the news that troopers, or 'traps' as the miners called them down here, were on their way, looking for Dave.

'Why me?' Dave asked, pausing mid-reel in surprise.

'They say you took their rum...'

'Took her? I'll have you know I paid damn good coin. Ask Smiggins at the depot.'

Jock shook his head. 'Smiggins is lying 'bout it. Apparently the troopers had ordered it in and he wasn't supposed to sell it so he's letting you take the blame.'

'Bastard,' someone muttered in the crowd. Smiggins the shopkeeper was unpopular as it was, ripping off the miners whenever he could and charging exorbitant prices for any food he could manage to get in. This would cost him in more ways than one but there were the traps to be handled first.

'Two bob on Dave throwing a punch,' muttered Jock.

'Done,' said a few men nearby.

Then a clatter of hooves sounded as the law arrived and Kieran stood alongside Dave to wait, clenching and unclenching his stiff right hand. Others in the crowd stood alongside them too and it was a united bunch that faced the traps as they strode in.

'You Dave Tumulty?' asked the leader, Curtis, a burly man with red whiskers along his chin. He was puffing out his chest but his belly was the only thing straining his navy white-crossed uniform.

'Aye, as you well know, Curtis,' Dave said. 'I hear you're looking for me barrel.'

'Straight to the point, ain't ya?' Curtis said, spitting on the floor. 'Must be keen for a stop in the lock-up.'

'Keen for an *ale* actually,' Dave told him, grinning and holding his up, 'although that barrel of she-rum will provide me with a right nice nightcap later on. Might even take her to bed for a cuddle.' There were chuckles around the pub but Curtis was unimpressed. The man placed his hand on the bludgeon on his belt and cocked his head to the side.

'I'm gonna mark that comment down to you being Irish and therefore daft. Get me m'barrel, Paddy. Now.'

'Now what's a man like you want with a lovely curved lass like her? Besides, I paid Smiggins for her; a good amount of coin too. If you have a problem with that I suggest you take it up with him.'

'I did take it up with him and *he* says you never paid him, so it looks like theft to me.' The trap moved closer, taking out his bludgeon. 'Take me to it now or feel the brunt of this.'

Dave looked at the weapon held up to his face and seemed to weigh up his options. There were many miners who would fight but the traps were all armed, one with a gun, and Kieran knew Dave would back down rather than men getting hurt for his sake.

'Well, if you put it like that,' he said, leading them out. Kieran followed, disgruntled mutterings and the settling of wagers in their wake, and Dave took the traps to their tent, going in to get the barrel and handing it over.

'That's better, Paddy. Next time less cheek, eh?' Curtis said, stroking his bludgeon smugly.

Don't say anything, don't say anything, Kieran begged Dave silently, but of course his friend couldn't resist.

'Oh, there'll be no cheek, unless it involves me kicking you up the arse.'

Curtis glared then reacted violently, smashing Dave across the chin with his bludgeon. 'Good luck with trying that,' he said as Dave fell to his knees.

He walked off, laughing with his cronies, and Kieran helped Dave up, wishing he could go after the man and beat him senseless for such a cowardly act, but now was not the time. Vengeance would come though, if not by him by someone else. Sooner or later the miners were bound to strike back against the traps but it wouldn't be today.

Dave had a nasty welt on his chin and was spitting blood and Kieran cleaned him up as best he could before they both settled for the night, figuring an early departure would suit them fine. Kieran was keen to get away for a break from the place and keener still to go roaming and continue his search around Melbourne, but when they left before dawn Dave made a quick detour, leaving Kieran in the cart as he disappeared for a while. When he returned Kieran had to shake his head and chuckle but he didn't say a word. And the half-full she-barrel sat up front in style, all the way out of town.

Twenty-Three

Ballan, Victoria, February 1854

The wind was strong today but it was also hot, hotter than Eve had experienced, not that she minded when her delicious little secret awaited. She climbed down the embankment to look at it contentedly, knowing Amanda Cartwright, her new mistress, would be completely scandalised but uncaring. Amanda was only a decade older than herself but lived like a timid old lady, having been cosseted her whole life as a sickly, if wealthy, child. She would never even consider leaving the main road into town and clambering through the bush, let alone do what Eve was about to do next.

The river was customarily smooth and it reflected the cloudless blue sky and overhanging gums like a mirror but the wind was sporadically rippling it today and Eve watched the movement, mesmerised. It was so beautiful, her new home, although completely different to anywhere else she'd ever been. There were so many shades of green and gold she lost count when she tried to number them but there wasn't time to even attempt that today. She'd have to be fast if she was to return from her errands before lunch and she stripped off her dress and underthings quickly now, hanging them over a bush and pinning her hair high.

The water greeted her like a friend, soothing her in a refreshing, liquid hug and she gasped with pleasure as it cooled her and moved softly against her legs. There was something about this guilty pleasure that she couldn't seem to resist. Perhaps because it was a river that had first greeted her when she arrived in Australia, when the rash decision to dive into it had ultimately led to her freedom from chains. Or perhaps it was simply the sensation of water on skin itself, a delicious feeling in such a hot climate. Like a lover's caress.

A flash of Robert's face passed through her mind but she felt nothing for him now. Her heart had long emptied of the love she'd once felt and any memories of pleasure had been wiped away, as if the very act of recollection would further damn her soul. Eve cast the last thoughts from her mind, unwilling to consider past sins anymore. Her life was one of redemption these days and she took simpler joys from it now.

She focused on the natural surrounds instead, allowing herself to just float and enjoy this fleeting time to herself. A flock of large white birds were feasting on something high in the canopy and several kangaroos grazed nearby, although the big male was simply scratching his belly and looking about lazily, one ear flicking. Eve smiled at him, thinking what a handsome fellow he was. She was rather fond of these strange-looking animals; the babies, especially, were rather sweet. 'Joeys', Arthur had told her.

The Cartwrights' overseer Arthur Blockley was an interesting man, doing the work of several despite being hampered by a missing leg. He'd been Captain Cartwright's first mate in the navy for a few years before losing the limb in a skirmish with pirates, and the captain had given him the job of caring for the farm by way of compensation. Eve had taken a liking to him immediately;

in some ways he reminded her of her father with his wealth of knowledge and gentle nature although his broad northern accent was far from cultured. He was good to her, though, and looked after her and Amanda dutifully while the captain was away at sea.

As for her mistress, Eve conceded Amanda could be endearing at times despite being terribly spoilt, but altogether the trio made things work. In fact, in all Eve would say she had a fairly easy time of it, even when the captain came home who, as it turned out, was more bluster than bite, and he obviously loved his wife dearly, which was nice to be around.

Ultimately, Eve knew she was incredibly lucky to have been chosen to come here that day in Parramatta. She may well be just a servant and bound to the Crown, perhaps still for life, but there were patches of freedom in her days once more. Moments like now. Looking up at that clear blue sky unhindered by ship hatches or bars, she knew she'd never take that precious state for granted again. And she'd never stop thanking God for his mercy in sending Kieran Clancy to her aid that day. The good Samaritan with the lilting Irish brogue. The kindest man on earth.

And it's no, nay, never
No, nay, never, no more
And I'll play the wild rover
No never, no more

Kieran sighed, looking back at Dave who lay in the cart singing loudly, wondering if he'd fall asleep soon and eventually sober up. He didn't usually mind Dave's wild ways but after drinking with him every night for a week he was tired, especially as he'd risen early each day to go out searching for Eve Richards while Dave slept it off. 'Near Melbourne' hadn't seemed an impossible area to cover on horseback in his mission to find Captain Cartwright's home when they'd first arrived in Victoria but that was before the full rush. Now the lure of gold had the town bursting at the seams and its surrounding areas swelling by the thousands. He'd managed to scour most of the northern and western areas on three separate visits to Melbourne with Dave but he still hadn't found anyone who'd even heard of the captain, let alone any members of his household.

He felt depressed about the fact, although he knew he wouldn't give up. There were only so many square miles to search and sooner or later he'd find the whereabouts of one fair-haired maiden. Dave thought him mad, saying he was thinking with his heart and a few other areas of his anatomy at times, but Kieran didn't care. Perhaps it was madness to seek out a girl you'd met only once, and a convict at that, but Eve was part of his destiny now. He'd become obsessed with her over the long lonely months in the goldfields and this was far beyond any old game of chase, this was a full-blown quest and Eve was his grail. That he could feel such a thing for a woman once more was, ultimately, a relief but at other times, like today, it felt more like torture.

They were only about two hours from home and Kieran peered up at the sky, thinking he really should snap out of his melancholy before he actually did turn mad, when a kangaroo bounded across the road. A kangaroo wearing a dress. Kieran stopped the cart to blink his eyes a few times and look again, momentarily stunned.

'Why'd you stop the…well, would you look at that fecken thing,' Dave said, turning around to sit up and stare too.

It wasn't an average kangaroo, it was a massive male, and it wasn't wearing the dress exactly, the dress was wearing him, somehow managing to have snagged itself in the animal's paw and now billowing behind.

'How the hell would it find a dress out here?'

They were sitting in the middle of a stretch of road several miles out of town and there were no farms in sight. Kieran shrugged. 'I've no idea. Somebody must own it though.'

Dave looked at him and began to grin. 'Well, it seems to me the damsel in distress might be needing our assistance, Kier.'

'But why would she…'

Dave nodded over through the trees where the darker green spoke of river banks nearby and Kieran began to grin too. ''Tis a hot day.'

'Aye.'

Eve decided she didn't like kangaroos anymore, not one little bit. It may not have been the animal's fault her dress blew over towards him but it was certainly most unchivalrous of him to bat it with his paw, have it catch, then take off in alarm. Her underthings clung to her as she searched for the big grey, and the undergrowth flicked at her legs as she climbed back up towards the road, praying no-one would come along and see her thus exposed. Reaching the verge she peered out. The animal had stopped a few yards away and was trying to rid himself of her gown.

'Come here, you wretched thing,' she hissed, hesitant to approach him, firstly because he was a big animal with muscular shoulders, and secondly because it was a public road. But there was nothing else for it. She couldn't very well turn up at home like this and explaining what had transpired would have Amanda in a fit of vapours. Not to mention the fact that if the captain found out, it could possibly get her fired and sent back to board a ship bound for Tasmania.

Eve crept out cautiously, only to find her underthings had snagged on a bush and were beginning to rip.

'Of all the…stupid…' She twisted this way and that but now the strings were loosening and she held on with one hand, trying to keep the blasted things on and free herself with the other. Then to her mortification came the tread of boots.

'You seem to be in a spot of bother there, miss. I'd be honoured if you allowed me to assist you.'

Eve froze, her exposed flesh suddenly on high alert, her heart skipping painfully. Then she closed her eyes, wondering if there was any way in the world she could be mistaken but as she turned slowly around there he was. Kieran Clancy, the kindest man in the world. Coming to her rescue once more as she stood wet in her boots and bedraggled, his good Samaritan smile in place. Only this time there was something else in those eyes besides pity and Eve was painfully aware of her half-naked state as she stood before him thus, in broad daylight. Then she noticed a second man behind him, openly gawking, and his bearded grin was anything but gentle.

'The uh…kangaroo took my dress,' she managed to squeak out.

'Aye, lass. Dave, if you wouldn't mind…?'

The second man approached the animal cautiously while Kieran helped un-snag her underthings and Eve tried not to flinch as his fingers brushed bare skin. Fortunately he didn't take too long to release her and she had a strong suspicion he was quite used to the workings of a lady's undergarments. The thought was strangely annoying.

'Here you go,' the other man said, swaying slightly, and she suspected he might be drunk.

Eve took it, blushing. 'Thank you, Mr…?'

'Dave's the name, miss. Dave Tumulty, at your service.'

She put the dress on quickly, then dared to look at Kieran once more. 'I must thank you too, Mr Clancy. You seem to have rescued me again, as if from thin air.'

'Aye,' he said, his eyes never leaving her. 'I've a feeling our fates must be entwined for some reason.'

Eve blushed even deeper, not knowing how to respond to that.

'We've a cart just around the corner – can we give you a lift home?'

Eve wanted nothing more than to hide away somewhere to recover from her embarrassment but the whole episode had her running late now and Amanda and Arthur would be wondering where she was.

'If it isn't too much trouble that would be much appreciated.'

'Where do you live?' Kieran asked as they set off around the corner to his cart.

'About half a mile out of Ballan.'

Both men seemed to find that rather amusing, in fact Dave was openly chortling, and she frowned at them in puzzlement. 'Is there something funny about that?'

'Oh, there's something funny about it alright,' Dave said. 'It's a right, funny old world, isn't it, Kier?'

'Where do you live?' she asked, wondering if that had something to do with it.

'Ballarat,' Kieran told her, pausing at the cart to take her hand and help her up. 'Not two hours from you this entire time.' He wasn't laughing anymore and he held onto her hand a little too long as he said it. Eve felt something flutter inside, something she'd long thought dead, and she pushed it down.

'Imagine that,' she said, trying to sound lighthearted, but she suspected it sounded more like wonder. Kieran smiled a little too knowingly then climbed up next to her while Dave sat in the back, whistling loudly then breaking into song.

And I'll play the wild rover
No never, no more

She was here. She had been all along, less than two hours away while he searched for gold and dreamed his dream of finding her too. He felt as if he'd discovered the greatest nugget on earth; like all his fortunes had literally come at once and it was all he could do to not grab her and kiss her for joy. He'd said she'd owe him one if he found her, after all. But there was a wariness there, he'd courted too many lasses not to see it, and he would need to bide his time before he claimed this holy grail.

He settled for talking to her instead, mostly so he could watch that face and bask in her exquisite beauty. If he'd thought her so that long-ago day in Parramatta it was nothing compared to now. She'd gained weight on that thin frame now, not much but enough for her cheeks to be soft and full, and her chest had strained at the bodice of her undergarments and now her dress. It was like sitting next to a feast when you were starving and Kieran forced himself not to stare too much lest he do something rash. Like kiss her. There was that impulse again, unsurprisingly. It was exactly what he shouldn't do.

'Is your mistress a kind woman, Miss Eve?'

Eve had been talking about her position and Kieran looked at the road and tried to concentrate on her words. It wasn't ridiculously difficult; she did have that lovely voice after all.

'At times, although she's mostly preoccupied with her health, understandably.'

Kieran nodded. She'd mentioned the woman had a poor disposition. 'Sickly people are often that way.'

'Heartsick ones are the worst,' Dave added unhelpfully and Kieran quickly sought another question he could ask her.

'Does she suffer much?'

'Yes and no. She detests both the heat and the cold and she's constantly congested but that's because her lungs are damaged. She almost died from pneumonia as a child.'

Kieran listened closely, marvelling that she could manage to sound captivating even when she was talking about sickness.

'Arthur, that's our overseer, is very good with her, making sure she always has a warm fire when it gets cold and helping her to the couch when she's too weak to walk.'

Kieran felt jealousy instantly consume him at the mention of another man's name and Dave of course made it worse. 'Strong fella, is he? All brawny and muscly like, from hard work on the farm?'

'I suppose,' Eve said and Kieran gritted his teeth, 'for his age. Years at sea have weathered him though. And of course it's harder when you only have one leg; a pirate took it in battle.'

Dave let out an inappropriate chuckle and she looked taken aback.

'You'll have to excuse him, Miss Eve. He's a bit worse for wear from ale today,' Kieran apologised, fighting the awful urge to chuckle himself but mostly from relief.

'A thousand apologies, Miss Eve. I was just reacting to such unexpected information and meant no *harrrm*.'

'I suppose it must have sounded rather odd,' she conceded, missing the pun. She was blushing again and Kieran couldn't help but smile at how sweet she seemed.

'And what of the captain himself?'

'He's often away,' she said simply and Kieran hoped desperately that he was kind to her.

Eve pointed down the road. 'Here's my turn-off. Please, don't bother driving me up, I'm happy to walk.'

'I'll walk with you then, just in case any kangaroos happen by,' Kieran said, seizing the chance to be alone with her.

'Oh no really, I'll be fine.' But he was already pulling up the cart and jumping down and he figured she could hardly refuse after his subtle reminder that a second rescue had just taken place. It felt a bit underhanded but the opportunity was just too good to miss. 'Well, I...I suppose. Just to the rise though.'

He guessed she wasn't keen on being seen with a man and assumptions being made about her day and he couldn't blame her for that.

'It's a pretty place,' he noted as they walked, nodding at the wildflowers that bordered the drive.

'Chocolate lilies and milkmaids,' she told him. 'I'm rather fond of their names.'

'Does it feel like home here?' he asked, looking around at what seemed a pleasant farm, then he wondered if that was an appropriate question.

Eve shrugged. 'I'll always be a servant so it's not really mine to call it such, I suppose, but it's a nice place to live. I've been lucky... thanks to you.' She gave him one of her rare smiles and Kieran almost let out a gasp at how pretty the dimples made her. He was certainly staring and she dipped her chin.

'I told you at the time you should be thanking yourself,' he said, dragging his gaze away and continuing towards the house.

'You're too modest, Mr Kieran. If it weren't for you my life would be a misery, perhaps even over. I never could have spoken up myself but you...you did that for me. A total stranger.'

'You didn't seem like a stranger,' he said, looking across at her again.

'...and yet I was.' She stopped as they'd almost reached the rise. 'I just wish I could repay you some day.'

Kieran swallowed hard and took his chance even though he knew it was too soon. 'There was some talk of a kiss should I ever see you again.'

'I...I think I've already given you one of those.'

He moved closer, leaning over to brush his lips against her cheek softly and she let out a shocked gasp. 'You gave me one like this,' he said, holding her gaze, their mouths inches apart. 'But I was really kind of hoping for one of these.' He took her in his arms and captured her lips properly then, before she could protest. It was warm and wondrous, the contact suddenly intimate and explosive in the light breeze, like nature herself caressed the moment. Like they'd always been here, doing this. It only lasted a few, endlessly precious seconds but it was as perfect as any kiss could be and, as he drew away it took a moment for her eyes to open, and he knew it had affected her the same way.

'When can I see you again?' he asked, pushing a strand of her hair back from her lovely face.

'I don't...think I should.'

'How often do you swim at the river?'

Her expression clouded and he suspected she felt ashamed at being decadent and ashamed for kissing him. Someone had got into her head or broken her heart somewhere along the line, he could sense it. He knew the feeling all too well, and ironically it was Eve herself who had revived his own heart. Kieran wanted to tell her that but a mask was falling now, drawing her back from him and blocking him out.

'I cannot do this, Mr Clancy. I am grateful to you but I just cannot. I'm sorry,' she added.

'I didn't kiss you because you owe me something...'

'Nevertheless,' she said, then she began to walk away.

'Miss Eve,' he called and she turned back, tears in her eyes now.

'There's no possibility that the Cartwrights would allow me a beau, Mr Clancy. You need to forget you ever saw me.'

There was more to it than that, something far deeper was swimming in those tears, but Kieran knew he'd be wasting his time trying to find out what it was now. 'We can meet to talk at least,' he said instead. 'There's no sin in that.'

But the shame turned to fear as he said the words and she didn't just walk away now, she ran.

Kieran puzzled over it all the way down the drive but it was a jubilant Dave that greeted him and his excitement was infectious.

'I thought you were mad for sure, Kier, but she's a beautiful lass, no doubting that, and a kind one too, I'd say.'

'Aye, she is that,' Kieran said, clicking the horse to go, 'although she's going to take some convincing.'

'If ever there was a man who could win her heart it must be you, her almighty rescuer. Surely that counts for something.'

'But I don't want her to feel beholden...anyway it wouldn't be enough,' he said, remembering her words.

'Just kiss her until she gives in. That usually does the trick.'

Kieran sighed. 'I just tried that and I thought she liked it but then she turned funny and ran.'

'You sure you were doing it properly?'

Kieran just gave him a look and Dave laughed. 'Ah, I'm only teasing. I wouldn't worry if I were you. A girl that goes swimming in the nuddy is one with fire in her blood, I'm betting. You'll heat it up with time.'

'If I can get time with her.'

'You'll find a way; after all you've found the girl at last,' Dave said, punching the air. 'You've found your girl, Kier! *Eureka!*'

Kieran laughed too then, his earlier exuberance returning.

'Now, how about a drink to celebrate?' Dave suggested, pulling out some bottles of ale. 'It's not every day you strike it rich.'

Kieran took a swig and they toasted, crying 'Eureka!' once more, and Kieran knew Dave was right: he would find a way to break through her shame, and her fear. He would heal Eve Richards's heart. Two rivers, two rescues, it was quite simply fate, and the same fate would surely lead them to find love, in the end.

Twenty-Four

The road seemed longer than usual today but Kieran forced himself onwards, hoping the heat would draw Eve down to the river again. It had only been a week since he'd found her but it felt like months and his insides fluttered with the thought that he might get to hold her again today. Kiss her and awaken that fire he hoped still lay within. Start to heal whatever was broken in her heart.

Long hours working during the week meant he'd no time to try to see her, but it was Sunday once more, a day of rest, and a day he suspected she usually bathed in the river. It was a tantalising thought and Kieran urged his mount, more eager with each mile.

It had been a tough week of waiting in more ways than one. Rogue hold-ups by thieves known as 'bushrangers' were rife and yet another gold bullion transit had been raided on Wednesday, despite a heavily armed escort. The general public's opinion of them ranged from fear to romanticism, depending on the character of the man or the gang, with a few of the more dashing, rebellious bushrangers popularly perceived as modern-day Robin Hoods.

From the miners' perspective, some were esteemed for sticking it to the rich, so long as it wasn't a fortunate miner travelling with his new-found gold; however, there was a more direct consequence that negatively impacted opinion. The thievery hit them right where it hurt most: their pocketbooks, and there was a general consensus that the high cost of licence fees would be far lower if more bullion arrived at its destination.

Regardless of monetary repercussions, there was also the danger of being shot to be considered and it was with wary eyes that Kieran travelled along a thick section of bushland now. He was glad he'd hidden most of his gold and money back at camp.

Other issues had been on his mind aside from Eve and gold-related news. He'd had a letter, a sad one from home. Liam wrote to say Eileen had become withdrawn and thin these past eighteen months since the baby's death and that he and Rory were becoming increasingly worried about her. She was usually so emotionally strong it was hard to imagine her struggling and Kieran knew he'd have to try to get to her soon and see what he could do to help her recover. She'd always been there for him and there was no question he'd be doing the same in return.

It put more urgency on trying to win Eve's heart; before someone else noticed a kind, beautiful and intelligent young woman lived nearby the goldfields, a place filled with thousands of mostly single, sex-starved men. Sooner or later one of them was bound to try to court her and convince the Cartwrights to let her marry or perhaps even steal her away. It made Kieran desperate just thinking about it.

The area where he'd found her was coming into view and Kieran dismounted and walked his horse now, climbing down towards the river and looking along. She was nowhere to be seen and he swallowed his disappointment, sitting down to watch and wait for a while.

An hour passed, then another, and Kieran knew she wasn't coming; the memory of her actually running away from him confirmed any doubt. Well, there was more than one way to approach this, he decided, leading his horse to the road and jumping astride. *Fortune favours the brave, if sometimes foolish*, he imagined Liam saying. He was about to be both so he prayed today it held true.

He'd been on her mind, she couldn't deny it. Despite busying herself with washing, cleaning, cooking, reading and every other preoccupation she could find, that reawakening of the flesh was impossible for Eve to block out. But she'd made up her mind: she refused to be weak again, even though the hunter was a different kind of tempter this time. Perhaps even truly the kindest man on earth.

However, Kieran Clancy was still a man, and a very handsome one, capable of clouding her mind until her body and heart ruled instead. He endangered her self-control and that endangered her new life, and even though he was the one who'd given her this fresh start she couldn't allow him sins of the flesh in return. Even if the Cartwrights could be convinced she be allowed a beau or, more remotely, a husband, she didn't want that power to rule her once more. She didn't want to walk back into Eden and she didn't want the apple.

And never again would she take a bite.

'Eve,' Amanda called and she went to her with the tea. 'Ah, there you are. Could you bring the smelling salts too? I feel quite faint in this heat.' Eve put the tea tray down and went to fetch them, as she was asked to do most days. Returning to her mistress, she noted she looked particularly listless today, her complexion pale against her curly dark hair.

'Would you like me to fan you, ma'am?'

'Yes, I suppose you may as well. You can read to me while you're at it.'

Eve fetched the large bamboo fan the captain had picked up in his island travels and fanned Amanda with one hand, reading from her mistress's favourite tome of Shakespearean sonnets with the other. It was a passage about love and Eve tried not to get lost in the beauty of the words, pushing even that temptation away.

Let me not to the marriage of true minds
Admit impediments. Love is not love
Which alters when it alteration finds,
Or bends with the remover to remove:
O no! it is an ever-fixèd mark
That looks on tempests and is never shaken…

'How true that is,' Amanda said, sniffing her salts. 'A pity all men don't take their vows as seriously.'

'Yes, ma'am,' Eve said, blanking all thought lest she engage with the sonnet's meaning too. 'Shall I read on…or would you prefer something else?' she added hopefully.

'No, no, continue.'

Eve went to do so, reluctantly, but there was a knock at the door and Amanda sat up, her smelling salts falling to the floor in her excitement at having a visitor. The Cartwrights knew almost no-one in Australia and had no kin, save one elderly aunt in London, but even she had recently passed away. Amanda's health prevented her from attempting to socialise and the delivery of goods provided her only variety of company. It was usually Barney, the Scottish delivery man from the local store, and she always told Arthur to invite him in for a chat.

'Well, who can that be then? We're no' expecting anyone today,' Arthur said as he came through from the kitchen to answer and the women waited to hear who it was.

'Good afternoon, sir,' an Irishman's voice could be heard and Eve felt a heady rush of instant recognition. 'Is this Captain Cartwright's home?'

'Aye,' Arthur replied warily.

'I wonder if I may enquire if you have a servant within by the name of Eve Richards?'

'Why would ye be wanting to know?' Arthur said.

'I'm an old friend and I heard she lived near town. The name's Kieran. Kieran Clancy.'

'Arthur? Arthur, do invite the young man in,' Amanda called out, looking over at Eve with surprise. Eve lay down the fan and book, her hands shaking with nerves at having to face Kieran again, fearing what he might say or what her mistress would make of her having her own visitor, especially a man.

He entered the room, good-looking as can be in his Sunday best, and Amanda looked impressed.

'How do you do, ma'am,' he addressed her, taking off his cap and bowing slightly then nodding over at Eve with a smile. 'I apologise for the intrusion but I just wanted to check in on my old friend, Miss Eve. I'm Kieran Clancy.'

'How do you do, Mr Clancy. I didn't know you had friends in Victoria, Eve,' Amanda said, watching them both with interest. 'Aren't you going to say hello?'

'Hello, Mr Clancy,' Eve said, nodding at him and attempting to smile, as would be expected of an old friend.

'Miss Eve,' he said with another slight bow. 'How good it is to see you again. I must say, you're looking very well.'

Eve tried not to blush but she could feel it creeping up into her cheeks. 'Thank you, sir.'

'I should think she is, with that constitution of hers. In our service over a year now and not a sniffle from the girl.'

'She's always been of hardy stock. Her family were all the same,' Kieran told her.

'Is that so? She's never mentioned that.'

Eve could have told him she'd never been asked about her past but it was just as well. Kieran seemed intent on making one up for her.

'A long line of robust lasses and stout lads in the Richards clan; not a day of illness among the lot of them, but of course it's probably partially due to the tonics we had in our village. My own sister Eileen made ones that could improve the health of most in no time at all.'

'Is that so?' Amanda asked, eyes round with interest. 'Whatever did she put in them?'

'Oh, all manner of marvellous things! Pigs root, truffle juice, wildflowers…' Kieran paused to clear his throat, which seemed to be itching him. 'Excuse me, but may I trouble you for a glass of water?'

'Of course, how rude of me and please, take a seat there, Mr Kieran. Arthur, bring some water. In fact, Eve, pour the tea,' she said, flapping at the pot. 'Wildflowers, you say? But we've fields full of them right here.'

Eve poured and Arthur went to fetch the water but he was eyeing Kieran suspiciously.

'Aye, but you'll be in no need of a tonic yourself, being such a fine, healthy-looking woman,' Kieran said, taking a seat on the settee smoothly, his irritated throat miraculously healed.

Amanda shook her head vigorously. 'No, no, Mr Clancy, in fact quite the opposite, I'm afraid. I've been sickly most of my life. I almost died from pneumonia as a child, as a matter of fact.'

'You don't say,' Kieran said, appearing shocked. 'Tell me, do your lungs suffer in the heat or the cold?'

Eve sank onto a stool nearby, watching Kieran play her mistress like a fiddle and helpless to do anything to stop it as they continued on.

'Terribly! I'm feeling quite poorly today, as it happens,' Amanda told him, leaning forward in her excitement to talk to someone about her favourite subject.

Kieran looked at her thoughtfully. 'I don't suppose...oh, but that's just daft. I'm sure a captain's wife has the best physicians available to her night and day. What would you be wanting from our village cures.'

'What were you going to suggest? Don't tell me...don't tell me you can make these tonics yourself?'

'Well, I could have a go from memory,' he offered, sipping his tea. 'I watched my sister make her potions for years and I do recall quite a bit of the process and ingredients. Meanwhile, if you like, I could send for some of her handmade ones. She lives in New South Wales though so it may take a few...'

'Oh yes!' Amanda said, eyes shining now. 'But you must let me pay you for your troubles.'

'Not at all, ma'am. I'm sure Miss Eve would be grateful to have an old friend do her mistress this favour.'

Amanda nodded. 'Well, if you're sure you have the time...'

'I'll find it,' he declared. 'In fact, what if we begin right now? I noticed some chocolate lilies and milkmaids along the drive that would be a good start for a vapour decongestant recipe; perhaps Eve and I could collect some. Do you have any baskets handy?'

Amanda was so enthused by the idea she went and fetched some baskets herself and Eve found herself bustled out the door and walking down the lane alone with Kieran within minutes.

'You were awfully quiet in there,' Kieran said after a pause. He looked ridiculously pleased with himself and it irked Eve immensely.

'It seemed unnecessary to speak when I was literally in the conversation in the third person.'

To her annoyance he chuckled at that. 'Very droll, Miss Eve, very droll indeed. What a clever mind you have there. Almost as impressive as that beautiful face of yours.'

Eve stopped in her tracks to glare at him now.

'Why are you saying things like that, Kieran Clancy? In fact, why are you even here, throwing everything I've confided to you back in my face to...to...'

He stepped closer, watching her struggle to articulate it. 'To spend some time with you, Eve?' he said, dropping the 'Miss'. 'Is that really too much to ask?'

Eve wanted to say yes but his kind eyes were boring into hers and the word seemed peevish now. 'Not if you only want my friendship and help, no. But if you're looking for more, I told you before, I can't give...that to you.'

'I'll settle for your friendship and help for now, but you won't be able to fight more when it comes. It's destiny, Eve, not me. It's bigger than we are.'

He smiled at her then before walking over and picking flowers and Eve stood for a moment, digesting his words. They were etching into her mind before she could manage to stop them and blank them out, finding their way in past the shelved memories of her sins. Somehow he'd managed to invite her on a different kind of hunt, one driven by kindness and beauty, and already her heart was listening as it swelled with the sweetness of his speech, more impactful than even a Shakespearean sonnet. For they were words driven by an inarguable, ferocious force: the simple power of truth.

Twenty-Five

He was later than usual and Eve was trying not to care but her eyes moved to the clock every few minutes and she cursed herself each time she did it.

'Mr Clancy should have been here by now,' Amanda said lightly, a knowing gaze flicking Eve's way. She chose to ignore it and focus on her reading instead.

Love's not Time's fool, though rosy lips and cheeks
Within his bending sickle's compass come

'Perhaps he's out in the sheds with Arthur,' Amanda interrupted her.

The overseer had warmed considerably towards Kieran over the past few weeks and the two men were often seen chatting and smoking their pipes as they discussed farming out there.

Amanda stood and walked to the window to see. 'Oh yes, he has arrived,' she said, waving. 'I wonder if he's got that new tonic ready for me? I've almost run out of Sleepy-o.'

Whatever fibs Kieran had fabricated to ingratiate himself into the woman's good graces, lying about tonic making wasn't one of them. Her mistress was in the best health Eve had yet seen her and there was a detectable spring in her step as she came back to her chair. Eve pushed away further musings on Kieran's character to read on.

Love alters not with his brief hours and weeks,
But bears it out even to the edge of doom.

This time it was men's voices that interrupted her and Eve put the book down, trying not to feel that delicious thrill that accompanied the anticipation of seeing someone you'd missed. For she had missed him, despite every possible effort not to. She could no longer deny that she cared for him, not only as her saviour but as a friend; however, any further admission was still out of the question, despite the butterflies flying about in her stomach right now.

The door banged open and in they strode, laughing about something, and Kieran doffed his cap and bent to kiss Amanda's hand, as was his habit now, and she smiled happily up at him. 'I thought you'd forgotten us today.'

'Now, to forget to visit you would be like forgetting to put on my trousers. I did do that today, did I not?' he said, pulling a comical face and pretending to check.

Amanda laughed and Eve smiled. Kieran's charm was difficult to resist.

'Hello there, Miss Eve,' he said, nodding over at her and she tried not to do her usual thing and blush. It was so frustrating when her body betrayed her like that.

'Hello, Mr Clancy,' she said. 'Would you like some tea?'

'No, no, don't trouble yourself...'

'Nonsense, Kier, I think we'd all enjoy a cuppa. Come on, Eve, I'll help ye,' Arthur said.

'No putting your sailor's rum in it now,' Kieran called after them.

'You hear that, Eve? He thinks yer trying t'get him drunk,' Arthur said.

Eve laughed, although the blush was deeper now and Arthur began to watch her as they took out crockery and put the water on.

'I wasn't sure what he were up to at first but I have to admit it: he's a fine man, yer Mr Clancy.'

Eve took out the milk and placed it on the tray before answering. 'He's not mine, as well you know.'

Arthur picked up some spoons and pointed them at her. 'Aye, but he could be.'

Eve shook her head. 'Don't even say such things, Arthur. The mistress would never allow it.'

'I think she finds the whole idea *romantic*, as you lasses say, but it's no' the mistress you need to consider, it's the master. Mind you, I think we may have powers of persuasion in our favour.'

Eve wanted to ask, 'Such as?' but refused to allow herself. Besides, Arthur seemed hell-bent on telling her anyway.

'In case ye haven't noticed, the captain's rather partial to his wife and if there's one thing he worries about, it be her.'

That was true, Eve conceded.

'He's going to be pleased as punch when he sees how much she's improved under yer Kieran's tonics,' Arthur continued. 'If ever ye had a chance at being allowed to have a man o'yer own...'

'Arthur,' Eve stopped him, closing her eyes against the conflicting emotions roiling inside her at his words. 'I don't need nor want a man of my own. I don't want anything except a peaceful life.'

'Come now, Eve, yer wanting more than that.'

'No. I just want to be a good woman in the eyes of God and to be left to serve out my days without any trouble and earn my redemption. That's why I'm here, Arthur. That's my fate and I'm grateful for it.'

Arthur put the last cup on the tray and lifted it for her.

'Loving a man isn't a sin, Eve,' he told her gently before limping away. Eve blinked at the effect those words had as she stood in the kitchen alone.

Oh, but it can be, Arthur, she wanted to tell his retreating back. *And it can cast you from paradise into the very darkest of hells.*

It was time to leave and it was time to tell her he was going but Kieran hated uttering the words almost as much as he hated to go. Mostly because he'd hoped she would have been able to love him a little by the time he went home to his family but also because he would miss seeing her each week. Seven days between visits would feel like nothing compared to the weeks or even months he would need to be away, and Kieran was already bracing himself for the longing and loneliness that would accompany him each day. But there was nothing else for it. The sun was low in the sky and he had to depart, and she had to know he wasn't coming back for quite some time.

They were walking down the drive in the fading orange light, their lover's lane as he thought of it now, the place he often visited in his mind when he missed her most, reliving that reward he'd claimed. That one perfect kiss.

Looking over at her, he searched for the right words but found none and she looked back at him, thoughtful herself.

'There's something on your mind, Eve,' he finally said.

The early autumn wind was whipping at her hair and she pushed it back. 'I could say the same to you.'

Kieran sighed, knowing the time had come. 'I'm leaving.'

Whatever she'd thought he was about to say it obviously wasn't that and she bit her bottom lip and nodded slowly. 'Why?'

'It's my sister Eileen. She's not doing too well and I need to go home to her and try to help.'

'What's wrong with her? Is she sick?'

'No, no, it's nothing like that. She lost her baby the day I left town, stillborn.'

'How terrible for her…' she said before frowning in confusion. 'But why did you leave then?'

Kieran rubbed his neck, wondering how much to reveal of his more troubled side, but then again that's what this might have to take. Perhaps if she saw a less cocky, more complex man she might see that he was vulnerable too and open up to him at last. 'I had a bit of an altercation with a doctor who wouldn't tend her. To be honest that's why I came down to Victoria, to lay low for a while.'

'Oh,' she said.

'You sound disappointed there, Eve.'

She shrugged her shoulders, not bothering with her hair now as it slipped its pins and swept about in burnished strands in the dusk. 'Why should I be? I just thought you came for gold, is all.'

'I did come for gold,' he said, daring to take a strand of her hair and place it behind her ear as he'd done that first day, weeks ago. 'I've found it too, only I'm having a hard time convincing it to come free.'

Her eyes never left his as he ran his fingers down her arm to take her hand and Eve shook her head. 'It's not that I don't care for you, Kieran…'

'I know that you do, lass, I can feel it. I can sense you've been hurt too and I know how that feels, believe me.'

'You can't possibly…'

'*So tell me then.* There's nothing left for it but for you to be honest with me now, Eve. I think you owe me that much at least.' That last comment upset her but he didn't take it back. Whatever it took at this point, even pushing her guilt.

'I...I can't tell you...'

'You can. You can tell me anything,' he said, running his thumb gently across the mark on her chin. 'We all carry scars, Eve. Whatever it is, I'll understand.'

'You can't understand this,' she whispered, struggling not to cry. 'How it feels...'

'How it feels when what?'

'When...when your entire world is ripped away, when you're betrayed and cast out...'

'People have tried to destroy me too, to take my life, my freedom.' He was impassioned now and took both her hands. 'I'm an Irishman, Eve. Some people think our blood isn't worth saving; that we should be starved or beaten from this earth. I know what it's like to be betrayed and to be broken down but if you give those people this,' he paused to place her hands over her own heart, 'then you give them your soul.'

'That's just it. It's not about the people who betrayed me,' she said so softly he could barely hear. 'I...I...'

'Tell me, love,' he begged. 'Tell me what it is.'

'I betrayed myself,' she said on a sob. 'I let...I let him hunt me down, I gave in to temptation. I'm truly Eve...and I am a sinner.'

He pulled her into his arms as she cried in earnest now and he stroked her back, softly crooning. 'There now, Eve, there, lass.' Then he pulled her back, holding her shoulders. 'I take it this man didn't offer you marriage?'

'He...he couldn't. He was the young m...master of the house.'

Kieran nodded, wishing he could punch the bastard who used her so, but he expressed himself more gently to her. 'It sounds to me like he was the one at fault.'

'No...he can't be held to blame entirely if I...if I let him.'

'I doubt he deserves such loyal words. Why didn't he protect you or fight for you?'

Eve shrugged, frowning now. 'I suppose I...I wasn't enough.'

'Then he was a fool, lass, and a cad at that.'

'But I was a fool first. That's why I'm afraid, Kieran, I'm scared of the way you make me feel. I can't let my foolish body and my heart take over my mind again. I can't be that *weak*.'

She said the word with such devastation that Kieran could have wept for her, a girl so riddled with guilt and unfairly punished for doing what comes naturally to all.

'We all sin, Eve. We all give in at times. Do you think I have never bedded a woman? Do you think me a terrible sinner then?'

'But you're a man.'

Kieran let out a short laugh. 'Aye, and so was Adam. I never understood why Eve copped all the blame when he took a bite of the apple too.'

She shrugged sadly. 'It's just the way of the world.'

'Well, it shouldn't be. And you shouldn't live a life of loneliness because you think all lovemaking is a sin.' He took both her hands again. 'It can be wondrous, Eve, when it truly is for love.' He dared a kiss then, a mere brush of lips, yet every sensory instinct seemed to live in that brief, sweet touch, and he was filled with sincerity as he declared the rest. 'I love you, Eve, and I want to marry you. There'll be no sinning involved this time, I promise.'

She was hesitating, staring at his mouth in the half-light, her face tear-stained, then she reached up to cup his cheek with her hand, so gently he didn't dare breathe, and leaned close to place a soft kiss of her own. Kieran's heart leapt that she was brave enough to do so, and with such trust. Then a rush of joy swept through him and he captured her mouth with his, pulling her against him and kissing her properly, unleashing everything he'd felt since they'd met; all those long months of yearning, the endless hours of loneliness, every ache of restraint from each look, word and touch.

It flowed between them like a great wave now, wondrously free to crash at last.

'I love you too,' she gasped, pausing to rest her forehead on his. 'How can I not when you're...when you're so kind?'

'Only kind?' he teased, although his heart leapt at the words. He kissed the top of her head and tried to calm his racing pulse and senses. 'What about devilishly handsome and charming?'

'And terribly modest too,' she said, smiling a little now.

Kieran chuckled, letting happiness override everything else. 'So when can I ask the good captain for your hand?'

'You truly want to do this?'

'More than anything in the entire world,' he said, tracing her lovely face with his eyes.

Eve smiled shyly again, her dimples darting. 'Well, he...he'll be home in August. Oh, but what if he says no?' she said, her face falling.

'Then I'll have to put a tonic in his tea.'

'But he could...'

'Hush, lass,' he said, kissing her again. 'You're forgetting about that Irish charm.'

'It's just that I...I never thought such a thing would be possible for me now.'

'Plenty of convict servants marry, and Arthur and Amanda don't seem to mind me hanging about. In fact, I'm reckoning Amanda will love the idea of having her own private tonic maker for life. She'll support this, Eve, I'm sure of it.'

'But if the captain still refuses...if he takes this away from me now I don't know if I could bear it.'

'Nothing will stop me from being with you, Eve,' he told her firmly. 'Not a sea captain, not even the ocean itself,' he said, sweeping his arms back dramatically to convince her. 'We've crossed one to be here, don't forget,' he said more softly now, taking her hands again, 'for different reasons and from different worlds, but somehow we're standing under the same sky.' He looked up and nodded at the twinkling lights appearing there, two pointing like an arrow towards others arranged in a cross. 'We're meant to be, you and I. Our fate is already written up there, in those southern stars.'

'The Southern Cross actually,' she told him. 'Arthur says it points due south, see? He said it directs you home when you're on the seas.'

'Then look to it while I'm gone, my love. I'll be looking too, thinking of you until I can follow them back.'

They held one another close then, under those guiding stars, grasping on to this moment for as long as they could, knowing it would be replayed over and again in their minds until he returned. Until that fate-filled sky brought him home.

Twenty-Six

Orange, March 1854

She was staring again, not at the place on the rise where Kieran would eventually appear but over at the creek where a tiny grave lay beneath a tree. It had a marker, just a simple one naming the baby and the date: *Sarah Mary Murphy, born 6th September, 1852.*

Eileen hadn't wanted it stated that she'd died at the same time. She hadn't even wanted to put Mary in her name, saving it for the daughter she still hoped to have, but Rory had wanted it included like a blessing so she'd agreed it could be added to the middle.

She would have been a year and a half old if she'd survived. Eighteen months and four days, to be exact. Eileen always counted each morning, like it meant something still. She'd be forming sentences now and have hair long enough to tie back or up, away from her dear little face. Her daughter would have been a beautiful child but God had stolen her life away. Even Mary, the sacred mother, had let her down in this, of all things, and Eileen couldn't forgive her for it, no longer placing flowers at the statue on the mantel or going to Mass. Her rosary beads now left in a drawer.

Rory said she needed to get past it, telling her that she had three other healthy children and that more would follow, but she couldn't. She didn't want to. It was as if she kept Sarah alive by thinking about her every day and talking to her soul up there in heaven, and if she didn't do so then her baby was truly gone.

And so she sat, and thought about her, what could have been, what was, and she went about her daily tasks, mothering her boys and caring for them all, but it was as if from a distance. She'd thought she'd known grief when she lost her ma and da but this was different. This was a pain that crippled and she couldn't find the will to send it away.

The children were playing near the gate and a sudden excited cry turned her head towards them.

'Ma! Ma!' they called out, pointing up the road.

'It's Uncle Kieran!' Thomas yelled, running now.

Eileen stood slowly as the place on the rise saw her prodigal brother return at last and something moved in her heart aside from grief for a change. If she could have mustered a smile she might have called it happiness or relief, but it was probably just love. And when it came to family, that was always hard.

'They're heartily sick of it around here, I can tell you that much,' Rory was saying as Liam brought more beer out onto the porch. 'Diggers are leaving their claims in droves to go south.'

'They'll find licence fees down there too,' Kieran reminded him.

'Aye, but they're less than up here and only adults pay. They're forcing lads as young as fourteen to find the coin now and throwing them in the lock-up if they don't.'

'How are they supposed to pay the fine to get out if they can't even afford the licence fee in the first place?' Kieran said, shaking his head and accepting the proffered cup from Liam.

'Now you're using logic, Kier. There's not a lot of it goin' on the goldfields in the north.'

'Not a lot of it to be found in the south either,' he told them. 'You're more likely to find gold and that's saying something!'

Rory and Liam laughed but Eileen remained quiet, sipping her beer and staring out over the fields to where the children were throwing stones at tin cups. She'd barely spoken a word to Kieran aside from welcoming him home and asking if he'd eaten and Liam could see his brother's concern mounting throughout the afternoon.

'So what of you, Eileen?' Kieran said, turning towards her now. 'How's your tonic making coming along? I don't mind telling you it's doing me some favours, remembering a thing or two you showed me.'

Eileen shrugged and Rory stepped in to fill the silence. 'How so?'

'Let me guess, there's a woman involved,' Liam said, lighting his pipe.

'Not just a woman, brother, an angel with flaxen hair and eyes so beautiful they can't seem to choose their own colour.'

'And terrible taste in men, I'm gathering.'

Rory laughed and Kieran put up his hand in protest. 'I'll have you know she sees something in me with those eyes of hers. She's…well, she's agreed to marry me.'

'Marry you?' It was Eileen who spoke and she was staring at him as if confused.

'Aye,' Kieran said, 'she has to get permission first though so…'

'Permission from who? Her father?' Eileen spoke again.

'Well, it's complicated you see…she's a servant.'

'A convict, you mean?'

'Well, yes, but she's a good woman, Eiles. She's…'

'What did she do?'

Kieran was looking uncomfortable and Liam almost groaned when he said the next words. 'I... er...don't actually know the full story.'

'What do you mean you don't know? You could be bringing an axe murderer into the family; have you not even considered that?' Eileen looked furious now and Liam and Rory exchanged glances, at a loss at what to do. It was the most she'd engaged in any conversation for months, though, so neither of them interfered.

'It's nothing like that! She was misused by the master of the house, I know that much, and cast out onto the streets so...I guess...'

'What? That she robbed a bank? Stole a horse? Turned whore someplace?'

There was anger in Kieran's voice now as he cut her off. 'You're not to say such things about her, Eiles. This is the woman I love and she is kind and brave and I've seen nothing but goodness in her since I met her. I will be marrying her and if you don't like it that's just tough.'

Eileen stood from her chair and stared him down. 'Well, she won't be putting a foot in the family home until I know why she's a criminal, do you understand me?'

'Eiles,' Rory warned, finally interjecting.

'These are your children too,' she said, turning to him. 'Don't you think they have a right to know if their new aunt is going to kill them in their beds?'

'Eileen, have a little faith in me, for Godsakes,' Kieran said, standing too. 'Do you really think I would endanger my own kin?'

'I don't know what to think, Kieran. I feel like I don't even know you, you've been gone so long.'

'You know that I love my family, Eiles,' he said more gently, 'and that your happiness is the most important thing to me in the world.'

'I'm not sure if I still believe that,' she said, her glare cold. 'I'm not sure I know anything anymore.'

She walked away then, down the steps and across towards the creek and Kieran stared after her. 'Do you think I should follow?'

'No, let her be,' Rory said with a sad sigh.

'That did her good, I'm reckoning,' Liam commented. 'At least she got some of that anger out. She barely talks these days.'

'Trust me to be the one who makes her angry,' Kieran said ruefully, sitting back down and nodding across at Rory. 'I've always been the one to set her off and you've always been the one to calm her back down.'

'What's my job then?' Liam said, smoking his pipe and watching his sister.

Kieran sighed. 'Figuring out a way to help her.'

'Where are you two off to?'

Kieran turned at the sound of Rory's voice and spoke for Liam as well. 'We thought we might head over and check out the pub at Ophir to celebrate the final payment. Want to come along?'

The last instalment had been made on their land debt and Rory seemed to consider the idea of joining them but declined. 'I think I'd best stay home. I need to finish mending the gate.'

It had been three days since Kieran arrived and the tense atmosphere was starting to wear on him. It didn't help that he was unable to show his face in town and had therefore been farmbound the entire time. His restless spirit had been sorely tested and when Liam suggested this celebratory adventure he'd jumped at it, especially as Liam had heard some travelling musicians were playing at a pub over there tonight.

They set off at a canter beneath a brilliant sunset, farewelling the children who ran with them down to the gate with excited shouts and waves.

'Bye, Uncle Kieran! Bye, Uncle Liam!' they called.

'Bring us back some presents!' added Matthew hopefully.

They hit the road and Kieran welcomed the bite of the air and the feel of horseflesh once more.

'Race you to the tree!' Liam called and they took off, whooping and laughing, feeling like children again themselves. Liam won and there was a fair amount of crowing that resulted in a second race, then a third, all of which Liam also won, and by the time they arrived at Ophir the horses were tired and the men were more than ready for an ale. It was well past dark by now and the party was in full swing. In fact it was standing room only, despite talk of the northern goldfields becoming more and more deserted, and Kieran felt right at home among a bunch of drunken miners once more.

The band was good, especially the singer whose face was obscured by a massive black beard but nothing could hide the man's height nor his heavyset physique. He was simply enormous, yet his voice was so melodic it could even be termed sweet, an incongruous combination. He was singing 'Wild Colonial Boy' and Kieran wished Dave was here to hear it.

Come along my hearties, we'll roam the mountains high,
Together we will plunder, together we will ride.
We'll scar over valleys, and gallop for the plains,
And scorn to live in slavery, bound down by iron chains

Kieran and Liam were soon singing along, downing ales and chatting to other miners as the merry evening wore on, and by the time the band finished their last song Kieran found himself feeling rather misty, so touching was the singer's rendition of 'The Girl I Left Behind'.

'Feeling alright there, are you, Kier?' Liam teased.

'Aye, you just wait. One day it'll be you and you'll know how it feels,' Kieran said, blinking fast.

'I'd best start going places that actually have women in them for that to happen,' Liam said, looking around at the sea of hairy-faced men in the room.

'There's always Mass?'

'Eileen has stopped going so we have too.'

Kieran paused mid-ale. 'Shite, she is in a bad way.' For his sister to lose her faith said more than even her anger or silence.

'Aye,' Liam said, looking despondent. 'I just don't know what else to do, Kier. I've tried everything I can think of to bring her back into normal life but it's just like...like something has died inside of her too.'

'You'd think the boys would be able to draw her out.'

Liam shrugged. 'She still manages them but it's almost as if she isn't there, you know? Like her heart isn't in it.'

Kieran nodded. 'Grief can be like that,' he said, thinking of his own experiences, 'but hearts can heal, Liam. She'll come back, you'll see.'

Liam looked to say more but the conversation was interrupted by the approach of the giant singer from the band, and to Kieran's surprise he walked straight up and stood before him, massive arms hanging by his side.

'I've got something for you,' he said, his dark eyes boring and the crowd around them quietened down and watched on with interest.

'For...for me?' Kieran said, nervously watching one meaty hand move. The man reached into his pocket and they all watched as a cap was produced.

'I never did get to thank ye for this.'

Kieran stared at the man's face, recognition dawning. 'Big Pete?'

'Just Striker these days. I got lucky on the fields, as it turned out.' He broke into a gap-toothed smile then, holding out the cap, and Kieran stared at his own name written on the inside brim.

'Well, how do you like that?'

'Take it,' Striker said, offering it to him.

'No, no, you keep it as a souvenir. At least you never forgot my name,' he added, nodding at the inscription.

Striker grinned again, putting the too-small cap on his large head and clapping Kieran on the shoulder. 'I never would have forgotten ye regardless. Drinks on me for this man tonight,' he declared and a few people cheered as Kieran almost fell then regained his equilibrium.

'This is my brother, Liam,' he thought to say, and the two men shook hands, Liam's dwarfed by Striker's huge paw.

'Pleased to meet you,' Liam said.

'Drinks for the brother too,' Striker called over to the barman.

'Well, that's mighty kind of you,' Liam said, looking enquiringly at Kieran.

'We...er, had an interesting night in Sydney together once,' Kieran said by way of explanation.

'Yer brother here is a good man,' Striker said, 'as I'm sure ye know.'

'Oh, he has his moments, although he couldn't win a horse race to save his life.'

'He's been known to win a bet on a fight on occasion though, or so I'm told,' Striker said, passing over ales while Kieran laughed.

'You can blame my mate Dave for that.'

'Seeing as he's not here,' Striker said.

'Exactly,' Kieran said, grinning. He sipped his ale and looked at Striker curiously. 'What are you doing singing in a band if you've found gold and you're...well, a wealthy man now, I'm guessing?'

Striker shrugged. 'The wealthy don't want the new breed of gentlemen that come from the fields. You can put on all the fancy clobber and ride about in a fine carriage but they'll no' give ye the time o'day and I don't fancy sittin' around trying to convince them to.'

Kieran had heard that. Of the few diggers he knew who'd struck it rich, most had either ended up blowing it on the wrong things and been left with nothing to show for their big find; or they'd met with ill fortune in one way or another, drinking themselves senseless and getting robbed or beaten up. Their dreams of fortune hadn't factored in the world where fortune lives; a place where most of the lower-class diggers would never belong.

'I imagine it must be a rich life in itself, to use such a god-given talent to give pleasure to others,' Liam said.

'Well, it seems the brother is a right nice fella too,' Striker said, looking pleased. 'Come on, let's get good and sloshed and ye can tell me yer life stories.'

They drank until the pub closed before moving on to a campfire in the bushland out back to yarn the night away. Striker brought along some of his bandmates so there were songs too, and much laughter until the wee hours, with the firelight orange against the trees and the smoke curling towards stars that shone clearly in the cold dark above. Eventually they crashed on blankets before preparing to make their tender way home in the morning, and Striker promised to look them up when the band went touring south later in the year.

'There're some mean troopers down there, mate,' Kieran warned him.

'Mean bastards everywhere ye go, Kieran, but I think I can hold me own.'

'He could hold several people's owns,' Liam muttered as they waved and rode away. 'Must be a handy man to have around in a fight.'

'That he is, brother,' Kieran said, 'although I wouldn't recommend betting on him unless he's fighting against the law.'

'Best stay clear then, Kier,' Liam said, looking over at him meaningfully.

'Aye,' he replied. But he was thinking it would be better to stay close.

Twenty-Seven

The kookaburras were swooping and making their laughing calls as the rain began to fall in hard pellets, releasing a refreshing, earthy scent as it met the ground.

'She'll be soaked,' Liam said. They were all watching her, the lone figure dressed in black down by the creek.

'She never seems to care,' Rory replied and he sipped his tea resignedly. His brother-in-law was looking older, Kieran observed, the lines around his eyes and mouth more pronounced now, telling a tale of sorrow.

'I don't think my presence here is helping,' Kieran told them with a sigh. 'Maybe I'm even doing more harm than good.'

Rory moved to sit on the bench and fill his pipe. 'At least you stir something inside her.'

That comment worried Kieran further. His sister's marriage seemed in a sorry way and even though he was sure Rory would always remain loyal it was tragic to see the once-happy couple broken down to such a state.

'I don't think any of us are helping, to be honest. I don't think we're capable; it has to come from her,' Liam said, his intelligent eyes sad.

She was returning and Kieran made up his mind that now was the time to tell them all what he'd decided beneath those southern stars last night. After three weeks there was nothing more for it: it was time for him to go.

'Nice walk, love?' Rory said as she mounted the steps but she said nothing so he simply handed her a cloth and she patted her hair dry, walking inside to where the children were resting.

'It's time for me to hit the road, I think,' Kieran said, knowing she was within earshot. 'Dave will be needing me back at the claim and I can't really stay here, hiding away from the world indefinitely.'

'So soon?' Liam said, looking disappointed. Kieran knew his brother had enjoyed having him here these past few weeks and he hated to part from him too.

'It's a life of freedom for me in Victoria, lads, and opportunity too.' He didn't mention Eve but he knew they realised she was the biggest part of the motivation. His late-night mooning outside kind of gave him away.

'When will you be back?'

'In a few months, I'm thinking.'

'A few months,' Eileen's voice could be heard and she came to stand at the door, her face expressionless and drawn. 'It was a year and a half this time. Soon it will be a few years and then you'll never come back at all.'

Kieran stood away from the porch rail where he'd been leaning to face her. 'I'll always come back, Eiles.'

'And bring the convict wife with you, I suppose.'

'If she's welcome.'

'She won't be welcomed home by me.' There was a tense silence interspersed only by the sound of the rain. 'She won't be welcomed because I won't be here.'

The three men stared at her and it was Liam who spoke. 'What do you mean by that?'

'I want to go south too,' she said, her voice firm with the decision. 'I can't…I can't stay on this land anymore.' Her gaze flickered towards the creek before coming to rest on Rory. 'I'm just… just…' Then unexpectedly her face began to crumple, the hardness she'd worn for so long falling away to reveal the rawest of sorrows. 'I'm just so e-empty inside.' Her voice broke into a whisper as tears filled her eyes and she shook her head from side to side. 'I can't…I just can't…'

Rory rushed to sweep her in his arms and Eileen collapsed into them, crying for the first time since Kieran had arrived, in pitiful tears that wrenched his soul. He and Liam came forward too, to place comforting hands on her back.

'It's a good idea, love,' Rory said, his voice choked. 'A new beginning together. A fresh start.'

Liam nodded, tears sliding down his own cheeks. 'It doesn't matter where we live as long it's on Clancy land together…and Clancy owned.'

'You'll love it down there, Eiles,' Kieran said, 'and it will heal your heart, I promise it.'

They stood together for a while then as the rain pattered on the farmhouse, built with such hope by a family from across the sea, and Kieran looked over past the creek to the horizon beyond, to where the town of Orange lay. Somewhere there lived a doctor whose hands Kieran would forever consider stained with blood and whose heart was as hard as the stone he'd cast through his window. He may have taken that tiny life from them but he wouldn't be taking this: their united Clancy hearts. Nor their right to choose to start again. And find a way to be truly free.

Twenty-Eight

Ballan, May 1854

She wasn't there. After all the weeks of longing and after all the sleepless nights in the saddle following that starlit cross south, Eve was out picking up supplies for the household. Kieran had struggled to escape Amanda who was overjoyed to have a fresh supply of tonics delivered but he'd eventually succeeded and was now hurrying towards the small town to find Eve. But, as the unseasonable heat of the autumn morning warmed his back, he had a sudden suspicion and turned his mount into the bushland alongside instead.

It was pristine, the light dappling through the trees that lined the waterway, and the river moved in idle flow as it came into view, like a living thing beneath a cloudless sky. And there, at its centre, floated a woman, hair fanning out from an exquisitely beautiful face that was filled with such rapture, such peace, that he could only behold the sight at first. But then suggestions of naked skin could be glimpsed below the water and Kieran dismounted to take off his boots, his shirt, his breeches. He made his way towards her, the cold silk of the water enveloping him, and the eyes in that face opened and widened in recognition.

'Kieran,' she whispered, her shoulders pulling forward as she stood before him and reached out her arms. It seemed the most natural thing in the world to walk into them, to pull that naked skin against his and to fall into drugging, worshipful kisses and blend as if into one.

'I love you,' he told her over and again, their mouths and hands gliding now, and he guided her to the river bank to lay her beneath him. Long water-soaked limbs entwined with his and the softness of her breasts and hips fit against him as each ragged breath was captured by the other. Eyes open and faces close in a merging of souls. He took her quickly, unable to hold back the tide of desire that had been building from that very first day, driving towards a climax intensified by love, exploding something deeper inside them both.

It was the sweetest of surrenders, unlike anything he'd ever experienced before, and he fell to the side and leaned his head on her arm, kissing the soft inside gently, his eyes still locked with hers. He saw no guilt there anymore and he was relieved, although he thought it best to cement his intentions just in case.

'When is the good captain expected home?'

'Three months,' she told him, stroking his hair.

'Best get thinking about a wedding dress, Miss Eve, although I think I prefer you like this.'

She blushed but she was smiling too. 'I don't think the priest would be too pleased.'

'It's not the priest you need to care about pleasing.'

He kissed her once more, slow and languid now, but she drew away after a while and he knew he was making her late. They dressed and he helped her mount his horse, loving the feel of her body pressed against his as he took her home. But soon they were standing on their lover's lane farewelling each other once more and Kieran hugged her close, loath to let go and lose her touch for a whole, long week.

'You haven't told me about your trip home,' she said, lifting her face to him.

'Apologies for that, ma'am. I was a little distracted.'

She smiled at that but buried her head against his chest, still a little shy, he supposed. 'How's your sister?'

'She was in a terrible way while I was there but I think she had a bit of a breakthrough in the end,' Kieran told her. 'They're selling up and moving south, actually, which is brilliant news.'

'Oh, Kieran, how perfect for you...and for her, I'm sure. Making a fresh start is always a good idea.'

'You'd be an expert on that subject. Mind you, this isn't something new for us Clancys either, what with packing up and leaving Ireland and so on.'

She smiled again. 'I've never had a sister. Can't wait to meet her, and the rest of your family.'

Memories of Eileen's disapproval flashed through Kieran's mind but he sought a platitude over the truth. 'I'm sure she feels the same way.'

Eve hugged him closer and sighed. 'I wish I didn't have to go. *Parting is such sweet sorrow*,' she added in a mutter.

'A lover of the bard, are you?' he said, kissing the top of her head.

'I read his sonnets to Amanda, she adores him, but he's been making me ache for you horribly.'

Kieran pulled back to look into her eyes. '...*that I shall say goodnight till it be 'morrow*.' He kissed her briefly once more then grinned. 'You know, that would have sounded so much smoother if we were under our southern stars.'

'As long as we're not star-crossed lovers,' she returned, looking slightly pensive for the first time that day.

'None of that now. Those same stars led me home to you. Besides, we are destined to be, remember? Rivers keep proving it.' He grinned and raised his eyebrows suggestively and it coaxed the laughter he was seeking, although she was blushing again. She pulled away and walked up the drive, turning constantly to wave as she went and he blew kisses and waved back, imprinting the vision of her on the flowered track in his mind. Love shone from her smile and her now-dry hair whipped in fair strands about her lovely face, a visage he was determined to wake up to every day of his life.

The image stayed with him as she disappeared and Kieran mounted his horse to return home with wondrous memories of the whole day replaying through his mind. He knew something far beyond the physical act of sex had occurred, something on another plane; an experience that he could only describe as 'spiritual'. In truth, he'd married her in that moment when he fell into her soul. In the eyes of God, if not yet man. They were joined together now, two healed hearts with one shared destiny. With surely their only cross a protective one, blessing them from afar.

Twenty-Nine

Ballarat, July 1854

'The traps are out today.'

The word was spreading quickly and Kieran watched as many diggers took off to avoid being checked for their miner's licence that afternoon, running into the bush to hide among the scrub, to lie and wait in fear. Lest they be hunted down like animals, by their own government, Kieran observed with disgust. Most of the unlucky miners couldn't afford to pay the exorbitant fees and Kieran knew Dave wouldn't have done so out of pure resentment that they be paid at all.

'You'd best lay low too,' Kieran said, pausing in his sluicing to turn to his friend.

'Feck them,' Dave said, continuing to work his cradle and frowning.

'Dave...'

'I'll no' run off and hide, Kieran. I'm heartily sick of the whole business!' Dave fumed, his usually amiable demeanour evaporating. 'Who the hell are they to charge us for the right to mine and take all our profits? And we're not even allowed to vote and get those bastard politicians to change the law.'

As a landowner, Kieran actually was allowed to vote but he and Dave had never talked about it. He supposed Dave just assumed Liam held the title, but now was not the time for such discussion.

'You need to go,' Kieran warned, looking along the creek bed nervously. 'Go hide out at Striker's.' Striker had been as good as his word in coming south and he was currently renting a house near the pub, where more and more buildings were popping up. It was more spacious than most with several bedrooms and, most fortuitously, a secret basement where harassed miners often hid out. He'd also managed to marry a very nice young woman called Betty who was as small as he was large, something they both acknowledged with good humour.

Dave stopped what he was doing, staring at the gravel and rocks before throwing the cradle down with a clatter. 'Aye, I'll go, but the day is coming, Kier, mark my words.'

He left, his stride angry, and Kieran looked after him thoughtfully. Usually he was the one with the flashes of temper; Dave handled most conflict with cheek, but things were changing in these muddy creek beds in Ballarat, Dave was right. You didn't need to be Irish to recognise the charge of rebellion in the air.

Kieran stopped to have a break, lighting his pipe and watching the traps move along the creek beds, past the crude timber channels that balanced overhead and the litter of equipment that the fleeing diggers had left behind. It was Curtis and his lackeys and Kieran knew they wouldn't bother with him. He always paid his licence, wanting no more trouble with the law now that he was soon to be a married man, well, God willing anyway. The captain would be home next month, according to Arthur. He'd sent word from Melbourne where he'd already docked but he was spending some time with the new governor, Hotham, before he returned to Ballan.

Rumour had it the Governor would be touring the goldfields soon and, gazing around, Kieran wondered what the man would make of it; whether he would see past the rough crudity of such an existence and support the miners' cause or turn a blind eye to the growing injustices here, like so many others. Kieran looked the remaining diggers over. Only about half had stayed, which went to show just how unaffordable the licences were, and already an argument was ensuing.

Jack 'Macca' McKenzie was getting a serve from Curtis. The young man was a native colonial and typical of those he'd met so far: brash, confident and unapologetically 'Australian'. Kieran remembered thinking he would call himself an Australian when he arrived here too, back when he was in Ireland and he'd naively believed oppression would stay there, on the other side of the world. But it had followed them here, of course, and the curse of being poor Irish or, indeed, any member of the underclass, marked them all as lesser beings. Unless you had the correct accent, upbringing and, indeed, blood, you had no voice in this new land either, and little hope for justice. Even having the right to vote amounted to little for Kieran if the rest of the population weren't granted the same. The majority of landowners were elitists who would always side with the Crown, rendering his opinion of little consequence.

Kieran listened to Macca, who was putting up a brave fight. Even as a natural-born Australian this man wasn't allowed to vote, although he certainly had a voice, and his relaxed stance in the face of violent authority was admirable to those listening on.

'Listen, if I say I'll pay it tomorrow then I'll pay it tomorrow. Ya know I'm good for it, sarge.'

Kieran chuckled at the way the man spoke. The colonial accent may not be good enough for the upper crust but Kieran loved it. They tended to drawl out their vowels in a leisurely way, as if the hot climate made them take things more slowly, even their speech. And they had a penchant for shortening words or adding an 'ie', an 'a' or an 'o' on the end, especially when it came to nicknames, Macca's own a case in point. Kieran found their lackadaisical speech both colourful and humorous. There was a freedom in it, an irreverence that Kieran enjoyed hearing, especially during confrontations like now. If there was anyone around to put a bet on it, Kieran would wager Macca would win the day on bravado alone, and he eavesdropped with interest.

'Ye either pay up or ye go in the lock-up. Ye know the rules, Macca,' Curtis said, spitting tobacco on the ground and tapping his bludgeon.

'Now why would you go ahead and do a thing like that when I can't make the money for ya in there to pay the bloody thing?' Macca said, gesturing at his set-up with a shrug. 'Seems to me we both win if ya let me stay at me digs.'

'Pay it now or it's gaol, Macca,' Curtis said, obviously losing patience now. The traps were rewarded with half the fees they collected and Curtis would surely be itching to move on and bleed more men dry.

'Oh, fair go, sarge...'

'Take him, boys,' Curtis ordered.

'Now, now, hold on a sec there, fellas,' Macca said, putting up both hands as if to surrender. 'I'm sure we can come to an arrangement. How about I come find ya first thing and pop an extra fiver in the pot for ya patience?'

That seemed enough to whet Curtis's greed. 'Alright, but nine o'clock tomorrow mornin' on the dot, ye hear me?'

'Righto, sarge,' Macca said cheerfully and Curtis moved on to the next digging as Macca swaggered back to his sluice, whistling now; the fact that he'd just talked his way out of gaol for the sum of five shillings seemingly of little import. Most wouldn't have got the words out let alone be believed.

'Brilliant,' Kieran muttered to himself with amusement, turning back to his own work now, but he was halted by a shout.

'Oi! Clancy! Tell ye mate Tumulty I'm looking fer 'im!' Curtis yelled. 'I'm bettin' he hasn't paid.'

Kieran said nothing but he gave the man a nod to appease him and Curtis and his men rode off, leaving Kieran to get on with his morning. The winter sun bore down in welcome warmth and Kieran spent a quiet day of it after that until Dave made an appearance mid-afternoon.

'Everything alright then?'

'Aye,' Dave said, picking up his pickaxe to crack more rocks. He seemed restored to his usual good mood after spending time with Striker and Betty whom they'd both made close friends with these past months and Kieran was glad to hear him humming under his breath. It made him hesitate to tell Dave Curtis's message but it really had to be relayed.

'Curtis said he's looking for you. Said he's betting you haven't paid.'

Dave paused, pushing back his cap to scratch his head with a sigh. 'Maybe I should go down and do it this time. He probably won't let up.'

'I think it would be for the best especially seeing as…'

But they were cut off by the sound of hooves as Curtis showed back up, going straight over to them before they had a chance to move.

'Where's yer licence, Tumulty?' he demanded with a customary spit.

'I was just about to go and pay it, actually.'

'He was, I can vouch for that,' Kieran confirmed, nervous now as Curtis dismounted and walked over.

'Well, see, I don't think ye were, now do I? Ye thieving Irish bastard.'

Dave's expression was becoming inscrutable these days beneath his growing mass of facial hair but his eyes gave away his anger. 'I'll pay you now, if you like,' he gritted out.

Curtis would normally have accepted this but he seemed on a vendetta. Kieran guessed the bully in him was likely dissatisfied at the lack of violence in his day so far.

'Nuh, I think we might have t'teach ye a lesson this time. Tie him up, boys.'

Kieran watched in shock as they grabbed Dave and hauled him over to a big river gum nearby, pulling his arms back to fasten him to it, leaving him vulnerable and exposed to whatever came next. It was a bludgeon, held fast by Curtis as he beat Dave in the stomach and chest in sickening, heavy thuds.

'Stop it!' Kieran yelled, rushing forward, but he was met by a punch in the face then held back as he stumbled against the traps.

'Please,' he begged, but despite a few guilty glances by some of the less violent men among them, he was ignored, and for the second time in his life he had to watch his mate suffer thus, helpless to aid him.

'There,' Curtis said, standing back, his face red from exertion. 'Maybe that will make ye remember to pay next time, eh?'

Dave was slumped in agony but Kieran knew he wouldn't stay quiet, despite Kieran's internal begging that he do so.

'Maybe next time I see you I'll shove that bludgeon up...'

He didn't finish. Curtis silenced him with a final blow to the face.

A small crowd had gathered, mutinous and glaring after witnessing the popular Dave be brought so low, and Curtis looked around at them all, a manic triumph in his voice as he addressed them. 'This is what ye'll get, the lot of ye, if ye cross me. Ye seem to be forgettin' that yer only here on the Governor's good graces. From now on that's yer fate if ye don't pay what's owin' to the Crown.'

'What good's the Crown to us if we can't survive over here?' one miner called out.

'Ye've enough gold fer yer grog so ye've enough fer ye fees. I'll tie up all of ye filthy scum if I have to,' he promised loudly.

'Ale only costs a penny, not thirty fecken shillings,' said one burly man and mutterings rippled across the creek bed in agreement. He began to swing a mallet at his side and Curtis's arrogance seemed to falter as a few others picked up pickaxes and spades. He mounted his horse quickly, like the coward he was, issuing one final instruction before he made a swift exit.

'No-one touch him till dark or the same will apply to ye.'

The sound of hooves retreated and Kieran ran to do the opposite, cutting a groaning, bleeding Dave free and cursing as he looked over the cuts and welts on his friend's face and body.

The others watched on in silence then heads turned as a man came from the bushes. It was Striker, his large form casting a shadow as he approached the group, his diminutive wife Betty watching on loyally from the shade. They knew him, of course, who wouldn't recognise such a man with such a voice. He sang for them all in the pubs, articulating what was in their hearts, hidden identity intact behind his thick beard and cap, but he tended to lay low around the diggings themselves to avoid the traps. Unable to offer his friend Dave physical help, he seemed intent on offering words to them all instead, not sung this time, but heartfelt just the same.

'Yer no' here on the Governor's good graces,' he said to the crowd, his voice clear on the cool, whipping breeze. Looking over at a groaning Dave, his tone became louder. 'Yer here because yer choosing to be free, not held to the Crown. Even the English among us are treated like *rats*. They have no care fer yer lives, fer yer dignity,' he paused, taking in their faces, 'and they think they can beat ye into submission and silence? Well, lads…the time's comin' to answer a question I'd say. Are ye goin' to let them treat ye the way they treat their own back there? You: Irishmen, Scotsmen, English, Welshmen like me…do you want the hells they made fer ye back home to be replicated in another land? And you: Americans, Canadians, Germans, Italians and all the rest, who are they t'say what this new colony should be? Why indeed a colony at all?' He nodded at the Aboriginal workers and Macca. 'Why not a free country?'

Striker walked over to stand by the side of Kieran and Dave. 'We're all different yet we all have one thing in common; one truth that unites us. We are diggers, yes, but we're more than that now.' He lifted his massive fist into the air. 'We're Australian.'

A cheer rang out as other fists lifted too.

'We need to stand as one! United, lads! With respect fer one another,' he added, looking meaningfully at Kieran. 'Every man has that right and they canna take it from us.'

The breeze carried the miners' murmurs of agreement as Kieran and Striker took Dave away to have Betty treat his injuries but there was more than words flowing within it now. That charge of rebellion was now palpable, the contagion alive and swelling as it passed from one man to the next. It would have to run its course until justice prevailed. Or until further blood was shed.

Thirty

'What really happened?'

Amanda had been fooled by Kieran's story about a horse giving him a black eye but not Eve, nor Arthur. They'd shared a sceptical glance when Kieran's fabricated excuse was done but now, as they walked their lane, Eve was ready to hear the truth.

'I don't really want to tell you, love,' Kieran said. 'It's not a very nice tale.'

'I think I've seen enough of the darker side of humanity to hear it,' Eve said, old pains echoing, and Kieran took her hand. 'So, what was it? A bar-room brawl? A fight over a girl?' She was trying to lighten things but that last comment actually cost her.

'I already have the loveliest girl in the world,' he said, kissing her hand now, and she smiled.

'Stop blocking me with that charm.'

'Well,' he said, looking at the ground, 'it was actually due to a punch from a trap. You know, the troopers on the fields.'

'Yes, I know who they are.' They were notorious to most by now. 'Who was it that hit you?'

'A man called Curtis. It's his job to enforce the licence fees along our creek, only most can't afford them. They're barely surviving over there as it is.'

'Yes, I've heard that too. Thirty shillings does seem extreme.' It was in all the papers, which she read aloud to Arthur and Amanda every Monday morning.

'Aye, and he's a violent man to be doing the job. He...well, he tied Dave up to a tree and beat him with his bludgeon because he hadn't paid.'

Eve dropped his hand and stopped walking to stare, horrified. 'And you got that for trying to help him, I suppose.'

'Aye.' Kieran gingerly touched the bruise.

'Why didn't the other traps stop him?'

Kieran sighed. 'It's hard to go against the man in charge, I suppose.'

Eve shook her head, angry for Dave yet worried at how far things had deteriorated. 'What will happen now?'

'To Curtis? Nothing. He gets away with whatever he wants,' Kieran stated with a shrug but there was fire in his eyes. She'd begun to recognise that side of him more and more, the passionate, rebellious man within. Originally she'd merely thought him kind and, yes, somewhat of a risk-taker to do what he did that first day in Parramatta, but now she saw a wildness in Kieran too. And there was danger in such unpredictability.

'The miners shouldn't have to stand for that,' she said, watching his reaction closely.

'No,' Kieran said, 'they shouldn't...and they won't be.'

Eve nodded slowly. 'Is there talk of unifying and protesting?'

'Some,' he said, 'although everyone is waiting to hear what the new governor will do. Here's hoping your captain will have positive things to say to support us.'

Captain Cartwright would be joining Governor Hotham on his tour of the goldfields in two weeks' time before coming home.

It seemed both events were going to have a massive impact on their lives now.

'Kieran,' Eve said, choosing her words carefully, 'if the captain says yes to us marrying...'

'You mean when,' he corrected immediately. Amanda and Arthur were openly accepting of the two of them courting by now and Eve's hopes that the captain would allow it were quite high too, so she smiled and agreed.

'Yes, *when*, are you hoping to...to become a farmer once more?'

'Well, we'd have to settle nearby until he lets you go from service...if he does.'

'But your family want to settle further south, didn't you say? How would you afford a farm of your own around here? Or are you planning on going to them and only visiting me occasionally?'

'Of course not.'

Eve knew he had no immediate plans at all, save marriage. And she knew why. 'You're not planning to farm at all for a while, are you? You want to stay on the goldfields with your friends having adventures.'

'*No*,' he said vehemently before collecting himself. 'I want to stay there,' he acknowledged, 'but not for adventures.'

'What then?' The truth sat between them and she waited for him to admit it.

'I...want to stay for all of our sakes, to see this thing through...'

He wouldn't say the word so she said it for him. 'Is there going to be a rebellion, Kieran?'

Kieran looked away, his hands on his hips. 'I don't know.'

'Because if there is I don't want you anywhere near it.'

His eyes flicked back at her and there was a warning there now. 'Eve, you cannot ask me not to stand up for what is right. This is about justice.'

'It's about *money* and...and *violence*. And you'd risk our very futures for it!' she said, losing all composure and throwing her hands in the air. 'Do you think an English naval captain will allow his convict servant to marry a rebel? *Do you?*'

'I...haven't thought about it...'

'No. No, you haven't,' she said, tears forming now. 'Kieran,' she said, grasping his hands in hers, 'I love you so much, but if you do this, if you rebel against the authorities and end up being caught, there'll be no hope for us marrying. And there'll be no hope for your freedom...or perhaps even your life.'

Kieran was listening but he was struggling too. 'You...you cannot ask me not to stand up for what is *right*, Eve,' he said again. 'It's who I am. It's the reason we met and you fell in love with me, remember? A decent man doesn't walk away when people he cares about need him.'

'And how decent or kind would it be to break my heart once more? To break your own? Would it really be worth it then, to rebel against a power you know you can never defeat?'

'Would it be worth it not to, and know I never tried?'

She dropped his hands, hating to force it but knowing she would have to make him choose now. 'It's either a life with me or a life of protest, Kieran. It cannot be both.'

She held her breath as he stared at her for a very long moment before pulling her into his arms. 'Aye, you're right, my love. You're right.' Eve buried her face against his chest, closing her eyes in relief. 'I'll keep my head down and when we marry I'll leave the goldfields for good.'

'Do you promise?' she said, needing his vow.

He hesitated and she waited anxiously until he did. 'Aye, I promise it, love. You have my word.' Eve held him tight as he sealed his declaration with a kiss and she loved him more at that moment than any before. Because he'd given her more today than his love and his word. He'd sacrificed part of his very essence: the Irish rebel that beat in his heart.

Thirty-One

He'd avoided running into him on the goldfields with Governor Hotham as he toured, but there was no avoiding Captain Cartwright now and Kieran stared at the door nervously before knocking.

'Come,' boomed the captain's voice and Kieran took one last look outside where Eve was reading to Amanda to pass the nerve-racking time before entering.

'Ah, Mr Clancy. I must say I never thought we'd meet again but it's a small world, eh what?'

'Yes, sir. Good to see you again.'

'Brandy?' the captain offered and Kieran accepted it gladly. 'So, I hear you're quite the apothecary.'

'Well, it's more my sister Eileen, although I did learn a bit from her growing up.'

'More than a bit I'd say. I've never seen Amanda in better health and she won't stop singing your praises, let me tell you! I'd be green with envy if I wasn't tickled pink to have my wife so recovered.' He chuckled at his own joke. 'Besides, there's someone else you have your eye on, I hear.'

The captain looked over his glass at him and Kieran knew this was it: his moment to pitch. *No pressure*, he told himself, *only your entire future at stake*. He drove the thought away and focused on pouring every drop of Irish charm people said he possessed into what he said.

'It seemed fortune smiled on me twice, to run into Eve in Parramatta and now here, of all places. She was always my friend but I never expected it to evolve into deeper affections.' He paused, taking a sip of his brandy before continuing. 'You've taken such excellent care of her and given her a life of comfort that she is so grateful for but if you could see it in your heart, sir, well, I would beg one further act of generosity from you. I'd like to ask for her hand.'

'Hmm, yes, so I was warned by Amanda, romantic creature that she is,' the captain said, taking out his pipe and stuffing tobacco in. 'She's an excellent maid, I must say, and Amanda and Arthur are both fond of her, so it seems. I wouldn't be willing for her to leave our service, you understand.'

'Yes, sir, I do.'

'Although perhaps in a few years,' he conceded and Kieran felt hope leap at the words. 'I've really only one concern left.'

That paused the leaping and Kieran waited anxiously.

'You're a farmer, as I understand, yet you have been working the goldfields these past few years. Why is that?'

Kieran took another long sip of brandy before answering. 'A bit of a lark, I suppose, but I'm ready to walk away and buy a farm nearby now. I've saved enough over the years to get a modest one.'

'Just for marital reasons?'

'Aye, the goldfields are no place for a lady.'

'Yes, I saw the class of woman near there,' the captain said, shaking his head. 'Let alone some of the men. In all my born days, was there ever so much hair on men's faces?'

'Yes, sir, they tend to favour the look,' Kieran said, joining the captain in a chuckle and glad he'd chosen to be clean-shaven.

'How do you feel about this licence fee business?'

Wham, there it was, the question he'd dreaded most. Kieran kept his tone light, knowing his answer was crucial. 'It's harder for some than others. I've been lucky that it's never been an issue for me.'

'Do you think them unfair?'

'I think it would be fairer if it were based on how much gold people found,' he said carefully.

'Humph, difficult to police though, eh? Hard enough for the troopers as it is, from what I've seen.'

It took a great deal of self-control for Kieran not to react to that comment but he managed to remain quiet.

'Anyway, enough of all that. If you want to marry the girl you have my permission. Now go away and tell the damn women before my wife needs another tonic.'

Kieran closed his eyes briefly to allow the good news to wash over him before standing to take his leave.

'Thank you, sir, from the bottom of my heart.'

'Eh, well it'll be a foolish heart from now on, son. Life's never the same once a woman worms her way into it. Off you go, off you go.'

Kieran walked out and through the house, opening the door to a brightly fine if cool August day, and he looked over to the fair-haired woman of his dreams as she read in the sun.

By holy marriage: when and where and how
We met, we woo'd and made exchange of vow,
I'll tell thee as we pass; but this I pray,

Kieran stepped forward into that brilliant sunshine, finishing the verse for her:

That thou consent to marry us today

Both women turned to see Kieran's grin, which said it all, and Arthur began to cheer, overhearing as he pruned roses nearby.

'Oh, bless my good husband!' Amanda exclaimed, her dark curls bobbing as she jumped up and down, clapping, but Eve stood slowly, the little book falling onto the grass. 'Well, don't just stand there staring, girl! Go get your kiss!' Amanda said, giggling happily as Eve ran to Kieran and he lifted her and spun her through the air.

Then he held her against him as she took his face in her hands and kissed him in that sunlight, with so much love and relief infused Kieran could feel it flow into him. He let it soak through, drinking it in like it was the most precious of elixirs, before sending it back in a wave of his own, and it filled them both with private, joyful promise.

'When's the priest due back in town?' he asked, pausing to gaze at her.

'Not till December,' Arthur said from nearby and Kieran realised they still had an audience.

'So long?' Eve said disappointedly as Kieran reluctantly released her.

'We could marry in Melbourne,' Kieran suggested.

'Oh no, I insist on you having it here! It's not so long away and we've never had a party before,' Amanda said. It was a testament to how isolated Amanda's ill-health had made their lives that well-off people such as the Cartwrights could have so poor a social life. Kieran wondered who on earth she thought she could invite to her convict servant's wedding, knowing it certainly wouldn't be the Governor...nor the miners.

He'd been so focused on gaining the captain's permission he hadn't thought about when they would actually marry but now that he did December made sense. 'I have to work the claim for a while anyway on account of my mate being er...away,' Kieran reminded Eve. Dave appeared to have several broken ribs and wouldn't be fit for months. 'A December wedding would be perfect, love, and we can buy land and build our house in the meantime, not too far from here, of course,' he said and Amanda clapped her hands again happily.

'Oh, this is going to be such fun! Let's see, how many months does that give me? I'll need a new dress...actually, I think I may have some ivory material packed away...' Amanda trotted off inside to investigate and Arthur walked back to his shed to celebrate by smoking his pipe, leaving the newly betrothed alone.

'We could elope to Melbourne now if you want to avoid this,' Kieran offered with a grin, glad to have her to himself once more and drawing her close.

'No, no, we have to do it the way the Cartwrights dictate and Amanda seems intent on wearing ivory and being the bride now so...' She paused as Kieran broke into a chortle and she began to laugh herself. 'We'll have to just watch the bizarre show unfold, I suppose. Anyway,' she added, 'there's always our river.'

'My beautiful water sprite,' Kieran said, capturing her lips for another kiss. 'I say we build right alongside it so we can make love in the water at night, beneath our cross.'

'Sounds perfectly sinful,' Eve said, then she blushed at the reference to her old shame.

'No, it won't be, my love,' Kieran assured her, kissing her fingers before going on to confess, 'actually, I think it's kind of sacred in its own way. It's where I figure we really got married already, you know, that first time, when it was just you and me...and the river...'

She was still blushing but beginning to smile too as she teased him. 'You weren't being this romantic at the time, as I recall. In fact, I'm fairly certain you suggested I wear a rather scandalous mode of dress when we actually did marry.'

Amanda leaned out the window then, waving excitedly and draped in ivory silk, a sparkly crown perched crookedly on her hair.

'I found it, Eve! Look! Oh, and my debutante tiara…you must come and see…' she called, narrowly missing knocking it off as she ducked back through.

'I think at this rate I'll be lucky to rustle up any kind of outfit for myself at all,' she muttered between giggles and Kieran chuckled too as he muttered back.

'Perfectly fine by me.'

Thirty-Two

Ballarat, October 1854

It was getting harder, even for Kieran. The licence hunts were bad enough but the fact that there was less and less gold to be found just couldn't be ignored. With Dave still too sore to do very much it was up to Kieran to dig, deeper and deeper each day until his back ached and the callouses on his fingers bled. It took enormous effort and yielded little reward, made worse by the intense mood circulating on the goldfields that day.

'He won't get away with this,' Dave said, for what must have been the tenth time that morning. 'I don't care who he is.'

'He's got friends in high places,' Kieran reminded him, yet again.

'But it's cold-blooded murder!' Dave was sitting on a boulder, well enough now to be out of his bunk in their tent and back on site at the claim, but still weakened overall. He was sifting for smaller gold particles absently as they talked, an activity so habitual he barely seemed to notice when he picked little ones out and set them aside. 'Just two ordinary blokes like us, Kieran, asking the publican for a drink.'

'Aye,' Kieran said, standing to stretch his back and looking over at Dave. 'Poor Scobie.' James Scobie, a Scotsman they'd met a few times, had been clubbed and kicked to death the previous week and his friend had been badly hurt. Several men had been arrested for the murder including the owner of the newly built Eureka Hotel, James Bentley, but despite his obvious guilt, rumour had it that he would be acquitted by the police magistrate, Dewes, a close personal friend.

'That bastard Hotham won't do a thing about it, you'll see.' Despite early hopes that he would be sympathetic to their cause, the new governor's appointment had proven disastrous for the diggers. He'd inherited an unhealthy state budget from his predecessor La Trobe and he was intent on fixing things by enforcing gold licensing even further. Twice weekly, increasingly brutal licence hunts kept the miners on edge, with many pushed to extreme poverty levels now that the gold was becoming scarce and they were still forced to pay. Kieran had been wondering himself if the Governor would intervene and judging by the yells of outrage at the next claim they were all about to find out.

'What is it?' Dave called out to Jock who was standing in the group.

'That bloody murderer Bentley's been acquitted!' he called back. 'Group meeting at the old pub!'

'Come on,' Dave said, standing up, but Kieran hesitated.

'You go, I'll just finish up here first.'

Dave stared at him. 'Work can wait, Kier. This is a man's *life*.'

Kieran wavered but then Eve's face came to mind. 'I'd rather not get involved at this point.'

'Not...not get involved?' Dave said, incredulous now. 'You're the one always carrying on about oppression and freedom and the like; chucking your rocks and getting in fights with these kinds of bastards. For feck's sake, it could have been me that died the other week, or any of us when we take a beating.'

'Aye, but would good can it do to retaliate?'

'What *good* can it do? It can *change things*, Kier. That won't happen if we just do nothing.'

Kieran looked at his friend and sighed. 'Eve can't marry a rebel, Dave.'

He stared back, digesting the full scope of what that meant before replying. 'Take action or no', Kieran, you can't change who you are at heart.'

Kieran watched him as he left, angry at this new injustice and even angrier at Kieran's stance, Kieran knew. Dave was true to himself, always, whether that meant acting the clown or giving cheek, his own brand of rebellion. But there was more anger in him since his latest beating at the hands of the traps and there would be more than words flung now. Kieran could feel the impending bloodshed like an oncoming stormfront and Dave would be swept straight into its eye. Rebellion was ingrained at birth in Ireland and Dave was right, you couldn't change that part of who you are even if you tried. They'd learnt from bitter experience that the more you let men take your rights away, the more dignity you were denied; that's why every generation before them had fought against being controlled.

Yes, a life without freedom isn't a full life, Kieran reflected, yet the rebel within would remain silent, regardless. He'd sacrificed that part of his heart willingly when he'd made his vow.

For neither is a life without love.

It felt strange not to be down at the pub with his mates a few hours later and Kieran couldn't quite shake a growing uneasy feeling of disloyalty. He took out a letter from Liam to distract himself instead, re-reading the lines with pleasure. The Clancys' new land was right down by the sea and Liam had used his way with words to paint the picture clearly for Kieran. He ran his eyes over them again.

Warrnambool is cold at times, but wonderfully so when the wind carries the salt, and the view from down on the road, Kieran, well it's as spectacular as any place I've ever seen. Great limestone towers stand alongside each other like giants walking in the sea, burning in a thousand shades of orange and gold when the late sun hits. They're called The Twelve Apostles (although I have only counted eight) and it's God's work, Kieran. The waves are mighty, thirty feet at least I'm reckoning, and they pound away day and night. It's wild and it's dangerous and shipwrecks are common, sadly, but the beauty of it is truly astounding.

The children love running along the beaches down in the coves and Eileen seems happier now although still quieter than she was. She does worry over the cliffs but then again what parent wouldn't, I suppose?

The house that came with the land has far more room than our last and I cannot wait for you to come and see it all and hopefully, eventually, move here with your Eve. I'm so looking forward to meeting her when you do.

Kieran put the letter down, wishing he'd asked his family to come to the wedding now, but the idea of Eileen confronting Eve on the day was too worrisome. Besides, it was destined to be a bit of a circus with Amanda at the helm.

He stood and walked outside, staring up hopefully towards the Southern Cross but it was cloudy tonight. And dull. Perhaps it wouldn't hurt to have a beer now and listen to what they'd all decided. It had been nothing to do with his input, after all. Kieran began to walk in that direction and before he knew it he was at the pub doors but it wasn't rowdy, as he'd expected. A Welshman was talking to the crowd, who were hanging on to his every word and Kieran slipped in and leaned against the wall, listening too.

'Squatters pay only ten pounds a year and have title to over a hundred thousand acres, and they can vote and basically control the legislative council in Melbourne. What we pay in comparison is ludicrous. For every tiny piece of earth you mine and pay tax on you could afford a farm – if the bastards would let you save any money to buy one!' Murmurs of agreement followed as he continued. 'We don't have to resort to violence, gentlemen; indeed our truest weapon is constitutional. We should be fighting with our words and demanding our right to vote and make equality the law. Moral suasion will give us more power and, in the long term, more rights.'

'We tried to reason with La Trobe last year and look where it got us,' said an Irishman Kieran recognised as one of the more riotous among the diggers, Timothy Hayes. There was general agreement.

'Just because we marched on Melbourne and had our say to no avail doesn't mean we shouldn't try again. We have even greater grievances now and surely no politician could deny that this is an abuse of our basic human rights.'

'I wouldn't bet on it,' drawled Dave, prompting a few chuckles.

'Why would they care about our rights? They don't care now, when we starve or are beaten mercilessly by their tyrants,' an Italian man called out. It was Raffaello Carboni, a well-known man among them all. He was fluent in many languages and was often heard translating conversations and speeches to other Europeans. He was also notoriously theatrical. 'They would happily watch us perish and be wiped from the earth only they need to extract money from the very sweat of our heavy brows.'

'Well, yes, but just think on it until next week, lads, and in the meantime keep your heads down. We don't want any more blood being spilt.'

'Except Bentley's,' said Jock and several around him agreed.

The Welshman didn't comment further and the room soon swelled with noise as Dave made his way over to Kieran, handing him an ale.

'Good to see you haven't completely gone soft.'

Kieran chose not to comment, asking instead, 'Who was that man?'

'Humffray. He's a smart fella, solicitor or something, but he doesn't believe in violence unfortunately, as you probably heard.' Dave had returned to his usual, more affable state but he still hadn't quite lost his anger. Nor his cheek. 'Perhaps you'd like him.'

Kieran ignored that one too. 'What was the general consensus?'

Dave shrugged. 'There's talk of forming a reform league and more meetings. Apparently a crippled man was arrested for assaulting a trap so they're also trying to get him out of gaol. It's all just a fecken mess.'

Kieran nodded. 'Just don't get yourself in any fights, Dave. You're still not in very good shape.'

'They're just meetings. Why don't you come along, if you're worried, help me talk my way out of things? That isn't rebelling exactly, more like moral persuasion or whatever he called it.'

'I can't see me being of much use. None of our Irish charms work too well on the traps for some reason.'

'True,' Dave agreed. 'We should stay close to Macca. He's like a hypnotist or something,' he added, looking over at the gangly colonial. 'I wonder if we can talk him into wearing a dress?'

'Will you go?'

'Aye, only to listen like. A promise is a promise,' he added to reassure her. 'It's really just a political meeting to discuss reforms and legal rights so I doubt there'll be any trouble.'

They were lying on the river bank, bodies drying in the sun, and Eve seemed in no hurry to get dressed and go today, which suited him fine. They'd made love in an urgent, heated blur but now they were satiated it was time for more sensual, lazy pleasures as he stroked her back and she ran light nails across his chest.

'I really should get back to the tools,' he said, looking over at the half-finished frame he'd been building for their new house. Fortunately this land had been considered available for sale and Kieran had used everything he had to purchase it. He'd been excited to start putting the foundations together this Sunday and had spent the whole day doing so. Well, most of it anyway.

'What's that section going to be?' Eve asked, lifting her head to look at the frame too.

'That's the kitchen where you can look out over the river while you bake me lots of lovely cakes.'

'Baking for you, am I? I think it will be a nice view for you when you do the dishes for me.'

'Well, I suppose I could help out while you knit my socks on the front verandah.'

'Oh, a verandah. How wonderful!' she said, ignoring his jibes and getting excited now.

It motivated Kieran to jump up and put on his breeches to show her his plans. 'I was thinking a nice long one here,' he gestured, 'with the table and kitchen over there and two bedrooms off the back.'

He went on to show her where the fireplace and stove would go, along with the larder and lean-to for storage, and by the time he'd finished they were both so excited about their future they ended up making love again. On a blanket, on the ground that would soon be the location of their marital bed.

Trouble may well be building over on the goldfields but Kieran was determined to leave it all behind him in December. There were other things to build in life that were far more precious.

The meeting itself had been sensibly conducted and Kieran had been impressed with the official format and intelligent approach the leaders of the Reform League were taking to present all the issues plaguing the diggers to Governor Hotham. A man called Thomas Kennedy, in particular, gave an eloquent and impassioned speech on the importance of justice being served regarding the death of James Scobie and there was loud applause at its conclusion.

A committee of seven men was appointed, mostly ex-Chartists from Ireland, political activists who were well used to fighting for democratic freedom, and among them was a man named Peter Lalor, known to be Timothy Hayes's mining partner. Kieran observed him keenly, having already learnt from Dave that his family had been involved in the Irish struggle for independence for two generations. He had that look about him, probably a similar ferocity of countenance that Kieran had often worn himself; proud, unyielding, fierce, yet with egalitarianism at its core. Those who fought for equal rights all tended to don that mask at times such as these.

By the time the meeting began to disperse several thousand men were in attendance. Passions were high as they began their walk home, but it soon became apparent that the traps were following them in large numbers. Their presence spread unease through the crowd, slowing them down as heads turned and angry voices stirred through their ranks, until outside the Eureka Hotel they came to a halt altogether and the dissention grew into a stirring pool of unrest.

'What's up here?' Dave muttered and Kieran watched as men began to jostle with the soldiers and police.

'Bentley's in there,' Jock told them, pointing at the man's impressive but now controversial new hotel. This was being passed around in an angry chant and someone hurled gravel at the window. Bits of wood, stones and bottles followed and the fine panes shattered as the mob pulsated in frenzied outrage, their appetite for destruction incited beyond control. Kieran looked nervously over at the traps, fearing retaliation, but they were far too outnumbered to do very much and within minutes every pane was destroyed. Suddenly, a man shot out from the hotel's rear on horseback, no hat or coat to be seen, and therefore easily recognisable as Bentley. Many ran to pursue him while others ran into the building itself and crashing could be heard as they began to tear it apart.

More and more men were arriving and the crowd swelled to enormous numbers in the afternoon light, but most just watched as the main agitators did their work.

Kieran knew he should leave but it was darkly mesmerising watching such a thing unfold, the miners crawling like harvesting insects, the thuggish traps watching on angrily, and it looked to be reaching a violent crescendo as more and more military personnel arrived. But the troopers were still vastly outnumbered, despite the reinforcements, and broke suddenly to run and station themselves in the bowling alley building behind the hotel instead. Kieran wondered briefly if the violence would now be thwarted, and he knew he should feel relieved if it turned out to be so, but the Irish in his blood was up, and it wanted more action. Revenge was a powerful drug when the hunger for it had been fed for a lifetime.

Just then rags and paper were brought forward by a miner and Kieran watched, ashamed of himself and horrified now, as the man stuffed them under the calico covering of the alley. Kieran was struck by how calmly and coldly he proceeded to light a match, blinking at the reality of such blatant revenge in motion, and the fire caught quickly on the downward wind. The military could do little to stop it with the water cask now tipped over and the stables catching too.

He watched transfixed on the fringes until the whinny of horses roused Kieran to action at last, and he and Dave joined a few others in running to save the livestock inside. Other miners seemed to realise things were going too far and too fast too, and some began helping the servants escape with their belongings.

But anything deemed of ownership by Bentley was quickly destroyed.

'Argh!' called the fire-starter from before as he threw what appeared to be Mrs Bentley's jewellery box into the flames. The lady herself was heavily pregnant, and was now being evacuated, and Kieran fleetingly registered the depths of her runaway husband's cowardice.

Fire crackled and licked and soon the hotel itself was lit too, in terrible, leaping flames that devoured it hungrily. What was once the new, upscale watering hole of some of the most hardened miners, ex-convicts, traps and even bushrangers was being reduced to charcoal, the heat of it forcing the crowd to retreat and stare in silence now. The air itself seemed to melt as the building collapsed as if to its knees, crumbling further and further into the earth until only the joists and ridge poles stood tall, like fiery ribs in a carcass. They too eventually collapsed, one falling on the fine new ballroom attached, which caught alight and burnt slowly against the wind in a reluctant kind of curling.

They picked up anything that remained of Bentley's fortune and finery to feed the smouldering remains: a fence, a dray, a shay-cart, until all of his possessions were wiped from the very earth where he took a digger's life. Then they hunted through the rubble for whisky and ale, and crowed to the night that vengeance had been won, as the embers glowed and the smoke blew free.

Striker and Betty came to stand alongside Kieran, his massive arm wrapped protectively around her, and the others turned towards him as he spoke. 'The rebellion has begun, lads,' he said, 'there'll be no stopping it now.'

'Aye,' Dave agreed, looking pointedly at Kieran. 'No turning away from it either.'

'Humffray would say violence isn't the way,' Kieran reminded them, 'that we should seek justice through law.'

'This is justice,' Striker said firmly. 'Sometimes ye have to make yer own.'

But as the triumphant diggers ransacked the remnants of a wealthy murderer's world Kieran couldn't quite believe that two such enormous wrongs could ever make a right.

Thirty-Three

29 November 1854

'Beastly weather,' the captain commented and Kieran agreed politely as he sat perched on the edge of the settee, sticky from the spring heatwave and feeling awkward as Eve poured the breakfast tea in her usual role as maid.

Kieran thanked God it was only one more week until the wedding when she'd be able to go home and live with him each night. It was harder for them both since the captain had returned. He expected Eve to behave as an invisible servant, unlike Amanda who wanted her company for entertainment, but right now the lady of the house seemed oblivious to anyone but herself.

'I must say, this new morning tonic your sister sent is wonderful, Kieran,' she told him, leaning back to sip her tea. 'I'm literally bouncing out of bed, aren't I, Charles?'

'I think bouncing may be pushing things a little far,' he returned but there was amusement there as he glanced at her above his spectacles.

'Pooh, I do so bounce,' she admonished. 'Oh, look at Arthur's roses. How lovely.'

Arthur was bringing in an armful of red and orange blooms and he laid them on the side counter before standing back to look at them. 'Pity they bloomed too early fer the weddin' an all but they'll brighten the house anyways.'

'What are these ones called?' Kieran asked. Arthur had been enjoying teaching Kieran about his hobby these past months.

'This 'ere's an Old Red Moss.'

'Well, that wouldn't have been very romantic,' Kieran noted. 'Still, they say a rose by any other name would smell as sweet,' he added with a flick of a smile at Eve.

'I'm usually a fan of Shakespeare but I can't say I quite agree with him there,' Amanda said, giggling. 'What are the cream ones for the wedding called?'

'Great Maiden's Blush.'

There was general laughter at that.

'As long as they're in bloom and ready in time, I don't mind. They'll be a perfect match for my dress,' Amanda said.

'I thought you were wearing green,' the captain said.

'Oh, Charles, that was *weeks* ago. Try to keep up, won't you?' she told him. 'I'm back to wearing the ivory that I found the material for in the trunk.'

'Shouldn't the bride be the one wearing that expensive guff?' the captain queried with a yawn.

'Eve doesn't care what she wears,' Amanda said, flapping her hand. 'She's just happy to be getting married, all things considered.' Kieran shifted in his chair uncomfortably and Amanda seemed to recognise she'd said something insensitive. 'No offence, at all. It's just that you don't get many beaus knocking on your door around here, now do you, Eve?'

'No, ma'am,' Eve said, and Kieran was glad to see she didn't seem offended. In fact, she was smiling.

'Yes, although there are plenty of men nearby in those goldfields. Fortunately they didn't know there was a decent-enough young woman nearby. We might have had another riot,' the captain said, flicking his newspaper and looking over at Kieran now. 'Any friends of yours involved?' he asked casually but there was a warning in the tone as the genial mood shifted.

It would be a mistake to answer in the affirmative. The headlines were bold and damning:

Melbourne reinforcements attacked by miners – soldiers injured.

'No, sir,' Kieran lied, knowing most of them were. It had been difficult to resist joining them over the past few weeks and it was especially hard today, when a huge meeting would take place on Bakery Hill.

The Reform League had gone to Melbourne to petition Governor Hotham and the Head of the Gold Commission, Commissioner Rede, to abolish licence fees, grant suffrage and democratic representation, and disband the Commission altogether. They'd also demanded the release of several men who'd been arrested over the burning down of the Eureka Hotel, but they were deemed demands too far, the lot of them. He'd refused to consider any of their requests at all and appointed a Royal Commission to investigate matters on the fields instead, but it was conducted by Rede himself, which was considered the biggest insult of all. Well, the miners knew he regarded them all as 'rabble'. Rather than listen to their grievances he'd increased police presence and summoned reinforcements. Brutal attacks had continued as the forces marched and an ambush to halt their approach seemed the miners only choice. Not that the captain knew any of those facts.

'They talk of democracy and yet they use force. Listen to this Humffray character: *It is the inalienable right of every citizen to have a voice in making the laws he is called on to obey…taxation without representation is tyranny*. Tyranny, is it? And what of attacking government troops? I know what I'd do with them if I were Hotham.' The captain flicked at his paper and Kieran reminded himself that the man was in the military himself and served the Crown. His views were to be expected, if ill-informed.

'Humffray is actually against using any force...'

'Well, he's not much of a leader if he has so little control over his so-called men, now is he?'

'He's their chairman, not their leader.'

The captain was staring at him now and Kieran knew he should shut his mouth on the subject.

'You seem to know a lot about this.'

'Difficult not to when you're still living among it,' Kieran replied, trying to sound nonchalant.

'Well, I don't see why *we* have to live near such people, yourself excluded, Kieran dear. You'd think the authorities would remove that shanty town and make way for proper society,' Amanda said, sipping her tea in bemusement. 'So much unpleasantness to deal with.'

Kieran swallowed his resentment at those words, knowing he'd already said more than he should, but somehow he couldn't bring himself to let that comment slide. 'It really runs rather effectively, for what it is. If there were less beatings over licence fee payments. I think we'd see an end to all of this "unpleasantness", as you say.'

'Humph,' the captain said. 'I doubt things would settle down so easily. I've seen enough war in my lifetime to know when a battle is brewing, I could feel it when I was there myself. This skirmish is nothing to what's coming, I dare say; I hope you've enough sense to stay well away, Kieran.' The captain looked at him sternly now and Kieran nodded solemnly, reminding himself of his vow.

'Of course, sir,' he said, his eyes flicking to Eve who was listening on nervously now, her beautiful eyes wide. 'A soon-to-be-married man has other priorities on his mind than getting himself involved with law-breakers.'

'Good man, good man. Dance with the devil and repent all your days,' the captain advised, 'marry a good woman and repent regardless, but at least you'll live.'

Arthur chuckled from where he'd been quietly listening nearby and Kieran joined him, although it was forced. The conversation changed then, flowing down safer, wedding-themed channels, but as he sat and sipped his tea and made polite small-talk with an English sea captain Kieran couldn't help but feel somewhat of a traitor. Then Dave's voice came to mind, unbidden yet difficult to silence.

Take action or no', Kieran, you can't change who you are at heart.

'I can't believe this is the last time you'll leave me here,' she was saying as they stood on their lane. Her face was partially shadowed by the treetops dancing in the late morning light and Kieran was mesmerised by it, as he so often found himself. It wasn't just her beauty, it was the kindness that poured out of her, lighting the depths of her eyes and bending her lips into easy smiles whenever she looked at him.

'I can't believe this time next week you'll be my wife.'

'Yes, and I don't know what I'd do if it wasn't so.' The smile was changing now, sliding into a worried expression and he took her fingers and kissed them, as he was prone to do whenever she appeared nervous. 'Kieran...I...I think it's time I told you something...'

Kieran watched her, confused, until it occurred to him what she was trying to confess. 'I think I understand,' he told her, in what he hoped was his most reassuring tone. 'I don't care what crimes you've committed in the past, love. I never did. It's the goodness that I see, that I *know* resides in you, that matters to me.'

'C...crimes?'

'Crimes, accusations...it matters none. I know the last thing you would ever do is knowingly harm another soul and that's good enough for me.'

'Well, I...I *would* like to tell you the whole story...one day perhaps...but not now...there's something else more...well, pressing.'

Her hesitation confused him and she was looking at him very strangely, a myriad of emotions crossing her face, and he quite honestly had no idea what on earth she would come out with. Certainly not what came next.

'I'm carrying your baby.'

Kieran's jaw dropped to a gape, the word soaking into his brain. 'Babe...baby?'

'Yes,' she said, a telltale blush surfacing, 'that's what happens when...well, you know...' She paused to watch him, biting her lip. 'Are you unhappy with the news?'

A rush of shock then wonder swept through him. 'Un... unhappy with the...' Then he lost all ability to speak and hugged her close instead, pure joy consuming him now. 'We're going to be a family...?'

He pulled back, incredulous and holding her shoulders, beaming his exhilaration until her expression lit too.

'Yes, yes a...family,' she said, as if tasting the word. It was one he'd always considered the most precious of all, even above freedom, and now, impossibly, even more so. It made him silently vow he would unite his siblings and nephews with her before the year was out. His wife and child deserved to know the Clancy clan too.

'I know I've told you I love you about a hundred times but it's never been stronger than right now.' She smiled then and he kissed her, pouring that enormous love into it and wishing he could find a better way to express how he felt than with those few short, clumsy words. Then a Shakespearean line came to him, perfection within it, of course, and he stroked her face as he quoted it. *'This is the very ecstasy of love.'*

She giggled. 'My goodness, how charming you are, sir.'

He grimaced then. 'I'm sure someone more dashing would have got away with it. Where's those damn destiny stars when you need them?' he added, looking up at the clear spring sky.

'It is not in the stars to hold our destiny but in ourselves,' she quoted.

'Bloody hell, she's even better at quoting Shakespeare than me,' he told the heavens. 'How is it you sound perfectly sensible saying that when I'd come across like a bloody great idjit?'

'Because I'm a woman and we're supposed to be sentimental,' she told him.

'Well, sentimental or not I bloody well do love you, Eve Richards, and I swear with all my heart that I can't wait for you to be Eve Clancy and have our baby.'

'Yes, I'd noticed that you were swearing it,' she said, giggling now.

'I don't know what it is about you,' he sighed, feigning defeat. 'I used to be quite the smooth-talker when it came to the ladies.'

'So what happened to you, then?'

He laughed as he drew her close, brushing his lips on her forehead. 'Cheeky minx. I suppose I'm far more interested in making dozens of sweet bairns instead.'

She took one of his hands, still smiling, and placed it over her stomach between them. 'Let's just start with one.'

He felt the spot reverently and it was an incredible feeling, knowing the woman he loved would produce a child that was a blend of them both, an actual product of that very bond. Kieran finally understood it, this parental wonder, but then Eileen's face suddenly leapt to mind and a protective rush moved through him instead.

'You'll have to be very careful from now on. No heavy lifting anymore and you'd best ask Arthur to fetch all the wood and water.'

'I'm fine,' she assured him. 'And I don't need mollycoddling. Besides, we'll have to keep this a secret and pretend it's an early baby when the time comes. Amanda would have a fit if she knew it wasn't really a white wedding.'

'She'd have to change her dress!'

Eve laughed hard at that and Kieran drank in the sound, committing it to memory before he had to leave.

'A week is too long to wait,' he told her, hating to go.

'It'll pass quicker for you than for me. There's a lot going on around you from I've heard,' she said, her voice faltering. 'Kieran…'

'You don't have to say it, lass. Only a true fool would mess with this destiny now.'

Those words followed him later, as he paused at the crossroads down the track. He'd gone to visit Eve early because he'd planned to work on the house for the rest of the day but he was torn now. He'd meant what he said: he wouldn't be getting involved with law-breakers and risk his Eve-filled future but he couldn't quite bring himself not to watch events unfold. This was history in the making, surely, something his old countrymen had long dreamed of: to make a stand for freedom that could possibly succeed. Kieran found himself heading home to witness it, doing what he really shouldn't do, where he was greeted by an excited Dave.

'You're coming to the meeting then?'

'I'm thinking about it.'

A flyer sat on the table and Kieran picked it up, reading the stirring words and trying hard not to be affected by them.

Down with the licence fee!
Down with Despotism!
Who so base as be a slave?

'Humffray's going to tell us they've had no luck with his latest petition,' Dave said, talking in a rush as he pulled on a clean shirt, his face fleetingly pained from his still-sore broken ribs. 'This is it, Kieran. I can feel it.'

'It's just a meeting,' Kieran reminded him, more to reassure himself that it was acceptable to be attending it.

'Aye, and look what happened after the last.'

Kieran followed Dave out towards Bakery Hill, past the new buildings and neat shopfronts above the diggings that sat paradoxically near the burnt-down pub, and he tried not to think of angry flames, telling himself he'd leave this time if it came to violence. The crowd swept him along, swelling into thousands, and voices rang out in a fevered way as they marched upwards, united by their common cause.

'Down with licences! Down with the traps!'

They formed an enormous circle around the Reform League delegation who announced the result of their dealings with Hotham. Bentley and his accomplices had been re-tried and found guilty of manslaughter but this was the only piece of justice the miners had been granted. Despite thirty thousand signatures, all demands for fairer licence fees, democratic representation and their right to vote had all been refused. Humffray's non-violent, political approach had failed in the eyes of the diggers and open defiance was fast taking its place.

Timothy Hayes, the rebellious Irishman Kieran had recognised before, stood tall and addressed them all loudly as the new chairman.

'If one man goes to the lock-up for not having a miner's licence would a thousand of you go to liberate that man? Would two thousand?' The crowd cheered and he held his arms wide. 'Would you be willing to die?'

The crowd erupted in shouts of agreement as the chant rose: 'Burn your licence!'

Many did, hoisting them high, and Kieran itched to burn his own as he watched Dave take his out and light it too but of course he couldn't go that far. Yet he could soak in the atmosphere as men from countries from around the world united together, their ties stronger now than ever before. Even the newly arrived Chinese joined them in their fight as fists punched the air and burning licences were flung.

It was a dangerous game but none seemed to care; they'd been pushed too far by injustice, poverty and brutality now. Most had fled their home countries to escape oppression and they wouldn't accept it here, in this new, hopeful place. It raged inside of Kieran, the desperate urge to resist too, deep in that rebellious core of his heart.

Dave's words continued to ring true: he couldn't change who he was. He couldn't just wipe a lifetime of tyrannical treatment away. There was only one thing capable of stopping him joining in as he clenched and unclenched his right fist tight: the sacred place inside Eve where his unborn child lay. For it wasn't about who he was, anymore. Now the only thing that mattered was the man he could be.

'The traps are out today.'

Out in force. Rede's reaction to the news that miners were burning their licences now had been swift and severe. Even Macca had been beaten at the diggings this morning and he lay in a bleeding, moaning mess as Curtis and his lackeys moved towards

Kieran, Jock and Dave. A large throng had gathered and mutinous murmurs were rising in pitch as they faced the trio.

'Where's yer licences, boys?'

'I seem to have misplaced it,' Dave said, glaring as Curtis reached for his bludgeon. 'I wouldn't take that out again, if I were you.'

A rock was hurled, landing at Curtis's feet and more men gathered close, restless and stirring.

'Soldiers are on the way from Melbourne,' Curtis replied loudly, although he looked nervous as the diggers encircled them.

'Bring as many of yer fancy redcoats as ye like. Ye'll no make us cower to ye,' came a voice and the huge form of Striker moved forward as Betty watched on, characteristically loyal.

Curtis was pale now, as well he should be in the face of such a goliath. Something inside Kieran swelled at the sight of a marked man facing the traps, defiant and steadfast by their side now.

More traps rode into the crowd and a flurry of rocks were hurled, the situation growing more intense by the minute as numbers on both sides swelled and attempted arrests were made on several miners, including a now fist-wielding Jock. Bludgeons swung, the thud of bruising and the cracking of bones could be clearly heard among the sudden rioting, and by the time Kieran could make sense of the blurred violence that had taken place he saw that eight men had been chained, including their friend Jock.

Shoving and abuse flooded across the mauling fray but still Kieran stood back, desperately resisting going to Dave's aid now as his weakened mate was thrown to the ground. Watching Jock cop a fist while his hands were cuffed and try to throw one back was likewise excruciating. And when a limping, bleeding Macca came over to support Striker's push against several traps beating on an Aboriginal miner, Kieran had to hold onto a tree branch to physically force himself not to go over and help.

'This is the last of it!' Striker yelled as the traps finally moved off, taking the defaulters with them, including a bloodstained Jock, and leaving an incensed, angry mob behind.

'There'll be no more of this!' Dave joined in, panting and spitting out blood as he looked over at Kieran who still held the tree. 'No more.'

Thirty-Four

1 December 1854

The flagpole was tall, eighty foot or so by Kieran's reckoning, and a great Southern Cross sewn on blue silk flew at its crest as a glorious new standard for the thousands of men who gathered in a ring below it. Kieran watched those familiar stars dance against a sky that was brilliantly lit as the sun approached the west, and the rays stretched out, lighting the clouds in gold as if God himself were blessing this moment.

Captain Ross of Toronto was responsible for the new flag on Bakery Hill and he stood below it, sword in hand, surrounded by the newly appointed rifle division.

Humffray was absent today as a new leader, a commander-in-chief, stood alongside chairman Hayes now, holding the muzzle of his own rifle at his side. It was Peter Lalor, strong and stern. The mask of rebellion in place.

Many of the thousands gathered were armed now, although few could afford rifles. Mostly they sported handmade weapons or gold-digging implements, but it was enough for Kieran to know that this would be the last time he would come. He could no longer ignore the fact that the miners weren't holding 'meetings' anymore. This was a declaration of independence from the Crown. This was war.

Lalor didn't waste time with speeches about legalities; it was too late for such talk now. Instead he began a ceremony.

'It is my duty now to swear you in, and to take with you the oath to be faithful to the Southern Cross. Hear me with attention. The man who, after this solemn oath, does not stand by our standard is a coward in heart. I order all persons who do not intend to take the oath to leave the meeting at once.'

Kieran tried to walk away but his drumming Irish heart wouldn't let him. Just a few more words; just to always remember that he was here this day to hear them. That that heart swore in if not his voice.

'Let all divisions under arms "fall in" in their order round the flagstaff.'

Several hundred men in freshly formed divisions came forward with their captains who now stood as one to offer the military salute to Lalor. They wore no unifying clothing, no signature motif to mark their kinship, yet there was no need for such distinction; their loyalty to one another was written in the strained lines of their collectively determined countenance. Lalor knelt then and raised his right hand towards the flag and his next words carried firmly across the thousands present.

'We swear by the Southern Cross to stand truly by each other and fight to defend our rights and liberties.'

'Amen,' said the throng, and right hands were raised to the silk stars that seemed to fairly blaze in the glorious sunlight. Kieran looked out across them all, at the sea of different coloured hair, skin, shaggy beards or no. Dave's hand was raised, as was Striker's who'd even removed his much-treasured cap. Betty held it, watching him with pride. Macca and Jock were making their oath too and it took every emotion Kieran felt for his bride and his unborn child not to raise his own hand as well.

Dave looked over at him, disappointment in his eyes, but Kieran would have defended his stance if the silence didn't feel quite so sacred. For there were other stars to follow, ones that would lead him to true freedom. Love had chosen where his real loyalties lay.

Thirty-Five

3 December, 1854

It was his wedding day but he was alone that morning. Dave would be unable to attend as best man, in fact none of his friends would have been able to come, even if Kieran could have talked the Cartwrights into inviting them. The violence had escalated even further these past few days with Kieran now hearing cracks of gunfire echo across the bush, a sickening and terrifying sound as the traps actually shot at fleeing unlicensed miners. It further justified the sight of Lalor's makeshift 'troops' training in fierce fashion under Hayes.

They were still barely armed but they'd certainly become increasingly more formalised as a military unit, even physically removing themselves from the diggings to form a base or 'stockade' as they'd taken to calling it. It was at a formerly quiet mining spot nearby called Eureka, but Kieran imagined it was, by now, a crowded den of industry as the miners barricaded themselves inside as best they could. Dave was over there, along with the rest of their mates, awaiting the law who would surely come to strike them down, and Kieran had spent the past few lonely nights sleepless with nausea and worry over their fate.

They were his last here on the goldfields, and the place felt eerie and empty with so many gone and facing such danger. Everything lay waiting: sluices, carts, ropes and pans, all left to sit in the dust and mud, idle as the diggers turned their hands to darker, more desperate pursuits. Kieran's own things were mostly gone now, with his wagon packed up, and he and Eve would move into their home tonight, which was now partially completed, enough for them to be protected from the elements at any rate. It should have been the happiest day of his life but, with the threat of bloodshed on the horizon, he couldn't consider it so. Maybe the government would see sense and negotiate. Surely they wouldn't stoop so low as to massacre hundreds, if not thousands, of poorly armed miners in cold blood.

It was no use in trying to sleep in with that in mind so he got up, deciding to take his belongings to the house and get ready for the day instead. It seemed strange to leave his and Dave's dwelling after so long, and looking around at the now bare bunks, the worn table, the empty barrel of rum that stood pride of place on their only shelf, Kieran felt concern for his friend swell into sadness that these times would never come again. He'd spent most days and nights in Australia in Dave's company and now he was choosing a woman over his mate when he needed him most. *You're choosing a family*, Kieran reminded himself, *and a home on Clancy land, Clancy owned.*

He sighed, putting on his coat and stepping out into the still-dark morning to place his remaining belongings on the wagon and begin his journey towards his new life. To a beautiful wife, a baby. That was true freedom, better than any brand of rebellion. And looking up at the stars he knew, despite his inner conflict, he was following the right cross.

It was a quiet journey, the wagon wheels and the horse the only sounds aside from insects and birds, the kookaburras making quite a racket. He spied a koala in the lamplight too, moving along the side of the track to climb a tree, its joey clinging to its back. It made a scratching noise as it went, moving faster than Kieran would have supposed, but then he saw a couple of emus running by, making a racket of their own, and understood the koala's desire to get out of the way. Emus liked to peck. They liked to march too, in their funny ungainly way; it even sounded like human marching. Kieran paused, pulling the horse to a halt. That *was* human marching and it definitely wasn't emus making the sound.

He turned off the lamp and pulled the wagon over to the trees, managing to hide it in a track that led to a homestead across the way. The sound of boots became louder and Kieran peered out to watch as soldiers began to march by. Hundreds of them, all in red coats, followed by rows of traps. This was no small contingent, this looked like an army, all carrying rifles and meaning business. Sent on a bloody errand, Kieran well knew: to wipe out the miners at the Eureka Stockade.

Looking up to where their stars were now fading in a rising mist, Kieran sent out an apology to Eve because he knew he would probably be late to their wedding today. But it was no flimsy excuse: the redcoats were coming to kill the best friend he'd ever had. And he didn't need to have sworn an oath to know he owed allegiance to that.

His horse was tiring but Kieran pushed him on as hard as he could, knowing he would beat the on-foot troops but not by long, and he needed to give as much warning to the diggers as he could. The stockade was up ahead, a makeshift, roughly constructed affair consisting of wooden planks and overturned carts with sharp pikes at the edges, and Kieran noted there weren't as many miners inside as he had supposed. Then again it was Sunday and a lot of the Irish Catholics would have slipped off to attend Mass. It was a crude, dilapidated affair but the Eureka flag fluttered proudly above it, the stars shining in the pre-dawn and firelight.

'Who goes there?' called out one man and Kieran told him who he was before dismounting and leading his horse over.

'Kieran?' called out Dave, coming out of the crowd and staring at him, incredulous. 'You came!' he exclaimed, rushing forward to shake one hand and clap him on the shoulder with the other. 'I knew you would, brother, I knew it.'

'I'm only here to…warn you,' Kieran said in a rush, still panting from the exertion of the ride. 'The redcoats…and the traps… they're on the way in their hundreds. They're heavily armed,' he finished, looking over at Peter Lalor and Raffaello Carboni who were approaching them now.

'Look,' called out Jock as he came over too, and he pointed to the horizon where the soldiers could be glimpsed, eerie and menacing in the pale, misty light, as they amassed with the traps to attack the stockade. Kieran knew his window to escape was closing fast.

'I have to go, Dave,' he told his friend. 'It's my wedding day…'

'Aye,' Dave said. 'I suppose you do.'

Striker had come forward, and now Macca and a few others Kieran knew well, and he looked around at them all, terrified as the sound of marching could be heard once more.

'God be with you,' Kieran told them, unable to restrain himself from giving Dave a quick embrace.

'Aye, mate,' Dave said, his voice breaking, 'and with you too.'

Kieran went then, running off behind the stockade and making his long way around back to the road, leading his horse then mounting. The miners were scurrying now, preparing for battle, and Kieran felt like the rat leaving the sinking ship but there was nothing else for it, especially today of all days. He'd been a loyal enough friend to warn Dave and the others but he needed to be a loyal husband and father now. Other vows needed to be made today.

But then the crack of gunshot sounded and Kieran closed his eyes as a cry of pain echoed among it.

'God be with you,' he whispered again, unwilling to open them and witness what was unfolding, knowing it would sear his mind and shadow his days. But then he found himself pulling the reins and turning to do just that. Something inside reasoned he could give them that much, at least.

It was difficult to even conceive what greeted him as the impossibility of the scene slammed into his senses, yet there was no denying the sight of uniformed soldiers and police advancing in orderly lines towards the ill-equipped miners in the fogged glow of early morning. They were fighting as best they could behind their flimsy barricades, but it was futile, and man after man began to fall, like toys being toppled over in a child's game from here, and yet they were flesh and blood. Being torn and ripped, to lie deathly still on the cold bush floor.

The gunfire was thick, and deafening now, but it couldn't quite drown out the cries of injured and dying men. The terrible cacophony jarred and assaulted in turn.

Sickeningly, the bullets found more marks and blood quickly stained shirts and jackets, draining the life from their wearers, too easily, too fast. Kieran tried to blink the images away as men he recognised, worked with, drank with, hardworking men as honest as the day was long, fell in defence of what was only their right to be able to exist, after all. But that right was being denied in fatal, violent fashion today.

The redcoats were trained to kill and doing a professional job of it, methodically mowing the miners down, who were hopelessly outclassed. Striker's big form was clearly visible, even from a distance, and Kieran watched in paralysed horror as the big man fell, still trying to wield his pickaxe as he went. Then, terrifyingly, Betty ran over from the trees, begging them for mercy, but they struck her too and Kieran's eyes flickered with shock as they beat them both to death. Pitiful, cold-blooded murder.

'Oh dear God...no...'

Another man was caught straight in the chest and flung across Striker and Betty's forms, adding to what was becoming an impossibly tragic pile of bodies, and the sight sent Kieran's focus reeling about now as he searched frantically for Dave. He found carnage wherever it landed, recognising far too many of the casualties, including Jock who was writhing on the ground holding a tattered leg. Perhaps he would survive, Kieran thought with a numb kind of desperation.

It should have been over in minutes. The miners soon surrendered, but many of the redcoats and traps ignored their capitulation. Hands were raised in the golden sunlight as dawn finally ignited the scene but they soon fell as merciless troops marched into the stockade, to bludgeon and stab at will.

'Stop it! *Stop!*' Kieran heard himself screaming, tears pouring down his face as arms and legs were maimed, stomachs cut open and finishing shots fired. Then he recognised Dave at last, cornered with his hands on his head, a bayonet at his throat. '*No*,' Kieran yelled, pushing his horse into a canter towards him, all vows evaporating as his loyalty-torn heart finally seemed to explode in a wave of terror and grief.

Then there was a shot, just a final single one, and everything in Kieran Clancy's world suddenly turned dark.

Thirty-Six

It was warm in the little church as the small party assembled inside waited in a strained hush, pocket watches sporadically checked as the endless minutes slipped away. Eve stared at the door, desperate for Kieran to materialise, her entire body rigid as fear mounted and spread, a small bouquet of Arthur's roses clenched in her hands. Her simple navy dress too tight.

Amanda broke the silence, asking if they should find out if anyone had seen him along the road, had he been robbed? Attacked? How could he not turn up? Her ivory gown rustled as she paced, cream roses bobbing as they poked through her tiara, and the priest asked if the bride would like a drop of church wine to calm her nerves. He was talking to Amanda.

Suddenly someone did appear at the door, only it wasn't who they all hoped for. It was Barney, the local delivery man, and he was white-faced as he told his news.

'There's been a battle…over at the Eureka lead.'

The captain came immediately forward. 'The miners?'

'Aye. They ne'er stood a chance though. The soldiers 'ave arrested plenty but there's many more who'll no' see the light o'day again.'

Eve simply stared at him as the words began to swim in her mind. Around and around. Incomprehensible.

'How many souls?' the priest asked.

'Dozens, I'd say, and a whole lot injured too, poor blighters.'

'Traitors to the Crown,' the captain reminded him.

'Maybe so, sir, but the bastards went in and butchered the injured and surrendering men, which is a mongrel act, if ye ask me. Pardon me French,' he added.

'B...butchered?' Eve said, dropping to a church pew now.

'Now, now, Eve. Kieran wouldn't have been involved, I'm sure of it. He'll come soon, love, you'll see,' Arthur reassured her, coming over to her side.

'Oh no! Kieran would never do such a thing – especially today of all days,' Amanda agreed, fanning her flushed face.

'He'd no' risk marrying you for anyone or anything,' Arthur said firmly.

But Eve knew with sudden, devastating certainty it was exactly what he'd done; it was too much of a coincidence that the battle had occurred at the same time as Kieran not turning up for their wedding. There was only one reason on earth he would do this, something even bigger than his love for her.

'To do what is right,' she muttered vaguely.

The others began to whisper among themselves although their worried eyes followed her as she moved to the church entrance to gaze out at the empty path. It was a glorious day as the world welcomed the first Sunday of summer in stunning sunshine but it just looked grey to Eve. It was as if all the colour had been stolen from the earth and, as she stared at the small cemetery nearby, a terrible dread came to the fore.

'I need to...to know...'

Arthur came to stand next to her. 'What was that, love?'

'I need to know, Arthur,' she said, urgently now. 'Please,' she begged him and he looked over at the captain who nodded his permission.

'Aye, I'll go see what I can find out. Why don't ye go home and wait...'

'No,' she said, immediately shaking her head. 'I'd rather stay here.'

Arthur nodded in understanding. 'To pray?'

'No,' she admitted, looking back outside. 'It's just where he'll come if he...if...'

If he's still alive, the unspoken words rang between them. But as he limped away a murder of crows called plaintively from the tower above, a death knell where wedding bells should rightly have been ringing.

It was late in the day when the wagon could finally be heard. The captain and Amanda had long returned home but Eve had been allowed to stay. In truth, they seemed relieved to let her do so. The captain had told her to 'hold fast' but no-one seemed capable of looking her in the eye.

But now one man was: Arthur, slumped in his seat, his countenance telling a story of devastation and now heartfelt pity. Eve's chest constricted in an unbreathable vice as he stepped down to take her hands in his.

'It's no' good news, Eve.'

She didn't speak. She couldn't. But he did, the next sentence uttered with impossible finality.

'I saw the list of the dead, love. His name was on it.'

'No,' she said, shaking her head. 'I refuse...I refuse to believe it...'

'Eve...'

'He cannot...be...'

A suffocating pain surfaced then as she choked on her words and Arthur gently held her as wrenching sobs began to escape; wave after wave of them as she heaved with unbearable grief.

'*He cannot be.*'

'Aye,' Arthur said, wiping tears too, 'I'm afraid so. I'm so sorry, Eve; he was such a good lad.'

Was. People would ever talk of him as something in the past now. The late Kieran Clancy. Her wonderful, charming, handsome fiancé. The kindest man on earth.

'I want to see him,' she whispered brokenly.

'They'll no' let anyone near, probably because o' the way they…' He didn't finish the sentence and she tried not to imagine how it would have ended. 'Anyway, they did give me his cap.'

Eve took it from his hand, stroking the worn rim where his name was written with shaking hands. 'I…I never saw him wear this one.'

'Perhaps it was only fer best. It was his wedding day after all.'

She raised her face to Arthur's red-rimmed eyes and shook her head brokenly. 'How could he have done this, Arthur?'

A tear rolled down his craggy face as he replied. 'Men have many kinds of loyalty runnin' through their veins, lass.'

It was the rawest of truths, and it tore at her. Once again in her life she hadn't been the one her lover was loyal to. She simply hadn't been enough.

Arthur led her to the cart, helping her up before climbing awkwardly on board himself and she stared at the little church and the gravestones nearby, knowing this place, this scene, would ever haunt her now.

Then the crows circled the sky as the curse of woman descended on Eve Richards once more and she lay her hand across her stomach. Helpless to change what lay beneath.

The captain and Amanda had debated it endlessly but his final argument eventually swayed her.

'It's not the right place for you anymore.'

'But it's over now. The troublemakers are all in gaol awaiting trial,' Amanda had reminded him. No mention had been made of the soldiers or police and the massacre they had performed, nor would the dead be mentioned, especially Kieran Clancy. Eve had known he wouldn't be. After Amanda's hysterics at the news of his passing the captain had declared his name not be spoken from there on. *Too distressing*, he'd termed it.

'Bah! You can't trust the rest of that rabble over in the goldfields not to keep stirring up trouble. The area's become unsafe, my dear; there's far too much violence on our doorstep.'

'Too much unpleasantness.' Amanda had agreed on that.

And so, a decision was made for the household to up and leave with the captain next week when he took his ship to Adelaide, the only Australian town to not be founded on convict settlement. A place worthy of an English sea captain's family.

And all the while Eve listened on as if from a distance, remembering that other-worldly feeling from days long past. That feeling that comes when you desperately dread something happening, and when it finally does you stop feeling any emotion at all. Because aside from her initial reaction she'd since been dry-eyed. Shocked, she supposed. But emotion would return, as she well recalled, and with it more of those rare comforting tears.

Yet it would take more than tears to cope with the months ahead when she was eventually thrown out, pregnant and alone, or sent back to prison in disgrace. Robbed of a life filled with laughter and love. Eve, the sinner, once more.

Letting her heart rule had destroyed her again but she still believed Kieran had meant his solemn vow, he just couldn't change who he was, in the end, any more than she could have stopped the inescapable force of loving him. And be willingly chased and caught.

Eve went to the window and stared out at the sky, to where their stars would appear when the sun went down. People said the miners had them on a flag now, she and Kieran's Southern Cross, brilliant against a sea of blue silk. The very stars Eve had thought would bless them, the ones that would lead him home, had stirred the rebel in his heart to action, and now she faced life alone.

And so Eve would board yet another ship, to start again, on another shore. Time would reveal the truth as her belly swelled and she'd be cast from the garden. Betrayed by that foolish heart; her weak and sinful flesh.

An unnatural life her destiny, after all.

By Any Other Name

Thirty-Seven

Warrnambool, Victoria, December 1854

The gulls were riding high and Liam watched them, mesmerised and feeling their flight as if it were his own as they soared, then dipped and sailed across the gigantic granite cliffs below. It wrenched at his soul more than usual, possibly because of the wildness of the wind that afternoon. It whipped at the ocean as it hurled itself in almighty thunderous crashes against the cliffs, dwarfing the cove entrances and making a mockery of the tiny human who watched on.

Indeed, he felt not only small but humble before such majesty and terror, well knowing the power this southern ocean could inflict on humanity, having seen numerous shipwrecks or at least their aftermath since arriving here six months ago. Whenever the emergency bell rang out from town it made his new preoccupation with loneliness seem insignificant, but it was there, all the same.

It seemed strange to be lonely when you lived with two other adults and three children but somehow Liam was. A new restlessness had begun since they'd moved here, a need for other companionship that stirred and crashed like this mighty sea, and he knew he would have to do something about it, but where to find it…or more precisely *her*, eluded him. He'd always liked women, of course, but back in Ireland he'd been shy where Kieran had been bold, awkward and tongue-tied where Kieran had been charming, and women had found him almost invisible next to his older brother as a result. But that was in the past now. He'd been living his own life in Australia long enough now to surely step out of his brother's shadow, as nerve-racking as that seemed.

Perhaps it was time for a trip, as Rory had astutely suggested the other day, a visit to Melbourne or Adelaide to see if he could summon the courage to talk to a woman somewhere, somehow. Lord knew there were few of them here in this tiny new town of Warrnambool.

Liam walked back along the road towards home, still deep in thought as Eileen waved frantically from a distance and he sighed. What on earth was his sister panicking about now, betting one of the children had wandered off exploring again. But it seemed there was real news that had stirred her as she held up a newspaper and called out.

'Hurry!'

Liam picked up his pace then, jogging to the front porch, out of breath as he took in the headlines.

'There was a rebellion, right near where Kieran is, hundreds of miners up against armed soldiers and police. It was a massacre, Liam.'

Rory stood beside Eileen, putting his arm around her. She was shaking visibly. Shock never came easily to her these days.

'Five soldiers gone, and thirty-four injured with twenty-two dead among the miners,' Rory confirmed as Liam scanned the headlines. 'Parsons says there's rumours of butchery after they surrendered.'

Parsons was the local storekeeper and the fount of all knowledge in the village, or so he had anointed himself.

'Any lists of the casualties?'

'Not that Parsons has heard of. And they'd no' have any idea how to contact us,' Eileen said, wrenching her handkerchief in her consternation.

'I've written Kieran letters that have our address,' Liam reminded her.

'But what if he didn't have them on him?'

Liam ran his hand through his hair, his mind working fast. 'Surely his mates would have identified him, that Dave or the other big fellow we met...Striker. Someone would have let us know.'

'Not if they were injured or killed too.'

Liam stared at his sister, acknowledging there was logic in that. 'He said he wasn't going to fight because of Eve,' he said gently.

'We all know him too well to believe that,' she said, eyes full now. 'Liam...'

'Aye, I'll go up there, Eiles,' he said, holding her shoulder briefly and looking up at Rory. 'But I'm sure he's fine.'

His brother-in-law nodded and agreed but the look he returned was anything but reassuring.

Liam packed quickly and was on the road within the hour, Eileen's worried tears prolonging his farewells, and he kept the horse at a trot, trying not to imagine the worst. But memories from Kilrush pricked at his senses and he could barely block them out: the sight of a broken body, the putrid stench of dock refuse. And the groan of near-death on the lips of the only brother he would ever know.

It took a full day in the saddle but as Liam entered Ballarat it felt far longer and he hurried to ask the first person he met where he could find out about casualties from the stockade.

'You related to a digger?' the heavily bearded man asked warily.

'Aye,' Liam said, 'although I'm hoping not to be related to anyone on that list.'

'It's pinned outside the traps' station, although they're still adding a few here and there.'

Liam wasn't sure if knowing there were casualties whose lives were still in the balance was a good or bad thing but he pushed the thought aside to ride over to the traps' station, staring at the list that held news of his brother's fate from several feet away before slowly dismounting and approaching. It fluttered in the breeze as if it were a mere advertisement for selling a horse or buying soap and Liam had a bizarre moment of non-reality considering the enormity of what it truly contained. Devastation. Eternal heartache. Gut-wrenching grief.

It felt as if he'd stepped out of himself and he squeezed his eyes shut, unable to face whatever was on there. Fear was driving him to the point of nausea, but he knew he had to do this now. Sooner or later he had to know. He opened his eyes slowly, scanning the first name, the second. He'd almost got to the end when the two words leapt out and they seemed to burn through his retinas and straight into his brain, searing it with instant, unthinkable pain.

Kieran Clancy.

Two words so dear, so agonising now, for they belonged only to the hole being torn in his heart. Suddenly he needed to see where his brother lay more than anything in the world, for surely those two words lied. Such an impossible fact simply couldn't be true.

'Where are they buried?' he asked the same miner from before, who had followed him over on horseback.

'Most are up near Eureka. Which one was it?' he asked, compassion softening his rough Australian accent.

But Liam couldn't say those two words aloud. To do so would make them true.

'Come on then,' the miner said, seeming to understand. They rode off and the miner directed Liam to a stand of great gums where a fresh row of graves lay. They walked along past a particularly small one then Liam paused in front of a far larger mound beside it. Someone had scrawled those two precious words on a temporary, rough cross and he felt a desperate urge to scratch them away.

'When did...did they...'

'Pretty much straight away. What those bastards did...anyway, I'm sure you've heard.'

'Aye,' Liam said, his throat closing now as tears pushed their way through.

'Brother, was it?'

'Aye,' was all he could manage again.

'Lost mine too,' the man admitted, looking along, 'although he didn't take as long to bury as yours. I heard one of the traps say it took three men to dig the hole. Guess it doesn't run in the family.'

Liam was confused and stared at him. 'Whose family?'

'Yours,' the man said, looking confused at Liam's lack of comprehension. 'Can't say I ever met him but apparently your Kieran was huge; even his cap was tiny on his head. But, of course, you'd know that. Didn't anyone send it to you or get in contact? I saw the bloke who collected it, if that helps.'

'A...a...cap?'

'A grey felt one with the name written along it in big letters; read it myself, sorry to say. Kieran Clancy alright, no mistake.'

He said it slowly as if fearing Liam had lost his mind a bit, which perhaps he had because suddenly he was digging with his hands at the grave.

'Hey...*hey*! Mate, ya can't be doing that. Come on now,' the miner said, grabbing and pulling his shoulders but Liam shrugged him away, desperately flinging earth now until a face started to appear, the pallor of death a sickening sight. But despite recognising it and being disgusted, Liam actually let out a gasp of relief, collapsing to sit in the dirt and simply stare.

'You...you right there, mate?' the miner said, looking almost frightened of Liam now. 'I know you've had a shock and all but I really think looking at him isn't gonna help.'

'I'm not looking at him,' Liam said, shaking his head as he stared at the familiar face.

'Yes, you are, I'm afraid,' the miner said, talking as if to a child now. 'That's his name on the cross, see? Kieran Clancy.'

'I'm not looking at him,' Liam said again, 'because that isn't my brother.'

Thirty-Eight

'Are you sure?'

'They don't make mistakes over something like that.'

Liam stared at the list of names of the men on trial as announced in the newspaper he held, wishing futilely his brother's name was on this one. But, as it turned out, he wasn't in a Melbourne gaol, nor was he in any of the surrounding bushland near Eureka that Liam had scoured, nor the goldfields, nor Ballarat. He'd asked every man he met but they'd either not been involved or they hadn't seen him there. His best hope was that he'd be among the hundred or so about to be released from the barn where many rebels had been locked up.

'Here they come,' the bartender said as the diggers began to walk down the street and Liam ran out to watch them, scanning every face until he had to accept Kieran wasn't among them. But he thought he recognised one man in a green waistcoat.

'Dave,' he called out, taking the chance, and the miner stopped and walked over to peer at him.

'Do I know you?'

'I'm Liam Clancy, Kieran's brother.'

He looked exhausted, and blood stained the waistcoat, but Dave's smile was warm as he shook Liam's hand. 'So you are! Are ye here visiting Kieran then?'

'No...that is, I can't find him. Was he...did he fight with you?'

'No, no. He came to warn us though, just before. It was his wedding day though so he had other plans.'

Liam was shocked to realise he hadn't known about that. Kieran hadn't mentioned it was any time soon let alone a date, probably because he couldn't really invite Eileen and therefore the rest of them.

'Do you know where he was going after that?'

'He's building a house, down the river. I can show you if you like.'

Liam looked over at the crowd of noisy diggers now piling around the bar. 'Don't you want to have a few ales first?'

'Aye, I wouldn't mind,' Dave said, 'but how about I just grab a bottle or two for the road?'

He was on the second by the time they were on their way in a borrowed cart and Liam was filling him in about the list and Striker.

'Aye, I saw it happen, cowardly bastards. Took four of them to kill him in the end.' He took a swig of his beer, his anger evident. 'And then they killed his little wife Betty while she tried to stop them. The poor wee girl,' Dave said, shaking his head against the tears that were forming at the memory. 'Anyway,' he said, wiping at them with his sleeve, 'it's done now. I hope they at least buried her next to him. She was always right by his side.'

'There was a small grave near his,' Liam told him, remembering.

Dave nodded. 'That's something, I suppose. But what a right shock it must have been for you to see his name and then to find out it wasn't him.'

'I'm still reeling from it, to be honest, but once I see him I'll be alright.'

They were approaching the river now and Liam leapt down with Dave to investigate the half-built construction near the bank but there was no sign of activity. Tools lay inside, and a few boxes, but it was obviously uninhabited.

'It doesn't look like anyone's been here for a while,' Dave said, checking out the cold ashes in the roughly stacked stone fireplace. 'That's strange.'

'Maybe they've gone on a honeymoon,' Liam said.

'He said he was staying here; besides, Eve wouldn't be able to leave anyway. I mean, you know she's...er...'

'Aye, aye, I know.'

They stared at each other, both confused and Liam's levels of worry were increasing again until Dave clicked his fingers.

'I just remembered I know where she works. Come on.'

They leapt back on the wagon Dave had borrowed and made their way up the road until they reached a laneway. It was a pretty place, lined with flowers, but Liam took scant notice as they hurried to the door of the farmhouse and knocked.

A man answered and Liam breathed a sigh of relief that this home, at least, held people inside.

'Can I help ye?' the man asked, his Scottish accent thick.

'Sorry to trouble you, sir, however I'm looking for a servant of yours, a Miss Eve?'

'A friend, are ye?'

He looked suspicious, so Liam simply nodded. 'The name's Liam and this here is Dave.'

'Barney,' he told them, seemingly satisfied as he continued. 'She don' live 'ere no more, lad. The whole family up and left on account o' all the trouble. I only jus' found out meself yesterday – left me a note asking me to keep an eye on things here, indefinite like.'

'But...but she was getting married. Did her husband go with her?'

The man shook his head again, his expression falling. 'A terrible sad business. He ne'er showed up. They thought she'd been left at the altar but then they found out the lad had been killed down at that stockade.'

Liam sucked in his breath. 'Because of his name being on the list?'

'Aye, they gave her his cap an' all. Written there plain as day: Kieran Clancy. They say it fair broke the poor lass's heart.'

'But he didn't fight at the stockade,' Dave said.

'And he wasn't the one wearing the cap. I'm his brother, sir, and I can tell you for a fact he's not the man buried in that grave.'

The man stared at them both. 'Well…well then why didn't he show up? The family took a good week to up and leave so he'd plenty o' time to come explain,' he added, looking from one to the other. 'She's a right beauty, that girl – seems a cruel thing to do.'

'He never would have done that to her,' Dave said firmly. 'Wild horses couldn't have kept him away.'

'Something did though,' the man said, 'because I was there that day and I'm telling ye: he ne'er showed up at that wedding.'

Liam looked over at Dave, a silent dread passing between them, because there were very few possibilities of what that something could be. And none of them held much hope.

Thirty-Nine

Melbourne, December 1854

'Come on, lass, ye'll be right as rain,' Arthur assured Eve but as she stared at the gangplank terrible memories assailed her of chains and that old cloak of darkness where unspeakable acts were hidden from sight. Even the sound of sails unfurling whipped through her ears in a terrifying rush. Arthur was the right person to have beside her, however, and he steered her elbow gently along until she was on board. It felt disconcerting to have the sway of water beneath her feet once more, unsteady like everything else in her world, and she held onto the rail tight, trying not to think about seasickness lest the nausea of pregnancy get the better of her.

Amanda was escorted next and she made quite a fuss of making sure all her luggage was carried with care. The captain paid scant attention. He was too busy marching about deck, issuing orders and looking every inch at home in his smart naval uniform.

'Look sharp there, Stevens! Nolan, tie that rope again...and someone fetch me my blasted eyeglass. We can't set sail without seeing where we're damn well off to.'

Eve would have been amused to watch had she not felt so wretched. This journey could only end badly for her and the clean bunk she would sleep on these next few days could well be her last nights of comfort. Already her stomach was beginning to expand and Eve knew she wouldn't be able to hide her condition much longer. Each day her desperation grew to find a way to avoid ending up back in gaol but her options were narrow. The only possible hope was that the captain and Amanda would take pity on her and allow her to stay on with her child but she doubted they would. She'd learnt first-hand that the world of the gentry held little tolerance when it came to servants and promiscuity. Even a young life of service hadn't saved her the last time she'd been caught out.

'Take yer things downstairs, Eve,' Arthur said, interrupting her thoughts and she followed his direction to a small cabin on the left. It was bare, save a water stand, trunk and narrow bunk, but it was clean and it had a porthole, which seemed an extreme luxury compared to what she'd endured at sea before. Eve stared at the blue water extending all the way to the horizon, trying to believe that some twist of fate would save her once more.

But the kindest man in the world wouldn't appear with his charming words this time. He was no longer even a part of this earth.

Eve touched the pane, wondering if that was the option to take now, to choose the gravest of all sins and take her own life. It would be easy enough to throw herself overboard in the night, to see Kieran again, perhaps, in an afterlife. But that was a mortal sin, if the Catholics had it right, and she would be doomed to hell while her good man resided in heaven, separated for eternity by God himself. Besides, it would also be murder, she realised, touching her hand to her womb in protection, even though this child would be better off without living its life. The baby of a convict, at best left to the streets when it should have been playing by a river, cherished by loving parents and blessed beneath those southern stars.

The ship began to move away from the land and shouts could be heard as mooring ropes fell, and she acknowledged that this journey was inevitable, as was her wretched future.

'Read to me,' Amanda was saying and Eve reluctantly picked up the well-worn volume of Shakespeare. Her mistress had been amusing herself by dressing Eve up in her gowns to pass the time, teasing her that she'd put on weight of late. Eve had hidden her dread at the words and even now she was blanching as the seam strained at the narrow waist of the blue muslin, digging in hard as she leaned over. It seemed to add to the farcical aspects of her life right now, that she must don a costume and prepare to play a part, but at least the truth remained hidden. For now.

It was blustery, the air invigorating after hours indoors, and Eve breathed it in gladly, hoping it would bring the colour back to Amanda's cheeks. She was proving a poor sailor. Her disposition, although much improved these days due to the tonics, was ill-suited to the constant motion of the open sea.

Eve was used to it again and she'd managed to push aside the earlier memories of her convict experiences, for the most part. In fact, despite all the turmoil within her, the ocean itself surprisingly offered some comfort. It was vastly different being able to see the waves that rocked you and smell the sea salt fresh on the wind. And the crests of white upon the blue fairly danced, hypnotising her as the great ship plunged its way through, cutting a fanning pathway of residual spray that drifted around them, cooling their faces.

It was soothing to Eve but it wasn't enough for Amanda who groaned as they dipped quite firmly now and the captain spun the ship's wheel and called out orders to his men.

'Read,' Amanda demanded again, ignoring him.

Eve opened the book to a random page and began, a part of her aching that it should be that old familiar verse from *Romeo and Juliet*.

'Tis but thy name that is my enemy;
Thou art thyself though, not a Montague.
What's Montague? it is nor hand, nor foot,
Nor arm, nor face, nor any other part
Belonging to a man. O! be some other name:

'Hold to port!' the captain yelled but Amanda waved her on.

What's in a name? that which we call a rose
By any other name would smell as sweet;
So Romeo would, were he not Romeo call'd,

The ship veered again and they both had to hold fast to right themselves.

'Best get below decks,' Arthur yelled, approaching awkwardly with his one good leg. 'Storm's brewin'.'

He nodded towards the horizon and Eve gasped at the sight of dark clouds building like a wall against the blue summer sky. They were notorious, these storms from the south. Eve remembered then that this was the shoreline many termed the Shipwreck Coast but she'd been so preoccupied with her grief, her predicament and her fear of ships themselves she'd not considered it. However, one look at Arthur's face was enough to convince her that the threat of danger was very real indeed. Then the captain came over to briefly reassure Amanda, telling her to 'hold fast', which only reminded Eve of the last time he'd said those words, to her in fact. On her wedding day.

Below in Amanda's quarters it didn't feel any safer, and Eve was starting to feel the terrible creep of imprisonment by the time the storm truly hit an hour later. And no amount of Shakespeare could help them ignore its ferocity. The great ship lurched and groaned as waves crashed against it, tossing it like a toy in a giant tub. Shouting could be heard between the ocean's roar, and water lashed angrily at the porthole glass where all visibility had been lost. It was growing darker too and Eve held onto the lantern in a desperate attempt not to panic. Amanda, however, was far beyond that point by now.

'Oh, God help us, *God help us*,' she cried out between screams, gripping onto the wall near the bench.

'*By…by any other name…*' Eve was still trying to read to comfort her but the dwindling light and terrifying noise were against her and now furnishings were sliding and falling to the floor. A plate crashed and Amanda screamed again as Arthur came stumbling into the cabin, his grey hair plastered by rain, water running in rivulets from his clothing onto the floor.

'There now, miss,' he said as Amanda grasped for his arm.

'What's happening up there? How much longer?'

'There's no way of saying, although I think we're near the eye of it. Captain says if we can only…'

But he was interrupted by an enormous sound of falling masts above them and splintering timber. Men cried out and wet sails could be heard drumming on the deck above.

'Shite,' Arthur said, clambering back out and Amanda stared at Eve in shock.

'Is it…is it falling apart?'

'No, ma'am, surely not,' Eve reassured her but pure fear was flooding through her now as the reality of the situation began to hit. 'Perhaps I should go and check…'

'Yes, hurry!' Amanda agreed.

Anything was better than sitting and imagining the worst, or so Eve thought until she reached the top of the stairs. She struggled to open the hatch but then she was met by winds so ferocious she immediately stumbled and fell back against the wall, eyes wide as lightning irradiated the horrifying scene.

The mizzenmast above the captain's cabin had broken in half and the sails lay drenched and useless, flapping among a tangle of ropes and broken timber. Eve pushed back blinding strands of hair to see men running about frantically, falling on the wet deck and battling against waves that loomed like black giants before crashing across the deck, pounding them into the sea. The captain stood at the wheel, straight-backed and focused as he tried to read what the ocean would do next, like David before an almighty Goliath. Eve prayed for him. She prayed for them all.

There was another scream from Amanda below, barely discernible above the cacophony of storm and sea, and Eve tried to get back to the hatch but the wind was driving her back. It held impossible force and it was inciting the ocean to swell and smash. To pound them all into submission. How foolish it seemed suddenly, to face such might. How small and defenceless they were in their flimsy vessel of wood, rope and sail.

Another huge wave rode towards them and she gripped on tightly as it exploded and obliterated everything from sight, dwarfing them into nothingness until all she could see was churning, running water. Then there was another almighty noise as the mid-deck collapsed under the pressure and Eve knew then, without any doubt, they were going down.

Amanda.

Eve fought desperately to get back to her mistress now, knowing she would be terrified, but the ship was beginning to keel as the ocean dragged them downwards, and she fell again, sliding towards the edge where men were horrifyingly, sickeningly, being thrust overboard. She grabbed onto a rope but it slipped from her grasp and the surging water drove her helplessly towards the scuppers that ran along the bottom of the side walls, spaces where her feet could become dangerously stuck. Eve knew if they did she would surely drown.

Eyes landed everywhere now as she fought for survival, something she wasn't sure she even wanted only this morning. But as Arthur pushed his way down to Amanda and the captain bravely stood his ground Eve knew with certainty she would fight for life too. It was purely primal, when it was real.

The ship began to sink in the middle and she knew she would have to make the jump off the side to avoid being sucked under when the great weight went. And so she stood and braced herself, with one last look at the helm where the captain now stared straight across to an emerging Arthur and Amanda. He locked eyes with his wife, whose dark strands of hair were plastered against her stricken face, and Eve could read the love there as the lightning flashed. Then he called something out just as the boat lifted high at the stern, and as she jumped the words rang in Eve's ears.

'Hold fast, my love. Hold fast.'

Forty

Warrnambool, December 1854

He was writing again, this time a letter to a lawyer called Lincoln Ellis that Parsons had recommended in Melbourne, but it was already his third of the day and Liam yawned and stretched as the morning light streamed through the window. He'd been at it since well before dawn, unable to sleep as the mystery of Kieran's whereabouts plagued at him. His best hope was that Kieran had hidden out from the law then gone in search of Eve, although it didn't seem much like Kieran's style to hide, nor did it seem likely he would have let Eve worry for the days in between their missed wedding and her departure.

There were other possibilities, of course, each thought a sickening one. He could be badly injured somewhere or imprisoned, although some wild ideas of his brother being taken by bushrangers had also occurred to Liam, as far-fetched as that sounded. It wasn't unheard of these days. He could also possibly be dead but Liam felt, deep down, his brother was somewhere on this earth still. He'd survived miraculously before and Liam still believed he was destined for great things. To even contemplate otherwise felt impossible.

Eileen was putting the kettle on and she called out to ask if he'd like a cup of tea.

'Aye, that'd be nice thanks, Eiles.'

His sister had that drawn look about her again and Liam knew she was just as worried about Kieran as he was. He walked out onto the porch and she joined him with the tea as he lit his pipe and stared out at a wet world that was drying in the sun.

'Quite a storm we had last night,' Rory commented as he rounded the corner from the barn, carrying the milk from their new cow, Backy. The boys had named her, although in truth it had been a compromise from them wanting to call her Mrs Backside. 'I thought the roof might come off at one point.'

'Roofs can be fixed,' Eileen said quietly, sipping her tea.

'That they can, love,' Rory said gently, kissing her cheek and producing a single red rose from behind his back. 'Grown just for you.'

That earned him a small smile and Liam marvelled at the gentle patience of his brother-in-law. It couldn't be easy to live with a wife who worried like that.

'Got some good milk from Backy today. I think we may have enough for you to make me some cream and scones.'

'And I suppose you're expecting I wait on you too. Set out the good china while I'm at it.'

'That'd be mighty fine of ye,' Rory said, grinning now.

Liam smiled too but that lonely feeling was surfacing once more at their banter and with it that now-familiar ache.

'I think I may head in to town and see if Parsons has the papers in yet,' Liam told them, finishing his tea. 'They should be…'

But he was interrupted by a sound dreaded in these parts as the faint peal of the emergency bell echoed in the clear morning air.

Rory and Liam were quick to react, grabbing their coats and tethering their horse to the cart before setting off fast to provide whatever aid they could. But as they reached the small town and the handful of people staring out at the cove there seemed little hope they could help the poor souls involved now. There had been a shipwreck alright, the rocks were strewn with debris, but it was mostly at the bottom of the headlands with little reaching the calm beach below.

'I'll go down and look,' Liam offered.

'Aye, I'll come too,' Rory agreed, and Parsons and a few more joined them as they descended down the narrow track. It was a magnificent morning with the sun blazing across the pristine scene: cresting sapphire waves, golden sand, stunning jewelled colours wet on the cliffs, but it was eerie to think of how it would have seemed hours ago, in the darkest ink of night. How terrifying to be tossed by mountainous waves only to sink to a watery grave, or, worse still, float for hours then be devoured by the great white sharks that patrolled these deeper waters. It was incongruous, this beautiful, terrible place.

The searchers spread out, some moving along the rocks, others walking in the shallows and peering out. Liam and Rory searched the beach and the caves that ran underneath the ledges, although Liam really felt that they were wasting their time. The likelihood of survival past those treacherous heads was low. The smell of seaweed was strong and the occasional human article reminded him of another search, long ago. A boot here, a broken bottle there. Splintered polished wood from what was once, perhaps, fine furniture. If only he could find Kieran now as quickly as he had in Kilrush, but this game was a slow one; drawn out and more painful with each growing day.

The last cave was deep and Liam walked all the way into it, bending to a crouch. He supposed he owed the victims that much: a proper search, but then something caught his eye. It was a dress, blue and covered in sand, and there was a white hand. And a face.

'*Rory!*'

He rushed over to check her pulse. She was still alive but it was thready and her skin was like ice. Liam immediately took off his coat as Rory arrived and stared in disbelief.

'Shite, let's get her out of here,' he said, collecting himself, and they both picked her up to carry her up the hill.

The irony wasn't lost on Liam that the last time they'd done this it was Kieran's life they were saving. Perhaps that was a good omen, he supposed, looking at her properly now. A beautiful sign.

'How is she?'

Eileen washed her hands and came out to sit heavily on her porch chair. 'She's clean and she's warm but I don't know if she'll make it. Certainly a fever would do her in.'

Liam knew she was merely being practical but he didn't like the offhand way she said it.

'Poor girl,' he said softly.

Eileen frowned. 'Aye, sorry. I didn't mean to sound so harsh. It's just that there's another complication; I'm fairly sure of it anyway.' She paused to pick up her tea cup thoughtfully. 'She's with child.'

Liam gaped, understanding now.

'I wonder…I wonder if her husband perished at sea?' Rory said, shaking his head slowly.

'We'll find out soon enough, I suppose,' Eileen said. 'That was an expensive dress. She's a wealthy lady, which means someone will come looking for her eventually.'

'Aye,' Liam said, 'I suppose so.'

'What's your name, lass?' he asked again.

Eve closed her eyes as if to stop the enormous twist of fate from arriving but already the words were forming, as if unbidden. For she couldn't be Eve Richards anymore. She couldn't choose a convict existence, a life in chains, her baby left to dire and uncertain fates. She was already a sinner, a convicted thief, by any other name.

'Amanda Cartwright.'

And now a thief of someone else's life.

Forty-One

Melbourne, January 1855

'Kieran. Kieran Clancy,' Liam emphasised, not that it seemed to be of much use. He'd searched painstakingly in Melbourne this time, going to every boarding house, pub, gaol and hospital, and now even the prison hospital, as grim a place as ever he'd been, but it was still a possibility and Liam waited. Yet again.

The man ran a thick, stubby finger down pages of names but eventually came to the end with no match made. 'Sorry, sir, he's no' here.'

Liam nodded and sighed before thanking him and moving off, wondering where else he could possibly look today. He'd been in town for over a week and not only was he feeling despondent, he was feeling homesick, not just for family and land this time. That lonely chasm inside had been filled this summer as the loveliest girl he'd ever met made her place in his home. And his heart.

As her belly grew his longing to marry her grew too, to give her a place to start again, but the death of her husband was still so fresh he held back on declaring his affections, unsure if they were returned in any measure anyway. For now it was enough just to watch her move and to listen to her cultured voice that made even the most ordinary of sentences beautiful. She was too good for him, he knew, the widow of an English sea captain no less, but he would end up asking for her hand anyway. He'd regret it for the rest of his life if he let the opportunity to marry Amanda Cartwright go.

She didn't know the reason for his trips, he and Eileen having decided it would be best not to mention they had a brother who was probably involved in the stockade and still missing. She was a genteel lady, after all, and it would be enough of a challenge getting her to marry him as it was; a criminal in the family wouldn't improve his chances. Eileen was sympathetic to his cause, having long worried about his bachelor state, and she seemed to like Amanda's company. It softened her, having another woman to talk to, and in all the future looked bright for the Clancy clan if only Kieran could be found.

Looking up at the prison hospital walls he wondered for the thousandth time where his brother could be, wishing with all his heart he could bring him home.

He was still convinced he remained here, somewhere on this earth, firmly believing that Kieran was stuck somewhere, for whatever dark reason that may be, and Liam's own life felt stalled until he could get to him; as if he was walking in circles, unable to move on. He'd always been patient where Kieran had been impetuous, but it was wearing very thin now. Too much lay unresolved.

It was hot and barely any relief could be found in the slight breeze that ran through the bars in the wall. He wondered why they bothered with them here. It wasn't as if any of them had the strength to climb down and escape, although every day he was gaining his back now. And every day his determination to get out of here was growing too.

Kieran Clancy walked over to those bars now, mostly to get away from the groans and wails of the man in the bed alongside him who'd been in agony since he'd arrived the day before. The poor blighter had some kind of problem in his groin area and Kieran pitied him, of course, but the noise made this echoing hellhole even more unbearable than usual.

Kieran forced each step, clenching muscles that had wasted away these past months to make it to the window to look out at the courtyard below. Freedom lay waiting and he could almost taste it now, each fraction of healing bringing him closer to that precious state.

He'd been shot close to his throat as he'd raced towards the stockade and the redcoats had taken him with the other seriously wounded back to Melbourne with them. Not that he remembered anything. All he knew was the painful recovery that had followed when, for the second time in his life, he'd nearly died at the hands of oppression. The injury had rendered his neck swollen and the subsequent infection that had near killed him meant he'd not been able to use his voice for months, a fact that had so far spared him being officially charged.

It also meant no-one knew who he was. Or where.

Kieran had mimed for pen and paper on numerous occasions but prisoners weren't granted such luxuries. They were barely even treated for their injuries and illnesses and the woeful lack of sanitation in the place meant you were lucky to survive a stay in here. At least he'd managed that so far and now he was focused on his next challenge, for his only hope for release lay in finding his voice. Without that he couldn't tell his family he was even alive, let alone protest his innocence and be acquitted, or charged. And without it he couldn't be free.

Kieran rubbed at his beard, bushy on his now-thin face, and began to exercise his throat muscles as he stood, trying to coax more sound than the mere grunts that had begun to form these past few days. It was painful but he persevered, focusing on the scene below to distract him from the discomfort.

A man was walking slowly across the cobblestones, seemingly deep in thought, and Kieran deeply envied his ability to walk out of here and get on with his life. He was determined his turn would come. He *would* find his voice and he *would* speak his family's name, for the woman he loved needed that name too, and his baby who would soon be born. Never had the word 'Clancy' seemed more valuable to him than now: when he was fighting to claim it out loud.

Just then the man in the courtyard looked up and over at the windows where Kieran stood and a surging wave of recognition moved through him. He grabbed at the bars, too late as the man turned away, heart thumping and his throat straining in agony as he tried to call out, but the only sound was a dragging and pitiful rasp.

Liam, his brain screamed. *I'm alive! I'm here!*

But Liam walked away and the words fell silent against the slumped shoulders of his brother's retreating back.

I am Kieran Clancy.

Forty-Two

Warrnambool, February 1855

Eileen knew without Liam saying anything he didn't have any good news but the children jumped all over him anyway, oblivious.

'Uncle Liam! Uncle Liam!'

'Did you get me a present?' asked Matthew, ever hopeful.

'Well, as a matter of fact...' Liam pulled some boiled sweets from his pocket and they clapped their hands.

'Matthew Murphy, your manners are disgraceful,' Eileen admonished but she smiled at how much they adored him. Sadly, if conveniently, they'd stopped asking about Uncle Kieran months ago and Eileen sincerely hoped they wouldn't bring him up in front of Amanda. He was going to be a difficult family member to explain. Not that she was ashamed of him; she was proud of her brother and would have been proud of him if he'd been involved in the Eureka Stockade too. She came from too long a line of rebellious Irish men and women who'd stood up against the Crown for her not to be sympathetic to the cause.

It was just that Liam was so obviously in love with Amanda and, as kind and lovely as the girl was, she was also finely raised and her brother would need every possible societal advantage they could wrangle to marry her.

Watching her pretty face as she greeted Liam now, Eileen acknowledged that she definitely liked Amanda too but there was something about her that niggled. A scar on her face that she said she got from falling over as a child, marks on her wrists that she said came from a horse and cart accident. And there was a general aura of preoccupation about her that Eileen couldn't help but pick up on, especially as Amanda was so often deeply lost in thought. But whatever her secrets, her character seemed genuine enough. Besides, any woman carrying her recently deceased husband's baby was entitled to brooding and, in fairness, she was probably still in shock. It was likely far too soon for her to see Liam in a romantic light but Eileen was certain she would eventually. He was just too good a man to ignore, surely.

Then again, she was biased.

Liam had always been such an easygoing, intelligent and gentle brother, never giving her a moment's worry, unlike Kieran of course. Eileen's heart ached as she thought of him and she would corner Liam alone as soon as she could manage to get him away from Amanda, who he was now chatting to with a look of adoration on his face. She certainly looked beautiful, despite her large, swollen belly, and her eyes had lit up at the sight of him, which was a good sign. But that could wait.

'Liam, can I have a quick word?'

'Now?' he asked, looking reluctant.

'Aye.'

'Back in moment then,' he told Amanda with a grin and Eileen walked away from the house with him, towards the fence line where Rory was mending the gate.

He waved over. 'Any luck?' he called.

Liam shook his head as Eileen handed him his mail.

'There's no news in there,' she told him as he picked a few out. 'I've read them all.'

Liam rolled his eyes. 'Well, I know I should tell you to keep your nose out of my private business, but I suppose that's too much to ask right now.'

'Yes, it is. And it was too tempting not to read them when I had them hidden under my pillow.'

That justified it well enough, although he defended Amanda straight away. 'She wouldn't pry like that.'

'Well, I wasn't taking any chances. Anyway, forget your mail. I've something far more important to discuss,' Eileen told him, seizing her chance. 'I think I've found a real opportunity to find out what happened.'

'What is it?'

Eileen held out the paper Parsons had given her yesterday. 'They're putting them on trial next month, all thirteen prisoners from the stockade. People say there're massive crowds going because so many are against them being convicted.'

'Really?' Liam pored over the story, scanning quickly.

'Anyone who knows anything will be at that trial, Liam. It's our best shot.'

'Aye, you're right about that. I'll go and see what I can find out.'

'Good lad,' she said and he grinned.

'Now, I'm getting a bit too old for that, am I not?'

'Force of habit,' she said, smiling herself at the slip. 'Sometimes I forget you're all grown up.'

'Aye, that I am, Eiles,' he said, as they walked back to where Amanda stood waiting, holding out his tea. 'That I am.'

'What are you up to in here?'

Eve jumped as Eileen walked into the kitchen and she closed the newspaper rapidly. 'I...I was just catching up on the news.'

'I wouldn't have thought that politics interested you much,' Eileen said, placing a basket of potatoes on the table and getting out a pot to wash them.

'Why would you say that?' Eve replied, pushing the paper aside to help her peel.

'Oh, I don't know, a lady such as yourself wouldn't be a fan of the rebels, I'm sure.'

Eve frowned, wanting to defend them but then again, why should she? The Eureka Stockade had ruined her life. Why she was even reading about them was beyond her but she couldn't seem to help herself. Anything that had touched Kieran touched her still and she doubted her grieving heart would ever be able to see it any other way.

'I'm a fan of justice,' she said, 'and I don't believe men should be convicted for standing up for their rights.' That much was true, but choosing to do so over marrying the woman you supposedly loved was another matter altogether. Grief wrestled with anger then and she swallowed them both. What was the point in feeling either?

'I'm betting your husband didn't see it that way,' Eileen said before pausing mid-peel. 'I mean being a naval officer and all. Sorry to mention him.'

Eve dipped her head as the captain came to mind, standing stalwart on the ship, his eyes locked on the woman he adored before they perished at sea. The woman Eve now said she was.

She didn't worry she'd ever be found out she was masquerading as Amanda Cartwright; the lady had no living relatives and no friends to speak of after such a sheltered life and all that she owned had been lost at sea, save the house. The few people who knew her were back in that tiny town of Ballan and Eve knew she'd never return there now, although she'd told Eileen she'd sent a letter 'home' to sort out her affairs.

No, it wasn't being found out by evidence that concerned her, it was the fear of her own guilt one day tripping her up and leaving her cast out once more. Perhaps these kind people would never have reported her as a shipwrecked convict to the authorities, had she originally told the truth, but if they found out now she knew they'd certainly never trust her again. And she would end up having to leave, pregnant, penniless and alone.

'He...he didn't approve of what they did but then again he didn't understand their reasons, I suppose,' she said, choosing her words with care. 'I'm guessing many of them felt they had no other choice than to rebel.' No other choice, save marriage and a child.

Eileen looked at her in surprise. 'Aye, very true, Amanda. Very true. We'll make a Clancy of you yet.'

Eve froze, her eyes locking on Eileen's, and she had the half-crazed thought that her guilty mind was being read at the use of the name. 'What...what did you say?'

'A Clancy,' Eileen told her, smiling fleetingly as she dropped a freshly peeled potato in the pot. 'It's our family name, well, Liam's still anyway. Haven't we ever mentioned it before?'

Eve continued to stare, just managing to say 'no'.

Eileen shrugged as she scrubbed at the potatoes. 'I suppose you only hear me saying Murphy but that's Rory's surname of course. We women give up too much when we marry, don't we? Not that I minded,' she added quickly, 'it's a natural state, to have a partner in life.'

Clancy. The word spun through Eve's mind, darting about like a moth around a lantern. Then the first names spun with it: *Eileen, Liam*. She forced herself to ask the question, past a tightly constricting throat. 'Is it...just the two of you then? Siblings, I mean.'

Eileen paused before responding. 'Aye,' she said, but there was a strange tone in her voice and Eve couldn't quite believe her. Nor could she possibly leave it alone.

'You hesitated.'

Eileen sighed, putting the potato she was holding aside. 'We haven't wanted to mention it but...we have another brother. He was involved with the miners at the Eureka Stockade and we just thought a well-bred lady such as yourself wouldn't quite... understand...'

'U...understand...?'

'Well, he's missing at the moment and we're trying to find out where he is; we're worried sick, to be honest. That's why Liam keeps going away, he's searching for him.'

'Searching...for...?'

'Kieran.'

Eve felt all the blood in her head drain and she could barely think at all now, only to realise his family didn't know he was dead. They still had something denied her forever: hope.

'I'm sorry now, that I didn't tell you upfront,' Eileen prattled on. 'I should have trusted you, I suppose. I just thought it might make you look down on us; the gentry have always treated we Irish with disdain, especially when rebellion rears its head and Liam...and I, well, we are fond of you, you see. We want you to stay here, with us, if you can forgive us for being dishonest, Amanda.'

Her own dishonesty hung in the air on the name and Eve struggled to bear it.

I am the liar. I am the rose by any other name. And now the greatest of terrible truths cannot be told because of my deceit.

Suddenly the room felt stuffy and she rose from her chair. 'I think I may have a little lie-down,' she mumbled.

'Are you alright...?'

'Yes, yes,' she managed, barely making it to her bedroom before collapsing on the blankets heavily to stare at the ceiling in shock and disbelief. This was Kieran's family. They would have been *her* family if those ill-fated stars hadn't stolen her new life away. And now she'd tried to trick those stars, to steal someone else's fate, but that curse of an unnatural life had found her. Once more.

The weight of her new sin was unbearable now; life with Kieran's family would be impossible to endure. Especially when they still believed he could be alive.

And especially when Clancy blood ran inside her too, in the form of his unborn child.

'Where's Amanda?' Liam asked Eileen.

The trial was starting in Melbourne in a few days and he was keen to get on the road, although he wasn't keen to leave the woman he loved. For he did love her now, hopelessly, for he doubted she returned it. She was fond of him, he was certain, but not in love, he knew. Perhaps when the baby came it would seem a more natural thing to her and she would see something in him too. Eileen said it wouldn't be long before the birth now, perhaps a matter of weeks. She certainly looked a good way along, in as much as Liam knew about these things; he just hoped he wouldn't be called upon to help with the event itself when he got back, an old pain echoing at the thought.

She was down by the gate, picking wildflowers awkwardly and putting them in a basket for Eileen.

'Here now, you shouldn't be doing that,' he said, taking the basket from her and holding her steady as she rose up.

'I'm fine,' she said, puffing. 'Eileen wants them for me actually. Something to help when...' She blushed then and his heart leapt a little at how beautiful she looked, even when she was feeling embarrassed.

'I wanted to talk to you before I went.'

'Oh,' she said, frowning. It was a relief that she knew about Kieran now but she'd become even more preoccupied than usual since she'd found out and she always lowered her eyes or left the room whenever his name was mentioned. Liam suspected she didn't approve of the rebels in general, despite what Eileen said to the contrary.

'We need to keep looking, Amanda,' he said gently, trying to help her to understand and more than a little disappointed that she didn't seem to. 'He is our brother after all.'

'Yes, of course,' she said; however, she was still frowning.

'You think he's some terrible criminal, don't you?' he said, deciding to be frank, but to his surprise her eyes filled with tears.

'No...'

'What is it then? What's wrong?' he said, daring to take her hand.

She was fighting against quite a lot of emotion now and he wondered at it. 'Are you worried for us, lass, is that it?'

She said nothing but gave a small nod.

'There now, don't take on so. If we still believe he's out there somewhere then you can trust that he is. Kieran does this to us on occasion; goes missing and leaves us thinking the worst but there's always a good story behind it in the end. Besides, I know...I'd feel it in here if he were gone,' he said, letting go of her hand and pointing to his chest.

Amanda shook her head but still didn't speak, looking so concerned for him he couldn't help but steer the subject towards his original, intended topic of conversation.

'It will all turn out fine, you'll see, and...and well, when I get back I was hoping, I mean after you have the baby and all, I thought it might be nice if we perhaps...' Liam paused, hating how bad he was at this but knowing he needed some sign of encouragement to take with him on this trip, however small. Anything to hold on to when he lay down his head at night. 'Would you allow me to take you out for a walk or a picnic or something…some time? We could go into one of the larger towns to dine if you like. Do it in style.'

Her tear-filled eyes were wide now. 'You…you mean, like courting?'

'Aye,' he said, relieved he'd at least made his point.

'Liam, I…I don't think it would be a good idea.'

It landed like a crush against his chest but he nodded as manfully as he could.

'It's not that I'm not fond of you, I just…I don't think this is the life for me here. I'm thinking I might go, I mean once the baby is a little older.'

'But…but you said you had no family, no-one to inform that you'd even survived, so where…?'

Amanda shrugged. 'I don't know yet.'

'Don't you,' he began, then paused to clear his throat, 'like us?'

That brought a fresh onslaught of tears. 'I think you're the kindest people I've ever known, but you deserve much, much better than me.'

He gazed at her lovely face and shook his head in bewilderment. 'How can there possibly be anyone better than you?'

She touched his hand then, lightly, and it took his breath.

'It's more than possible, Liam,' she said, tears falling once more. 'I don't deserve you all and this isn't my fate.'

'But how can you know such a thing?'

She shrugged sadly. 'It seems to be written in the stars.'

He was confused by that but as she walked away he vowed he would change her mind, even though right now it seemed as if he'd need to reach up and rearrange the sky.

Forty-Three

Melbourne, 22 February 1855

The crowds could be heard through the window bars and Kieran figured they numbered in their thousands as the rebel trials began. The prison patients were restless as they listened, those who were well enough to be aware of what was going on anyway, their only source of information the chatting they could hear among the guards and staff. At least they could all manage that much now that the wailing man had been released.

The Eureka prisoners were charged with high treason and Kieran recognised a few of the names, in particular Raffaello Carboni and Timothy Hayes. Kieran doubted the latter would be found not guilty considering his role overall. Rumour had it Peter Lalor was injured and hiding out, and so far the police had failed to find him and charge him too, which gave Kieran some satisfaction, at least.

The miners had paid a terrible price for their right to exist. Twenty-four of them were dead and now these thirteen charged faced execution, with many more missing or hiding out. The trials would soon show whether anything had been gained from all the bloodshed in the end. It seemed unlikely, yet Kieran liked to dream that justice would prevail and that laws would be changed. That this fractured population from all the ends on earth could find a way to leave foreign oppression behind; to find freedom in this land that held such hope. Such potential.

Sitting behind bars, Kieran knew the truest value of that precious word 'freedom' now, understanding at last that it really resided inside. If you were free to just exist, to be happy, to love, then you needed little else. Except physically being able to do that, of course. To be with the people that fulfilled those needs, those who fed your heart until it overflowed with the wondrous stuff. All the choices in life that had directed his fate; all the games he'd played, the adventures he'd undertaken, the risks he'd exposed himself to, were really in search of that internal freedom.

Images flashed through his mind as the crowd outside stirred, moments when he'd grasped it. Galloping under an Irish moon with a stolen horse and a stolen bride, getting beaten up then saved because he'd doffed his cap, rescuing a girl by a river who was in a spot of bother, daring to cast a stone. Riding unarmed on a horse straight into a war. It was all to be free to exist, to be happy and to love, and without Eve he doubted any of the three would be possible because she was more than the woman he loved now. She was, essentially, his freedom.

And so he sat in a bleak, wretched place and forced sounds through a pain-filled throat, dreaming of all the words he would one day soon say:

I am Kieran Clancy…and I'm innocent.
You are my freedom.
I love you.
I do.

And all the while, as Kieran dreamed his dreams, the swell of a greater freedom rumbled in the streets of Melbourne below.

'Liam!'

He'd never seen such crowds and, as he made his way towards Dave people jostled against him, the atmosphere alive with passionate yelling and animated conversation. Few would be here by accident and, by the looks of things, few would be silent today.

'How are you, Dave?' he asked, shaking the miner's hand. His beard had grown even longer than last time Liam saw him, almost as long as his waistcoat, and Liam remarked on it.

'Badge of honour, me friend,' Dave told him. 'Come on, let's grab an ale before we go in.'

The pub was busy to the point of overflowing but they managed to get a drink and find some standing room near the door.

'Do you know many who are on trial?' Liam said, practically shouting over the din then looking about self-consciously.

'Aye, a few,' Dave told him, drinking his beer thirstily. 'Hayes is the one they'll be hunting first, I'm reckoning, and that Italian bloke, Raffaello. He's the one who organised a lot of the Europeans to fight; speaks a ton of languages. Hey, Macca!' He paused to wave and a lanky, fair-haired man waved back from across the packed room, a few other heavily bearded men with him. 'There's a couple of us here but we best lay low.'

'You're not thinking they'll still make more arrests, are you?'

Dave shook his head. 'You never know but I doubt it. They're keen to find Lalor though, make no mistake. Did you hear they had to amputate his arm? Woke up in the middle of the operation and told the doctor to have more courage! That's guts.'

'Aye,' Liam said, shocked.

'Anyway, apparently he's alright and the Governor's put four hundred pounds on his head, but no-one's turned him in.'

'I'd heard that,' Liam said, thoughtful now. 'You don't suppose...'

Dave shook his head again. 'I've already looked into it. Got it on good authority Kieran's not with him.'

Liam sighed and nodded, drinking his beer.

'There're thousands of people here today,' Dave reminded him, 'and I'm betting someone knows something. Let's see if we can't talk our way into that courtroom, start at the heart of things like.'

It seemed like the best idea to Liam, to hear every detail of that day from those who witnessed it first-hand, because some tiny clue might come out that could shed light on Kieran's disappearance, however small.

'Aye,' he agreed, 'let's hear the entire tale,' and so they drained their glasses and made their way down to the Victorian Supreme Court.

The crowd was enormous now, filling the heart of town in their thousands, and the noise was deafening as many called out in support of the miners. Some even held placards and Liam read a few: *Australians against tyranny, We all deserve the vote, Fighting for freedom isn't a crime.* They came from all walks of life too, with workmen shouting alongside businessmen, well-dressed women next to bearded miners and students clutching satchels, their youthful faces impassioned. Hundreds of them were trying to get through the doors but Dave used pure deviancy and bribed a guard to let them through.

'No wonder you're friends with Kieran,' Liam said and Dave laughed.

'Come on.'

They sat behind the press and family members, far enough away to be inconspicuous yet close enough to hear the banter up front.

But pregnant, married or no, he sat by her bed all afternoon and slept in a chair nearby, all through the night.

It was dark and cold, colder than anyone could ever imagine, and the water clung to her, pulling her down; demanding she give in to the deathly world below. But all the while Eve held fast, gripping her numb hands around the broken piece of deck that was keeping her afloat and forcing her exhausted body and mind to stay awake lest she pass out and let go.

'It's alright now, you're safe, lass.' It was a man's voice, talking in a gentle Irish brogue.

Kieran.

But no, he was gone from her now. Beyond the reach of the living.

So let go.

But she clung on.

Warm hands were taking hers, unclenching her fingers that she realised weren't gripping the wood at all. They held onto sheets instead, clean and dry, and Eve opened her eyes to stare into a face she'd never seen before but was somehow familiar, just the same.

'You're safe,' he said again, and Eve noted that his eyes were very kind.

'Is she awake?' came another voice and she turned to see a dark-haired woman entering, carrying a tea tray. She put it down and rested her hand across Eve's forehead then took her wrist to feel her pulse. 'Much better,' she concluded, satisfied. 'Must see if we can't get you to eat something, girl. Would you like some toast?'

Eve nodded then looked back at the man who was smiling at her now. 'You've been through quite an ordeal. Do you remember what happened?'

Eve nodded again, blinking away images of black walls of water and the anguished countenance of the captain going down with his ship.

'Did...anyone...else...?'

'I'm afraid not, lass,' he said very gently but the words slammed straight through her heart. *The captain. Arthur. Amanda.* 'We're... er, not sure who you were travelling with or who may be looking for you now. Have you any family you'd like us to contact?'

Eve stared for a moment as the shock and sorrow registered then slowly shook her head. There was no-one else who would know if she were dead or alive. No-one who would care.

'What's your name?'

No-one who would even know who...or what she was.

'I...' Eve began to speak again but her mouth was dry.

'Let's get something to drink for you first. Are you hungry?' the woman said. Eve nodded and allowed her to help her sit up slowly and prop her up with pillows so she could eat.

'Our storekeeper Parsons said it was in the news that you were headed to Adelaide,' the man said.

'Fifty-seven souls...' the woman tutted but the man gave her a warning look.

'Do you want us to send word to anyone there?'

Eve shook her head again and ate slowly as the ramifications of her new situation dawned on her. Yes, grief dragged at her heart but the will to survive was still strong and at the fore. *Another new beginning*, came the thought, *on a new shore.*

Amanda's blue muslin hung by the window next to a vase containing a single red rose and something began to tick in the back of her mind. There was no-one who would need to be told of the death of a sea captain and his wife, either.

'I'm Liam, by the way, and this is Eileen.'

Such familiar Irish names. So painful to think they could have been common in her life if Kieran had lived. Her very own family.

'Thousands of people trying to get in today, Ebenezer,' called out one.

'Aye, I guess they'll just have to read all about it in the papers,' came the reply.

Liam knew at once who the two men were: Ebenezer Syme and David Blair, journalists from *The Age* newspaper that Liam particularly enjoyed reading. They were known to be sympathetic to the rebels' cause and were a good part of the reason the public were getting behind the miners.

It was a mark of just how serious the case was considered that the Attorney General himself, William Stawell, had been appointed prosecutor. Not only was he against democratic reform, he was a close friend of Governor Hotham and Liam knew he would be doing everything he could to convict the miners and squash the rebellious spirit that was spreading throughout the colony. This trial had moved beyond the diggers now; this was political warfare.

The defence was led by Richard Ireland and, as he spoke to the other lawyers nearby, Liam noted his thick Irish accent matched his name. Ireland was reported to be defending the miners for free, which gained him Liam's admiration in advance.

The jury took their seats then the thirteen miners were led through and Dave swore under his breath at the state of them. Each and every man was filthy and bruised, their hair and beards matted, and they stood shoulder to shoulder from countries all over the world. Hayes was Irish, as were a few others, and Raffaello was of course Italian, but Liam had read in the papers that there was also an American, a Scotsman, a Dutchman, a Jamaican and a native Australian on trial.

'All rise for Chief Justice William à Beckett,' came the call and they stood as one as the judge entered.

Stawell began his opening address then and the seriousness of the case silenced the room. 'The charge is that you did on the 3rd December, 1854, being then in a warlike manner, traitorously assemble together against our Lady the Queen, and that you did, while so armed and assembled together, levy and make war...'

Looking across at the countenances of the miners Liam could feel their fear. It was terrifying even witnessing thirteen lives on trial.

'...and attempt by force of arms to destroy the Government constituted there and by law established, and to depose our Lady the Queen from the kingly name and her Imperial Crown.'

The fact that this had become a trial of treason and sedition seemed ludicrous to Liam. None of these men could possibly have been thinking to overthrow the Crown with their few hundred men and poor weaponry, they'd simply wanted to be able to live affordably and in peace without getting beaten up or shot at.

Stawell concluded reading out the charges then called for Timothy Hayes to stand trial first, as most people had expected. He had the most notoriety and, if convicted, the others would surely follow suit.

'Your Honour, we have a plea of abatement for Mr Hayes,' Ireland informed him, pausing proceedings. 'There is an affidavit that states an omitted reference in the charges to my client's place of abode.'

'Your Honour, this is just an objection in order to stall,' Stawell protested.

The judge agreed. 'Yes, it is insufficient, Mr Ireland.'

Stawell looked pleased but Ireland was unruffled. 'I am afraid, then, that we cannot proceed with Mr Hayes's trial as we did not anticipate he would be standing today. We have no witnesses.'

'But if Your Honour would allow us to delay...' Stawell blustered.

'The court will do no such thing. Who's next?'

There were looks of amusement passing around the press now and Liam was impressed with Ireland's clever strategy in using a small personal detail to bring about such a big advantage. The defence stood a far better chance in acquitting a less prominent man early, and Liam wondered who the first one would now be. Then one of the prisoners stood up and dared to speak himself.

'Please, Your Honour, I am Raffaello Carboni and I...'

'Oh, be quiet!' the judge said, dismissing him with a wave of his hand.

There was general chuckling around the court at the reputedly eloquent and theatrical Carboni being so swiftly shut down.

'Your Honour,' Ireland said apologetically, 'er...*we* actually ask for abatement for Mr Carboni in that his witnesses are also not available today.'

Stawell gaped at that. 'I just saw one of them outside!'

'Well, go and call them in,' the judge said.

The bailiff went and called the names but no-one came forward and Stawell marched about, furious now.

'Who's next?' the judge said again.

Another man's name was suggested but Ireland informed the court that his counsel was unwell and couldn't be here today. That was enough to make Stawell so frustrated his wig was beginning to topple but then one of Ireland's associates suggested another name: John Joseph. The Jamaican.

Convicting an Irish rebel was a far safer bet for Stawell but he was left with little choice now, and so the task began for him to convince the jury that condemning a runaway slave to death for being involved in the stockade was a justifiable thing to do. The man looked particularly vulnerable, standing and holding his hat close against his heart, his eyes huge in his dark face.

The first witness was a soldier, a redcoat, who swore he saw Joseph at the stockade from fifty yards away, firing a shotgun that felled the soldier alongside him. Stawell made a good job of painting Joseph as a murderous rebel but Ireland's associates soon tore a hole in his testimony.

'Were there any other coloured men present that day?' the defence's lawyer asked.

'A few.'

'How many?'

'I'm not sure...ten maybe.'

'Well, with other dark-skinned men present, how can you possibly be sure it was this man you saw?'

It was a good ploy to undermine the man's credibility but the answer unravelled its effectiveness.

'I arrested him.'

Liam groaned inwardly. Still, this was far from over. The next soldier told the same story but this time the defence lawyers made better work of trapping him.

'So you're telling us that you could see a coloured man from fifty yards away in the near-dark? And that, with hundreds of bullets flying about, you can be sure his bullet was the one that hit the man next to you?'

'Yes.'

There were murmurs in the court and a few people laughed with derision. Better, Liam decided.

The next witness was grilled about licence burning and Stawell made quite a deal over the fact that Joseph didn't have a licence when he was arrested and must have burnt his; however, the defence made the court chuckle once more by suggesting it might have fallen out while he was trying not to get shot. Stawell was red-faced with anger now.

'He was breaking the law, which is an act of sedition! He had taken up arms behind a barricade and was witnessed firing against soldiers of the Crown, which is *treason*. Therefore he must be found to be guilty.'

That concluded the case for the prosecution and the judge asked the defence if they would like to call their first witness.

'We have no witnesses, Your Honour.'

It was an astoundingly brazen tactic, to rest so heavily on the jury's sympathy, but the concluding statement was so brilliantly delivered it soon made sense.

'Do you really think that this man, this simple field worker from Jamaica, would be capable of plotting to overthrow the Queen of England?' They'd obviously schooled Joseph to look as dim-witted as possible as he began to scratch his head and adopted a very docile expression. There was a lot of sniggering around the court and, even though it offended Liam that they were suggesting the man was simple because he had dark skin, the strategy was seeming to work. By the time they'd concluded, Liam was feeling optimistic for an acquittal but Stawell wasn't done.

'Are we to assume that because this man is a man of colour he has no independent thoughts? That he is innocent of firing his gun? You have witnesses that have told you...'

'Liars!' called out one man from the back and the judge ordered silence in the court.

'You have to do your duty,' Stawell concluded, 'and you know what that duty is.'

Then the judge made it worse by pointing out that the prisoner had made no effort to remove himself from the situation and was there willingly. 'The Crown has proven his character, now you must discharge your duty, as has been said.'

The jury filed out to make their decision after that and Liam looked over at Dave and shrugged. 'I thought they'd won it but then the judge...'

'Aye. He's thrown a spanner in the works now. Come on, let's grab a quick smoke.'

The mood in the corridor was likewise doubtful among the defence lawyers and press but Stawell and his team looked quietly confident, even smug. Liam was starting to think the miners would face more deaths after all but then the jury returned and it was clear a quick, unanimous decision had been reached. Although which way it had fallen was impossible to tell.

The court was completely silent as the head juror stood and the judge addressed him gravely.

'Have you reached your verdict?'

'We have, Your Honour.'

'And what say you?'

There was a pregnant pause before the words swept across the room. 'Not guilty.'

Relief flooded across Joseph's face and the courtroom erupted in cheering and shouts of victory. Ireland and his team went to shake Joseph's hand, who was crying now. A jubilant Dave clapped Liam on the back, saying, 'Get a load of Stawell's face,' which Liam observed was so incredulous it made him laugh.

Joseph was escorted from the room by a triumphant throng and Dave and Liam followed them out to watch the reaction of thousands of people who now celebrated in the streets, hugging and cheering at the news that the first man had been set free. It was a victory for democracy. An open piece of defiance against English oppression, and one that held political clout, at last.

The crowd lifted Joseph on a chair and paraded him down the streets of Melbourne and Liam felt an enormous shift take place in that moment. Something had been born today, something unique now to this place, this Australia. The people had said yes to a common man's right to exist and to his right to defend himself against elitist tyranny. It would change things, he knew, because the general public had tasted power, and with it came the knowledge that anyone else involved in the rebellion could be acquitted too.

And that realisation gave Liam something he needed more than anything else right now: another reason to hope.

Forty-Four

Warrnambool, March 1855

The sun shone across the deep blue ocean beyond the cliffs, as peaceful and as smooth as a mirror that morning, although the great waves that battered the rocks were still at play. They never ceased in their enormous flinging and fanning, terrifying yet breathtaking too. Eileen wondered how Amanda felt about watching it as she observed her wandering along ahead then pausing to stare out. The breeze lifted the hair away from her pretty face and Eileen knew deep thoughts ran beneath it, but thoughts of who?

Was it the husband who'd perished out there only months before? Was it the man who'd carried her up from the cove and so tenderly cared for her as she recovered? Was it someone else? The last thought had begun to visit her since Liam had been away, or more accurately since she'd mentioned Kieran's name, and Amanda had turned quiet and withdrawn ever since, although strangely it didn't seem like disapproval that drove her behaviour. It seemed more and more like guilt furrowing the woman's brow, which puzzled Eileen immensely. What would she have to feel guilty about? It wasn't her brother who'd got himself messed up with the rebellion. She had nothing to do with him.

'Amanda,' Eileen called but she didn't turn around. '*Amanda*,' she tried again.

Amanda did turn towards her then, holding back her hair self-consciously, and Eileen walked over to stand by her side. 'You seem very thoughtful. Everything alright?'

'Oh, yes,' Amanda said, shrugging but not meeting her eyes. 'I just get melancholy by the sea.'

'Well, that's understandable,' Eileen replied, 'you've had a terrible experience. It would be strange not to be affected by it.'

Amanda nodded but as they turned to stroll back to the house it wasn't her belly that she held onto, as she so often did these past few weeks, it was her wrist. And something in the way she rubbed at it made Eileen wonder what memories she was really trying to push away.

The boys were playing cricket with Rory out in the front paddock and Backy the cow watched on, flicking her ears with interest whenever the ball was hit her way. Eileen's husband had never really made time for such things back in Ireland but nowadays he took things a bit easier. Living by the sea seemed to have mellowed them all. If she didn't have the constant worry over Kieran plaguing her, Eileen would have said they were content here. Leaving Orange really had given them all a fresh start and although a day never passed that she didn't mourn her little girl she'd made her peace with it too. There were plenty of blessings in her life and she smiled as Matthew finally connected his too-large bat with the ball and Rory cheered him on as he ran between wickets, dropping his bat altogether in his excitement.

The worry she felt over Kieran was now flowing into her concern for Amanda, the connection still puzzling her, but she was trying not to think about it today. Liam was in Melbourne with Dave, and a few others he said knew their brother, and she was certain something would come of it. She'd even go as far as to say she knew it, somehow. Maybe it was some kind of blood connection, a Clancy intuition. Or maybe it was simply superstition because a kookaburra had sat on the rail and sung to them all that dawn.

Eileen shoved it all aside for a moment, regardless, enjoying watching her boys for a little while longer before walking back to the house to get the dinner on. Amanda was outside, staring at the horizon from her chair on the porch, her knitting idle in her lap.

'Those booties won't knit themselves,' Eileen told her as she approached.

'Oh,' Amanda said with a start. 'I think I'm getting a bit soft in the head.'

'It's the baby,' Eileen told her, 'I always got vague towards the end too.'

'Want some help with dinner?' Amanda asked, rising slowly and changing the subject. Eileen had told her the story of her own stillborn baby and Amanda always tactfully redirected any conversation that dwelled on her own pregnancies. She was very considerate like that.

'Only if you sit down. I'll not have you trying to stoke that fire like yesterday.' She was a hard worker too. In fact, Amanda really knew her way around a household for a gently brought-up woman. 'Did the papers arrive then?' Eileen added, seeing some on the bench as they walked in.

'No, Parsons just gave me some old ones to read to give me something to do.'

Eileen picked one up. 'Liam will enjoy these; we didn't get *The Age* until this year,' she said, scanning a few lines. 'Huh! How's this? *The licence fees will surely be abolished under this new governor. There'll be no need for violence over this issue once sense has prevailed.*'

'Yes, some of it is most ironic,' Amanda said, although a shadow passed over her face once more. The one that echoed with guilt.

They went about their tasks then, cutting vegetables and meat and kneading damper for the oven, an Australian food they'd all taken to enjoying on a daily basis. Eileen chatted away but Amanda was quiet until the subject of gravy came up.

'I can make that if you like. Mrs Matthews used to say...'

She stopped abruptly, her face suddenly flaming.

'Who's Mrs Matthews?'

'Our...our old housekeeper. She taught me how to make gravy years ago with her mother's own recipe.'

Eileen stared at her, trying to read what was really going on. 'Why would a housekeeper teach a lady such a thing?'

Amanda looked even more flustered now. 'Oh...just to pass the time, I suppose.'

'You know, you seem to be adept at a lot of things that I wouldn't have expected, Amanda. You can knit and sew, cook and clean. It seems a strange thing for a servant to teach her young mistress how to wait on others.'

'Yes, I suppose...' Amanda said but she was looking to the door towards escape now. 'I think I might just have a lie-down...'

'Is there something you're not telling us?' Eileen interrupted, getting a bit fed up with all the mystery now.

Amanda stood and Eileen noticed she was trembling.

'Oh, now...oh, dear, don't take on so,' Eileen said, immediately sorry for her bluntness. 'I don't mean to pry...it's just that I get the feeling, well, I can see you're carrying something difficult inside and I don't think it's just about your husband, is it? Something's bothering you, Amanda. You can trust me if you need to let it out; I won't judge you, I promise.'

Amanda hesitated and for a moment Eileen thought she would open up but then her mask slipped back in place and she shook her head. 'No, no, I'm just tired and probably a bit vague, as you said. Excuse me,' she said, making her exit, and Eileen sat back down, staring at the door.

Why so much secrecy? Why not just open and up and tell the truth? Then she remembered how she had felt, after losing her daughter. The months of grieving, her retreat into silence. Perhaps it was only Amanda's grief that plagued her and the guilt that can come with it, especially if you'd survived when others had perished.

Eileen stared at the papers and vaguely began flicking through them, thinking about all that had transpired and reflecting that yesterday's news often felt more like fiction than fact. It was all just stories, after all, and everyone had them to tell, a long line of them that linked together to form the tale of a life. Then she saw an illustration of a couple in the pages, telling the end of two such tales, of a man and a woman who had perished at sea.

An English sea captain and his dark-haired wife.

Rory stared at the black-and-white image and Eileen watched various emotions cross his face: confusion, shock, some anger. 'Why don't you just confront her straight out?'

Eileen shook her head. 'No, she needs to confess it herself when she's ready,' she said, having decided that almost immediately. 'She has her reasons why she's using an alias, and she's obviously got plenty to hide, but confronting her isn't the answer. We can't take the chance that she might run off this late in her pregnancy and lose her baby through lack of care. I wouldn't wish that on anybody.'

'Aye,' Rory said, sighing now as he watched his sons play. 'We can't have her doin' that.'

'She's proven herself hardworking and she doesn't put on airs and graces, which says something about her character, I suppose, but she'd better have a damn good reason for doing this to us... and especially to Liam,' Eileen said, heated now as she mentioned her brother. 'He deserves more than a bunch of lies.'

'Whoever she is it's no' the baby's fault that she's done what she's done.'

'Aye,' Eileen agreed, staring back at the house. 'The sins of the mother cannot be cast upon the daughter or son.'

Forty-Five

Melbourne, March 1855

The day was finally here: the trial of Timothy Hayes.

After a second man was found not guilty Stawell had been swift to use his clout as Attorney General and had the jury and judge both sacked, and new ones appointed. The jury were an unknown quantity but the judge was one of Stawell's personal friends, a Mr Redmond Barry, something that had greatly angered the defence lawyers and their supporters.

It had meant a three-week delay during which time the journalists at *The Age*, Blair and Symes, had done everything they could to further incite public outrage and build support for the remaining prisoners. Commentary on the unfairness of having such an elitist form of democracy sat alongside articles condemning Stawell and Hotham himself, to the point that suggestions were being made in the newspapers to ban the state prosecution altogether.

Meanwhile, the two reporters had taken to speaking openly in the streets, stirring the crowds by reminding them that the miners had been forced to defend themselves against violent thugs, as many knew the traps and redcoats to be. Public sympathy was easily garnered there – the corrupt forces weren't only the bane of miners. Blair, in particular, was very vocal that the public demand Hotham himself give the prisoners amnesty and spare their lives, considering his forces were at fault, with no further trials to be held. But held they would be and today it would be Hayes who would stand, Stawell's best hope of a conviction, and he had insisted it not be delayed again.

However, there was more at stake here than one man's life, or indeed the lives of the other ten. The freedom that had swept through Melbourne those few short weeks ago had gained momentum. This was history in the making. This was for the rights of every Australian now, the right to have a voice.

'Listen to this,' Liam said as they sat and read the paper outside the court, waiting to go in, '*Who are the traitors? The sets of officials at the heads of our government departments, up to His Excellency himself, are public servants, and if they turn against society, plot against its liberties, goad with an insolent and petty tyranny, we say they are the traitors.*'

'Hear, hear,' said Dave, dragging on his pipe. 'Look out, it's Macca again. Over here, ye gangly bastard!' he called out.

The miners present in the crowds had relaxed since the first two acquittals, figuring more arrests really were pretty unlikely now, although if Hayes were to be convicted they might change their minds. Macca ambled over through the crowd and shook their hands with a grin.

'How's it goin', mate?'

'Good, good. This here's Liam Clancy, Kieran's brother,' Dave introduced him, 'and this here is Macca, as smooth a talking colonial boy as you'll ever meet.'

'Nice to meet ya,' Macca said. 'Sorry to hear about Kieran. I've been keeping a lookout for 'im but no luck so far. Sure he'll turn up though – probably still in hiding like a lot of fellas are.'

'Aye, that's what we're praying for,' Liam said. 'Every acquittal is giving me hope, although today will be a tough fight.'

'Are ye coming into the courthouse then?' Dave asked Macca.

'Nuh, happy to wait at the pub. Not keen on law courts, to be honest. Bloody awful places in my experience.'

'They're scary alright,' Liam agreed.

''Sides, got a mate just released from prison for nicking then falling off a bicycle. Spent a month in that useless hospital of theirs then, bam, three days in a cell and he's out.'

'Why'd they keep him so long in the hospital?' Dave asked.

'Got the handlebars straight in his you-know-what then it got infected and he screamed so much they thought he was dying. I reckon they kept him in there because they figured he'd never be comin' out.' The others laughed as he continued. 'Said the poor bloke next to him didn't sleep for days, only he couldn't tell 'im to shut up because he'd been shot near the throat and couldn't talk.'

'Imagine that,' Dave said, still half-laughing, 'poor blighter. I'll bet he never wanted to tell someone to shut his bloody trap more in his life.'

'I'm reckoning ya right there. Anyway, best be off. Give Hayes a nod for me, won't ya?'

People were beginning to pile through the doors so they set off too, bribing the same guard as before and moving into the courtroom.

The new jury and judge were soon in place and Liam noted that Stawell's smug expression was back, as was his ferocious and passionate language, and he opened with a damning tirade directed towards a beaten-looking Hayes, the prisoner's anxious wife looking on.

'Not only was this man the chair of the meeting on November twenty-ninth last year, he was also heavily armed and drilled the men in a warlike manner,' Stawell stated, his gaze sweeping across the jury. 'Hayes incited them to burn their licences with him and he did *all of this* under a flag other than the Union Jack.'

There was a stir around the court as he concluded and the first witness was brought in, a trooper by the name of Mr Goodenough, which set Dave off into chuckles. This was further enhanced as they overheard someone in the press mutter the man's nickname, 'Judas Iscariot'.

Stawell's questions started predictably enough: were you there that day? Do you recognise the accused? But then he reached beneath the bench and took out something that made the crowd gasp: it was the flag itself, somewhat torn apart by soldiers seeking souvenirs that fateful day, but still large enough to impress the crowd in its audacity as Stawell held it high. He wasn't only fired up today, he was quite the showman. Then he asked Goodenough if he'd heard what Hayes had said to the crowd that fateful day.

—'He said it was useless to try to deal with Hotham through legal means because he refused to even listen to their petition.'

'Did you see him the day after that?'

'Yes. I saw him armed with a double-barrel shotgun. He called his men "gentleman soldiers" and asked them to come forward and volunteer to stand up and fight for their rights and liberties. Then I saw him drill them the next day.'

Stawell looked more than satisfied with those comments and sat down as Ireland took over.

'Mr Goodenough, didn't you state previously that Hayes actually said to the men that it was "necessary to take the law into their own hands"?'

'I may have done.'

'Will you swear it?'

'...well, no, I won't swear it...but he said something like that...'

'But you won't swear they were the exact words?'

'What's the difference anyway?'

That caused a stir court-wide and Dave looked over at Hayes's wife, muttering, 'Because it's a fecken man's life.'

Goodenough was dismissed under glares and hisses and the next witness, Andrew Peters, came out, wearing civilian clothes. After stating under Stawell's questioning that Hayes acted as a sergeant and instructed that sharp pikes be used in order to pierce men on horseback, Ireland came out with a completely different line of questioning that had the court instantly entertained.

'What clothing were you wearing when you went to these meetings?'

'Same ones I'm wearing now.'

'But you're a policeman, are you not?'

'Yes.'

'I think someone was spying...'

The crowd rippled with amusement and Ireland had a little more fun with this for a while, unsettling Peters further before deftly returning to the central reason for the trial.

'Did you hear anyone say anything against the British constitution or about establishing a republic?'

'I...couldn't swear that I did...'

'Hmm. And was there a search for licences that Thursday?'

'Yes.'

'And did you hear that shots were fired by the troopers at men that didn't have them?'

'Not by the troopers...by the ground police...'

There was a loud reaction from the crowd now and several of the jury shook their heads as Ireland cornered the man further. He tried desperately to backtrack but he couldn't change his own words. Police had shot at unarmed men for not having licences days before the stockade had ever taken place. Unprovoked. It was simply now a fact.

There was a recess not long after that controversial moment and Liam and Dave piled out with the crowd onto the street to find Macca and tell him all the news.

'Apparently there's a priest taking the stand testifying Hayes was with him that morning and wasn't even at the battle, let alone armed, but I think the fact miners were shot upon days before gives him enough justification for retaliating, regardless,' Liam reported, having eavesdropped on the journalists as they'd left the courts. Dave, Macca and his fresh-out-of-gaol mate Roger listened on with interest. 'Mind you, this isn't some unsophisticated miner we're talking about. Hayes represents everything the government doesn't want Australia to become. He's an anarchist and he's particularly dangerous to them because if he gets off it tips back some of the control to commoners...and Hotham knows it.'

'Yeah, well I hope 'e does get off,' Roger put in. 'Those bastards treated us like animals in that hospital gaol.'

'Yes, Macca was telling us about your...er, stay,' Liam said.

'Did they tell you about me screaming blue murder? The poor bloke next to me couldn't even object, all shot up in the neck as he was. They wouldn't even let 'im have a pencil and paper to write down what he wanted to say. Now how can ya treat a man like that? He don't have no voice, at least give 'im that.'

'Aye,' Dave agreed. 'How's he supposed to even get word to his family that he's okay if he can't...' Dave's expression froze. '...He can't...'

He paused then, staring over at Liam.

'...speak,' Liam finished the sentence as his heart began to race. 'Did...did this man have dark hair and...and eyes...like mine...'

Roger looked closer at him. 'Yeah, I'd say so. And he was wearing his Sunday best too, or what was left of it, which I thought seemed a bit odd if he was down at that stockade.'

'What makes you think that's where he'd come from?' Dave said and Liam held his breath.

'Because I heard a guard say it one day, that he'd been shot in the neck because he was galloping over towards the rebels yelling "stop" at the top of his voice. Said it was the shot of the day, according to the traps,' he told them all, 'the gutless bastards.'

Liam and Dave jumped up as one to grab their coats and Macca did likewise.

'Hey...hey, where are you all going?' Roger asked, confused.

But no-one bothered to answer him as they ran for the door. It wasn't every day you found a man once thought dead.

He'd been listening to the guards discuss the trial from his usual position at the window, glad to hear that Hayes was being defended so well and feeling encouraged that the miners might all be acquitted in the end. It boded well for when he could finally state his own case for freedom too. But then three men appeared below and the time to do so suddenly arrived with urgency. He'd need to find his voice today even if it did feel as if razors were engraving each sound on the inside of his throat.

It was Liam again, this time with Dave and Macca, and they were running, which meant only one thing: they suspected he was inside.

Kieran made his way to the guards, something he'd never done before, and they paused mid-sentence from their animated discussion.

'What d'y'want?' asked one, a particularly lazy man Kieran knew as Sullivan, and the moment of truth arrived as Kieran worked harder than ever before to get words out.

'I...I...am...'

The man began to laugh. 'Oh, this should be good. Go on, you're what? A filthy Paddy? A colonial bastard? A dirty digger who'll rot in here forever?'

'I...'

Voices came from below as his brother and friends pleaded on his behalf but even Macca didn't seem able to persuade the guard to allow them entry.

'Don't waste our time, lad,' said a slightly more reasonable man named Reynolds. 'When you're ready to speak come to us then, but now obviously isn't the time.'

'*Kieran*,' called Liam desperately from below as the guard ordered them away. '*Please…*' he begged.

Kieran closed his eyes and took a deep breath, drawing on every piece of strength that lay inside.

'I…am…Kieran…Clancy.'

Forty-Six

They'd worked all night and all morning but the Hayes verdict would dictate whether or not they'd go ahead with their plan. It was a risk, a big one, but Kieran wanted it this way and Liam could well understand why. Between grunted sentences and written ones, they'd pieced his story together in the presence of the lawyer Parsons had recommended and Liam had written to months ago, Lincoln Ellis. He was a smart man, and a compassionate one. It had only taken a matter of minutes to convince him to come to the prison hospital and assert Kieran's legal rights to be charged and go to trial, or have the matter dropped altogether, the injustice of his brother's story speeding his actions.

'You're sure it's him?' was his only hesitation.

'They only brought him out to the top of the stairs, just so we could identify him, but aye, I'd never mistake him for another, Mr Ellis,' Liam had told him, unable to halt tears at the sweetness of the memory. He was thin, bearded and unkempt but his eyes held the soul of the most precious man in Liam's world: his only brother. 'They said they couldn't do any more than that without a lawyer.'

'Well,' Ellis had said, 'you've got one of those now. Come and let's see what we can do for him.'

The guards were completely outmanoeuvred from there on and Kieran had finally been allowed to talk to them all, well as best he could anyway, but firstly Liam had needed just to embrace him. All the grief and worry of the past months had emptied as they both broke down, and Liam was so grateful he was alive he could barely let him go, but there was freedom to be claimed and this was the moment to claim it. When most of Australia was sympathetic to its cause.

And so Liam sat in the courtroom once more, alongside Dave, who'd never left his side and was still red-eyed from the tears he'd shed in finding out Kieran had been shot because he'd been trying to protect him.

'To save the best mate I've ever known,' he kept saying, echoing the words Kieran had written down when the lawyer had asked why he'd finally rushed to the stockade. 'I can't believe he risked his life for me, in the end.'

But Liam could believe it. Kieran had lived his whole life passionately and impetuously, almost like it was all a game, however serious or dangerous things may be. The challenge, if they could set him free with their plan, would be to stop him running off and searching for Eve straight away, when he was still so weak, and Liam knew he'd have a battle on his hands too when he told him no-one knew where she had gone. Kieran had already told Ellis all urgency lay in getting word to, then marrying, his fiancée, but Liam couldn't focus on that next hurdle right now. All that mattered was Kieran being heard at last, acquitted from any charges, then set free from the hospital prison. The timing of when best to attempt that was everything.

The judge came in and they rose collectively to watch history unfold, but Liam's eyes were on the side door where Ellis would appear at the day's end, to throw Kieran's fate into the winds of change. But only if they blew favourably today.

It was the defence's turn for witnesses and Ireland had a few more confirm the fact that bullets had been fired at unarmed miners before the stockade and that Hayes had been there, forced to watch but unable to help. The potential for Hayes's acquittal felt strong to Liam now but he watched Stawell stand and approach the witness nervously, just the same.

Stawell started with a different line of questioning, on a subject that Liam had always known he would eventually hone in on: that brilliant Southern Cross flag.

But Ireland was well prepared for this part of the case.

'Your Honour, would Mr Stawell please confirm that he himself gathered under a similar flag that was not of this colony's a mere three years ago as part of a group?'

Stawell gaped. 'Your Honour, that was for the abolition of convict transportation to this colony.'

'So, you did meet under a non-colonial flag...' Ireland continued.

'Your Honour, meeting with positive intentions under another flag is hardly the same as arming yourself behind a stockade with plans to overthrow the law.'

'It has not been proven Mr Hayes was armed or even at the stockade.'

Stawell faced him now, livid. 'I have six witnesses saying he was.'

'And I have witnesses stating he wasn't. *And* I have evidence that proves these men were shot upon, unarmed, days before, then attacked at Eureka under government orders, which makes the stand *self-defence*, not an overthrow attempt,' Ireland countered, facing him too.

'*I have court records, facts that the miners fired first...*' Stawell yelled.

'*You know the truth, Stawell!*' Ireland yelled back.

'Silence!' thundered the judge. 'Counsel will direct conversation through me, not towards each other.'

There was a moment of mutinous glaring before they conceded.

'Your Honour,' Ireland said, calmer now, 'it is my intention to show that the miners were forced to erect a stockade, a place of safety where they could not be shot at, beaten and abused by soldiers and police for being unable to pay exorbitant licence fees. We already know for a fact that the ground police attacked several men three days prior to the morning of the third of December...'

'It is not a fact!'

'He was your witness, Mr Stawell,' Ireland said, not even looking at him now. 'As I said, they were *forced* to erect a place of safety and when they did they were attacked there by heavily armed Crown men, without any warning. And I can prove this with a single document which I would now like to read out loud...'

'Objection, Your Honour,' Stawell said.

'Your Honour, it is simply a copy of the Government Gazette.'

'If it isn't already submitted as evidence you cannot read from that, Mr Ireland,' the judge replied.

Ireland appeared frustrated but said: 'Then I will endeavour to deliver its content from memory as best I can.'

'Your Honour,' Stawell objected again but the judge allowed Ireland that much and it was Stawell's turn to look frustrated.

'It is a memorandum printed on the fifth of December that reads as such: "On the second of December I was informed that the rebels had taken up arms and formed a stockade. As such, I ordered back-up forces from Melbourne to *attack this camp* at daylight and the troops were ordered to assemble at two-thirty in the morning."' Ireland paused and held the gazette up to the jury. 'Who wrote this report, you may be wondering? It was penned by a good friend of the prosecution, as a matter of fact…Governor Charles Hotham.'

The court erupted in a maelstrom of outrage, the judge unable to silence the noise this time, and a swell of fury swept through Liam too. These men, friends of his own brother and even his brother himself, had been attacked and many slaughtered under orders from their very own governor. Dave looked at him with pained eyes, the grief and loss from the violent massacre still freshly written there, and Liam simply shook his head at what he and those other miners had endured. It could never be justified now.

'They had taken up arms,' Stawell tried to argue over the mayhem.

But Ireland's voice was loud and clear. 'It was an *attack*, designed by the Governor…'

'You always knew it was so, Stawell!' a man shouted from the crowd.

'Order!' called the judge. 'Evict that man!'

'Hotham is a murderer!' cried out another.

A few were indeed evicted, and silence was eventually restored but the atmosphere remained heavily charged now that the full extent of the government's tyranny had been revealed. By the time Ireland had concluded his case Liam could already sense a victory in the air, but it didn't stop Stawell from making one last, desperate attempt to convince the jury otherwise. Then he turned to his old friend, Judge Barry, as his last hope. Perhaps he would urge the jury in the prosecution's favour, as had the first judge.

'Gentlemen of the jury,' the judge began, 'from the evidence presented to you, you must irrevocably conclude two things: that treason has been committed and that Timothy Hayes is guilty of it. If you believe the prisoner has committed this treason then you should convict him.' He paused then. 'However, I have an opinion on this matter, one that you may choose to disregard but nonetheless: I believe that you should *not* convict this prisoner.'

Shock rippled across the courtroom and Liam looked over at Dave in amazement, who began to shake his head in disbelief. Then they both turned to observe Symes and Blair who were sitting back with enormous satisfaction at the expression on Stawell's face, which was alternating somewhere between outrage and disbelief. The jury left to deliberate but most observers didn't bother to move for sure enough they were back swiftly and Timothy Hayes stood to await his verdict.

'Not guilty!' came the cry and there were tears from his wife as Hayes came out of his cordoned-off cell. He held her close and the noise in the court near deafened those within, so euphoric was the crowd at the tenderness and elation of the moment. Ireland beamed and lawyers shook hands but Stawell merely stared into space in shock as the enormity of what had transpired seemed to hit him.

He had lost a case most considered impossible to lose; an Irish rebel, an anarchist who had taken up arms and helped raise an army against government soldiers would walk free. It made the Irishman in Liam want to shed tears of joy. And, as the day wore on, one by one other miners were set free as well, each trial more farcical than the last. Finally, the day was done, the judge looking immensely relieved as he left, and the lawyers gathered their papers and shook hands, although not Stawell who'd left straight away, unsurprisingly, his chin low.

There was a sense of completion and jubilation for most but Liam and Dave sat on the edge of their seats, staring hard at that side door. Then he came, Mr Lincoln Ellis, and they watched with pained breath as he approached Ireland and his associates, begging God that the defence would extend their generosity to just one more miner this day.

Liam watched as discussion ensued in hushed tones and at one point looks were extended their way.

'Aye,' he heard Ireland say, and one of the junior lawyers left, carrying a letter Ellis had handed over. Liam closed his eyes, praying that he would succeed.

It seemed an eternity but it was certainly only a matter of minutes because Ellis was still chatting away with Ireland and the others when the young man returned. More hushed conversation ensued until Ellis suddenly left the group and walked over towards Liam and Dave.

'It seems the judge is very tired of this whole affair after today –' Liam felt disappointment well, '– so tired, in fact, he said there was no point in the police even bothering to press charges against an unarmed man at the stockade. Kieran is free to go.'

He handed over a letter that the judge had signed to confirm it and Liam broke down as he took it into his hands. 'I can never thank you enough…'

'Ah, thank Ireland. He's the one who pulled the strings,' Ellis said, and Liam and Dave looked over at the man tearfully.

The lawyer merely smiled and called over: 'Go and buy the poor fellow a drink. He could use one, from what I've heard.'

'One? We'll buy him a hundred! Come on, Liam,' Dave said and they rushed for the doors, to spill out onto the erupting streets of Melbourne this historic day.

Never had Liam felt more joyful than this moment as they ran to have Kieran released, through a triumphant, exuberant Melbourne crowd. All of their lives finally, so wonderfully, had been turned around today. Kieran was free, which meant Liam was free too, and Eileen and the family, free to follow whatever their hearts desired. And, as he reached the courtyard and looked up at the bars that would no longer come between them, Liam felt a surge of conviction that the Clancys would be blessed from now on.

Kieran would find his Eve and Liam would win Amanda's love because they'd beaten all the odds now, finding life where there was surely death, freedom where there was gaol. Surely a peaceful life on Clancy land would be their fate now, with nothing else to stand in its way.

Forty-Seven

Warrnambool, April 1855

She'd known it as soon as she'd opened her eyes that this would be the day. It was only a slight pain but she recognised the feeling from her miscarriage years ago: the baby was definitely coming. Eve rose to look outside, at what kind of day it would be when her baby was born, but it was a strange sort of one, with heavy clouds blocking the sunrise and patches of blue in irregular arrangement. It was windy too, as if the weather was just generally confused, and she smiled, thinking it may mean her child would be unpredictable, and perhaps a little wild.

She could smell the porridge cooking, which meant Eileen was already up but Eve prolonged telling her she was in labour for now. She needed her help but not her too-knowing looks that had begun the day Eileen had confronted her about hiding something and she knew, somehow, that Eileen had figured out her deceit. Eileen wasn't a very good liar and she often let remarks slip, insinuating Eve wasn't who she said she was. Sayings like 'you can't make a silk purse from a sow's ear' had begun to pepper her conversation and questions about the marks on her wrists and her housekeeping skills kept popping up until Eve wanted to scream the truth.

But, of course, she never could.

She could make up some other name and background for herself, she supposed, a less genteel one that would be more believable, but Eve really didn't want to throw more lies upon her lies. It would just have to suffice that soon she would leave with her child and let these people live in peace, without a thief in their midst. And without someone who had loved their deceased brother and could steal away all their hope that he still lived.

For some reason her father came to mind then, and with it his advice about being honest. Something she'd long forgotten in the turmoil of the past few years.

Look for truth and act truthfully, Evie, and remember: you teach people how to treat you, with each and every thing you do and say.

She'd taught these people nothing but her own deceit and she didn't deserve to live with them, reinforcing it each day.

How far I've fallen, Papa, she told his spirit now, *too far for God's forgiveness, even you would have to see that. I'm so sorry...*but then a contraction tore through her and she gasped, knowing she'd have to tell Eileen soon. She was saved from having to do so, however, as a knock came at the door.

'Amanda, are you...oh dear lord, is it today? Into bed with you now,' she scolded after taking one look at Eve doubled over and grimacing as she held onto the windowsill. Eve allowed her to help her back to it and she lay down, trying to prepare herself for what the day would bring. But whatever physical agony it gave her it would be nothing compared to the emotional pain that would come when she took Kieran's child away, separated forever from the only family he or she would ever know.

Forty-Eight

Ballan, April 1855

'I'm telling you, they just up and left.'

'But they must have told somebody something.'

'They were funny like that,' the man whom Liam had introduced as Barney told him, 'kept to themselves most of the time on account o' the lady's poor health.'

'Yes, I know that,' Kieran said, exasperated. His throat was paining him too but at least his voice was back now, thanks to some numbing tonic he and Liam had made up and he'd used regularly over the past few days. It was raspy, and he had to keep his sentences short, but he could communicate, which was just as well because now it seemed he had quite a search ahead of him. 'Surely they left some clue.'

'Not so far as I know of,' he said with a shrug. 'You've a needle in a haystack ahead o' ye now, son, but I'll tell ye one thing: ye fair broke that poor girl's heart. I'd waste no time in finding her, if I were you.'

Kieran walked outside the shop where the man worked and ran his hand across his newly shaven face, frustrated at the dead end and wondering wildly what to do now. He'd known she wouldn't be here, of course, Liam had told him that much, but he'd thought he'd be able to trace her movements if he started in Ballan. Now it seemed she could be anywhere, perhaps even in another country for all he knew. Thinking he'd chosen his mates and the rebellion over her. Thinking he was dead.

Liam had filled him in on the tale of the cap and the mistaken burial yesterday, waiting until the day after he was released lest he rush off to find her straight from hospital. It had shocked him, causing him to hurry and get on the road to here before he'd even had a moment to think straight, but now there was time to think, alright. And he needed a plan fast.

Liam was holding the horses, watching him closely, and Kieran looked to him for answers. He was always so clever, perhaps he could see a place to start.

'It's no use trying to begin from here,' Liam said, reading his mind. 'We need to consider how they would have travelled and where.'

'Melbourne seems likely,' Kieran said, taking out his tonic. 'We need to go and check,' he began, pausing for a swig, '…coach houses and ship records.'

'Aye, but you need to make a detour, Kier. It isn't fair not to see Eileen before you go, not after all the worry she's been through.'

'You can tell her I'm alright.'

'It's less than a day's ride. Besides, you need to rest and pack and do this properly. Who knows how long it may take?'

Kieran nodded, seeing the sense in that. The cart he'd left by the side of the road back on that fateful day of the battle had long disappeared, along with all his belongings. Besides, it was still early so they'd be able to get to Warrnambool late and spend the night. A sensible option in all. 'Come on then,' he said and they mounted and began to move off. 'I can't stop longer than overnight though. Every day...' he paused then, wondering how to break the next to his brother. Directly, he supposed. He was hardly one to waste words anymore. 'She's having my baby.'

Liam stared at him, taken aback. 'That...that complicates things.'

'Aye.'

'Do you...do you think she's being treated well? I mean, a servant isn't supposed to...well, you know how people are.'

Kieran shook his head. 'I can't imagine them just casting her out. Amanda is a bit selfish and spoilt but she isn't cruel.'

'Amanda,' Liam said, surprise crossing his face once more. 'Funny you should mention that name. I...er...have some news of my own.'

His brother was blushing now and Kieran started to smile, glad to focus on someone else for a moment. 'Don't tell me you've found a girl?'

'She found us, actually,' Liam said, still blushing and now fiddling with the reins. 'You know how I told you about all the shipwrecks we get down on the coast? Well, she was washed up on shore, the only survivor, and...'

'You swept her into your arms?'

Liam laughed self-consciously. 'Well, not quite as gallantly as all that, but she has been staying with us ever since.'

'And have you declared your feelings as yet, brother?' Kieran was thoroughly enjoying watching Liam's discomfort. It was the first time he'd ever been able to tease him so.

'In a way, but that's complicated too. Her husband perished at sea and she's, well, she's having a baby too.'

Kieran stared at him, then shook his head. 'Oh, what a pair we are, eh?'

'Aye,' Liam said with a sigh, 'but at least your girl loves you, well, will do once she knows you're still alive. Mine's in mourning and, I don't know, there's something else going on with her too. She doesn't seem to believe in herself, almost as if she sees herself as cursed.'

'Eve used to feel that way. Probably does again now, I'm guessing,' Kieran said, sad for her at the thought. 'But you can't focus on that; you have to push through it,' he advised, 'convince her you're meant to be.'

'How am I supposed to do that?' Liam asked, and Kieran looked up at the sky.

'Just follow your heart, brother,' he said, adding with a grin, 'and maybe try a little Irish charm.'

Forty-Nine

Warrnambool, April 1855

She didn't need to be told something was wrong. Endless hours of childbirth had weakened her to the point of pure exhaustion and Eileen was pacing and frantic.

'Get me a fresh pitcher of water,' she instructed Rory, who had been turning whiter by the hour, painful memories no doubt assailing him.

Eileen had even brought in a statue of Mary, placing flowers in front, and Eve could feel the desperation in the room. It was lit by several lanterns but they were fading into a blur now as Eve struggled to stay conscious.

Another contraction ripped through her and she cried out against it, her world turning to stars as she squeezed her eyes against the excruciating, slicing pain.

'Hold on, Amanda, you're almost there.'

Eileen was holding her hand and Eve clutched at it, screaming now, before the agony finally receded and she slumped back in the pillows.

Perhaps this was it, she thought dazedly, the end of her unnatural life. Her day of reckoning here, after all the others she'd survived. Memories of judgement days long past floated through her mind and she could hear the voices as if their owners stood in the room, like spectres.

You are to pack your things and leave our service immediately.

...sentenced to transportation to the colony of Australia...

I saw the list of the dead, love. His name was on it.

'No, no,' she groaned, her head thrashing back and forth.

'Amanda,' Eileen called to her, but the stars were coming her way again, not southern ones to bless or curse, the ones that heralded pain.

'Hold on, love, oh dear God,' Eileen's voice came through vaguely. She was crying now and Eve knew the memories for her must be horribly raw.

'I'm sorry,' she panted, 'I'm sorry this has to be you.'

Eileen stroked her brow with a cloth and Eve managed to open her eyes and focus as the wave receded once more, like the ocean pulling back, only it would hurl at her again, she knew. She was fighting for life in an inky black sea of pain, clutching on to survival, mocked by those stars.

Eve grasped at the sheets, fighting it all. Holding fast.

'The baby is stuck, Amanda, like mine was. I'll have to go in and pull it out.'

Tears streamed down Eileen's face and Eve reached out to grasp her hand. 'Eileen...I'm not...'

'Save your strength, love. Everything is going to be alright,' Eileen told her and Eve knew she was lying. But lies couldn't save her now, nor could they save her child, and it was time to let them all go.

'I'm not Amanda...'

Eileen nodded, fresh tears rolling. 'I know. I saw her picture in the newspaper.'

'I'm...'

But then the pain crashed once more and she was drowning in it, and those stars exploded where sight should be, and she could hear the apocalyptic sound of horse hooves as the end drew near.

They were exhausted but Liam was practically running after they dismounted and went up the porch stairs. It made Kieran smile, hoping his brother would receive a warm welcome from his lady.

'I've a present for you,' Liam announced, but the room was empty and he turned to Kieran before they both walked over to another door and Liam pushed it open to a scene that was so familiar it hurt to watch it; bowls of bloodied bandages, an ashen-faced Rory, a woman in agony on the bed. Then Eileen turned and her face told the tale before something else took its place: pure love and the sheerest of relief.

'*Kieran,*' she cried and fell into his arms. 'Oh Liam, I knew you'd do it, I knew.' She was sobbing and they both held her close.

'Kieran,' Rory echoed, coming over to hold them all too and Kieran closed his eyes momentarily at the love he felt for them all. But then a third person said his name, in a voice weakened by pain, but it was impossible not to hear the shock within it. Nor the soft-cultured accent that underscored the sound.

The spectres had gone and they'd sent an angel in their place, the dearest one of all. The kindest man on earth who now lived in heaven.

He was walking over to her, so real and lifelike, yet she could see the fresh scar on his neck, the bullet that must have killed him.

'I'm dying, my love,' she whispered, 'I'm coming to you.' God was being merciful, after all. She would make it into heaven too.

'Eve,' he said, his face filled with shock. 'Oh, my girl.' He kissed her and his lips felt warm. Oh, if only that was real, she told her fuddled mind, but now the stars were coming once more.

'Do something!' she heard him cry out, before even the stars turned black.

Eileen took Eve's hand that was now limp at her side. 'It's the same as what I went through, I think,' she told the room but then she turned to Kieran. 'What did you just call her?'

'Eve,' he said, staring in horror at her unconscious face. 'You have to save her,' he begged, 'that's my child. That's my Eve, Eiles, my love.'

'Your...your...'

It was Liam who spoke and Kieran turned towards him, the full impact of the whole truth unravelling in Kieran's mind now. Shipwrecked. Alone. A convict servant with someone else's identity there for the taking, no other choice save gaol once more. 'This is your Amanda?'

'Aye,' Liam said vaguely, his face drawn with shock. 'She...she can't be both.'

Eileen wiped Eve's brow and stared over at her brothers, tears streaming but her voice firm. 'Whoever she is, we need to get that baby out because she's...she's...'

'No,' Kieran said. 'Liam,' he turned back. 'Please...please, you have to help her.'

'I couldn't do it again...I...'

'You're the only one who ever has,' Eileen said, her eyes so pained Rory turned away at the sight. 'There may still be a chance.'

Liam was still and Kieran grabbed his arm, begging now. 'Liam...I can't lose her. Please do this for me. *Please.*'

Liam nodded then and began to move, washing his hands, moving into position and waiting until Eileen had coaxed Eve back to consciousness with cold presses and movement.

'Just one push now, love,' she coaxed. 'It's all we'll ask of you.'

'On the count of three,' Liam said, 'one, two...'

'Arghhhh...' came Eve's pitiful cry as her body arched and Liam pulled out the child, unwrapping the cord from around its neck and holding it in his arms momentarily before raising his eyes to Kieran.

'She...she's...'

Then a sound filled the room, more precious than any Kieran had ever heard as his daughter cried out her presence to the world.

'Oh...oh thank the lord,' Eileen said, dissolving into tears.

Liam handed the baby into Kieran's arms and he stared down at a beautiful heart-shaped face that was puckered up with her distress at the ordeal of being born, and he did the only thing he could think to do. And the only thing that could possibly save Eve now: he placed her in her mother's arms.

The stars were gone and the waves had stopped and now there was another angel, this one even more beautiful than the last. Eve's eyes kept wanting to close but she fought against them to behold this dear little face. The cherub had been distressed but now she was content, and watching her with curious eyes, and Eve felt a surge of love so strong she began to cry.

The darkness pulled her but she fought against it, some small strength born from this new emotion, this power. And looking at the Kieran angel now alongside her, she decided whatever this in-between world was, this was where she would stay. She'd survived many forms of hell on that other place they called earth. And heaven could just damn well wait.

Fifty

Ballan, June 1855

It was cold and Kieran rose to stoke the fire, sparks flying up the chimney as the flames began to leap and dance. It was getting quite late but the mail had arrived and he'd sat up to read the papers and the long-awaited letter from Liam, which he'd read twice. He was in a place called Murwillumbah, a long way north on the coast of New South Wales, and Kieran could read between the lines, well enough to know his brother was enjoying his travel adventures, even if he hadn't quite got over his broken heart. It was a terrible cost for Kieran's own happiness but it couldn't be helped. Just another twist in his and Eve's star-crossed fate.

Kieran rose to stare outside, deciding to smoke his pipe despite the icy air and, as he stepped out, he noticed the stars were, in fact, very bright tonight as the Southern Cross twinkled above them like diamonds on the dark velvet sky.

How those stars had changed things, not just for him but for all Australians now. He'd just read that all free men had been granted the right to vote and that Peter Lalor himself would sit for parliament, an extraordinary turn of events. Licence fees were greatly reduced and miners could now buy their land as what seemed impossible a year ago came to pass.

And all because men had united under the Southern Cross, that sky-flung symbol of freedom, and the Australian public and her juries had refused to allow them to be punished for doing so. For ultimately all they'd wanted was fairness and equality, two things they would now hopefully build this land on, giving future generations a parliament where all classes could be represented, from all the nations on earth. Giving them something Kieran would never again take for granted: a voice.

Kieran reflected back on his own part in the Eureka Stockade, to that critical moment when his heart had chosen to protect his mate Dave, even though so much of it belonged to Eve. But he'd learnt there was room for many people inside; your heart simply swelled when faced with the privilege of loving more than one. And it chose your loyalty for you, overruling all thought, or any vow, made by your mind. It rendered sense insensible and logic illogical when it came to the moment of truth.

Staring up at the stars Kieran reflected that it really wasn't ever about who or what you loved more, it was just, simply, about love.

The door creaked open then and out came his new wife, Eve, and he wrapped his arms around her under those southern stars.

'Is she asleep?'

'Ages ago. I just adore watching her though. She really is rather angelic, even though I'm sure every mother thinks such things.'

'That she is, my love, and a little star too, our Aurora. I hope we have a dozen more just the same, all girls and all just like you.'

'I keep saying I think she's more like you, but love is blind, I suppose,' Eve said, kissing his cheek then yawning. 'Anyway, I'm off to bed, are you coming in?'

'Aye, I'll be there in a moment. See if I can't get you in a spot of bother.'

Eve smiled and moved closer to be wrapped in his arms.

'Don't take too long,' she said, her fingers tracing his chin, but then they found the scar on his neck and her expression turned pensive.

'It's all in the past, my love,' Kieran said, watching her closely.

She nodded but the shift was still there. 'Sometimes I...I still fear this is just a beautiful dream, some kind of trick God is playing on me before I wake up alone or in chains. That you and Aurora aren't real because this life is too good to be true. Like I still don't...I don't deserve it.'

'You've always deserved a free and happy life, my beautiful girl, and a life filled with those who show you that every day. This is your fate now, Eve, *our* fate, in fact. You can believe it, I promise.'

Her smile returned at those words. 'Are you rescuing me again by a river?'

'I'm pretty sure you've always been the one saving me.'

She laughed then and he kissed her once more before she went inside and Kieran turned back to look at the sky and finish his pipe, thinking how incredibly fortunate his life had turned out to be too. This great southern land was wild and unpredictable, sometimes savage, sometimes beautiful, but like anywhere there was opportunity, if you sought to find it. Looking far above him he knew he'd been blessed here, under that cross, for in the end he truly had struck gold.

It was simply freedom, by any other name.

With Respect

I would like to acknowledge the traditional custodians of this land, with respect for your culture and history.

In particular, I would like to acknowledge the Gadigal and the Dharug from the Eora nation, the Wiradjuri and the Wathaurong. I deeply regret that the period that this novel is based on is underscored by the horrific injustices you suffered at the time.

Acknowledgements

I'm a very lucky author because I have so many wonderful and colourful people in my life who inspire a myriad of traits in my characters. To my husband Anthony, the kindest man on earth (well, according to me anyway), my determined, passionate son Jimmy and my gentle, reflective son Jack, much of the Clancy brothers' spirit was derived from your amazing souls. Thank you for your everyday inspiration.

Thank you too to my support team: my incredibly wise and beautiful Mum, my sisters Linda and Gen, my brothers James and Tom, my brothers and sisters-in-law, and my precious girlfriends Theresa and Zoe, Carmie, Chantal, Bobbie, Lara-Fi, Thuy and Gemma. And to Guy Whitington, Chris Naismith, Richard Welch and Lincoln Ellis, thank you for suggesting so many hilarious ideas and for all the 'blokey' chats.

There's more but I'm starting to sound like I'm giving an Academy Award speech so I'll finish with my intrepid agent Helen Breitwieser and my wonderful team at HarperCollins: Jo Mackay, James Kellow, Sue Brockhoff and the ever-amazing Annabel Blay, editor extraordinaire. I will forever thank the southern stars that led me to you.

I am also a lucky author because I am blessed with much fodder for the imagination for the stories themselves. In particular, my close and extensive family have provided many wonderful anecdotes over endless cups of tea throughout the years. With so much story at my disposal it is little wonder, then, that family history has ended up being woven into my fictional works and *In a Great Southern Land* is no exception. How fortunate I am to have such inspiration and input and I particularly thank Chris and Daphne Ashley, my cousins, for their research into this time period. It led to many hours of daydreaming, culminating in this novel.

I had often pondered why anyone would decide to leave their homeland to travel to the other side of the world, particularly when the clippers of the time were often no match for the treacherous seas. Yet, not only did my maternal ancestors take such a daring chance, they brought the entire family with them.

This novel was inspired by their tale, one of adventure and hardship, and I've given our fictional family their real-life name: Clancy.

Six generations ago in 1841, five Clancy siblings lived on the banks of the Shannon River in Killaloe, County Clare, Ireland, and, when their parents passed away (we have long assumed from one of the many diseases that plagued Ireland during this time) they decided to pack up and move to Australia.

It was very moving to research what life was like in this part of Ireland back then and their reasons for leaving soon became apparent. As described in the novel's early chapters, it was a harsh existence, with little opportunity, and oppression was rife. I can well imagine why the lure of the great southern land would have proven too much to resist.

It was a difficult and dangerous undertaking to cross a vast ocean as a family, some married with young children. Sadly, one little girl, Sarah Clancy, perished at sea and I named Eileen's stillborn child after her in the novel. It feels like a small token but I wanted to bring her to Australia at last, if only on paper. (I also have a cousin named after her in Western Australia). My direct ancestor was the original Sarah's cousin, Dennis Clancy. He was nine years old when he arrived in New South Wales.

The Clancys were sponsored emigrants and many were uncommonly literate, in fact family folklore has it that neighbours would come from far and wide to hear my ancestors read from the papers.

Dennis Clancy's son John and his wife Anne Mackey

There was much opportunity as the wild west of New South Wales opened up to settlers and my forefathers' timing was certainly fortuitous. Skilled farmers from Britain were highly prized by the government at the time as the colony began to wind down the transportation of convicts, seeking a more ambitious, financially prosperous future at the expense of its traditional indigenous past.

Dennis's family eventually settled in Orange, New South Wales, where my grandmother's family, the Richards, had also emigrated to from Ireland. The house they built still stands today. It is where my grandmother, Gladys Mary Veronica, was born (see below, with my twin cousins, Anne and Tricia Colgan in the 1970s).

I've long loved the town of Orange and the rich history it holds. I spent many happy days there in my youth and some of our family still reside in this beautiful place and on the rolling farmland nearby. There've been halcyon days and harsh seasons of drought, but the Clancy line still lives on there after a hundred and seventy-five years, which is why, perhaps, I always feel part of me belongs there too. It was a labour of love to paint the landscape with words. Thank you to the Colgans, in particular, for your enduring hospitality, with especial gratitude to my inspirational and wonderful Aunty Beryl who sadly passed away while I was writing this novel.

For whatever reasons our early settlers came, be it opportunity, desperation, adventure or hope, they laid down the foundations for Australia's future. The decisions they made formed what would eventually become our collective voice, first raised with fledgling independence in 1855 when a jury stood and proclaimed a rebel Irish miner 'not guilty' for taking arms against tyranny.

We have a colourful past, some of it inspirational, some of it tragic, some of it incredibly moving. I am very grateful to be Australian and hope we can continue to try to build it into a land of empathy and equity, never forgetting that powerful energy that whipped through the air on that fateful day in Melbourne, long ago. That we can strive to truly be a place where justice is every person's unquestionable right.

And where freedom can reside within us all.